Love at first sight

Deep emerald eyes bore into Amy's, singling her out as he angled his horse toward her. His glossy black gelding breathed close, but she felt no fear, for the man held her safe with his piercing green gaze. She felt as though he could see through her eyes right into her soul.

He tipped his plumed hat. Flustered, she turned and glanced about, certain he must be saluting someone else. But everyone was laughing and talking or watching the procession; no one focused their attention his way. She looked back, and he grinned as he passed, a devastating slash of white that made Amy melt inside. Long after he rode out of sight around the bend, she stared at the place where he disappeared. . . .

Amethyst

Lauren Royal

A SIGNET BOOK

SIGNET
Published by New American Library, a division of
Penguin Putnam Inc., 375 Hudson Street,
New York, New York 10014, U.S.A.
Penguin Books Ltd, 27 Wrights Lane,
London W8 5TZ, England
Penguin Books Australia Ltd, Ringwood,
Victoria, Australia
Penguin Books Canada Ltd, 10 Alcorn Avenue,
Toronto, Ontario, Canada M4V 3B2
Penguin Books (N.Z.) Ltd, 182–190 Wairau Road,
Auckland 10, New Zealand

Penguin Books Ltd, Registered Offices:
Harmondsworth, Middlesex, England

Published by Signet, an imprint of New American Library,
a division of Penguin Putnam Inc.

First Printing, February 2000
10 9 8 7 6 5 4 3 2 1

Printed in the United States of America

PUBLISHER'S NOTE
This is a work of fiction. Names, characters, places, and incidents either are the product of the author's imagination or are used fictitiously, and any resemblance to actual persons, living or dead, business establishments, events, or locales is entirely coincidental.

For my husband, Jack,
because I couldn't write about true love
if he hadn't shown me what it means

Acknowledgments

I wish to thank:
Terri Castoro, the most patient critique partner on the planet, for going *way* above and beyond; Elaine Koster, my incredible agent and the first "real" person in the business who believed in me; Audrey LaFehr, my editor, whose confidence and boundless enthusiasm keep me going; Genny Ostertag, her assistant, who cheerfully answers my endless silly questions; Jack Royal-Gordon, the world's most understanding husband, who puts up with month after month of no clean laundry and nothing planned for dinner; my son Brent, for designing and maintaining my website and telling all his teachers that Mom wrote a book; my son Blake, for keeping so happy and busy I almost never feel guilty ignoring him to write; my daughter Devonie, for all the precious kisses and hugs even though I am far from a perfect mommy; Ken Royal and Margot Harris, the brave, generous people who read my early attempts and gave me encouraging feedback; the Rockin' Robins, my online writer's group—Nancy Phillips, Elaine Ecuyer, Diana Brandmeyer, and Amanda Murphy—for always hanging in there; Rebecca Forster, mentor extraordinaire, for turning the lightbulb on in my head; the Orange County Chapter of RWA, for everlasting support, a wealth of knowledge, and the willingness to share it; Rita Adair-Robison, for all her encouragement and dragging me to RWA in the first place; the Rising Stars of Romance, for all the uplifting camaraderie; the Painted Rock Research Listserve, for having an answer to every question no

matter how obscure; Elise Misiorowski, from the Gemological Institute of America, for her wonderful insight into old jewelry manufacturing techniques; Mark Zana, for exhaustive research into England's confusing monetary history; Herb Royal, for explaining all about obsolete guns and the resulting wounds in excruciating detail; Teri Royal, for invaluable firsthand experience in the mechanics of sibling rivalry; my oldest friends—Julie Walker, DeeDee Perkins, and Diena Simmons—for their Blind Faith (even though our favorite band growing up was the Who); Del Amitri, for writing and performing such incredible music for me to listen to as I write; my first readers and biggest cheerleaders—Joan Royal (head cheerleader), Dawn Royal, June Jørgensen, Karen Nesbitt, Taire Martyn, Alison Bellach, April Mann, Beth Sher, Tobey Seidman, and Sandy Shniderson—for reading my stories and laughing and crying in all the right places . . . and anyone who bothered to read all this, for your amazing fortitude. Thank you.

Prologue

London
Monday, April 22, 1661

"Here, there's room!" Amethyst Goldsmith shouldered her way through the crowd, her parents and aunt murmuring apologies in her wake. "Come along, 'tis starting!" When she finally reached a few bare inches of rail, she clasped it with both hands and turned to flash them a victorious smile.

Hugh and Edith Goldsmith came up to join her, shaking their heads at their daughter's tenacity. Laughing, Hugh's sister Elizabeth squeezed in behind. Ignoring the grumbling of displaced spectators, Amy spread her feet wide to save more room in the front. "Robert, over here!"

Robert Stanley tugged on her long black braid as he wedged himself in beside her. She shot him a grin; he was fun. Although he'd arrived only last week to train as her father's apprentice, Amy had known for years that she was to marry him. So far they'd gotten along fine, although he'd been surprised to find she was far more skilled as a jeweler than he. Surprised and none too pleased, Amy suspected. But he would get over that.

She might be female, but her talent was a God-given gift, and she would never in this lifetime give up her craft. Robert would just have to get used to the idea.

With a sigh of pleasure, Amy shuffled her shoes on the scrubbed cobblestones. "Look, Mama! Everything is so clean and glorious." She breathed deep of the fresh air, blinking against the bright sun. "The rain has stopped . . . even the weather is welcoming the monarchy back to England! Have you ever seen so many people? All London must be here."

"Even more from the countryside, I'd wager." Her mother waved a hand, encompassing the crowds on the rooftops, the mobbed windows and overflowing balconies.

Amy looked up as a handful of tossed rose petals drifted down, landing on her dark head like scented snowflakes. She shook them off, laughing. "Is it not beautiful? Just look at all the tapestries and banners."

"Just look at all that wasted wine," Robert muttered, with a nod toward the fragrant red river that ran through the open conduit in the street.

Amy opened her mouth to protest, then decided he must be fooling. "Marry come up, Robert! You must be pleased King Charles will be crowned tomorrow. Twelve years of Cromwell's rule was enough! Now we have music and dancing again." She felt like dancing, like spreading her burgundy satin skirts and twirling in a circle, but the press of the crowd made such a maneuver impossible, so she settled for bobbing a little curtsy. "We've beautiful clothes, and the theater—"

"And drinking and cards and dice," Robert said pointedly.

"That too," Amy agreed, turning back to ogle the mounted queue of nobility parading their way from the Tower to Whitehall Palace. Such jewels and feathers and lace! Fingering the looped ribbons adorning her new gown, she pressed harder against the rail, wishing she too could join the procession.

"Where did they possibly find so many ostrich feathers in all of England?" she wondered aloud, then burst into giggles.

Her aunt laughed and wrapped an affectionate arm around her shoulders. "Where do you find the energy, child? You must come to Paris. Uncle William and I could use your happy smiles."

Amy hugged her around the waist. Aunt Elizabeth had lost her three children to smallpox last year, and Amy knew she still bore a heavy heart.

"We need her artistry here," Amy's father protested, poking his sister with a grin. "Your shop will have to do without."

"Ah, Hugh, how selfish you are!" Aunt Elizabeth chided. "Hoarding my niece's talent all for your own profit." She aimed a mischievous smile at her brother. " 'Tis no wonder we moved to France to escape competition."

Amy giggled. Aunt Elizabeth and Uncle William had been forced to move their shop when business fell off during the Commonwealth years. But they'd flourished in Paris, becoming jewelers to the French Court, and would not think of returning now.

"I'm glad you came for the coronation, Auntie. 'Twould not be the same without you."

"I'd not have missed it," Elizabeth declared. "Old Noll drove me out of England, but though my home is elsewhere now, 'tis God's own truth that no one here is happier than I."

"Listen!" Amy cried. A joyous roar rolled westward toward them, marking the slow passage of His Majesty in the middle of the procession. "Can you hear King Charles coming? There are his attendants!" The noise swelled as the King's footguards marched by, their plumes of red and white feathers contrasting with those of his brother, the Duke of York, whose guard was decked out in black and white.

All at once, the roar was deafening. Amy grasped her mother's hand. " 'Tis him, Mama," she whispered. "King Charles II." Glittering in the sunshine, the Horse of State caught and held her gaze. "Oh, look at the embroidered saddle, the pearls and rubies—look at our diamonds!"

Amy cared not for horses—she was terrified of them, if the truth be told—so she paid no attention to the magnificent beast himself. But three hundred of her family's diamonds sparkled on the gold stirrups and bosses, among the twelve thousand lent for the occasion. "Oh, Papa, I wish we could have designed that saddle," she breathed.

Aunt Elizabeth laughed, then her hand suddenly tightened on Amy's shoulder. "Charles is looking at me," she declared loudly.

Amy's father snorted. "Always the flirt, sister mine."

Amy's gaze flew from the dazzling horse to its rider. Smiling broadly beneath his thin mustache, the tall King waved to the crowd. His cloth-of-silver suit peeked out from beneath ermine-lined crimson robes. Rubies and sapphires winked from gold shoe buckles and matching gold garters, festooned with great poufs of silver ribbon. Long, shining black curls draped over his chest, framing a face that looked older than his thirty years; the result, Amy supposed, of having suffered through exile and the execution of his beloved father.

But his black eyes were quick and sparkling—and more than a little sensual. Some women around Amy swooned, but she just stared, willing the King to look at her. When he did, she flashed him a radiant smile.

"No, Auntie, he's looking at *me*."

Before her family even stopped laughing, the King was gone, as suddenly as he had arrived. But the spectacle wasn't over. Behind him came a camel with brocaded panniers and an East Indian boy flinging pearls and spices into the crowd. And then more lords and ladies, more glittering costumes, more decorated stallions, more men-at-arms, all bedecked in gold and silver and the costliest of gems.

Yet none of it mattered to Amy, for there was a nobleman riding her way.

'Twas not the richness of his clothing that caught her eye, for in truth his was plain in comparison to those around him. His black velvet suit was trimmed with naught but gold braid, his wide-brimmed hat decorated with only a single white plume. He wore no fancy crimped periwig, but his own raven hair fell in gleaming waves to his shoulders.

Deep emerald eyes bore into Amy's, singling her out as he angled his horse in her direction. His glossy black gelding breathed close, but she felt no fear, for the man held her safe with his piercing green gaze. She felt as though he could see through her eyes right into her soul. Her cheeks flamed; never in her almost-seventeen years had a man looked at her like that.

He tipped his plumed hat. Flustered, she turned and glanced about, certain he must be saluting someone else. But everyone was laughing and talking or watching the procession; no one focused their attention his way. She looked back, and he grinned as he passed, a devastating slash of white that made Amy melt inside. Long after he rode out of sight around the bend, she stared to where he had disappeared.

"Amy?" Robert tugged on her hand.

She turned and gazed into his eyes, pale blue, not green. They didn't make her melt inside, didn't make her feel anything.

Robert smiled, revealing teeth that overlapped a bit. She'd not really noticed that before. " 'Tis over."

"Oh."

The sun set as they walked home to Cheapside, skirting merrymakers in the streets. Her father paused to unlock their door. Overhead, a wooden sign swung gently in the breeze. A nearby bonfire illuminated the image of a falcon and the gilt letters that proclaimed their shop GOLDSMITH & SONS, JEWELLERS.

There came a sudden brilliant flash and a stunned "Ooooh" from the crowd, as fireworks lit the sky. Amy dashed through the shop and up the stairs to their balcony. Gazing out over the River Thames, she watched the great fiery streaks of light, heard the soaring rockets, smelled the sulfur in the air. 'Twas the most spectacular display England had ever seen, and the sights and sounds filled her with a wondrous feeling. If only life could be as exhilarating as a fireworks show.

When the last glittering tendril faded away, she listened to the fragments of song and rowdy laughter that filled the night air. Couples strolled by, arm in arm. Robert stepped onto the balcony and moved close.

His voice was quiet beside her. "This is a day I'll never forget."

"I'll never forget it, either," she said, thinking of the man on the black steed, the man with the emerald eyes.

Robert tilted her face up, bending his head to place a soft, chaste kiss on her lips. 'Twas their first kiss; she was supposed to feel fireworks.

But she felt nothing.

Chapter One

Five years later
August 24, 1666

"Are you telling me *you* made this bracelet? A woman? This shop is Goldsmith & *Sons*, is it not?" Robert Stanley puckered his freckled face and made his voice high and wavering. "Where are the sons?"

From over by the stone oven, Amethyst Goldsmith's laughter rang through the workshop. "Lady Smythe! A perfect imitation."

"Well done, Robert." Her father smiled as he brushed past them both and through the archway into the shop's showroom.

Robert's pale blue eyes twinkled, but he stayed in character, cupping a hand to his ear. "Imitation? Imitation, did you say? I was led to believe this was a *quality* jewelry shop, madame. I expect genuine—"

"Stop!" Amy struggled to control her giggles. "You'll make me slip and scald myself."

Robert's gaze fell to Amy's hands, watched her pour a thin stream of molten gold into the plaster mold. His expression sobered. "I like Lady Smythe," he muttered. "At least she buys the things *I* make."

"Oh, Robert." She sighed. "Why should it matter who made something, as long as we're selling a piece?"

"I'm a good goldsmith . . ."

"You're an excellent goldsmith," Amy agreed. Although she also thought he was a bit unimaginative, she kept it to herself. "What does that have to do with anything?"

"You're a woman."

She clenched her jaw and tapped the mold on her workbench, imagining the gold flowing to fill every crevice of her design. "I'm also a jeweler," she said under her breath.

"Never mind." He walked to his own workbench and plopped onto his stool, lifting the pewter tankard of ale that sat ever-present amongst his tools.

Ignoring him, Amy picked up a knife and a chunk of wax, intending to whittle a new design while the gold hardened. The windowless workroom seemed stifling today—hot, close, and dark. She dragged a lantern nearer, but the artificial, yellowish glow did little to lift her mood.

Five years she'd lived and worked with Robert Stanley, and still he didn't understand her. She couldn't believe it. She was marrying him in two weeks, and she couldn't believe that, either.

Once it had seemed like a lifetime stretched ahead of her before she had to wed. She'd put it off, and put it off, then last spring her father had announced she was twenty-two and it was time to get on with it. He'd set a date, and that had been that. No matter that Robert thought his wife should stay home and mend his clothes; no matter that he resented it when her designs sold faster and she received more custom orders than he did.

No matter that she didn't love him. Not the way a wife should love a husband. Not the way it was in the French novels she read. Not the way she had felt, five years ago at the coronation procession, when that nobleman's emerald eyes had locked on hers. She'd never forgotten that feeling.

She would learn to love Robert, her father said. But it hadn't happened—not yet, anyway. Not even close. Amy sighed and lifted the braid off her neck, rubbed the hot skin beneath. She had set out to talk to her father dozens of times, but her courage had failed her.

Since the death of her mother in last year's Great Plague, it seemed she could take anything but her father's disapproval.

When the casting was set, Amy plunged it into the tub of water by Robert's workbench. She rubbed the mold's gritty plaster surface, feeling it dissolve away in her hands, watching Robert's knife send wax shavings flying as he sculpted a model. She scowled at his curved back. "I believe I fancied you more as Lady Smythe."

Robert turned and stared at her for a moment. He hunched over suddenly, and his face transformed, taking on a definite Lady Smythe look as his voice rose in pitch. "Are you certain, madame? I hear tell you've had dancing lessons and speak fluent French. Such pretensions. I don't hold with women reckoning account books, you know. Not at all." Then his voice deepened into his own. "Or making jewelry, either."

Amy flinched. She pulled the casting from the water and carried it to her workbench to brush off the last remaining bits of plaster.

He rose and came up behind her, tilted her head back with a hand beneath her chin. "Two more weeks, and a proper wife you'll be." With little finesse his mouth came down on hers. The faint scent of his breakfast had her squeezing her eyes shut, praying for the end to this torment. "Part your lips, Amy," he demanded against her mouth. She didn't. She wished he'd use one of those newfangled little silver toothbrushes Aunt Elizabeth had sent from Paris.

Finally he raised his head. "Two weeks," he repeated.

Her eyes snapped open and burned into his. "Papa would never allow you to keep me from making jewelry." She looked down and brushed at the casting harder.

"Hugh Goldsmith will not be here forever." His hand moved to snake down her bodice, but Amy's gaze flickered toward the showroom in warning. "At least soon he'll not be able to threaten me with bodily harm for sullying his virginal daughter." He strode back to his workbench, back to his ale. "Two weeks." Raising the tankard in a salute, he flashed a grin. A grin that Amy had once thought boyish, engaging . . . but of late had made her uneasy.

They both turned as the bell on the outside door tinkled. "I'll get it." Amy stood and whipped off her apron.

"Your father is out there," Robert reminded her. "He can handle it."

She paid him no mind, but smoothed back a few damp strands that had escaped her braid. Pausing to straighten her gown, she put a shopgirl smile on her face, then headed through the swinging doors into the cool, bright showroom.

"A locket," a young woman at the case was saying, smiling up at a gentleman with his back to Amy. Deep red curls draped to the lady's bare shoulders; her lavish golden brocade gown had a neckline much lower than Amy's father would ever allow. The man's mistress? In the years since the Restoration, the nobility had taken King Charles's lead as far as morals were concerned, which is to say they had very few.

The tall man addressed Hugh. "My sister would like a locket." He urged the lady—his sister, not his mistress—forward. "Go ahead, Kendra, see what you fancy."

Amy took a step closer, though the gentleman seemed determined to work with her father. Hugh smiled. "Have you a style in mind, or a price, Lord . . . ?"

"Greystone." The man waved a hand. "Whatever she likes." Although his back was to Amy, she sensed his impatience by the set of his wide shoulders under his hunter green velvet surcoat.

Hugh cleared his throat. "Perhaps my daughter can help you decide. Amethyst, please show Lord Greystone the lockets."

She took out a tray and moved to set it on the counter, smiling at the man's sister. Lady Kendra nodded and grinned in return, her beautiful red curls shimmering to rival the glitter of jewels in the case. Amy's hand went reflexively to her own head, as if she could rearrange her hated black hair into something more fashionable than her serviceable braid.

She picked up an oval locket with tiny engraved flowers. "See the gold ribbons forming the bale?" As her father had taught her, her voice was sweet and confident, reflecting her certainty of both the quality of the piece and her ability to sell it. She snapped open the locket and extended it, looking up at Lord Greystone.

" 'Tis—" Her voice failed her.

Hugh nudged her, frowning. "Amy?"

" 'T-'tis quite feminine," she stammered out.

It couldn't be he.

Emerald green eyes locked on hers—as they had done five years earlier. It *was* him . . . the nobleman from the coronation procession. Her heart seemed to pause in her chest, and for a second she thought she would drown in those eyes; then she looked away, with an effort, and down to the locket she was holding.

Lady Kendra reached to take the locket from Amy. "Oh, look how pretty it is, Colin." She held it up to her bodice, turning to model it for her brother.

With seeming reluctance, Lord Greystone swung his gaze toward his sister's chest. "I know not that I care for it."

"Notice the fine engraving, my lord," Hugh rushed to put in. " 'Tis truly first quality."

Lord Greystone ignored him and looked back to Amy. When his eyes narrowed, Amy found herself studying him in return. Classic symmetrical features, carefully sculpted. A long, straight nose; a slight dimple in his chin; his clean-shaven complexion more golden than was the fashion. God in heaven, she had never seen such a handsome man.

Her heart sped up when he finally spoke. "Have you a locket with . . . amethysts?"

His voice, smooth and deep, sent a shiver down Amy's spine. *Amethysts* . . . She opened her mouth to answer, but the words refused to come out.

"No, my lord, we do not," Hugh said. "But emeralds would suit the lady—"

"Yes," Amy interrupted, finally finding her voice. "Yes, we do have amethysts! If you'll but wait one moment . . ." She reached to grab the key ring off her father's belt, then turned and bolted for the workshop.

"We'll wait," Colin murmured, watching her disappear through the swinging doors, her braid flying behind—a long, thick, ribbon-entwined braid his fingers itched to unplait.

She was back in a flash. An orange-haired man followed her out, wiping blunt hands on his apron, leaving streaks of abrasive gray slurry. He lounged against the archway and fixed Colin with a distrustful light blue stare.

"Here it is," Amy announced proudly, handing the locket to Colin. She kept her gaze on him even while she plunked the key ring into her father's outstretched hand.

Colin wasn't much for jewelry, but he blinked at the piece in his hands. " 'Tis beautiful . . . 'tis truly beautiful."

Amy beamed. "It does have amethysts, my lord, and diamonds, too."

"I can see that." Wrought in shimmering gold, the locket was exquisite. On top, a cutwork pattern of diamond-set leaves surrounded an amethyst flower. The lozenge-shaped locket dangled beneath, encrusted with amethysts and diamonds, its lid enameled with delicate violets. Swinging from the bottom, a large baroque pearl gleamed.

Colin had never seen anything quite so splendid. He looked up at the jeweler. " 'Tis remarkable . . ."

"*I* made it." A pink flush blossomed on Amy's cheeks.

Kendra's mouth dropped open in surprise. Colin's startled gaze swung to Amy, over to her father, who nodded proudly, and then back to Amy. "I don't believe it. You're—"

"A woman?" There was a challenge in her amethyst eyes.

He grinned, caught out. "However did you learn to make something like this?"

Her father cleared his throat. "We'd not much to do during the Commonwealth, my lord. I expect you were abroad?" Colin nodded his assent. "Well, jewelry was much frowned upon, other than some mourning pieces. I had time aplenty to train Amy in the arts of goldsmithing. She's a natural—even did the enameling herself." He placed a possessive hand on his daughter's shoulder.

"I must—I mean, *Kendra*—must have it."

The jeweler shook his head. "I'm afraid it is not for sale. 'Tis Amy's own keepsake."

"Of course it is for sale, Papa." Amy regarded Colin with a speculative gaze. "But 'tis very expensive."

"I'd expect so. We'll take it."

Kendra turned to him, a frown creasing the area between her light green eyes. "Are you sure, Colin?"

He looked down at his sister. "Do you not like it?"

" 'Tis lovely, but . . ."

"I said I would buy whatever you chose for your birthday. I want you to have it." Colin knew he was acting out of character, but in all his twenty-eight years he had never met anyone like the girl who had made this piece, and he wanted his sister to own it. He fished a pouch of coins from his surcoat. "Here. Take what is fair. Include a chain; I want her to wear it now."

Colin watched Amy fumble with the pouch, taking note of her distraction, the way her gaze darted back and forth between the coins and his face. She felt it, too—this compelling, undeniable attraction. He smiled to himself. It made a man feel good, though nothing would ever come of it.

"Papa?" Closing the pouch, Amy showed her father the gold she'd taken.

Hugh nodded. " 'Tis fine, Amy." He pocketed the coins and placed a chain on the counter.

As she returned the pouch to Lord Greystone, he handed her the locket. His fingers brushed her hand, and a brief, warm shiver rippled through her. Her breath caught; she hoped he didn't notice.

She stiffened when Robert sullenly pulled a cloth from his apron pocket and moved from the archway to stand beside her. He polished the counter as she threaded the chain through the bale on the locket, then held it up for Lady Kendra to see.

"Ooh . . ." Lady Kendra breathed. "Will you put it on me?" She turned, and Lord Greystone lifted her hair so Amy could fasten the clasp. Lady Kendra faced Amy and touched the locket reverently. "Thank you so very much. I'll treasure it always."

"Thank *who*?" Lord Greystone prompted with a smile.

"Thank you, Colin."

When Lady Kendra turned to embrace her brother, Amy bit her lip, feeling an unexpected twinge of envy for this woman's shiny red curls and low-cut gown. But most of all, she envied the way Lady Kendra was hugging Lord Greystone. She looked down at the counter, lest Robert catch sight of her telltale eyes.

Lord Greystone ushered his sister outside, then lingered in the doorway, looking oddly reluctant to leave.

"Can . . ." The long fingers of one hand drummed against his muscled thigh, then stopped. "Can you make a signet ring?" His question came low across the small shop, to Amy, not Hugh.

"A signet ring?" she said with a small smile. "Of course, 'tis a simple matter." Beside her, Robert stopped polishing.

"Good." Lord Greystone paused, frowning a bit. "I'll send a messenger with a drawing of the crest," he said at last. "And the address to deliver it when you're finished."

Amy nodded, feeling a quick stab of disappointment that she'd not be seeing him again. Robert's hand resumed its deliberate circular motion on top of the counter.

"I thank you," Lord Greystone said. Then he melted

out the doorway and into the teeming streets of Cheapside.

Amy stared after him until her father cleared his throat.

"I cannot believe you sold your locket," he remarked. "I thought it was your favorite piece."

"It was," she answered dreamily. "But I can make another one." Her stomach fluttered with happiness, just knowing Lord Greystone admired her craftsmanship and his sister would be wearing her locket. And soon, *he* would be wearing her ring.

"If you ask me, 'twas a clod-headed idea," Robert put in with a shake of his carrot-topped head. "You'll never find time to make another locket with all the custom orders you get."

Amy and her father shared a quizzical look.

"Besides, I didn't like him," Robert added. "I didn't like the way he looked at you."

Amy lowered her gaze and brushed past him into the workshop. She'd liked the way Lord Greystone looked at her, very much. Very much indeed.

Colin entered their carriage to find Kendra seated inside, her arms crossed. "What took you so long?"

He sat opposite her and looked out the window. "I ordered a signet ring."

"You *what*?"

He brought his gaze to hers. "I need it, for a seal."

Kendra shot him a look of patent disbelief. "You couldn't even afford this locket." She shook her bright head. "Something happened in that shop."

"Nothing happened." His younger sister was observant as hell, and it could be deucedly inconvenient at times. "I just thought it was a beautiful piece of jewelry, and I wanted you to have it."

"Od's fish, Colin, you're the one always lecturing us about saving funds . . ."

He turned off her voice in his head, instead considering the possibility of landing that enticing little jeweler in his bed.

". . . planning for the future."

She was completely off limits, of course. Not a widow, not an actress, not a lightskirt . . . not a highborn member of King Charles's licentious Court.

"And you ordered a ring. You never wear jewelry."

A sheltered young woman of the merchant class, 'twas most likely she would never bed with any man outside of marriage. And Colin Chase, Earl of Greystone, had no intention of marrying beneath himself.

"I cannot believe you bought this locket in the first place."

Besides, he was already betrothed to the perfect woman.

"I do love it, though."

As they passed Goldsmith & Sons, he glanced out the window. He would never go back there. It had been a harmless flirtation, nothing more. He couldn't remember the last time he'd set foot in a jewelry shop, and . . . no, he had no reason to ever return.

"Thank you, Colin. I truly do love it."

He blinked and looked at Kendra. She was sighing, gazing down at the locket and fingering it possessively. What had she been saying? Oh, she loved it. "I'm glad. Shall we go buy our brother that telescope he's been hankering for?"

"Oh—are you sure? Ford will be thrilled." Kendra bounced on the seat, then settled her skirts about her, as though she'd just remembered she was grown up. "Can it be from me, too? Sometimes he drives me mad as a Bedlam wench with his scientific obsession, but he is my twin, and I love to see him happy."

Colin gave his sister a fond smile, hoping the man she finally consented to marry would have more energy than he did. "Yes, it can be from you, too. Now, where do you suppose we might find such a contraption?"

Chapter Two

"Ring-a-ring o'roses
A pocket full of posies
A-tishoo! A-tishoo!
We all fall down."

"Hold still, if you please."

Amy looked down to the seamstress who knelt at her feet, pinning up the hem of her wedding dress. "I'm sorry, Mrs. Cholmley." She sniffled, and a tear escaped and splashed on the older woman's hand.

Mrs. Cholmley glanced up, concern marking her kind hazel eyes. "Reminds you of your poor mama, don't it? The children playing outside, I mean?"

Amy nodded mutely, blinking back more tears. She concentrated on the gown's belled-out lavender lace skirt, counting the love knots—small satin bows sewn loosely all over, one for each wedding guest to tear off after the ceremony, as a keepsake. Fifty-eight, fifty-nine—

" 'Tis only a game, dear. D'ye think they even know what they're singing?" The seamstress reached absently for more pins, talking to herself, so far as Amy could tell. "Roses, the rash; posies to sweeten the putrid air. The ring is . . . the plague-token, of course." She sighed. "My Edgar had one—black and pus filled—he screamed so when the doctor cut into it. Lud, I still hear him in my dreams. Turn, please."

With a sigh of her own, Amy dutifully turned. She

stared out the window at the sky, gray with smoke from the incessant burning of sea-coal.

"And your mama? Did she suffer one?"

Her gaze dropped to Mrs. Cholmley's gray head. "Suffer what?"

"A plague-token."

Would this woman never stop chattering?

Amy's fists clenched. "We know not. At the first sign of fever, she begged us to go to Paris and stay with Aunt Elizabeth." Her voice dropped to a whisper. "I was in Paris. I know not what happened to her."

"Hard to believe a year has passed. It feels like yesterday they painted that red cross on my door. House after house marked for the quarantine and staffed with guards, all up and down the street. I thought I was like to meet my maker, right enough. And the death carts rattling by . . . 'Bring out your dead; bring out your dead.' " Mrs. Cholmley shuddered and pinned. "My Edgar was buried in a plague pit. Your mother, as well?"

Amy shut her eyes and bit a mark into her lower lip. "We think so. We've found no grave." No grave to put flowers on, nowhere to go talk to Mama, to tell her about the upcoming wedding, all her misgivings.

The heavy, sweet stench of decaying bodies had hung over London for weeks after Amy returned from Paris. She'd read in the *London Gazette* that one in five Londoners had died. But that had been months ago, and London had recovered its usual bustle.

Mrs. Cholmley had apparently talked herself out. Beyond the window, the children's voices faded, replaced by the ordinary sounds of busy London. Swiping the tears from her cheeks, Amy listened. Creaking wheels, animal snorts, the familiar din of grumbles, shouts, and the singsong chants of vendors.

She opened her eyes. The remembered reek of decomposing corpses shifted to the scent of new, starched fabric. At a gentle touch on her knee from Mrs. Cholmley, she turned again. Her fingers worked at the love knots on her dress. She wished she could tear the little bows off now—or better yet, tear the whole gown off and into shreds. Ten more days and she would be Robert's wife. Ten days! It seemed impossible.

For six months now, her father had gone about making wedding plans, and she had done nothing to stop him. It had given him something to think about in the wake of his wife's death, and Amy had not found the strength to fight him. It had all seemed so very far away.

But now her wedding day was almost here. Every morning she woke up wishing it were no more than a bad dream. She had to find the courage to call off this wedding before it was too late. Now.

"Are you finished yet?" she asked, her voice sharper than she'd intended.

Mrs. Cholmley sighed and stood up, flexing her arthritic joints. "All done," she said, smiling in a sympathetic way that made Amy feel even more guilty. "You nervous brides." Clucking good-naturedly, she drew off the wedding dress. Amy's maid pulled her periwinkle gown from the wardrobe cabinet.

Underskirt, overdress, laces, stomacher, stockings, shoes . . . dressing seemed to take forever. At last Amy went down the corridor toward Hugh's room. The closer she got, the faster her heart beat and the slower her feet dragged.

She paused in the doorway and stared at her father's back, struck as always by how empty the room felt without her mother's presence.

"Papa?"

Hugh jerked, startled. He stood slowly and turned to face her. "What is it, poppet?"

A familiar, dull pain briefly squeezed Amy's heart as her gaze dropped to the miniature of Edith, its oval gold frame cradled between her father's work-worn hands. "She was lovely, was she not?"

"Yes, she was." He smiled down at the picture. "You have her delicate chin, and her beautiful amethyst eyes."

"And *your* unruly black hair." Hugh didn't react to her gentle teasing tone. "Sometimes, Papa . . . sometimes

I think that if you could wear out a painting by looking at it, Mama's image would have disappeared from the canvas a long time ago."

He looked up, offering her a wan smile. "We shared a rare love, poppet."

'Twas a perfect opening; she couldn't let her courage fail her now. She lifted her chin. "Papa, I . . . I always dreamed of a love—"

"Have you seen those ruby earrings your mother wore to see *Henry V* the week before she—she—"

Amy crossed her arms, sympathy and impatience warring within her. Impatience won. "Papa, I need to talk to you."

"I just want to see them," he said gruffly.

She knew his moods, and there was no arguing with his retreating back. Determined to say her piece, she picked up her skirts and followed him down the two flights of stairs and into the workshop.

While he started unlocking their safe chest, she tied on an apron and sat at her workbench. More to calm herself than to accomplish anything, she unfolded the sheet of paper Lord Greystone had sent her and smoothed it flat against the table. She squinted at the drawing and steeled herself to broach the subject again.

The last bolt clunked into place, and she heard Hugh throw open the lid and begin removing trays to access his private collection in the bottom. Amy dragged a candle closer to study the Greystone crest. She listened to the soft metallic sounds of her father sifting through centuries of treasures.

She had to just say it. "Papa—"

"Mmmm . . . I've always loved this piece." Exasperated, Amy turned to watch her father sit back on his heels and hold up a pendant. It sparkled in the lantern light. Drawn despite her low spirits, she rose and moved to him.

"Let me see. Who made it?"

"Your great grandpapa, a master with enamel. Look."

"Ahh . . ." Amy studied the piece, a merman, his

entire torso consisting of one huge, perfectly formed baroque pearl. His tail was an enamelled rainbow of colors set with cut gemstones. He wore a miniature necklace and bracelets, and carried a tiny shield and saber. The entire, elaborate pendant was less than four inches tall, including three pearls that dangled from the bottom. " 'Tis exquisite. I remember it now."

"He was inspired by Erasmus Hornick's design book." Hugh still had the treasured book, an ancient leather-bound volume from Nuremberg that Amy was almost afraid to touch. "But the workmanship was his own. He outdid himself with this one, do you not think? In almost a hundred years, no one in the family has ever been able to bring himself to sell it."

"I'm glad."

He replaced the piece and hunched over the chest, resuming his search for the ruby earrings. He was mellow, Amy thought, maybe now . . . "Papa—"

"Your talent came from him, you know. Through the generations. A gift—and an obligation."

Amy swallowed and took a deep breath. "Papa, I—"

"I know what you're going to say, Amy." His knees creaked as he stood up. "You think I know not how you feel? 'Tis naught but nerves. Every bride has them."

Amy shot him a hurt look, shocked that he'd known all along that she wanted to call off the wedding, yet chose to do nothing about it. Her own father. She returned to her workbench and set Lord Greystone's ring into a clamp attached to the table.

"You bear a responsibility. Here in this shop, our people have worked for generations, for you. You can do no less for your own children. And you cannot do so as a woman alone."

Amy heard her father's footsteps, then a small *clink* as he placed the earrings on her work surface. Pear-shaped, blood-red rubies were bezel set and *pavéd* with diamonds on long, graceful drops. Amy's heart clenched as she remembered how her mother had protested they were too fancy, but then held her head high that night at the theater, to show them to advantage.

"Life is fragile, poppet." Hugh's voice cracked. "I want to see you settled before something happens to me, too."

The rubies seemed to wink in the candlelight, a poignant reminder of her mother and her mother's expectations. Amy's throat closed with emotion, and she had to force the words out. "Nothing is happening to you, Papa." Averting her eyes from the earrings, she dug in a drawer for a stick of engravers' wax and heated one end in the candle flame, then rubbed it over the top of the ring.

"This family has hoarded gold, coins, and gems for centuries—*centuries*, Amy—making certain no Goldsmith will ever suffer a moment of insecurity. The shop sold almost nothing during the Commonwealth. Could we have lived through it as we did—with servants, and nice clothes, and good food on the table—without that legacy handed down from our ancestors?"

She stilled, a sharp-tipped tool in her hand. "No." The word was directed toward Lord Greystone's ring, its hard-won shine dimmed by engravers' wax and the blur of unshed tears.

"And now that the good times have returned, we work every day to replace what we were forced to use. 'Tis my responsibility, and one day it will be yours."

With the quick, sure strokes of an artist, she traced a reverse image of the crest into the wax, then lifted the graver. The murmur of Robert assisting two customers came through the arch from the showroom, but Amy and Hugh's silence grew tight with tension. Hugh sighed. "These marriages—'tis the way our trade works. I want your word that Goldsmith & Sons will go on. I need your promise."

"Nothing is happening to Goldsmith & Sons." Amy started engraving, meticulously carving out tiny ribbons of gold from the signet's top. She felt her father's gaze on her, knew he wanted an answer, not a denial. An answer about Robert.

The tool slowed as she focused on the ring—and the man it was for. A hazy image of Lord Greystone's handsome dark features hovered in Amy's mind. He'd just looked at her with his piercing emerald eyes, and she'd felt warm all over and had known that it would never, *just never*, be that way with Robert.

She hurried to finish, set down the graver and held the ring to the candle, studying the reverse crest for imperfections.

"Promise me," Hugh pressed. "You have a gift that cannot be wasted, an obligation in your blood. Promise me."

She dripped a shiny blob of red sealing wax onto the design sheet and pressed the ring into it. It made a perfect imprint of the Greystone coat of arms, but she didn't feel her usual surge of satisfaction. Sighing, she turned to search her father's concerned blue eyes. " 'Tis just Robert, Papa. He . . . he does not understand me."

"He does not have to understand you. You were promised to him years ago, and he knows his place. As a second son, he's lucky—very lucky—to be marrying into a wealthy family, with his wife-to-be the sole heir. Without you, Robert has nothing. He knows it. He's the right man for you—the right man for Goldsmith & Sons."

Her father didn't understand her, either. "He scares me when he touches me."

"You know naught of the marriage bed, poppet. 'Twill not scare you for long."

Tears stung the backs of her eyes. She sat up straighter. "He wants me to stop making jewelry."

A short, harsh bark of laughter followed that statement. "The man is feeling impotent now. When his apprenticeship is finished, he'll feel differently. He'll not care to do without the income from your designs."

He reached for the ruby earrings, turned to put them away. She watched him gaze at the jewels, then kneel to tenderly place them in the bottom of the chest. Her fingers clenched tight around Lord Greystone's ring as the tears that had been threatening welled up, and before she could stop herself, she dropped to her knees beside him.

"Papa, look at me. Me!"

She reached for his hands and grasped them in hers, the ring trapped somewhere amidst the tangle of their fingers.

"Papa! Remember you told me I'd have a love, a love like yours and Mama's? You promised, but it's not happened! I do not love Robert." She felt a tear escape and roll down her cheek as her desperate eyes implored his pained ones. "If something happened to him, I'd not stare at his picture, I'd not—"

"Enough!" Hugh stood so abruptly that Amy fell back. Never had he raised his voice to her. Now in his fear, his loneliness, he lashed out. "I loved your mother—I still do—and she's gone! I cannot work—I stare at her painting—I loved her so! Better you and Robert think straight. Not like me!"

His shoulders slumped, and his voice dropped to a husky whisper. "Not like me."

She watched him draw a shuddering breath as he reached a hand to pull her up. "I'm sorry, poppet." His eyes fluttered closed and then open as he ran a shaky hand through the black tangles of his hair. "That it has come to harsh words . . . I'm sorry. But there is more to life than love. 'Twill be better for you this way. You must see a bigger picture. Tradition, continuity . . . this is how our guild has survived for centuries."

The hard edges of the heavy ring bit into Amy's clenched fist. She blinked back the tears. Like the vast majority of betrothal agreements, hers was not binding until consummation. No money had yet changed hands. There must be another way for her that would still preserve the business. "Surely there is another jeweler . . ."

"Ours is a small industry. Others were apprenticed a decade ago. These matches are made for children, and you're twenty-two. 'Tis God's own truth I've been patient, but 'tis past time your future was cemented." He moved to wrap an arm tight around Amy's shoulders, as though willing her to understand, to accept the realities of her life. "Robert is a good goldsmith, a good man. You cannot have everything, Amy."

You cannot have everything. The words echoed in Amy's head, summing up her destiny. She was stuck, as sure as an insect in amber.

Shrugging out of her father's grasp, she picked up a cloth embedded with reddish rouge powder and rubbed the ring absently, a final hand-polish to make it gleam. It felt solid in her hands, this thing she'd created from nothing more than raw metal and elusive inbred artistry. She could never give up making jewelry. She was born to it.

Her gaze swept over the cluttered workshop. Tools, hunks of discarded wax, and half-finished pieces of jewelry littered every available surface. A thin veil of the reddish rouge powder dusted the tabletops and stained her fingertips.

This was where she belonged. And if her father said that Robert belonged here as well, that was the way of it. The fire below the oven snapped, and she blinked, then knuckled the last trace of tears from her eyes. *You cannot have everything.*

"Promise me, Amy. Promise me that Goldsmith & Sons will not end with you."

"You have my promise."

"I love you, poppet," Hugh said quietly.

He only wanted what was best for her. As she turned into his arms, the ring slipped from her fingers and clattered to the wooden floor.

"I love you too, Papa," she said.

'Twas a long time before she bent to pick up the ring, an even longer time before Robert came in to find her staring at it.

He stood over her. "You still working on that damned ring?"

She looked up at him, but could not find the energy to summon as much as annoyance.

" 'Tis finished," she said. "I'll have it delivered in the morning."

Chapter Three

"Colin! Down here!"

From along the ridge where he and nine others were grappling with a huge block of limestone, Colin glanced to the path below to see his brothers climbing from the carriage and Kendra leaning halfway out the window, waving wildly.

"You're early," he called a minute later, heading down the rise. He wiped gritty palms on his linen breeches, his shirt billowing in the light wind that buffeted across Greystone's quarry.

"Early?" His older brother Jason laughed, pointing at the sky. Colin glanced straight up and then west to where the sun was nearly setting.

"Sorry." He shrugged. "I've been about since six this morn. In the woods, the fields . . . I reckon I lost track of the time."

"I reckon you lost your hat, as well?" Kendra fixed him with a half-serious frown of reproach. "Look at you, brown as a gypsy!"

With the back of one hand, he wiped at the sweat on his forehead. "Have you come to see the renovations, or to harp on my appearance?"

"To harp on your appearance," Kendra's twin, Ford, answered for her. "But I've a curiosity to see your new kitchen. Pipes and taps . . . do they work due to a siphon effect, or is it simple gravity? In Isaac Newton's new paper, he says—"

"Od's fish—how the hell should I know? I'm a farmer,

not a bloody scientist. They work because the mason put them in right."

"What *I* want to know"—Jason patted his stomach meaningfully—"is whether we'll find food in this kitchen?"

"Hell, yes." Colin laughed. "Benchley's been slaving since dawn, I expect. Go on up to the castle, and I'll follow along shortly. Four quarrymen are down with the ague, and we've two more slabs to bring up."

"God, 'tis quiet here." Kendra paused before climbing from the coach into Greystone's little courtyard. "Listen." A few low birdcalls, distant bleating from the fields, a faint rustle from the smattering of trees that stood sentinel around the tiny circular drive. "It sounds like no one's home."

"No one *is* home," Jason reminded her. "Colin has only Benchley for company until the renovations are further along—and he's likely in the kitchen."

"Let us go see the kitchen." Ford urged them along. "Those pipes—"

"That food—"

"Those Chase stomachs!" Kendra laughed as they walked toward the door to Greystone's modest living quarters. "I cannot say I'm surprised that Colin restored the kitchen first."

"A man's got to eat," Ford declared.

"I could feed an entire village on what you three pack away in a day. Look . . . the door is part open." She stopped, her hand on the latch, and turned back to watch their carriage pass under the barbican gate, the driver heading out to Colin's stables. "And the drawbridge is down."

Jason's green eyes sparkled with suppressed laughter. "It's probably not been up in a hundred years. What would be the point? There's naught in this old place of interest to anyone."

"Something doesn't feel right."

"There she goes, leaping to conclusions again." Ford

pushed open the door and stepped inside the plain, square entry. "Good Lord, what is that on the floor?"

"What?" Kendra took a step back.

"Ouch!" Jason wrenched his foot from under hers. "Why do you insist on wearing those blasted high heels?" He shouldered his way past the twins. "Something spilled, is all." Leaning down to touch one of the dark splotches, he rubbed the substance between his fingers, then sniffed and turned back to them slowly.

" 'Tis blood."

"Blood?" Kendra squeaked.

"Don't get overwrought." Suddenly Jason grinned. "I'd wager 'tis just another of Colin's practical jokes."

Kendra took another step back. "Real blood a joke?"

Ford put a hand on his sister's shoulder. "Perhaps Benchley butchered something outside and failed to notice it dripping when he brought it through here. Look, the drops trail under the door to the Great Hall, toward the kitchen. I wonder what it is? I'm hoping for suckling pig."

The Great Hall's door was ajar, as well. Jason led the way into the gutted, roofless chamber, its pitted stone floor still scattered with rusted cannonballs from Cromwell's last siege.

"How could he not have noticed it dripping?" Kendra's voice was a whisper, her gaze riveted to the bloody trail. " 'Twas pumping out here, from the looks of it." She fixed Ford with light green, accusatory eyes. "A suckling pig!" she exclaimed, her voice rising. "More like a cow, I'll warrant you. I've never seen so much—"

At the other end of the Hall, Jason reached for the door, then jerked back his hand. "The latch . . . 'tis covered in blood as well."

Kendra bit her lip. "Maybe we ought to wait for Colin."

"Don't be a goose." Jason kicked at the door with one booted foot, and it gave, swinging open with a prolonged creak.

Meandering bloody footprints traversed the short corridor. "I don't like this," Kendra insisted, gingerly picking her way past the dark red marks.

They paused at the entrance to the kitchen. "Benchley?" Ford called, running a shaky hand through his wavy brown hair. "Benchley, are you here, man?"

"It appears not," Jason said unnecessarily.

"Oh, my God," Kendra breathed, pointing to one of the two sunken wells.

"What now, Kendra?" Ford glared at her.

"Do you not hear the dripping?"

"Dripping?" Jason started toward the well, then suddenly flung out an arm. "Stay back!"

Kendra ducked to avoid being knocked in the teeth. "What? What is it?"

"This is no joke. Ford, fetch Colin *now*!"

Despite Jason's warning, Kendra rushed forward, then let out an earsplitting scream before whirling to muffle her face against his broad chest. "He's dead, he's dead, he's dead," she panted. "Benchley's dead. Oh, my God, Benchley's dead!"

Disregarding Jason's instructions, Ford threw his arms around them both, his breathing labored though he'd failed to utter a sound. Squished between her brothers, Kendra turned her head and cracked open one eye, just to make sure.

Bent at the waist over the crossbar that spanned the well, Colin's manservant dangled, his clothes streaked with red. More blood dripped from the sopping mass of his prematurely gray hair, echoing as it plopped into the water far below.

At the grisly sight she let out a whimper and promptly reburied her face.

With an unnerving suddenness, mad laughter burst out behind them. The siblings broke apart and stared, dumbstruck, as Colin strode in and leaned over the well.

A plaintive voice resonated from the depths. "My back is killing me. Will someone help me out of here?"

Kendra blinked, finally figuring out what had happened. The color rushed back to her cheeks. "You lout! That was mean."

Colin grinned at her, raising one black eyebrow.

"But a good one," Ford admitted sheepishly, starting to chuckle. "Definitely one to be proud of."

"A devil of a mess, but worth it." Colin's voice was ebullient. He reached down to hoist Benchley up. "If you could only have seen your faces."

The manservant's shirt was plastered to his short, wiry form. "I'll be going to clean off now," he said with the greatest of dignity. Back ramrod straight, he thrust his beakish nose into the air and strutted from the room.

"Hurry back; we're fair starving," Jason called, before the siblings burst into peals of laughter.

Jason leaned on both hands against the large, scrubbed wooden worktable, his long black hair falling forward to hide his face. "I cannot credit that I fell for it," he muttered. "I even said at first . . ." He looked up at Colin. "By God, but your betrothed will be sorry she missed this one."

"Bosh!" Kendra waved a hand. "She would say 'twas a childish waste of time."

Ford sniffed at a covered platter. "Suckling pig," he mumbled, hiding a smile as he made his way over to one of the basins and reached for a bronze tap.

Her eyes sparkling with mischief, Kendra turned to Colin. "When are you and Lady Priscilla Snobs setting the date?"

"Lady Priscilla *Hobbs* and I have yet to decide. She'll not move to Greystone in the condition 'tis in." Colin scanned the shelves, looking for something he could use to clean up.

"Gravity," Ford declared, opening the tap, then shutting it again. With obvious glee, he repeated the motion. "Definitely gravity."

Kendra nodded absently and turned back to Colin. "Priscilla could live at Cainewood with us."

"Not likely. This family is a bit too, uh, high spirited for Priscilla." He dropped a wad of rags on the biggest puddle of pig blood, poking at it with one booted foot. "She's an only child, you know—used to peace and quiet."

"She's a snob, you mean. Otherwise—"

"Kendra!" Jason's leaf-green eyes glared into his sister's lighter ones. "Lady Priscilla is a perfectly nice person. More important to Colin, though, she's pretty, titled, and the only heir to an enormous fortune. If it takes her a while to get used to us, we'll just have to put up with it." He turned to Colin. "How are the rest of the renovations coming along?"

"Slowly." Colin looked up from where he crouched on the floor, mopping the last of the bloody trail. "My study and one bedchamber are finished, enough for Benchley and me to stay here and work. But for Priscilla . . ."

Jason's hand went to his narrow black mustache, stroked one side, then the other. He nodded. "I'm sure Priscilla requires a small army of servants, as well as a proper suite and a couple of receiving rooms, at the very least." He tossed Kendra a warning glance. "On the other hand, she's not going to wait for the entire castle to be remodeled, is she?"

"God's blood, no." Colin shook his head vehemently. "It stood vacant since '43 when the Roundheads laid the Great Hall in ruins. I'll warrant we'll see another quarter century before 'tis fully restored."

"See this lead pipe?" Ford gestured at the stone wall. "I'd lay odds there's a cistern on the roof. This second tap controls outflow—the River Caine lies downhill from here, does it not?" He grinned, his deep blue eyes flashing with satisfaction. "Gravity."

"Fascinating," Jason said dryly.

Standing up slowly, Colin twisted the new gold ring on his finger, considering the enormity of the task ahead of him. "No, Priscilla wants to wed and start a family soon. Just a few more rooms . . ." He sighed. " 'Tis all so damned expensive. The problem is I've been spending more on farm equipment and livestock than renovations.

I need to get the estate into shape before it can generate a decent income."

"Poor Colin." Kendra walked around the kitchen, reaching up a hand to trail along the mantels of the three immense fireplaces. "I suppose I cannot fault you for wanting Priscilla and her 'enormous fortune,' but can you not hurry it along a bit?" She stopped and cocked her head at Colin, who was busy lighting candles to ward off the encroaching dark. "Manage to compromise her, or something?"

"Kendra!" Jason scolded.

Ford snorted, his attention finally diverted from the pipes. "*Compromise* her? At King Charles's Court? Just what would that entail, do you suppose?" He wandered over to break off a piece of the fresh-baked manchet that Benchley had left on the table. "I'm afraid 'compromising' went out with knights in shining armor—or Cromwell, at the very least." He sank his teeth into the fine white bread, talking around a mouthful. "Colin could ravish her on the hazard table at Whitehall Palace, and I doubt anyone would take notice—other than to push them out of the way so they could get on with the game."

He reached for more bread, but Kendra slapped his hand away. "I'm not a half-wit." Due to her three brothers' exasperating diligence, she was certain she was the only virgin at Court. "I was trying to put it delicately, but what I meant was, why not just get her with child?"

Colin had held his tongue during Ford's tirade—facts were facts, after all—but this went beyond his gentlemanly sensibilities. "I cannot believe you would suggest such a thing."

"I cannot believe you've not thought of it. I'm sure you all have, in fact, and you'll just not admit it!" Kendra's lips thinned with irritation. "You and your *honor*. If Priscilla Snobs had half the honor of any one of you, she'd swallow her pride, marry the man she supposedly loves, and help him rebuild his home. She can afford to live simply for a few months; 'twould not kill her. Or she could move in with us, or live in the town house."

Colin gave a resigned shrug. "We've been over all our options." One by one, he took four goblets off the shelves and set them on the table. "The town house always has people coming and going—'tis no place to actually live—"

"I like living there." Kendra reached for some napkins and started folding them into triangles. "London is exciting."

"Well, Priscilla feels differently. She's a very calm person. I like that, you know. Having been dragged halfway around the world most of my life, I'm looking forward to staying in one quiet place, with one quiet family . . ."

Kendra straightened the fourth triangle, then looked up. "You'll be bored to tears in no time."

"Kendra's right enough," Ford put in. "It sounds like Priscilla's main attraction, other than the aforementioned 'enormous fortune,' is her talent for putting one to sleep—"

"Enough!" Colin's gaze flashed around the table, resting on each sibling in turn. His expression was thunderous. "Perhaps I've yet to set a date, but I *am* marrying Priscilla Hobbs, and I'll not have you discussing her this way any longer. I *like* her. I like her appearance, I like her demeanor, I like her background, and yes, I like her title and her fortune. She's exactly what I've been looking for all these years, and I'm not going to let all of you ruin it for me!"

There was a rare silence among the Chase family. Colin considered they might even have stopped breathing; the only motion seemed to be the candlelight that flickered against the whitewashed stone walls.

"I'll be right back," he muttered after a minute, then stalked off down the corridor to the buttery.

Though he took his time selecting a bottle of wine, the silence still reigned when he returned. Jason shifted uneasily on his feet, Ford traced aimless circles with his finger on the tabletop, and Kendra seemed to be studying her shoes. Colin almost felt sorry for them.

"Colin?"

"Yes, Kendra?"

"Do you love her?"

He sighed impatiently and set to uncorking the wine. "Our parents loved one another, and what did it do for all of us? They were very passionate people, were they not? Passionate about each other, the monarchy . . . we were born of their passion, not because they wanted children." He looked straight at Kendra, his eyes burning into hers. "No, Kendra, I don't love Priscilla, but I do like her. And I think it is better that way."

Colin filled the goblets, the sound of pouring wine unnaturally loud in the tense atmosphere. Jason took a careful sip, then set his goblet back on the table, his expression betraying a faint touch of sadness.

"You've thought about this a lot, have you?"

Colin's chin went up. "Yes, I have."

Jason shook his head, almost imperceptibly. " 'Twas not really like that, you know. Our parents—all of us—were victims of the times. I felt very wanted as a small child. During the fighting, I missed them terribly, and I'm certain they missed us. Damn Cromwell!" He slammed his fist on the table, making the empty bottle dance and the wine sway in their goblets.

"I miss them now," Kendra said quietly. "I always will."

"Well—"

Colin's thoughts were interrupted by Benchley's sudden return. The small man skidded into the kitchen, panting, water from his freshly washed hair puddling on the stone floor.

"My lord, you must come!" A lantern bobbed in Benchley's trembling hand; Colin leapt to grab it before it might crash to the floor. "I went outside the walls to dump the water, and—Holy Christ, you must see it!"

"See what?" Colin asked, but the words were directed to Benchley's retreating back. They followed him at a run, through the darkened castle and outside the turreted walls.

A hush seemed to fall over the countryside as the five of them gazed toward London. At the edge of the jet-black night sky, a dazzling red glow hovered at the horizon.

Kendra's whisper shattered the silence. "What is it?"

"A fire," Jason stated grimly. "And it looks big."

"London, on fire?" Kendra's voice was tense with fear. "Or is it closer?"

Jason put a hand on her shoulder. "Don't trouble yourself, Kendra. 'Twill not reach us here. The night is so dark that it seems to light the sky, but I'd wager that in daylight we'd not see it at all."

"But it looks enormous. Whitehall Palace could be burning, or St. Paul's or—our town house! Oh, God, what if the town house is on fire?"

By the dim light of the lantern, Jason's gaze met Colin's over their sister's head. "We must go help," they said together.

"Ford, you'll come as well," Jason continued. "Colin, you've extra horses? Carrington will fetch Kendra home in the carriage. Let's move."

Chapter Four

Colin paused to lean and pat his skittish gelding's black, lathered neck as Jason and Ford rode ahead. " 'Tis all right, lad," he murmured, though he knew the endearment was likely swallowed by the sounds of chaos that engulfed them.

"Colin!" Though they'd barely fought their way into London, Jason's voice was already hoarse from smoke and overuse. "Come along! We'll lose you, man!"

Usually dark and deserted at night, London's streets were alive with an appalling incandescence and a crush of displaced humanity. Colin's skin prickled with heat as he picked his way around people, animals, and debris. Bits of ash drifted down, dotting his clothes and hair. Squinting into the haze, he searched the maelstrom for his brothers.

There they were, their familiar forms near a commanding presence riding tall on a huge black stallion: King Charles with his own brother, James, Duke of York. Colin watched, mesmerized, as the King reached into a bag flung over his shoulder and threw a handful of guineas to the workmen, encouraging them in their efforts to create a firebreak. The gold coins shimmered in the light of the flickering blaze, as though hung suspended in the thick, smoky air.

"Sweet Mary," Colin breathed, finally catching up to his brothers. "Where to start?"

"Here's as good a spot as any." Jason twisted in the saddle, looking for a safe place to tie up their horses. His gasp made the brothers turn.

Hands white-knuckled on the reins, Colin could only stare at the terrible splendor of St. Paul's Cathedral, all ablaze.

"God's blood," he murmured.

"I was *there* last week." Ford jockeyed his horse closer to Colin, shaking his head in disbelief. "Lady Tabitha and I—we carved our names into the lead on the roof."

"They're erased now," Jason said grimly. "Along with six centuries of other signatures." The molten metal ran down in fiery streams, the glorious dome rising like a torch from the sea of flames made by thousands of structures burning all at once. Jason shook himself, then reached to touch Colin on the shoulder. "Come, there's work to do."

They wheeled to see King Charles dismount and toss his reins to a liveried groom, who led the enormous horse to a makeshift penned area crammed with other aristocratic mounts.

"There's a likely spot." Jason's eyes lit with relief. They left their own horses—along with a fair amount of coin to guarantee they'd see them again—and headed down Warwick Lane on foot, jostling through the swarm of firefighters.

A bucket brigade broke apart and reformed to include them, and before he knew what was happening, Colin was accepting pails from Ford and thrusting them at King Charles. From all evidence, the King and his brother had spent the night wading ankle-deep in trenches and splashing through mud and water; their silks and laces were drenched, sooty and scorched.

"You've been here since when, Sire?" Colin yelled as the King turned to take a bucket.

"We came downriver yesterday noon." Charles twisted to pass the bucket, then turned back to Colin. "Would have ventured out Sunday, but the Lord Mayor assured me 'twas nothing."

"Nothing? We saw it from Greystone!"

"If I recall aright, Bludworth's words were 'Pish! A woman might piss it out!' "

His Majesty gave a snort of disgust that may have been tempered by weary amusement, then stepped from the line when James thrust a shovel into his hands.

The Royal brothers trotted off into the smoke. The fire was giving Charles his first opportunity as king to play the hero in person—and he performed the part superbly, Colin mused in some vague recess of his mind, passing along another bucket.

"Help!" The cry, thin and distressed, came through the shouts of the workers. "Help! My brother!" A hand tugged at Colin's breeches, and he looked down into a grimy young face.

"Where?" Colin asked. Sensing that he'd finally attracted someone's attention, the boy grasped Colin's hand and yanked him out of the queue—a feat made possible by desperation, given his scant five foot height against Colin's six-plus. The next bucket landed in the dirt, soaking Colin's boots and spewing mud into the frightened boy's face. "Where?" Colin repeated.

"P-Paternoster Row!" The lad was off like a rocket, brown hair flying as he threaded his thin form through the confusion, trusting Colin to follow at his heels. Rounding the corner and skidding to a halt, the boy pointed up at a fourth-story window.

Behind the mottled glass, a pale face hovered, small nose pressed against the pane. The child's tiny fingers clawed helplessly at the glass.

Cursed bad luck, the lad was trapped in one of the few houses in this old neighborhood that actually boasted glass windows. The ground floor was engulfed in flame. Black smoke billowed out, cloaking the street, a typically narrow, dirty alley lined with tall houses leaning forward until they nearly met their opposite neighbors. Colin peered through the haze. Flames leapt from roof to roof, eating their way toward them.

Without conscious thought, he went in the other direction, bolting past another burning house to a third that was deserted but yet unscathed. He booted open the door and sped up two flights of stairs, coming out on the balcony.

The houses were crammed together. It was an easy leap to the balcony next door, and then once again to the one under the boy's window.

"Stand back!" he implored the terrified face. Climbing onto the balcony's rail, Colin stretched toward the upper story to hack at the window with his sword. The boy disappeared into the smoke-filled room; Colin saw flames licking up the far wall, and whacked at the window harder. But his elegant rapier blade was no match for the thick, uneven glass. He dropped to the deck of the balcony and whirled in desperation, relieved to see Jason and Ford among the crowd that had gathered in the street.

"Rock!" he yelled, and the next second a chunk came sailing up; he caught and hurled it through the window in one smooth motion. A swipe of his blade cleared most of the glass from the sill. He dropped the sword and struggled out of his surcoat, tossing it up to drape over the frame before he jumped to catch the window ledge with his hands and hoist himself inside.

The small, towheaded child cowered against a side wall, wide eyed with terror. Fed by the fresh air supply from the broken window, the blaze thundered. The fire seemed alive, a hideous monster come to devour all in its path. Colin's lungs burned as he swept up the boy under one arm and leapt out the window. They landed hard on the balcony, tumbling into a tangled heap, Colin's surcoat twisted around one foot. Flames followed, orange and white and blue tendrils snaking through the window, threatening the wooden structure on which they huddled.

Colin unsnarled the garment and threw it over the rail to his brothers. He stood, pulling the boy up with him, and jammed his sword back into his belt. Below the balcony, several men waited, a quilt stretched tight between their hands.

"We're going to jump!" he shouted to the child over the roar of the flames.

"No!" The boy squirmed out of his grasp. "No! No!"

Colin snatched him back. A devil of a time to be scared of heights, but then again . . . Colin's gaze focused on the quilt. Three stories, his considerable weight plus the lad's . . . there was not a chance in hell they'd survive anyway. Hot flames licked at his back; black, billowing smoke choked his air supply. Through tear-blurred eyes, he searched out Jason's face, far below.

"Rope!" he bellowed, the word tearing at his raw throat.

Time ticked away while he watched his brothers argue with a man intent on securing his worldly goods, then give up and simply filch the rope from his laden cart, Ford tugging while Jason brandished his sword in the obstinate fellow's face. A moment later, the lifeline snaked up, thrown in a wide arc by Jason.

With shaking fingers, Colin knotted it to a balcony post and pulled tight. He hauled the child onto his back, yelled "Hang on!" and they were speeding toward the ground. After sliding to the dirt, Colin had the presence of mind to grab the boy and roll out of harm's way as the balcony fell to the street, landing with a mighty crash and a deadly shower of sparks.

Safe for the moment, Colin and the boy lay tangled together, coughing their lungs out.

"John!" The boy's brother rushed forward and scooped him up. "Oh, Johnny! I thought for sure you were dead!"

The child dissolved in tears. The older boy rocked him as, one on either side, Jason and Ford helped Colin stand and shrug back into his surcoat. They urged him down the street, further from the threatening flames, and Colin in turn tugged the boys after him.

"Wh-where are your folks?" he croaked between coughs.

The older lad shook his head. "I know not," he yelled over the deafening racket. "They told us to wait, but that was"—he tilted his blackened face to the sky—"yesterday, maybe." The smoke was so thick it looked like dusk, but the sun had risen, bathing the city with an unearthly glow.

The boy stopped walking. Hugging his sniffling brother to his side, he shoved the tangled brown hair from his face and fixed Colin with pleading eyes. "My lord, can you help us?"

"I . . ." Nonplussed, Colin looked to Jason and Ford. They shrugged.

"Can you help us? *Please?*" Not waiting for an answer, the boy grabbed his brother's hand, pulling him along as he shouldered his way purposefully through the throng.

Colin's gaze was glued to the lads' vulnerable backs. With a last glance at his own brothers, he called, "I'll see you at Cainewood!" and took off after the children, chasing them through the teeming confusion of the intersection and onto Friday Street.

They ducked into a space between two buildings. Seven more children huddled there, most of them in tears. "Davis!" a few cried in unison, running over to embrace the tall boy. They pulled little John into the center of their circle, a small island of camaraderie amongst the misery.

Colin's heart squeezed. These children could have been himself twenty years ago, and Jason and Ford and Kendra. They were commoners, not nobility, and they were most likely lost, not abandoned. But the desperate feeling was the same.

Davis withdrew from the group first, coming back to Colin. "We all live near each other, by Ludgate," he explained breathlessly. Though tall for his age, the lad could be no more than ten or eleven. "We waited there together, but our folks will never find us now. We had to move, to Warwick, then we found that empty house on Paternoster, then here . . . but my brother didn't make it here. Oh, I thank you, my lord." He fell to his knees in the mud. "You saved my brother's life."

Colin absently patted the boy's head, leaning back to look into the street. "The hell of a lot of good 'twill have been if we all burn anyway," he muttered. " 'Tis headed this way. Wait here; I'll be back."

He darted before a creeping wagon, its bed laden with a hodgepodge of domestic goods. With Colin's palms outstretched to press against the two horses's muzzles, the wagon ground to a quick halt.

"Hey!" the driver shouted. "What the devil do you think you're about?"

"I want this vehicle." Colin came around and leapt up next to the man, who shook his slick, bald head indignantly.

"Folks paid good silver for me to save their belongings. I'm bound for Moorfields, for the refugee camp." The man's accent branded him from the countryside, no doubt come into London to assist the victims' flight—and turn a handy profit in the process. A simple cart had suddenly become a high-priced asset, and this was a sturdy wagon.

"Silver, hell. I'll pay gold." Colin fished a pouch from his ripped surcoat and pulled out a guinea. He jumped to the street and started unloading the wagon, suffering a pang of guilt at his cavalier disregard for others' belongings. But a line from one of Dryden's poems came to him unbidden: *"And thus the child imposes on the man."* Surely children's lives took precedence over men's possessions.

The man bit on the coin and then pocketed it, climbing down from the bench and watching with disbelieving eyes. Colin tossed him another guinea.

"There's for your flea-bitten horses. And there's another in it for you if you'll help me unload. The fire's gaining."

A quick glance toward the flames had the man throwing goods off the back end, heedless of the clutter it added to the street. He grabbed the third coin, then took off at a run toward Cheapside, disappearing into the wretched mass of newly homeless.

The children clambered up into the wagon bed, their faces masks of relief under the tear-streaked soot. Waves of heat lashed at Colin's back, spurring him to move on.

He shrugged off the hot coat and stood up on the bench seat, plucking his damp, grayish shirt away from his body as he peered through the smoke toward the west. Priscilla lived in that direction, and the town house was there too, in Lincoln's Inn Fields. Thankfully, the area still looked untouched. The fire was heading north now; west was the best way out of London.

And out was where Colin intended to head—out and to his brother Jason's home, Cainewood. There was no sense looking for the children's families until the fire died down, which could be days. And there was no space for them at Greystone.

He sat down and picked up the reins. Traffic was unbearable, and they moved at a crawl. A quarter hour later, they'd traversed one block of Friday Street and made the turn onto Cheapside. Just three or four blocks, a little further from the leading edge of the fire, and then—

"Papa, no!" The voice cut through the roar of the crowd; an oddly familiar voice, though he was sure he'd never heard it raised before. His fingers went unconsciously to his ring. "You cannot, Papa!"

His head whipped around. There it was, Goldsmith & Sons. And the girl, Amethyst. He jerked on the reins as her father shoved her stumbling into the street, flames thundering in the shop behind. A small trunk came out after her, then the man gestured wildly and ducked back inside. Colin saw him start up the stairs—stairs already engulfed in fire—before a blast of heat slammed the door shut.

"Papa!" Her wail was a knife to Colin's heart.

"Davis, take it," he barked, throwing the boy the reins. He jumped to the street, lithely dodging cross-traffic as he made his way toward the girl. She hastened up the street in the direction her father had pointed, not making much progress, weighed down by the trunk she dragged in the mud.

They both whirled at the sound of an ominous crash. She let out an anguished scream as the roof of her home caved in, sending a column of sparks into the sky that was extraordinary, even in stark daylight.

"Papa!" She dropped the trunk and rushed back to the door. The gilt shop sign crashed to the street, but she lifted her skirts and leapt over it without missing a step. Colin reached her just as she grasped the door latch, but she jerked back, staring at her palm, where angry red welts were already rising. Cradling the hand, she doubled over, oblivious to the soot and ash that rained down on her head.

"Papa!" The cry was a whimper now.

Black smoke puffed out from beneath the door, swirling around her grayed skirts. She didn't move. Flames licked at the shop's windows. God's blood, the blaze would consume her in a moment, and she wasn't moving.

Colin grabbed her good hand and pulled her toward the wagon.

"No!" She wrenched from his grasp, bunching her skirts in one hand for insulation as she reached again for the searing metal handle.

Colin couldn't believe his smoke-blinded eyes. He clutched her by the waist and yanked her back against his body.

"No!" She slammed into him and immediately lunged forward. "Papa is in there—I must save him!" The door's paint was now blistering, writhing, bubbling. At any moment the planks would flare up. Yet she tugged against his restraint, aiming a shoulder at the door, clearly intending to batter it down.

With both hands on her shoulders, he dragged her back a yard . . . two . . . three.

"No! Let me go!" She twisted and turned in his grip. Heat battered them in scorching waves. *"No!"*

"Yes!" He spun her around and, desperate, gave her

a shake meant to rattle some sense into her fevered brain. "You must leave!"

"I have to save him!" Head down, she kicked at his shins. Still he hung on, jostled by the torrent of evacuees, dragging her stumbling toward the wagon as she struggled. "Let go of me!"

Jaw clenched, he stopped and took her face between his hands, forcing her eyes to his. "He's dead!" he roared over the deafening noise. "He went up the stairs and the roof collapsed! Now come, before you're dead as well!"

She froze, and a glassy look of despair began to cloud her amethyst eyes as she went limp beneath his hands. Before her knees buckled, he scooped her into his arms and ran to the wagon.

He flung her light frame up front, next to Davis, then made to climb up after her.

She stiffened, bolting straight up. "My trunk!" she screamed, pointing at the homely object. It sat mere feet from the shop, flames from the front wall reaching deadly fingers in its direction. But one look at her face told him he'd have to retrieve it, or she'd attempt to do so herself.

"Go!" he shouted at Davis, slapping the nearest horse on the rump for emphasis. Davis lifted the reins, and the wagon lurched, inching down the street.

The heat was incredible. A window burst as he raced toward the shop, the blast scattering glass and releasing clouds of smoke that seared his lungs anew. Coughing, his eyes streaming tears, he knelt to lift the trunk.

Hell and furies, how was a small trunk so heavy? He let it drop and, grabbing one handle, dragged it clunking down the rutted street to where the wagon crept along. Waving the children back, he managed to heave it into the wagon bed, then ran around and swung up to the bench, taking the reins from Davis, who scrambled to join the others in the back.

"Are you hurt?" He forced the words past his raw throat. "Amy?"

At the sound of her name, she looked up, her glazed eyes registering first confusion, then disbelief.

"Lord Greystone?"

Before he could respond, she threw her arms around his neck and burst into tears.

Colin placed one arm around her, gingerly and then tighter. The sobs wracked her slight body. Hot tears soaked through his shirt, wetting his shoulder.

Long, gut-wrenching minutes passed, and they progressed several blocks before she choked back the tears and slowly lifted her red-rimmed eyes to meet his. Dark purple smudges marred the delicate skin beneath her eyes; the fire had been burning since Sunday; she'd likely not slept for days.

"I'm sorry," he said.

She nodded her head miserably.

"Where can I take you?"

Sniffling, she gave a vehement shake of her head. "Nowhere," she said in a trembling whisper. "I have no one." Her eyes filled again, threatened to brim over.

Discomfited, he turned back to the road. No one? It couldn't be so; surely she knew someone who would take her in. Her father had perished, true—he'd seen that with his own eyes—but what of a mother? A relative? A neighbor?

Against his body, he felt her take a shuddering breath. Shooting him an exhausted glance, she pushed aside his discarded surcoat, then lay down on the bench, her knees drawn up like a small child. Less than a minute later, her breathing slowed and evened out in the rhythm of sleep.

He drove on, absently smoothing the loosened, tangled hair off her face, letting his gaze wander over the melting softness of her slumbering body draped along the length of the seat. Something vaguely disturbing fluttered and settled in his stomach as he turned onto Lothbury and headed west.

Chapter Five

"She's touching me."

Rubbing his dry, burning eyes, Colin glanced over his shoulder at the children in the wagon bed.

"He's looking at me oddly."

Colin clenched his teeth and turned his attention back to the road, where it seemed every inhabitant of London was ahead of him. A leisurely coach ride from London to Cainewood Castle usually took five hours, but the sun was setting, and after six hours they were naught but a quarter of the way there. They could walk to Cainewood faster than they were moving, he thought irritably.

"She'll not stop humming."

"Ouch!"

They had to find somewhere to stay before major warfare broke out. For the past hour, he'd stopped at every inn along the way and sent Davis to inquire about available lodging. Colin was beginning to believe every room in the kingdom was taken. When Davis came out of the last one, shaking his head "no," he'd briefly considered bedding outdoors for the night. But although it was warm, there was a persistent wind, and he shuddered at the thought of trying to make nine children comfortable with not so much as a blanket. Nine children and Amy Goldsmith.

He glanced down at her grimy face. Amethyst Goldsmith—whoever would have thought? He'd left her shop two weeks past with no intention of ever going back, ever seeing her again, ever buying another piece of jewelry. And now here she was, dropped—literally—right in his lap. God's blood, 'twas incredible! What had he done to deserve this?

She'd moved up in her sleep, and her head now rested on his thigh. He smiled to himself; he'd warrant she'd turn red with embarrassment if she knew. She was so different from the women in his circle, but 'twas more than a lack of sophistication. 'Twas a freshness, an optimism in those clear, innocent eyes—untouched by the Civil War, the years of the Commonwealth, the Restoration—all the calamities that had such a large part in the shaping of Colin and everyone he knew.

For the dozenth time, he allowed himself to touch her, thanking God she was alive. He ran the backs of his fingers along her delicate jawline and down her graceful neck, then slid his palm down her arm. He lifted her hand, lightly encircling her slender wrist. She stirred, and he hastily replaced her hand, setting it back on her curving hip.

Amy murmured something incoherent, flexed her lithe body a bit, then settled back into sleep, her long black lashes feathery crescents on her tear-streaked cheeks. Colin tore away his gaze and stared straight ahead at the congested road. Why did an innocent touch leave him so . . . disturbed? His betrothed, Priscilla, was the perfect woman for him, yet when he touched her—or made love to her, for that matter—his skin never tingled like this.

He was more familiar with Priscilla, he decided, more comfortable. He wasn't *supposed* to touch Amy this way—indeed, he'd not dare if she were awake. 'Twas the excitement of the forbidden, that was all.

Besides, he wasn't looking for passion in his marriage. He had told his sister as much just last night.

God's blood, had it been but a day since his family's visit to Greystone? He felt ages removed from the lighthearted man who had pulled that prank. It seemed like he'd not slept in a week.

He pulled up before another inn and sent Davis to investigate. Scuffling sounds and a high-pitched shriek came from the back of the wagon. Colin's empty stomach complained, loudly, and he came to a decision. They were stopping here. To eat, if nothing else.

They were in luck—of sorts. Davis came running back to report that there was room in the inn. One room, to be exact. With two beds. For eleven people. Well, 'twas shelter, and Colin was inclined to think there might be nothing else available between here and Cainewood. He sent Davis to claim it before someone else pulled off the road.

Amy washed down a bite of meat pie with ale, allowing the children's anxious chatter to lull her. Wedged on the bench between a girl of five and a boy of six, she kept her gaze on her plate and avoided Lord Greystone's eyes across the table. She had no wish to talk—given her choice, she'd not even be awake. She'd managed to spend the past few hours in oblivion, casting the time away. Dreaming . . . warm hands caressing her . . . comforting. Now that she was conscious, she felt guilty, having such a dream when her father was dead.

A sudden sharp pain of loss overwhelmed her, and she struggled to force it back inside. She couldn't think about it now—it was too fresh, and she was too broken.

"Bread, Amy?" Lord Greystone's rich voice cut through her thoughts. She slowly brought her gaze to his.

"No, thank you."

"Cheese?"

"No, I'm really not hungry."

She could see Lord Greystone eyeing her barely eaten pie, so she stuck her spoon in it.

"You have to eat." The statement was matter-of-fact, but his voice was filled with concern. "You'll fall ill."

When she dropped her spoon and lowered her eyes again, Lord Greystone cleared his throat and stood. "Well, let me just take the children upstairs. You stay for a bit and finish your supper. Will you wait for me here?"

Amy raised her chin and nodded up at him.

"I'll come back down for you," he promised, and took himself off, the children trailing in his wake.

She toyed with her food for the next quarter-hour, breaking up her pie, the spoon awkward in her left hand. She attempted a couple of bites, but the meat had turned cold and stuck in her throat, nearly making her gag. Gulping down more ale, she pushed her plate away; she'd not been hungry in the first place, but Lord Greystone had insisted on setting it in front of her.

When her ale was finished, she stared at the pattern in the oak table and blanked her mind until, out of a corner of her eye, she glimpsed Lord Greystone coming downstairs.

He'd cleaned up, combed his hair and pulled it back, donned his surcoat. 'Twas ripped a bit, but he'd brushed it clean of the ash and soot. His grayish shirt showed between the unbuttoned front. He needed a shave, but looked strong and male—and *there*. She watched as he went through a swinging door into the kitchen.

Amy ran her fingers once more through her tangled hair. Earlier, she'd scrubbed the grime from her face and undone her disheveled braid, but found nothing with which to brush it out. Their tiny room had no mirror—she was sure she looked a sight.

Not that she cared.

Colin backed through the kitchen door with two bowls full of sloshing liquid in his hands, some strips of cloth draped over one arm, and a jar of honey wedged between chin and shoulder.

He put everything on the table and straddled the bench beside Amy, motioning his head toward her plate. "Finished eating?"

"I reckon, yes."

"May I have a look at that hand? We really should clean it."

"I suppose so."

As she offered him her hand, Colin wondered if he were up to the task of drawing her out of this dreamlike state. He had to figure out something to do with her, but he was unlikely to get much help in the matter if she persisted in answering him with three-word sentences. He looked at her hand and winced.

"Ouch!" he said, giving a mock shudder.

" 'Tis not so bad."

"Bad enough." He gently placed her hand in one bowl. "We'll soak it for a few minutes, shall we?"

She wiggled her fingers. "What is it?" Her long black lashes swept down upon her cheekbones as she squinted at the bowl.

He smiled distractedly. "Cream."

"Cream? You mean, from milk?" She gave a slight shake of her head, and her dark hair shimmered in the flickering light. The glossy waves tumbled almost to her waist, and throughout the entire supper, Colin had been quite unable to keep his eyes off them.

"Why cream?" she asked.

"Huh?" He shook himself. "Good question. Does not everyone put cream on burns?"

"I think not," she mused, drawing her eyebrows together. Then her face cleared. She lifted her left index finger and raised it as if to make a point. "Butter. In my family, we put butter on burns."

"We always use cream," he asserted. "As well as honey. I hear tell that butter's no good."

"That's not what I've heard," she said dubiously.

"Well, how does it feel?"

She paused, considering, then tilted her head. "A little better, I guess."

"See?" His smile was triumphal.

Amy smiled back; 'twas shy and more than a little bit sad, but a smile nonetheless. Colin congratulated himself.

"That should do it." She started a little when he took her hand, but he pretended not to notice. While he held it over the bowl, watching the cream run off in tiny rivulets, the air between them crackled with unasked questions. Her hand stopped dripping, and he rinsed it in the bowl of water.

Her eyes closed, and he felt her relax, her hand limp as he swished it around, pulled it out and turned it over.

"Hmmm . . ." He dabbed gingerly at her palm with one of the linen strips. " 'Tis clean now, and a bit less red." He held it up for her to see. "What do you think?"

Her eyes popped open. " 'Tis fine."

But she was grimacing, and the longer she looked at it, the more he felt her body stiffen. 'Twas no wonder; the puckered blisters were an angry hue. He dabbed at her hand again.

"It should be perfectly dry. There. Now the honey . . ." He opened the jar, dipped in a spoon, drizzled the sweet thick substance onto her injured palm, spread it gently with one finger.

She sat silent as he wound a fresh linen bandage around her hand, tucked in the end and rinsed his fingers in the bowl.

"Davis is watching the young ones." Wiping his palms on his breeches, he rose to his feet. "Would you care to take a walk?"

Without waiting for her answer, he took her by the elbow.

The road out front was noisy, crammed with the endless stream of people fleeing London. A well-worn path in back of the inn led up into the gently rolling hills, and it was here that he guided her.

'Twas a cloudless night, the wind having blown away every wisp of smoke over the horizon, and Amy could just make out Lord Greystone's profile, dark against the moonlight. Aided by what seemed a million stars, her eyes adjusted to the darkness. As the lines of his face became more distinct, she decided his features were so perfect, so symmetrical, that he straddled the line between handsome and beautiful. Then, without warning, he stopped and turned to face her. His magnetic eyes burned into hers, searching, and she decided he was not beautiful after all. He was much too intense to call him that.

Twisting the gold ring on his finger—the ring she had made—Lord Greystone cleared his throat and looked away.

"How is your hand?"

"Not too bad."

"Are you right-handed, or left?"

"Right."

" 'Twill be a spell before you can write, then."

She shrugged. "I expect so."

Lord Greystone sighed, and the fingers of one hand drummed against his thigh. "Amy . . ."

His voice sounded serious; she did not want to discuss it. Not yet, not tonight. Maybe tomorrow. Or, if God was just, perhaps this was all a horrible dream, and tomorrow she would wake up back in Cheapside.

She took strength from Lord Greystone's presence, but she wished they were back at the inn, sitting side by side with tankards of mind-numbing ale, not saying anything. If he were going to insist on talking to her, she would have to make sure the conversation stayed on safe subjects.

The drumming stopped, and she took a quick breath. "You . . . you're very good with the children."

"Thank you." He looked relieved. "The lad Davis is an enormous help."

"Why are you . . . doing this? Caring for these children, I mean. 'Tis very nice, but . . ."

"But why am I shepherding children when every other able man is still in London, fighting the fire?" Lord Greystone led her up a rise to where he'd spotted an ancient, broken stone wall. He seated himself upon a low section. " 'Tis difficult to credit, but I've always felt a kind of . . . sympathy, I suppose you could call it, for children who are lost or abandoned. Perhaps I would have been of more use fighting the fire, but—"

"No, not at all." Amy levered herself up to sit on the wall, then turned to face him. "The children needed you.

Thousands are fighting the fire; one more would make no difference."

Lord Greystone hesitated, then shrugged. "I know how those children feel. When I was young, my parents left me a lot. Most of the time, in fact. And I was lonely and scared all the time. I wasn't a very brave lad," he admitted ruefully.

"They left you?" Amy could barely conceive of such a childhood; her parents had never left her for so much as a day. *Until today*, she realized suddenly. She felt a brief, sharp stab of grief, then pushed it down, down, far inside, like stuffing one of those new jack-in-the-box toys back under its lid.

She bit her lip. Lord Greystone was watching her; his hands came up, then dropped back to his lap. As long as she kept asking him questions, she'd not have to think about it.

"Why . . . how could they do that?"

He cocked his head. "They were passionate Royalists. Cavaliers. King and country came first. We—my brothers and sister and I—were such a distant second we barely even counted."

"But . . . where did they leave you?"

"Oh, with other Royalist families. They weren't cruel—they didn't actually abandon us. But to a child . . . well, it felt as though they did. To me, anyway." He paused, twisting his ring again. "My brother Jason—he's two years older than I—feels differently. But he was older when the war started."

"How about your sister?"

"Kendra and her twin, Ford, were so young that I don't think they remember any other kind of life. They're twenty-two—about your age, I think?"

Amy nodded. "And now?" she asked. "How do they feel about it now? Your parents, I mean. Are they sorry?"

"They died. At the Battle of Worcester, fifteen years ago."

His parents were dead . . . just like hers.

"Oh . . ." Her voice trailed off.

Mistaking her renewed grief for sympathy, Lord Greystone rushed to reassure her. "Say not that you're sorry. 'Twas Charles's last stand against Cromwell, and my folks would not have missed it for the world. I was a strapping thirteen by then, safely ensconced with other Royalist exiles in Holland. I didn't miss them much, since they were hardly ever around anyway."

He sighed, gazing out into the endless dark rolling hills.

"Was your family Royalist, Amy? During the War, I mean?"

"No," she said slowly, pausing as she thought how to explain it. "I mean . . . we weren't *not* Royalist, either. We were—nothing, I guess. Papa just tried to keep doing business no matter what happened." To Amy's surprise and dismay, her mention of Papa released a floodgate of emotions. She could no longer hold herself in check; tears started welling in her eyes. "I'm sorry," she whispered, chagrined that she couldn't control herself.

"Don't be sorry. Whether you were Royalist or nay—it doesn't signify. It seems a fine survival tactic to me."

She couldn't answer. Her throat seemed to close up, and a warm teardrop rolled down her cheek and splashed onto her clasped hands.

"Amy?" Lord Greystone probed. "Where is your mother?"

She tried to swallow past the lump in her throat. "She died," she answered in a quavery voice. "Of the plague. Last year. She fell ill and we had to leave. We went to France, and I never saw her again."

"I'm sorry," he said softly. He moved over on the wall and placed an arm around her shoulders. "I'm truly sorry." His voice was low and compassionate, but she wasn't ready to accept comfort yet.

"I . . ." His fingers tightened on her shoulder. "I don't understand. Your father . . . why . . . why he went back inside. When the shop was aflame."

Slow tears overflowed, quiet tears, not a storm like

earlier in the day when he'd found her. They burned in her eyes and traced hot paths down her cheeks. She was so exhausted.

"He wanted a painting of my mother." She brushed at the tears with the back of her good hand.

"A painting?" She could feel Lord Greystone beside her, shaking his head in disbelief.

"He *had* to have that picture. He used to sit for hours, staring at it. Perhaps—perhaps he didn't really want to live without her," she said, with a flash of insight that stabbed deep in her heart. "Now I have no one. I'm all alone."

He jumped down and stood before her, took her face between his hands. "You're not alone, Amy."

"Yes—yes, I am. My parents are gone . . . my home is gone . . ." There was Robert, but . . . there was no one to make her marry him, now.

"You must have family, somewhere?"

"Only my Aunt Elizabeth." The words came out a whisper, forced through her painfully tight throat. "She lives in Paris. Last year when I stayed with her I was miserable."

"Your mother had just died," he reminded her gently. "You would have been miserable anywhere." With him standing and her seated on the wall, they were of a height. His eyes searched hers, an intense gray, their color neutralized by the darkness. " 'Tis not so bad as all that."

More tears brimmed over, and she saw his brow crease in response.

"I wish I were not alive," she whispered, dropping her head to escape his penetrating gaze.

He lifted her face with strong, caring fingers under her chin, wiped her wet cheeks with his thumbs. "Never say that," he said, his voice gruff with emotion. " 'Tis good to be alive. Never ever say that."

In a violent motion, Lord Greystone caught her to him and held her tight. Amy felt his cheek against hers, rough with unshaven stubble, but warm and vital.

She rubbed her face against his, almost imperceptibly, feeling a human connection for the first time since she saw her father disappear into the raging inferno that used to be her home.

"God in heaven," she whispered.

In his arms she felt safe, removed from her hostile reality, and she wished she could stay there forever. She breathed deeply of his scent, smoke and healthy male sweat, mixed with a faint underscore of fragrant soap. Slowly her arms came up and stole around his neck, her fingers entwined in his hair.

Dimly realizing that his attempts at comfort were edging too far toward impropriety, Colin tried to pull back. But Amy came off the wall with him, sliding down his body until her feet came to rest on the grass, her head beneath his chin, her face pressed into his chest, her tears soaking the thin linen. Holy Christ. Despite her gut-wrenching misery, he couldn't help but think she felt too damn good in his arms.

Then he stopped thinking altogether.

When Amy raised her face to him, he pulled her even closer and brought his lips to hers.

The travelers rumbling by in the background, the crickets in the hills, the wind blowing past . . . all faded away like magic. Only the two of them existed.

The caress deepened and his lips parted hers, sending a shockwave through her entire body. Somewhere in the back of her mind, she marveled at the new feelings, for his kiss was nothing like the ones she had tolerated from Robert. She was overwhelmed by the way Lord Greystone's mouth claimed hers. His kiss was like a potion—it made her body melt and her consciousness dim—suddenly she remembered neither who she was nor what were her problems.

His tongue invaded her mouth, searching for hers, and he tasted of ale, but sweeter, and 'twas shocking and wonderful. She leaned into him, reveling in the feel of his hard body against her softness, and his hands wandered down her back, cupping her bottom and pulling her closer still. A low sound of pleasure escaped her throat.

It brought him back to reality.

He dropped his hands and broke away from her mouth. What was he doing? Seducing an innocent girl, taking advantage of her grief and loneliness, her vulnerability, her overwhelming need to feel alive and connected? He was not that kind of man—he had always prided himself on being cool and logical, not ruled by his emotions. And certainly a gentleman. He knew there were different rules for the women in Amy's class than for the promiscuous ladies in his own. He was thoroughly disgusted with himself.

Amy stared at him, dazed, her knees weak.

"I'm sorry," he said.

He didn't sound like Lord Greystone, Amy thought. His voice was rough, and he did look sorry—ashamed, even.

"Sorry?" Amy's senses were still spinning. She wasn't sorry, not one bit. She had wanted that feeling to go on forever. She'd never imagined any person could make her feel like someone else, in a different time and place.

And, unless she was mistaken, he had felt much the same. Surely he couldn't have kissed her like that if he hadn't. Or could he? She was admittedly ignorant of such matters. "You're sorry?" she repeated.

"Well, not sorry exactly," he said in that unfamiliar rough voice, fumbling for the words. " 'Tis just . . . I should not have done that . . . taken advantage of you like that. Not that I didn't want to—oh, bloody hell!" He took a step toward her and put his hands on her shoulders, holding her at arm's length, clearly exasperated. "You're a proper young woman, and I've a responsibility to send you to your aunt in the same condition I found you."

Amy would have agreed with him yesterday. But today, alone in the world and having tasted the sensations of being in his arms, she wasn't sure of anything.

"My lord—" she began.

"Colin," he interrupted, irony in his voice. "Once you've had a man's tongue in your mouth, you're allowed to call him by his Christian name."

Amy blushed furiously, thankful for the cover of darkness. Still, she tried the name in her head. *Colin.* She'd never called a nobleman by his given name, and it should feel wrong. But now she thought *Colin*, and it made her feel warm all over.

"And if you were about to tell me it matters not," he continued, "you're wrong. It matters a lot."

"But—"

"No 'buts,' Amy. 'Tis late, and we're both very tired. We have a long ride to Cainewood in the morning. Let us get some sleep."

He grasped her good hand and pulled her toward the inn. She followed reluctantly. There was no arguing with him, it seemed.

Her hand tingled where it nestled in his. She had held hands with Robert and never felt anything at all. Even with her limited experience, she knew this could not be normal. Was it not the same for him?

It was.

Colin had a vast record of experience and knew this was not one jot normal. But 'twas absurd. He was betrothed, and she was a commoner, a woman who, as of this morning, had nothing whatsoever to her name.

He was tired; that must be it. He was very, very tired.

If his hand were tingling—if his whole body were vibrating, as a matter of fact—'twas because he was tired.

After a good night's sleep, he'd feel differently. He'd be more himself, back in control. They'd go on to Cainewood, wait a couple of days until the roads were clear, then he'd take her to Dover and buy her passage across the Channel. They'd never see one another again. His pride would be intact, not to mention her virginity.

They arrived back at the inn and trudged wearily upstairs, to find four little bodies bundled in each of the two beds, crosswise, and Davis curled in the only chair, snoring softly.

Colin stood with his mouth open.

"You expected what?" Amy whispered. "That they'd all lie down on the floor and leave the beds to us? I'd say they settled themselves quite fairly."

"I thought they'd leave *part* of each bed to us," he complained loudly. "Greedy little devils, are they not?"

"Shhh! You'll wake them."

"I wish they would waken, so I could rearrange them," Colin stated wryly. "But you're not well acquainted with children, are you? Nothing short of a cannon blast would wake them."

Despite the sleeping evidence, Amy still couldn't bring herself to talk out loud. "I have no brothers or sisters. How should I know how children sleep?"

"I'll go downstairs and fetch some more blankets," he said, turning on his heel. He stopped short of slamming the door behind him.

Amy slumped against the wall, wondering what had made his mood change so suddenly.

She slid down and waited, her knees to her chest. Alone, the depression started creeping back. She'd not think about it. She'd think about his kiss . . .

She felt her lips burning at the memory.

At last he returned, two threadbare blankets in hand. " 'Twas like negotiating a treaty," he declared, "and they cost me a pretty penny. I'd be willing to wager they're her own personal blankets." He sniffed at them suspiciously. "They smell as bad as she does."

Amy wrinkled her nose, remembering the stout, flushed innkeeper's wife and her greasy hair.

Colin began to hand her the smaller blanket, then glanced at Davis uncovered in his chair.

"Hell," he muttered to himself. There was nothing for it; he was going to have to share a blanket with her. *Why?* What had he done to deserve all this temptation thrown in his path?

He covered Davis and gently tucked him in. "Sorry," he grumbled. "This is what I was afraid of." He spread the other blanket on the floor and sat on it to pull off his boots.

"Afraid of?"

"We'll have to share this blanket," he explained crossly.

"Is that what you were so vexed about?" Amy's features lost some of their tightness. "Strangers sleep together all the time when inns are full. Of course, they generally have a bed," she reflected.

"They're generally the same sex," he said pointedly.

"Oh."

"Yes. Well, come then, take off your shoes." He shrugged off his surcoat and rolled it up to make a pillow. "If they're anything like normal, these children will be up at first light."

He lay down. Amy slowly removed her shoes, then joined him at the edge of the blanket and arranged herself on her side, carefully separated from him. He threw the other half of the blanket over them both.

Her tears were silent, but Colin could feel the blanket tug slightly when her shoulders started shaking. "Damn," he murmured under his breath. He turned toward her and positioned himself against her back, spoon-fashion. "Shhh," he whispered, although she wasn't making a sound. "Shhh. 'Tis all right. I'm here."

She fit him perfectly.

Presently her tears stopped, and she reached back for his hand and tucked it around her middle. She shuddered once more and was still.

His whole body was rock hard.

His last waking thought was that he was lucky he was so exhausted.

Damn lucky.

Chapter Six

Amy trailed listlessly behind Colin as he hustled the children to the wagon. Leaning against the side, she watched them clamber into the back, wondering where she'd find the energy to climb up herself. She felt like she'd not slept a wink last night; barring some catnaps Monday evening and her uneasy slumber in the jostling wagon yesterday, she'd been awake for almost three days.

"Keep an eye on them, will you?" Colin asked.

She nodded, watching Colin's broad back and easy stride as he headed into the inn. Thank God he was here . . .

Closing her eyes, she shook her head in a vain attempt to clear it. She had to think straight, figure out a plan. 'Twas easier to let him take care of her, but she didn't belong here; she couldn't rely on Colin. A tempting comfort, but a false one. She meant nothing to him.

Her thoughts drifted to last night. How could she have talked to him about himself and his past as if everything were normal, as if her father had not just died? And God in heaven, had she actually kissed him? Her face flamed at the memory. What kind of a daughter was she? She deserved not to enjoy *anything*, ever again.

She opened her eyes to see Colin returning, her trunk balanced on one straining shoulder.

"What the devil's in here?" He set it on the floorboards with a decided *clunk*.

"Everything I own," she said in a broken whisper, her gaze riveted to the wooden slats, the leather straps, the brass fittings. Dear God, her father's life's work was in there. Suddenly, her throat constricted and she seemed unable to breathe. Colin pushed the trunk under the bench, making a hideous scraping noise.

Amy felt the grief bubbling up inside her. A weight settled in her stomach; a fist closed around her heart. Her eyes filled with hot, blinding tears. 'Twas rising, threatening to overwhelm her, and this time she couldn't stop it.

She stumbled up to the bench, but she couldn't sit upright, so she sank to the boards and covered her face with her hands. Then she let it rise up and out, the pain and the tears and the great, tearing sobs.

Her breath came in hysterical gulps. Colin stroked her hair, but she shook off his hand, though she knew it might hurt his feelings. The children were silent; she could feel their pitying gazes. She cared not. Her father was dead. She would never see him, never touch him, never hear his voice again.

She was jostled when the wagon started moving, but the tears wouldn't stop. Wordlessly, Colin stuffed a handkerchief into her fist. Before long 'twas sopping wet and twisted in her hands.

The world retreated until she was a mass of wretched pain. Her father was dead; her home was gone; she had no immediate family, no family at all except one aunt in a foreign country.

'Twas all her father's fault. He'd gone back inside their burning house and robbed her of her life in the process.

Damn him, she thought. *Damn him to hell!*

Bolting upright, she gasped and covered her mouth as though she had said it out loud.

She felt Colin's gaze, his compassion, but it helped not at all. When he drew her hand away from her mouth and threaded her fingers through his, she levered herself up to the bench and leaned against him, closing her eyes. The tears leaked slowly, tracing new paths down her raw cheeks. Her head throbbed; her eyes burned, hot and swollen. But no physical pain could match the anguish in her heart.

She had damned her father to hell, and for one split second, she had really meant it.

Standing next to the wagon, one hand resting possessively on her trunk, Amy watched, dazed, as Kendra led two children by the hand toward Cainewood's immense double oak doors, the raked gravel of the drive crunching under their feet.

"I cannot believe you did this, Colin." Kendra turned on the steps to count the young ones. "Nine children! You must have had your hands full."

She paused on the threshold, eyeing Amy speculatively. "Though it looks like you had help."

Colin didn't respond, but Amy slipped him a guilty sidewise glance. She bit her lip, knowing she'd been less than helpful. She'd not even been decent company. They'd been on the road for the better part of the day, and she'd strung no more than five words together the entire time.

But she had no time to dwell on herself, not with Cainewood Castle before her in all its ancient glory.

The living quarters formed a U around the quadrangle's groomed lawn. She looked up, and up. Four stories.

"Ninety-eight rooms," Colin said beside her, as though he'd read her mind. "Most of them closed up. Jason has years of restoration ahead; Cromwell sacked the place twice." He pointed, and she turned to see the marks of cannonballs in the high, crenelated wall. Beyond the smooth green grass of the quadrangle, a tall, timeworn tower rose majestically.

"The original keep," he explained. "I believe it dates from 1138. Cainewood's been in our family, save during the Commonwealth, since 1243."

"Oh . . ." Blinking, she turned and stared up at him, his bold features shadowed by the turreted curtain wall. A *huge* castle's wall. Other than Whitehall Palace, 'twas the largest structure she'd ever seen. And his family lived here . . . back in her shop and at the inn, Colin had seemed almost ordinary.

She glanced away, embarrassed when he shifted under her stare. He pointed again. "Beyond the keep, that's the tilting yard. Obsolete, these centuries past. Jason doesn't bother caring for it." His wave indicated the vegetation, untamed and ankle high. Still, a tilting yard . . . she could picture knights of old, mounted on glittering steeds, jousting, their lances held high. She'd been reading a medieval history—she'd left it on her bedside table. It must have burned—

"Come, Amy." His rich voice rescued her from those thoughts. "I know you're tired. Come inside and you can rest."

He shooed the last of the children up the steps and motioned her after them, through the massive doors. The sun was setting, and she expected the entry would be dim. But a chandelier dangled from the vaulted ceiling, blazing with candles that flooded the cream-colored stone chamber with light.

In awe she moved toward the slim columns that marched two-by-two down the center of the three-story hall. An intricate stone staircase loomed ahead. At intervals along the gray marble handrail, carved heraldic beasts held shields sporting different quarterings of . . .

"The Chase family crest," Amy said softly.

"How did you . . . ?" Colin set down the trunk and blinked at her. "Oh, you carved those symbols on the sides of my ring."

She smiled to herself, taking in the ornate iron treasure chests that sat against the stone walls, alternating with heavy chairs carved of walnut. Tapestries enriched and softened the effect.

" 'Tis . . . impressive, no?" Colin cleared his throat. "We, uh, used to have somewhat of a fortune," he said, rather sheepishly. "Before the War, that is."

Amy looked up to the balcony that spanned the width of the hall. "I've never seen the likes of it," she admitted. " 'Tis magnificent. The workmanship . . ."

"My home, Greystone, is nothing like this; take my word for it."

She didn't reply, mainly because her gaze wandered back down the stairs and settled on Kendra. From the top of her coiffed head, with her striking dark-red ringlets wired out on the sides, to the quilted slippers that peeked from beneath her mint-green satin skirts, Kendra was the picture of perfection.

Amy glanced down, mortified. Her own wrinkled, smoke-stained skirts had started out lavender on Monday, but now looked positively gray. She could only imagine what her face and hair looked like, all dirty and disheveled. She wanted to drop into the floor.

"Kendra, you'll remember Mistress Amethyst Goldsmith?" Colin's words prompted a small smile from Amy. Only harlots and pre-adolescent girls were called "Miss," and in light of her behavior last night, she considered herself lucky that Colin considered her neither.

"I'm not certain . . ." A frown wrinkled Kendra's forehead.

"You met Mistress Goldsmith last month in London," Colin reminded his sister. "She made your locket."

"Oh, of course!" Kendra's face lit up at the memory. She scrutinized Amy more closely, then smiled. "I—I didn't expect to see you here."

Convinced 'twas more likely Kendra hadn't recognized her under all the filth, Amy warmed to her immediately. "That makes two of us, Lady Kendra. I didn't expect to be here myself."

Kendra's laughter tinkled through the hall. "I suppose you didn't, at that," she conceded. "And please, call me just Kendra. May I call you Amethyst?"

"My friends call me Amy," Amy returned hopefully. She badly needed a friend right now.

"Amy, then. Um . . . might I guess you'd like a bath?"

"Oh, yes," Amy breathed gratefully.

"And some supper," Colin interjected. "She's not eaten in two days," he explained to Kendra.

Amy shook her head slightly. "I just want to sleep." She was certain she couldn't eat yet.

"Warm chocolate, then," Colin insisted. Amy nodded acceptance. "With brandy in it," he added decisively. "And some soup."

Amy sighed. "Perhaps some soup. The chocolate sounds nice." The brandy sounded nice. The brandy and bed. She'd be willing to wager the beds in a place like this would be nice and soft.

"Well, up you go, then." Colin gestured toward the stairs. "Up you all go, in fact," he declared in a raised voice, striding over to the children huddled in the back of the hall, whispering amongst themselves. "Baths for everyone, first thing. Then supper, then bed."

There were audible groans at this announcement. "Could we not just wash up a bit?" Davis spoke for the group. "We'll not really have to take *baths*, will we?"

Heading up the stairs together, Kendra giggled under her breath, and Amy smiled to herself. She knew that at home, Davis probably bathed twice a year, if that. Cleanliness was considered an invitation to infection.

"Oh yes, you will," Colin stated firmly. "Kendra, two at a time. And fresh hot water after each bath." Behind her, Amy heard the children's startled breaths. Such lavish use of water was unheard of in the City. She met Kendra's amused eyes, then watched as her new friend's face took on a mock-serious expression.

"Tell Cook to prepare supper—lots of it," she called down toward her brother's dark head. "Then, for God's sake, come up and give me a hand. *I'm* not the one who volunteered to play nursemaid."

"The mews was over there." Colin pointed through the keep's glassless window. The children clustered around him, craning their necks to see out.

He felt a small tug on his breeches and looked down. Noon sunshine streamed into the ancient roofless tower, dancing on a small lad's red-gold mop of curls.

The child cocked his head. "What's a news?"

Colin smiled at his puzzled look. "A *mews*," he corrected gently. "A building where the lord kept his falcons. 'Twas destroyed by the Roundheads in the siege of 1643."

"The same time the holes in the floor happened?" another boy asked.

"The same time," he told the child, a sturdy apple-cheeked lad. "But that only makes it more fun for hide-and-seek and treasure hunts, does it not?"

The boy and Colin shared a smile before the boy sobered. "When can we go home?"

"Yes, when?" the others echoed.

"Today?" The smallest girl's blue eyes looked so hopeful in her angelic little face.

His heart aching for them all, Colin brushed a golden ringlet off her tiny forehead. "Not today, Mary, but soon, I'm hoping." As a disappointed silence seemed to permeate the stone walls, he sighed, twisting his ring. "Very soon."

"Did you live in this keep when you were a little boy?"

Colin chuckled, gazing down into a girl's large brown eyes. "Heavens, no—how old do you think I am?" When the girl blushed, he reached over to ruffle her straight flaxen hair. "No one's lived in here for centuries. 'Twas open to the sky long before my boyhood days. Would you like to see the wall walk?"

The sound of a clearing throat rang from the doorway. Colin turned, startled.

" 'Tis dinnertime," Kendra announced.

He frowned. "How long have you been there?"

"We want to hear another story," piped up a chubby towhead, Davis's little brother, if Colin remembered right. After a good night's sleep and cleaned of the soot and ash, he looked a different child.

"That wasn't a story," he told the boy, then looked up at Kendra. "I was just explaining a bit of history."

"It is time for dinner now," Kendra said firmly. "Lord Greystone will tell you another story later."

"I will?" Colin raised one arched eyebrow.

"Yes, you will." Kendra shot him a teasing grin. "You brought them here, you're responsible for their entertainment. You owe them a bedtime story, at least." She motioned to the children. "Come along, you all need to wash before eating."

"But I promised to show them the wall walk," Colin protested.

"Oh, very well, but quickly. You know how sulky Cook acts when her lovely meals grow cold."

Beckoning, Colin led them all into the stairtower and down the winding steps to the archway. The children ran out along the top of the crenelated wall, shrieking with delight.

"Not too far," he yelled after them, "and be careful!"

"Dunderhead," Kendra chided. "When did you ever know a child to be careful?"

"Never." He smiled sheepishly.

They both turned and faced outward, rested their forearms on top of the ledge, and gazed out over the River Caine and the fields and nearby woods. Like most medieval castles, the tower at Cainewood was built on a tall motte—a huge mound of earth. Up on the wall walk they could see for miles in all directions.

"You're wonderful with the children," Kendra said quietly.

"I remembered playing in the keep—'twas so much fun. I just wanted to bring it to life a bit for them."

Kendra sighed wistfully. "I never got to play in the keep." The War had started before she was born, and as well-known Royalists, the family had adjourned to less obvious lodgings. Even that had failed to stay Cromwell from bringing his wrath down upon their home.

"I know, Kendra." Colin placed a hand over hers where it rested on top of the ancient wall. 'Twas peaceful up here. The days of war were long over, thank God.

"How is Amy?" Kendra asked suddenly.

"Still sleeping. Sixteen hours."

"She was exhausted." Kendra flashed him an arch

smile. "I saw you shaking her when I walked by her chamber."

He grinned in return. " 'Twas to no avail. She'd rouse for a few seconds at most, then drop back into sleep." He shrugged. "I thought she'd be wanting some dinner. She'd eaten but a few spoonfuls of broth, though her chocolate cup was empty."

"And her hand?"

"Blisters, but no telltale red streaks of infection. Thank the Lord for small favors. Coping with a grief-stricken guest is enough—I feel unequipped to deal with one who is fever ridden, in addition." He stared out into the distance. "I changed the bandage, applied fresh honey. I believe it will mend without incident."

Kendra hesitated. "You like her, don't you?"

"She's a talented girl," he answered cautiously. He kept his eyes trained on an outlying field.

"No, I mean you really like her. You're attracted to her."

"I suppose I am, physically anyway, at least a bit," he admitted. "Nothing will ever come of it, though." He turned to her, searching her light green eyes. "How did you know?"

Kendra gave an unladylike snort. "I remember that day in her shop. The way you talk about her, look at her, take care of her . . . and you put her in the Gold Chamber." The beautiful room was usually reserved for honored guests. "Colin—"

"I'm betrothed," he stated firmly.

"But—"

"No 'buts,' Kendra. I—"

"I hate it when you say that!"

Colin glared at her. "As I was about to say, I know you dislike Priscilla, but I *am* marrying her. And dangling a penniless commoner in my face, no matter how beautiful, is not likely to change that fact."

"But *why*? I've seen you with Priscilla—you don't love her, I can tell."

"I don't want to love her; I've told you that. She's wealthy, she's pretty, she's—"

"Cold."

Colin ignored that. "—she's titled—"

"As though we care about such things. We're titled, and what did it get us? Nothing! We were paupers on the Continent, dragged from Paris, to Cologne, to Brussels, Bruges, Antwerp—wherever King Charles wandered. We had no home, no one who really cared about us. People are what matters. Titles are worthless."

"Ah, but that's where you're wrong. That title kept us fed, allowed us to tag along with the Court, obligated them to take us in. 'Twas all we had, the only thing of value our parents gave us. And my children will have no less—and a lot more."

"You're an earl, for God's sake. Without the War, the Restoration, I would understand your mindset. If you failed to marry wealth, you'd have to live off Jason's largesse, or take a commission in the military, or a religious vocation."

'Twas Colin's turn to snort. "Not that, I'll warrant. You'll see a Chase in the pulpit the day the devil takes residence in heaven."

"You have a point there," Kendra conceded with a sheepish grin. "All right. But Charles owed a debt to our parents, and he gave you the earldom. Your children will inherit. You've no need to marry a title."

Colin's jaw was set, his voice firm. "They'll have titles from both sides. They will never know a day of insecurity."

"What a bunch of blatherskite! You're using this as an excuse to avoid caring about someone—someone like that beautiful girl asleep in the guest chamber. 'Tis what's inside that counts—the Chases care not about titles."

"This Chase does."

Kendra's coloring was high. She stamped her foot. "Oh, you're so stubborn!"

"No more than you are, sweetheart," he returned. "It runs in the family."

"Hmmph!" Kendra crossed her arms and turned from him, facing outward.

"Hmmph!" Colin did likewise, in imitation.

She burst out laughing. But Colin's attention was already diverted elsewhere.

"Od's fish!" he exclaimed under his breath. "I cannot believe I was blind to this earlier."

Kendra squinted her eyes, searching for something of note. "What? I see nothing."

"*Exactly*. 'Tis London. *Not* burning."

Sure enough, although a dark cloud of smoke still hung over London in the distance, it seemed to be lifting, and there were no visible flames underneath.

"Oh!" Kendra's voice went up an octave in her glee. "Ford and Jason are on their way home already, I'll wager."

"And I'll take the children back to London first thing in the morning. We can only pray 'twill not prove too difficult to locate their families."

"And Amy? Will you return her to London as well?"

"Of course," he snapped.

He was relieved when Kendra didn't comment on his annoyance. "Come along," she said. " 'Tis dinnertime. We can tell the children the good news."

He led the way down from the tower. Once in the quadrangle, the children ran ahead, racing noisily to the entrance. Crossing the lawn more sedately beside Kendra, whose fashionable high-heeled slippers discouraged running, Colin suddenly stopped in his tracks.

"Now where am I supposed to find a story, I ask you? No one found time to tell *me* fairy tales when I was little, I'll warrant you that."

"Oh, you'll think of something." Kendra flashed him a teasing smile. "I have complete and total faith in you, Colin Chase." Then she took off across the grass, running anyway.

* * *

Colin gently tucked the bandage and set Amy's hand back on top of the quilt. It looked tiny and delicate lying alone, with the rest of her buried beneath the covers. He licked a bit of honey off his finger, staring at her heart-shaped face. She'd missed dinner, and now supper . . . he glanced behind in case his sister might be watching, then, feeling foolish, shook Amy's shoulder again. Nothing.

He put one hand on her forehead. Still cool, and he could tell by the rise and fall of her chest she was breathing. He felt beneath her chin for a pulse. Nice and steady.

His knuckles caressed her cheek, then he flicked open his pocket watch. The children were waiting for that damned story he—no, Kendra—had promised them. One story, then he'd take everyone back to London in the morning. Surely Amy would be awake by then. And by tomorrow night, his life would be back to normal.

Sighing, he gave Amy one last long look, then walked out into the corridor. The door closed behind him with a soft click, and he headed for the drawing room.

The children waited on the black and salmon carpet, sitting with their backs to the fire. Weary after the stress of the past two days, their bellies full of Cook's good hot supper, their eyes were already drooping.

Their chatter died down as Colin seated himself facing them in one of the salmon-colored velvet chairs. Kendra sat off to the side in its mate, her head bent to her embroidery, failing to hide a smile.

The castle was cool and drafty in the evenings, the thick stone walls effective insulation from the warm summer nights. Kendra hitched herself closer to the fire and jabbed her needle through the fabric. He caught her movement, amused to see her engaged in such a ladylike occupation. 'Twas quite foreign to her nature, but he supposed she considered embroidery a fitting pursuit for a lady passing the evening surrounded by children.

He hoped she'd stick herself in the finger.

"My lord, what story are we to hear tonight?" Davis

prompted. The children shifted impatiently on their bottoms.

Colin glanced up at the carved wooden ceiling, but there was no help from above. All around the room, large gilt-framed portraits of solemn ancestors watched over him, waiting for him to prove himself a worthy entertainer of children. Finally, as his gaze fastened on a newly commissioned painting of his King, inspiration hit.

"Tonight, you will hear the story of the Royal Oak," he announced. The children scooted forward in anticipation. Kendra looked up and smiled in Colin's direction, one eyebrow raised in congratulation.

Colin cleared his throat. "After the Battle of Worcester," he began, "our King, Charles II, endured great hardships in escaping his enemies."

"Were you there?" Davis's little brother interrupted.

Colin smiled. "No, I was only thirteen at the time. But my parents were there." Heads nodded, and big round eyes stared up at him. He saw no reason to tell them his mother and father had died in the battle. They were worried enough about their own parents as it was.

"For nearly six weeks, King Charles was hiding and sneaking about," he continued. "Sometimes he hid with persons of high rank, and sometimes with those of low, but he was treated with the utmost loyalty by everyone. He'd been declared an outlaw, you see, and was hunted for his life, but the people still saw him as their lawful sovereign and willingly risked their own lives to save his."

"Our King was hunted?" asked the girl with the straight flaxen hair. "For real?" Her large brown eyes looked doubtful.

"Yes, certainly. Cromwell wanted him well out of the way." The girl nodded, and Colin went on. "Charles rode hastily away from the scene of his defeat, in the company of a few faithful friends. Whenever they came within hearing range of anyone, they spoke French to avoid detection. His friends brought him to a lonely farmhouse on the borders of Staffordshire, called Boscobel, where five brothers named Penderel lived. 'Twas death to anyone who dared to conceal the King, while a large reward was offered to any who would betray him to his enemies, but these honest farmers cared neither for threats nor rewards."

"How much was the reward?" Davis asked.

"One thousand pounds."

"A *thousand* pounds? Are you sure?" Davis shot Colin a sidelong glance. A thousand pounds was an absolutely vast sum, more than the average workman would earn in a lifetime.

"I'm sure," Colin reiterated. "They dressed Charles like themselves, in clothes belonging to the tallest brother, William Penderel. The King wore a green jerkin, gray cloth breeches, a leather doublet, and a greasy soft hat. He had to wear his own stockings with the fancy tops torn off, because his feet were so big they could find none to fit him. He cut off his famous thick black lovelocks so no one would recognize him. The brothers outfitted him with tools, and every day while the Roundheads were searching the countryside, they all went together into the forest and set to work as though they had simply gone to cut wood."

Colin smiled at the children's rapt faces. They would have been on the edges of their chairs, had they had any.

"His life with the Penderels was a hard one," he said, "for even if they'd had the power of treating him more according to his rank, they would not have dared do so, for fear they'd betray him. So he lived as they did: straw for his bed, and plain country food. And the clumsy country boots they gave him were too small, so he was forced to tramp around all day in great pain."

The apple-cheeked boy grimaced, and Colin grinned. "In fact, his memory of those boots is so strong that today King Charles has the largest collection of shoes in the land, each pair made to his exact specifications." The children looked at each other, tittering a bit.

He glanced at Kendra. She was still smiling down at

her embroidery, though she'd yet to ply the needle so far as he could tell.

"What happened then?" An impatient little voice reclaimed his attention. The girl had long black hair and large gray eyes, and Colin realized with a pang that she reminded him of Amy. For a fleeting moment, he wondered what a little girl of Amy's would look like.

He banished that thought. "I'm just getting to the good part," he assured the child. "One day, while the King was working with the brothers in the forest, they found a gallant Royalist soldier, Major Carlis, concealed there in the woods. Major Carlis had stayed 'til the very end at Worcester, and told Charles that he'd seen the last man killed there."

Colin sat straight up and lowered his voice, as though something frightening were about to happen. "Suddenly, the Parliamentary soldiers came upon them. Quickly, Charles climbed up an oak tree and crouched amid the leaves. Major Carlis joined him there."

"How long did they stay up in the tree?" interrupted four-year-old Mary.

"More than twenty-four hours, a whole day and night. The soldiers were certain they had seen more men and rode back and forth searching all that time."

"How many soldiers?" Mary asked.

Colin shrugged, frowning down at her head of blond curls. "I don't know, sweetheart."

"How many?" she persisted.

In a quandary, he glanced again at Kendra, and she looked up this time, biting her lip to keep from laughing. No help there.

"Seven," he announced finally. "I'm certain there were seven." When the little girl smiled happily, Colin flashed Kendra a triumphant smirk before resuming the story.

"Charles slept for a time in the tree, his head on the lap of Major Carlis, on a cushion sneaked up to them by the Penderels. When he woke, the soldiers were directly under his tree, talking to each other and saying how glad they should be to catch him. Charles held his breath; he was so frightened they might discover him there."

Hearing the children's own indrawn breaths, he was satisfied with his expertise as a storyteller. "Finally, the next day, they rode off and left him to get down in safety." Little breaths were released. "That tree, in memory of the good service it had done him, was afterward named the Royal Oak, and if ever you go to Boscobel you can visit it," he said by way of conclusion.

The children were not about to let him off so easily. "What happened *then*?" asked a girl with wavy light brown hair and golden eyes. "How did he escape?"

Colin glanced toward Kendra, but once more she smiled down at her handiwork. "Yes, Colin," she said to a misshapen embroidered flower. "What happened then?"

"Hmmph," he said, wishing she were close enough to kick her. "The brothers were afraid the Roundheads would come back when they couldn't find Charles elsewhere, so they moved him to another house, owned by a man called Colonel Lane, a few miles away. They had to find him a horse to ride there, because he couldn't walk that far on his aching feet. The boots, remember?"

Nine little heads nodded.

"He hid in a priest-hole in the Colonel's house, and he was very cramped and uncomfortable in there, for Charles is over two yards tall."

"Like you?" little Mary asked, staring at Colin as though he were the tallest man she'd ever seen.

"Yes, Charles and I are almost exactly the same height." Colin nodded solemnly, but a smile quirked at his lips. "Charles needed to get to Bristol to catch a ship and escape England," he continued. "But he couldn't go as a woodsman, since no one would believe that as a traveling disguise. So they dressed him as a manservant, in a plain gray suit, and a cousin of Colonel Lane's, Lady Jane, rode behind him on a horse, posing as his employer. He decided to call himself William Jackson, and they made up a story that they were on their way to a wedding."

"Whose wedding?" Mary asked. A smothered laugh came from Kendra.

Colin's mind raced. His gaze swept the chamber. "Lord Cornice and Lady Chimneypiece," he said.

He would swear Kendra was choking. Not that she didn't deserve to. He cleared his throat. "Charles and Lady Jane playacted all the way to Bristol. One day Charles's horse cast a shoe, and as he held the mare's foot for the blacksmith, he asked the man if there was any news since the battle."

"What did the man say?" Mary's big blue eyes were round as saucers.

"He told Charles that some of the Royalists had been found and arrested, but not yet Charles Stuart. The Roundheads called the King by the name of Stuart."

"Then the blacksmith was a Roundhead," Davis surmised. "Was Charles not worried to talk to him?"

"Not Charles. But Lady Jane, she was having a fright. And what do you suppose our good King said then?"

"What?" the children chorused.

"He told the smith, 'If that rogue Charles Stuart is taken, he deserves to be hanged, more than all the rest.' "

"He didn't," Davis breathed.

Colin nodded sagely. "He surely did. Charles enjoyed his jest, but Lady Jane wanted to die right there."

"I blame her not," said the girl with the golden eyes. "Not at all."

"Me, neither," Kendra put in with a raised brow. "That prank brings to mind one of my brothers."

"Let me finish," Colin scolded. "Lady Jane breathed more easily when the shoeing was over and they could be on their way. But at Bristol they were disappointed. For a whole month, there was no ship sailing to France or Spain. So Charles had to hide about the countryside again until, finally, a ship was found sailing from Shoreham to France. The ship was named the *Surprise*, but has since been renamed the *Royal Escape*."

He stood. "And *that* is the end of the story. Time for bed, children. We've a long trip back to London in the morning." He flexed his shoulders and stretched.

Applause came from the doorway. He turned to see his brothers, faces and clothing black with the soot of London's fire, jumping to dodge the children running from the room.

"Welcome back!" Kendra sprang up to greet them, her embroidery landing unceremoniously on the floor. She hugged them each in turn. "How did you like our storyteller?"

"Watch your gown; we're both sorely in need of a bath," Jason admonished. He aimed an exaggerated nod toward Colin. "I would have liked to attend the Cornice–Chimneypiece wedding. Pity that we were too young." He grinned. "The tale was magnificent."

"Yes, he certainly rose to the occasion," Kendra agreed. "I all but forced him into it," she explained, "in a sisterly way, of course." Colin snorted at that, and she flashed him an innocent smile. "Whatever made you think of that particular story?"

"Are you serious? We must have heard Charles tell it a hundred times on the Continent. 'Twas practically our nightly entertainment." He blinked at Jason. "You brought Ebony with you, I'm hoping?"

"We're both fine," Jason drawled. "Thank you so much for asking." He turned to Ford. "So nice of him to inquire after us before thinking of his horse."

Ford shrugged. " 'Tis not as though we've spent three days battling flames, exposing ourselves to the dangers of falling walls and debris—"

"No, nothing like that," Jason agreed. "Nothing that would compare to the hazards of telling tales to a pack of children."

"Oh, that's not all he's been doing. You know not the half of it." Kendra laughed, rolling her eyes toward where Amy slept upstairs, and Colin moved closer, intending to elbow her in the ribs. She dodged out of his way, giggling. "You two go clean up, and we'll meet you back here with some supper."

Amy woke to the sound of low voices nearby. She kept her eyes shut tight—she had no intention of letting anyone know she was conscious, just yet—but even so, she could tell from the color inside her lids that 'twas morning. Finally.

Several times during the interminable night, she'd awakened and floated to the surface of awareness, first hearing the soft crackling from the fireplace, then feeling the persistent burning in her right palm. And then she'd remember—and immediately force herself back into the depths of slumber. Back to where it was last week, and she wasn't alone in the world, and her only worry was her upcoming nuptials.

Once, she'd sensed a presence in the chamber and opened her eyes a bit, peeking through the slits to see Colin watching her, his profile dark against the light of the flickering fire. She'd shut her eyes and lain perfectly still, feigning sleep until he left. He'd sighed heavily before closing the door behind him. Was it a sigh of concern, she'd wondered vaguely, already lapsing back to her troubled dreams, or a sigh of exasperation?

He certainly seemed to be exasperated now.

"Bloody hell," she heard him say. "I want to take her with me. I need this episode over and done with. I've work to do."

"Well, 'tis not to be," a male voice answered reasonably. Ford or Jason, Amy reckoned. So they were back. "You'll have to deliver the children without her. You're not going to haul her around the countryside unconscious, are you?"

"Of course not!" Colin spat out.

"Shh!" cautioned another unfamiliar masculine voice. The other brother, she supposed. "She might be ill, you know, if she's been sleeping this long."

Amy heard a couple of footsteps, then a warm hand

pressed onto her forehead and rested there a few seconds, caressing almost. Colin. It had to be. "She's not hot," she heard him say, his voice closer now. "I checked her hand again last night. There's no infection."

Amy's heart fluttered at the thought of him caring for her while she slept. Perhaps she should let him know she'd awakened . . .

No! He'd take her away, ship her to France, and she wasn't ready to go. Aunt Elizabeth was kind, but she'd smothered Amy with concern following her mother's death. She couldn't face that yet; she needed a few days to think about things, to come to some kind of peace within herself. Better to pretend she still slept.

" 'Twill not be a simple matter to find a chaperone in London right now," Amy heard Kendra pointing out. "And you cannot just plop her on a ship by herself."

"That is true," he admitted grudgingly.

"You'd better go, Colin," Kendra advised. "The wagon is packed, and the children are waiting. She's not going to magically wake up, and even if she did, 'twould take her too long to get ready. She's not eaten in two days."

"More like four days," Colin grumbled. The voices receded, accompanied by footsteps. "I suppose you're right."

"We'll have her ready and waiting when you return," Amy strained to hear Kendra say. Then the voices faded away entirely.

Amazingly, Amethyst Goldsmith woke up the minute Colin's wagon rattled over the drawbridge.

Chapter Seven

"I came back here to take her to Dover and put her on a ship, and damn it, that is what I'm going to do!"

After three days spent weeping, thinking, and healing, Amy had sought out Kendra that very afternoon and shyly asked about joining the family for the evening meal. She'd been certain she felt ready for some human interaction.

Now Colin was home, and she was not so sure.

In the corridor outside the drawing room, she stood frozen in place, listening. 'Twas an incredible racket. Amy and her parents had rarely shouted at one another; the Chases seemed to use shouting as their main mode of communication. Even when they'd discussed her at her bedside, she reflected, they'd shouted in whispers. Tonight, they were none so circumspect.

"I promised her, Colin!" she heard Kendra wail. "I promised she could stay here until she's ready."

"Ready? What the hell is that supposed to mean? She's awake, she's ready."

"I'm not quite certain she's awake," another male voice put in, with more than a little amusement. "She's been wandering around here like a ghost."

Amy winced. Was that what they thought of her?

"She has not!" Kendra leapt to Amy's defense. "Her father just died, for God's sake. I promised her."

"A pox on your promises! I need to get back to Greystone. I needed to be there a week ago."

"Ja-son . . ." By the tone of Kendra's voice, Amy imagined her looking toward Jason beseechingly.

"A Chase promise is not given lightly." Jason, the voice of reason.

"A pox on you, too!"

"I agree with them, Colin. Promises aside, she's in no state for travel." So Ford was on her side as well.

"A pox on all three of you! I care not in the least who agrees with whom. I brought her here, and I'll take her away when I damn well please."

"I promised her!"

"You sound like one of those newfangled cuckoo clocks, Kendra. 'I promised her, I promised her, I promised her.' Well, cuckoo all you want; I'm not changing my mind. We're leaving come morning. Where is she? You said she was coming to supper."

Amy took a step back down the corridor.

"Your arrival probably scared her into the next county!" Kendra said.

"The both of you are acting like children!" Amy heard Jason shout, although she was steadily backing away from the room. "Colin, 'tis out of your hands. Go to Greystone in the morning. Ford or I will arrange for Mrs. Goldsmith's travel when she's ready. Kendra, go fetch her now. We'll meet you in the dining room in half an hour."

Amy fled up the stairs to her chamber and was sitting primly on the edge of her bed when Kendra arrived.

Her friend stood in the doorway, frowning. " 'Tis almost time for supper. You're . . . not planning to wear that gown, are you?"

Amy looked down to her skirts. The lavender dress had been laundered and pressed while she slept, but there were a few tiny holes where embers had landed, and little gray spots where the soot had stained it permanently. She'd worn it three days straight already. Her face burned.

"I haven't another," she said to her lap.

"Just a minute." Kendra started to leave, then reappeared in the doorway. "Oh, Colin is back." She disappeared again, yelling "Jane!" as she went.

Wondering what Kendra was up to, Amy ran her hand down the gilt bedpost beside her for what seemed like the millionth time since she'd awakened in this beautiful room a few days ago. 'Twas not the costliness of the gold that stole her breath away, for gold was so soft and pliable that she could hammer a single ounce into a hundred square feet of gold leaf. But she thought the intricately carved bed looked like nothing so much as a gigantic, exquisite piece of jewelry, and with a fresh stab of grief, she wished she could show it to her father.

All the room's furnishings were gilt, marble, or golden brocade. 'Twas like living in Queen Catharine's bedchamber. A floral fragrance suffused the air. Amy shuffled her smoke-damaged shoes where they rested on a plush patterned carpet of brown, cream and gold. At home, the floors had been polished wood, though her family had owned two precious Oriental carpets. The larger one had adorned a wall, the smaller, a table. Before arriving at Cainewood, she had never considered actually *walking* on anything so expensive as a carpet.

Kendra came back leading Jane, a plain-faced young maid with a kind smile and an armful of dresses. Kendra grabbed a yellow one from the pile and held it up to Amy's cheek. "No, too sallow," she muttered, tossing it aside. The next was peach. "Too pale." Jane handed her another, a burgundy satin. "Perfect," Kendra declared.

Before Amy knew what hit her, her gown was off and Kendra's dropped over her head. A rose scent wafted from the fabric. Wiggling into the dress, she inhaled deeply of the luxurious fragrance, thinking the Chases lived a different life indeed.

'Twas not *her* life, though. Her life would never feel complete without the joy of working with gold and jewels to create lasting bits of beauty.

Jane laced up the bodice, attached the stomacher, tucked up the skirt to reveal a shell-pink underskirt. She plucked Amy's chemise through the slashed sleeves, which were caught together at intervals with pink ribbons. Then she seated Amy before the oval gilt-framed mirror and started fussing with her hair.

"I cannot figure out how to braid it myself." Amy tugged up her lace-edged chemise to fill in the gown's low neckline. "Our maid used to entwine ribbons somehow."

"Oh, curls are the fashion now." Kendra waved a hand. "Have you decided what you're going to do?"

What *was* she going to do? She stared at her reflection. Without her father to force the issue, the one thing she would *not* do was marry Robert Stanley. She would have to write soon and tell him so.

"I know not," she sighed, sitting very still as Jane wielded a hot curling iron. "Go to Paris, I suppose, where my aunt and uncle have a jewelry shop." She toyed with a bottle on the marble-topped dressing table. "I—I promised my father I would never give up my craft . . . and jewelry is my life. I know no other."

"Well, you needn't leave until you feel ready. *I* promised you that."

"Thank you." Her eyes met Kendra's in the looking glass. "You're a good friend."

Jane tied a pink ribbon in Amy's hair and stepped back to view her handiwork. "What do you think?" She reached out and tweaked a curl.

"Beautiful," Kendra said.

Amy gazed at her reflection, touched a finger to her lips. The lips Colin had kissed. Maybe, just maybe, she would find a man—another jeweler—in France. A jeweler who could make her heart beat like Colin Chase did.

"No time for cosmetics," Kendra sighed. "We're late already."

"Where are they all?" Ford poured himself a second goblet of wine. "Kendra and Amy I can credit . . . women always take forever to ready themselves. But Colin—"

"Speaking of Colin . . ." Jason drummed his fingers

on the mahogany tabletop. "I think Kendra is scheming to match him with Amethyst Goldsmith."

"Huh?" Ford shook his head. "Whyever would Kendra do that?"

"Damned if I know. Mrs. Goldsmith has nothing to offer monetarily. 'Tis debatable whether a well-to-do merchant could match Greystone's needs, and now her family's shop has burned to the ground, rendering the question pointless."

Ford grinned. "The wench is a rare beauty."

"What the hell has that got to do with it?" Jason lifted his goblet. "I've seen nothing to recommend her in the personality department. I know Priscilla doesn't top Kendra's list of favorite people, but for her to push this match—" He stopped and took a quick swallow of wine. "Colin, there you are."

"Did you find the children's families?" Ford asked.

"Yes—and no." Colin took his seat. "It seems the littlest one, Mary, is an orphan. Her parents died in the plague. Neighbors had taken her in, but now that they're homeless . . ." He shrugged. "I brought her back with me."

Jason's goblet hit the table with a *clunk*. "You cannot be planning to keep her?"

"Priscilla would never put up with it." Ford reached for some bread.

Colin flashed him a scathing glance. "No, I'm not planning to keep her." He turned to Jason. "I was hoping you could find her a home in the village."

"I expect I can." Jason's hand came up and stroked his mustache, his eyes thoughtful. "Could you not have sent her to a foundling home in London?"

"I could have, I suppose." Colin leaned for the wine decanter. "The authorities are handling such problems. But I had not the heart to leave her in such chaos. Moorfields is a sad scene. The grass is littered with rescued belongings that people are wary of relinquishing, interspersed with ashes—"

When Kendra and Amy walked in, Colin paused in

midsentence. Jason frowned. By all appearances, his brother had fossilized upon glimpsing Amy.

He cleared his throat and kicked Colin under the table. "Colin?"

"Um, yes." Colin's hand dropped, and the wine decanter thudded to the mahogany surface. He blinked and came back to life. "Good evening, Amy."

"Good evening," Amy murmured, gazing at him from beneath lowered lashes. Kendra caught Jason's attention, raising one eyebrow as though to make a silent point.

"Will you not sit down?" Jason waved his hand, and a servant started ladling soup while two others pulled out ladder-backed chairs on either side of the rectangular table, at the end where the Chase men had seated themselves.

Kendra craftily slipped into the chair next to her twin, leaving Amy no choice but to sit beside Colin. She lowered herself to the chair, her body turned slightly toward Colin's. Colin listed over in her direction.

In the guise of reaching for a piece of cake, Kendra leaned close to Jason. "A current flows between the two of them," she whispered in his ear. "You'd have to be addlepated not to notice."

"Colin was just telling us about returning the children to their families," Ford explained to Amy. "Sounds as though 'twas a hellish mess out there."

" 'Tis getting organized somewhat," Colin disagreed, putting down his spoon. "Charles arranged for public buildings to store the goods of the homeless, and provided army tents and bread, all without charge. 'Twas impossible to get about to find anyone, but they've set up a missing persons area. I waited there until all the children were claimed—all except Mary, that is."

A frown appeared between Kendra's brows. "The little girl with the golden curls and the never-ending questions?"

He nodded. "And the big blue eyes." Eyes that were as sad as Amy's looked now. "I brought her back with me. If I'd a shilling for every question she asked on the way here, I'd be able to restore Greystone tomorrow."

Kendra smiled. "And our town house?" She spooned a bite of cake into her mouth; Kendra always ate dessert first, claiming she might not have room for it later.

"The town house is safe—Lincoln's Inn Fields was never in danger. The fire stopped short of Chancery Lane and Essex House. The burned parts smolder so hotly, though, no man would venture in. The first rain started falling this afternoon as I left, and I reckon that will help."

"It rained for but a few minutes." Kendra glanced out the diamond-paned windows. "I'd not think it would help much."

"Perchance it rained more in London." Colin shrugged. "Though with all the homeless, perhaps we should hope not." His mind wandered and his words trailed off. 'Twas difficult to concentrate on the conversation with Amy so near. A rose scent drifted over from her direction.

Having left her grief stricken and sleeping, he'd been shocked when the old Amy entered the dining room. No, not the old Amy exactly. This Amy was subdued instead of animated. She was sort of a Kendra-ized Amy, wearing a dress he recognized as Kendra's, her hair coaxed into long Kendra-like ringlets.

But he felt the same pull toward her nonetheless. The gown, which had never looked quite right on Kendra, was magnificent on Amy. 'Twas perhaps an inch too short and a bit tight across the bosom, but the deep burgundy color suited her perfectly. Despite the obvious touches of Kendra, the conspicuous lack of jewelry separated her most from the old Amy. That, and her reserve.

He wanted to fold her into his arms and coax the sparkle back into her eyes.

"And Charles?" asked Ford.

If Colin inched his chair to the right, perhaps he could brush up against her arm. No, too obvious. Maybe he could just move his foot under the table . . .

Ford banged down his goblet. "Colin? How is the King holding up?"

Jason kicked Colin again.

"Ouch!" Colin blinked. What had Ford been asking about? "Oh, Charles. Od's fish, he's in his glory. Not much time to chat, though." He leaned to rub his ankle, deciding he'd deserved the kick. Why did he always think about touching her? Thank God he was leaving for Greystone in the morning, before he turned into a complete animal. He redoubled his efforts to stick to the conversation.

"Did you visit with Charles at Whitehall?" Kendra asked.

At Whitehall? Amy mouthed silently, startled. Was this family on intimate terms with His Majesty? She sneaked Colin an incredulous sidelong glance, then chided herself. Why should she be surprised? They lived in a castle, after all. Jason was a marquess, Colin an earl, Ford a something-or-other . . . a viscount, that was it. Titles all granted by Charles, Kendra had told her, explaining the unusual situation.

Colin shifted beside her. "No, Charles rode out to Moorfields. 'Twas an incredible scene. He sat on his horse in the midst of the woebegone crowd, the ruins of St. Paul's in the background, wisps of smoke rising from the rubble of the City. The stories of his heroism during the fire spread quickly, and those who didn't witness it are as loyal as those who did. He vowed, by the grace of God, to take particular care of all Londoners, by means of exciting plans for rebuilding. Great cheers went up . . . old Charles is a popular man these days."

Painted by Colin's vibrant words, Amy could picture the scene in her head: her King, seated tall atop his horse, addressing his adoring subjects. 'Twas history in the making, and she loved history. She sighed in satisfaction.

"What are these plans?" Jason asked. "Did he elaborate?"

"He issued a proclamation that all new construction

should be done according to a general plan," Colin informed them, "so that London would—let me see if I can remember his words—'rather appear to the world as purged with fire to a wonderful beauty and comeliness, than consumed by it' and 'no man whatsoever shall presume to erect any house or building, great or small, but of brick or stone.' I think I got the words right, but that was the gist of it, in any case."

Amy smiled to herself at Colin's precise descriptions; it had been the same when he showed her the castle. Dates, words . . . a man who paid attention to detail. And one detail she was certain of was that he didn't want her here. He had as much as said he couldn't wait to get rid of her. Still, she could swear she felt a warmth emanating from him, as if he wished he could pull her into his arms. 'Twas confusing. She shifted on her chair, her satin gown sliding on the fine needlework seatcover.

"It sounds like a good plan," Ford remarked.

Colin nodded. "Charles also decreed wider streets so buildings on one side cannot catch fire from the other. He's appointing Christopher Wren as . . . let's see . . . 'Deputy Surveyor and Principal Architect for Rebuilding the Whole City.' " Colin smiled at the grandiose title. "Wren is charged with drawing up a plan of boulevards and plazas and straight streets."

"Charles announced all of this?"

"He told me of Wren privately. 'Tis not official yet. Wren was supposed to have the plans ready to submit today, and then an announcement will be made."

"A new London, rising from the ashes," Amy murmured, staring at one of the chamber's enormous tapestries, but imagining instead what this bright new city might look like.

Colin looked at her. "What did you say?"

"Nothing," she mumbled, her cheeks flaming.

He hesitated, then cleared his throat and turned back to the others. "Did you know that Wren's plan for restoring St. Paul's was accepted by the Commission just two weeks ago?"

"And now St. Paul's is burned to the ground," Jason mourned. He slowly shook his head. "If I'd not seen it with my own eyes, I would never have believed this much destruction possible."

"Two-thirds of London is gone," Colin lamented, "and more than half the people are homeless. Miraculously, it seems that only eight lives were lost." He put a hand on Amy's arm. "I'm sorry that your father had to be one of them."

Colin's touch startled Amy out of her vision, dragged her back into the real world. She nodded, but couldn't meet his eyes. *'Twas not fair!* Only eight dead, and her own father one of them . . . She paused, her spoon halfway to her mouth, swallowed a swiftly rising lump in her throat, and fought to bite back the tears. 'Twas a losing battle. Suddenly, she stood up. Her spoon clattered in the bowl where she dropped it.

"Excuse me," she apologized huskily, running from the room.

"You lout!" Kendra threw down her spoon. "This was her first supper in company."

"What did I say?"

" 'I'm sorry your father had to be one of them,' " Ford mimicked in a mincing voice. "Hell, Colin, *I'm* the one who's supposed to be tactless."

"I said I was sorry," Colin protested feebly. He twisted his ring, listening to Amy's footsteps fade as she reached the top of the stairs and turned down the corridor.

"Leave Colin alone," Jason said. "He's confused enough as it is."

"What the hell is that supposed to mean?" Colin demanded.

"Just that you're attracted to Mrs. Goldsmith, and you've not decided what to do about it."

"What?" Ford burst out in surprise.

Kendra snorted, rolled her eyes toward the arched stone ceiling, then focused on her twin. "You are so oblivious. If something cannot be weighed or measured, it fails to command your attention."

Colin's hands clenched. "I am not the least bit attracted to Amethyst Goldsmith—"

"Col-in." With a pointed stare, Kendra reminded him of their conversation last week on the wall walk.

"She's a wreck," he stated firmly, pressing his lips together.

"So what?" Kendra asked.

"So I'm leaving in the morning, most likely before she rises, and one of you will see that she gets to France, where she will recover in peace and never see any of us again. That's what."

"Now, Colin—" Kendra began.

"Leave it be, Kendra." Jason looked at each sibling in turn, signaling that the conversation was at an end. Then, food being the typical Chase cure-all for most unpleasant situations, he rang for the servants. "I'm ready for that roast venison. How about the rest of you?"

Chapter Eight

Amy bit her lip and added another crumpled ball to the small mountain of paper that was growing on the gilt dressing table in her bedchamber. Why could she not get this right?

She flexed her hand. The blisters had healed, but sometimes it still hurt if she overused it. One more try. She dipped her quill in the ink.

26 September, 1666
Dear Robert,

Perhaps you already know that I lost Papa and the shop in the fire. I am devastated. I've lost everything. My entire life has changed, and I'm afraid yours as well. Please forgive me, but I cannot marry you—

"May I come in, Lady Amy?" Small fingers tapped on her shoulder.

She looked up to see big blue eyes in an innocent face framed by golden curls. "I think you already have, Mary." Smiling, she set down her quill and pulled the little girl onto her lap. "And I'm not a lady, sweetheart. Plain Amy will do."

"You look like a lady."

"Oh, but that is only because I'm wearing Lady Kendra's dress." Mary hopped off her lap, and Amy smoothed the apple-green satin of her borrowed gown. She watched the child wander to the bed and climb the bed steps, winced when she stretched out her arms and, with a whoop of delight, flung herself facedown on the costly brocade counterpane.

"I am wearing Lady Kendra's dress too," Mary declared, the words muffled against the golden fabric.

"And so you are!" The dress hung loose on Mary's small frame and was hopelessly out of style. But she was thrilled with her new wardrobe. Kendra had found an old trunk filled with her childhood gowns, and Mary had worn a new one every day since her arrival. "And a lovely dress it is. Are you a lady then, Mary?"

"Nah." Mary giggled and rolled onto her back. "Are you sure you're not a lady? You live in this pretty place."

"Not really." Amy's gaze swept the gorgeous gilt chamber. "Before the fire, I lived all my life in London."

"Like me?" The child sat up and pointed a thumb to her own chest—a thumb, Amy saw, that looked recently sucked.

"Just like you. In Cheapside."

"My house was in . . ." Her little face scrunched up as she thought. "Ludgate."

"Ludgate Hill? Then see, we were almost neighbors."

Mary's feet swung back and forth off the end of the bed. "And your mama and papa are dead like mine."

Amy nodded patiently. An eavesdropper would never guess they'd had this conversation at least a dozen times already. "Yes, my mama and papa are gone, as well."

"And they're never coming back."

"No." She bit her lip. "They're never coming back. But I think about them all the time, so their memory lives on."

Mary jumped off the bed. "How many days has it been?" One little hand reached up to the marble-topped dressing table and snagged a silver comb. "How many days since the fire?"

"How many days was it yesterday, Mary?"

"Um . . ." She tugged the comb through her curls. "Twenty-something?"

"Twenty-one." Amy took the comb from her, and Mary faced away so Amy could untangle her blond ringlets. "So today, how many days has it been since the fire?"

The girl raised one short finger, then popped up another. "Two. Twenty-two." Her small voice was full of pride.

"Very good, twenty-two days." The comb made a pleasant swishing sound as she drew it through Mary's hair again and again.

"My mama died of the plague. How many days since that?"

"Oh, sweetheart, I couldn't tell you." Amy sighed. "A lot."

"More than a hundred?"

"More than three hundred."

Amy watched Mary's eyes widen in the mirror. "That *is* a lot," Mary said.

"Surely it is." Amy turned her around and tucked a golden curl behind one shell-pink ear. "And inside, it hurts a little bit less every day, does it not?"

"Maybe. A little bit." Mary's lower lip trembled for a second, then she picked up Amy's letter and stared at it uncomprehendingly. "Who're you writin' to?"

"A man I knew." Amy set the comb back in place. "In fact, I think I'm finished."

She took the letter from Mary's small hand. 'Twould have to do. 'Twas blunt, but she couldn't seem to get the words right no matter how hard she tried. Perhaps Robert would be relieved. He might think that her promised value as a wife had been reduced by the loss of the shop. He'd be free to wed elsewhere, someone who could meet his expectations of a wife.

If he could locate another heiress in the trade to marry.

Amy picked up her quill, dipped it in the ink, and put a period after the last word she'd written. *Please forgive me, but I cannot marry you.* Mary's thumb went into her mouth as she watched Amy sign her name: Amethyst

Goldsmith, very neat and formal. After blotting the ink with sand, she folded the letter.

She wrote Robert's name and his father's address on the back, then set it aside, adding no return address. There, 'twas done.

And Robert would not be able to find her.

"How about this one?" The thumb popped out, and Mary waved another letter. "Who is this one to?"

"My aunt in Paris. I'm going to move there and live with her soon. But not too very soon, I'm hoping." Amy pulled the girl tight against her, enjoying her comforting, childish scent. "I like it here with you."

"I like it here, too." A sigh wafted from the child's rosy lips. "But I wish I had a mama."

Amy turned Mary to face her, put her hands on her small shoulders. She locked her gaze on Mary's big blue eyes. "Lord Cainewood is going to find you a new mama very soon. He promised, did he not?"

The child nodded.

"A Chase promise is not given lightly."

"What?" Her tiny brow creased.

"He always keeps his promises."

Apparently that was good enough for Mary. She waved the letter again. "What did you say to your aunt?"

"I told her how sad I am about my father." Amy rose from the dressing table and wandered to look out the diamond-paned window. Below, a servant hurried across the quadrangle, carrying a basket of laundry, leaving footprints in the damp grass. "Sometimes it helps you feel better to write a letter about your sadness."

"Like if I wrote a letter to Mama?"

On the wall beside her, Amy traced a finger around the oval gilt that framed a painting of a woman. Colin's grandmother, perhaps. Or great-grandmother. Her clothes looked like they belonged to the previous century. "You surely could write a letter to your mama. It might make you feel better." Neither she nor Mary had pictures to remember their ancestors by.

When she turned to her, the child's eyes were wistful. "I cannot write."

"Would you like me to write your letter for you?"

She nodded, looking hopeful. "All right."

Amy walked back to the dressing table and sat down, set a blank piece of paper on the marble surface. "What would you like to say?"

Mary stepped close and stared at the sheet of foolscap. A delicate breath sighed out through her parted lips.

"Dear Mama, I love you, Mama. I miss you, Mama."

Slowly Amy dipped her quill and wrote, her throat closing painfully as the words scrolled onto the page. She swallowed hard. "Anything else?"

" 'Tis all I can think of," the little girl said gravely.

" 'Tis a perfect letter." Amy kissed the top of her curly head. "Would you like to sign your name?"

She nodded quickly, and Amy lifted her onto her lap and handed her the quill. With a look of utter disbelief on her face, Mary thrust it joyfully into the ink, splattering the page, then scribbled something that Amy took for a signature. For good measure, she added a very crooked heart and a couple of stick figures that Amy thought might be Mary holding her mother's hand. She was afraid to ask if she were right or not.

"Here, sweetheart, you can fold it."

Mary did, and if the edges didn't line up, well, it certainly mattered not. "Will Mama get it in heaven?" she asked.

"If you give it a kiss, she'll get it right away."

The little girl puckered her lips and kissed the letter gently, leaving a tiny wet mark. Amy imagined 'twas exactly the way she'd kissed her mother. She hugged the girl tight, and when Mary turned in her arms and pressed her lips to Amy's cheek, her heart melted.

"Did Mama get my letter?"

Amy touched the sweet damp spot on her face, blinking back tears. "Surely she did."

"Even though 'tis still here?"

"Even though. There is special mail delivery to heaven."

The girl nodded. Children were so trusting. "Will Mama write me back?"

"In your dreams, sweetheart," Amy promised, needing to believe it. "When you go to sleep tonight, your mama will visit your dreams and remind you how much she loves you."

"I've never been in a fancy carriage." Mary bounced on the leather seat. "It goes slow. Why did we not ride a horse?"

Jason laughed. "Your friend Amy doesn't like horses. We would have had to leave her at home."

"No, I want Amy." She jumped up and onto Amy's lap. Amy held the girl close while she peered across at Jason. "Did you really find me a mama?"

He angled sideways to stretch his legs in the cabin. "I surely did, Miss Mary."

"When will I meet her?"

"In a few minutes, as soon as we get to the village."

Mary's thumb went into her mouth, then slid back out. "Why does she want a little girl?"

"She lost her husband last year, and she needs someone to love." And the money that Jason would provide for Mary's care, Amy knew. 'Twas the perfect solution all around.

"If her husband is lost, why does she not just look for him?"

Amy stifled a laugh. "He died, sweetheart. In a mill accident."

"Oh." The girl's legs swung back and forth, kicking Amy's shins until she put down a hand to stop them. "Why do big people say that someone is lost? Why can they not just say he is dead?"

Jason reached out to tweak a curl. "My, you are full of questions, aren't you?"

"Will I have any brothers or sisters?"

"I'm afraid not. Mr. and Mrs. Bradford never had children of their own." Jason's hand went up to smooth his mustache, then he smiled. "That's why she wants a little girl so badly."

"Will she love me?"

"How could she not?" Jason chucked her under the chin. "And you will love her too, Mary, I promise."

"A Chase promise is not given lightly," Mary quoted solemnly.

"What did you say?" His jaw went slack in surprise.

"That means you always keep your promises. Amy told me."

"Oh." Jason and Amy shared a smile over the child's small head. "Well, she's right, you know."

"Amy is always right." Mary craned her neck to see out the open coach window. "Is that the village? Ooh, pretty."

Amy's gaze went to follow hers. "Much prettier than London, is it not? And cleaner."

"It smells nice, too. Every house has flowers."

Mary watched, rapt, as they passed several more houses and rolled to a stop before a small white cottage with a thatched roof. The coachman had not finished opening the door and lowering the steps before Clarice Bradford rushed out to meet them, holding a new rag doll.

Mary bounded down the steps and right into her outstretched arms.

For a long moment they clung to one another, then pulled back to give each other a considered look. Clarice reached trembling fingers to caress Mary's bright curls. She turned to Jason, who had followed Amy from the carriage into the cottage's tidy front yard. "Oh, she is beautiful, my lord."

Mary's head tilted up, then slowly went down as she took in the glossy brown braided bun that sat atop Clarice's head, the gray eyes set in her pretty face, her simple tan dress, and the plain black shoes that peeked from beneath her skirts. "You are beautiful too, Mama."

The gray eyes filled with grateful tears, and though

Clarice was an attractive woman, in that moment she truly did look beautiful.

"Did you make this doll for me?"

"Just for you. I sat up all night working on it." Too excited to sleep, Amy guessed. Yesterday when she and Jason had approached Clarice about taking Mary for a daughter, the woman had been overwrought with gratitude.

"Thank you, Mama. She is beautiful, too. I will name her Amy." Mary clutched the doll close as she watched the coachman and outrider carry Kendra's trunk into Clarice's cottage. Her blue eyes widened. "Do I get to keep all those clothes?"

Jason smiled. "With Lady Kendra's compliments."

"And . . ." Amy moved closer, pulled something from her pocket. "Lord Cainewood gave me permission to leave this with you, as a memento of our time together. I'm sorry I've nothing of my own to give you to remember me by."

The engraved silver comb sparkled in the sunshine as Mary took it, staring at it as though 'twere one of King Charles's crown jewels. "Oh, my lady—I mean, Amy! I will 'member you always." Amy knelt on the grass, and tears came to her eyes as Mary's little arms wound around her neck. She hugged her back fiercely.

When Amy rose, Jason ruffled Mary's curls. "Will you be needing anything else?"

"No." Mary glanced up at him, then over to her new mother. She scurried to Clarice's side and reached up to take her hand. "I am home now."

When, Amy wondered, would *she* be home?

Chapter Nine

Kendra dashed into the library and leaned against the large globe, breathless. "Amy," she panted. " 'Tis Colin." She paused for more air. "He's here. What are we going to do?"

Amy felt as though she'd been punched in the stomach. "God in heaven," she whispered. "He's come to take me away, hasn't he?" She looked up to the carved wood ceiling, her eyes tracing the intricate design while her mind wrestled with denial.

"There's nothing we *can* do," she said finally, her gaze dropping to Kendra. "I'm lucky he stayed away this long—"

"You fit in here. I don't want you to leave."

Kendra's words warmed Amy's heart. She rose from the chair and gave Kendra a brief, sisterly hug. "Thank you for saying that; you'll never know how much it means to me." She sniffed back tears. "I've loved every minute of my two months here, but 'tis not my place. I have another life."

"A life in Paris?" Kendra's brow furrowed in concern.

" 'Tis not so bad as all that," Amy said, remembering Colin telling her so outside the inn, after the fire. A long time ago, it seemed, but now she believed it. "As much as I love it here, my fingers ache to wield a knife on wax, to cast and polish and engrave."

Her hands clenched, then relaxed as her gaze dropped to the red-carpeted floor and ran along the wide decorative golden stripes, down the length of the long, narrow room to the fireplace. Kendra remained silent while

Amy stared into the distant flames, struggling with her feelings of being uprooted once again.

'Twas the only way. Robert must have received her letter and accepted her decision by now . . . and if not, well, he would never find her in France. She would work at Aunt Elizabeth's shop while she prepared to open her own. She'd vowed that Goldsmith & Sons would not die with her, and she meant to honor that vow.

Her trunk was gathering dust in the corner of her bedchamber, her inheritance locked inside. More than enough jewelry to stock a small shop, plus gold to pay for tools and equipment—gold that would be faithfully replaced as soon as she was able. She would never deplete the Goldsmith fortune. Like the generations before her, she bore an obligation.

Kendra heaved a heavy sigh. "If you leave, I'll miss you."

Her doleful tone snapped Amy out of her trance, and she shot Kendra a conspiratorial grin. "I'll hide here 'til Colin leaves. Up on the balconies—no one ever looks at the books there except me. You can sneak up food and tell him I've gone to Paris."

Kendra's laugh echoed through the two-story library. "I vow and swear, for a minute there I thought you were serious." She relaxed and leaned back against the brass mesh set into the bookshelf doors, then looked at Amy sharply. "You *are* fooling, are you not?"

"Marry come up, Kendra!" Amy offered her a small, wistful smile. "Have you ever heard of anything more ludicrous?"

"I'll go find out what Colin wants."

She reached to touch Kendra's arm. "We both know what Colin wants."

"*Colin* knows not what Colin wants," Kendra stated wryly. "I'll just see what kind of ideas I can plant in his head." And with that cryptic statement, she left the room.

Amy plopped back into the chair. The history books in front of her had seemed fascinating a few minutes ago, but now they had lost their appeal. She pushed them aside and laid her head on the exquisite mosaic table, the tiles cool under her cheek. She would miss this family, but she knew her life was destined along another path. *You cannot have everything*, she heard her father say.

She sighed and rose to go ready herself for supper. If she hurried, perhaps she would have time to take a walk around the grounds and think things through. But deep in her heart, she knew there was really nothing to think about.

This was it. Her time was up. Colin wanted her gone, and this time he would see it done. She had no excuses left.

Jason had plenty of excuses.

Colin spared Kendra not a glance when she walked into the drawing room. "*She's still here?* I cannot believe it!"

"It's not been that long," Jason stated calmly.

"Nine weeks! Don't tell me she's not recovered enough in nine weeks."

"I never asked her," Jason admitted. "She does seem to be getting on fine, though."

Colin stormed over to where Jason lounged against the carved stone mantle. "You never asked her?"

"I just said so, did I not? We've been quite busy these past weeks."

"You've been busy?" Colin spat. "Too busy to take a day or two to deliver her as promised?" His fists clenched. It had not been easy to walk away from Amy, but he'd done it, trusting he would never be tempted by her again.

"Yes. With the end of the harvest, Ford and I have been out collecting rents. 'Tis that time of year, you know."

"Yes, I know." Colin forced the words between gritted teeth. Jason's nonchalance wasn't ameliorating his mood in any way. "*I've* been busy. Disposing of the harvest, looking after the livestock, overseeing the quarrying and logging operations, collecting rents, directing restoration work, working on the damned account books—and all by myself with just Benchley for help. *You* have Ford and a battalion of servants, and you had not the time to—"

"Amy's been doing my ledgers for me," Jason interrupted. "I reckon she'd be willing to help you out. She's quite grateful, you know."

Colin made his way to one of the salmon-upholstered chairs and dropped into it, defeated. "She's been doing your ledgers," he stated in a dead voice.

"Oh, yes," Kendra bragged, "and she's much faster than Jason ever was. Why, she says she's just about caught up."

"That's a miracle," Colin allowed. "However did this come about?" They were bound to tell him anyway, so he might as well cooperate.

"I was showing her the portraits in the picture gallery," Kendra explained brightly, "and the door to Jason's study was open. He invited her in to look around, she asked what he was working on so hard, and that was that. She kept the books for her father's shop." Kendra smiled in a way that set Colin's teeth on edge. "She's so smart, Colin, you'd not believe it."

"Oh, I'd believe it all right." Just one more thing to add to the shining qualities of Amethyst Goldsmith.

"She became great friends with little Mary." Jason made his way to the chair next to Colin's. "Why, you should have seen her with that child. She's a born mother." He sat and stretched out his long legs, crossing them at the ankles. "I found a home for Mary in the village, with the widow of one of my men who was killed in that mill accident."

"Good." Wonder of wonders, his brother had actually followed through with something he'd asked of him. "Thank you for taking care of that."

"My pleasure."

With a gleam in her eye, Kendra turned to her heretofore silent twin for assistance.

"We've been discussing Amy's fine education," Ford put in helpfully. "She's interested in science"—Ford was forever complaining that no one in the family shared his fascination with science—"though she prefers history. She spends hours and hours in the library."

"She does, does she?" Colin crossed his arms and leveled a stare at Jason. "When are you taking her to Dover? You *are* taking her to Dover?"

"Of course, Colin. Whyever would you think not?"

"She should stay here," Kendra protested. "She's clever and sweet and helpful and a good friend and she has no one—just one aunt—and she fits right in with the family." Kendra paused for a deep breath and squared her shoulders. "You should marry her, Colin. We all think she's wonderful."

Colin had seen it coming. He raised one eyebrow. "Then you can all marry her," he suggested lightly, rising to go out the door. "I'm going to get cleaned up."

"Wait!" Kendra yelled after him.

He whirled around. "*You* wait," he returned fiercely. "I'm marrying Lady Priscilla Hobbs, or did that slip your mind somehow?" He turned to Ford. "You want Amy in the family? *You* marry her."

Ford's blue eyes widened at the mere suggestion. "*I'm* not ready to get married!"

Undaunted, Colin turned on Jason. "You marry her, then. You seem to enjoy having her around."

"I'm—I'm not attracted to her," sputtered the unflappable Jason. "She's—she's a bookkeeper!"

"Exactly." Colin turned on his heel and headed up to his bedchamber, shaking his head. Sometimes his family was more trouble than they were worth.

Kendra, especially. *You should marry her, Colin.* Hmmph! He'd get Kendra for that one. Tonight. He'd get her good.

A nice warm bath would calm him and inspire a clever idea.

* * *

"Defending the castle?"

Amy turned to see Colin framed in the arch to the stairwell. Taken off guard, she gazed at him, her hands tightening on the iron grille set into the keep's window. The last time she'd seen him, he'd been mentally and physically exhausted. Now the circles were gone from under his eyes. He looked relaxed and rested, his body hardened by healthy manual labor.

She swallowed hard. "Defending the castle?" she echoed.

His smile reached his glittering emerald eyes. "This is where the castle guard lived, and you were watching through the window."

"Oh." She blushed, feeling thick-witted for not catching the reference. What was it about him that robbed her ability to think straight? "I was just . . . ruminating." She glanced out the window, struggling for some relevant comment she could make. "How could they see to guard? The windows are so narrow."

"The better to deter arrows in days past." Colin moved toward her, then abruptly stopped. She thought she saw a frown flit across his tanned features. "In truth, they only lived and stored weapons in here. There was a level above us where they took turns day and night, watching through the notches in the battlement all around."

Amy looked up at the sky, streaked with colors from the setting sun. She imagined the guards up there, pacing back and forth, clanking around in their armor. Colin's words seemed to do that to her: make her imagine other times, other places. She stole another glance at him.

His gleaming black hair was loose for a change, cut just to his shoulders, easy to manage if not fashionable. 'Twas odd, but the color she hated on her own head looked just perfect on his.

She'd been convinced that her response to his kiss, that one time that now seemed so long ago, had been an outgrowth of her grief, a method for escape, but suddenly she knew she'd been fooling herself. It seemed each time she saw him, the pull was stronger.

She took a step closer. "I can picture the knights up there when you talk about them."

" 'Tis a romantic image, but they weren't knights all decked out for battle." Colin took a step back and leaned against the wall, crossed his ankles and arms. "Just regular men, mostly. Each of the lord's vassals—all the men granted use of his land—was obligated to spend part of his year as a member of the castle guard."

"I've been wondering what it was like to live here."

"Well, Kendra sent me to find you for supper, but I can give you my famous tour on the way down."

Amy laughed, a happy sound that tapered off into the night. He led her to the stair tower and down a level.

" 'Tis hard to imagine living in anything so primitive as a keep today," Colin's words floated up to her, "but in the twelfth century, it would have contained the best residential lodging for the lord. In those days, others lived in the smaller towers set into the castle walls, while the rest of the imagine had their homes constructed against the inside surfaces of the enclosure."

When they came out on the second floor, Amy wandered to a window where she could oversee the quadrangle. "No wonder 'tis so big," she said, imagining hundreds of people milling below.

"The castle was like a small town, and this keep was the ultimate in luxury accommodations." He joined her at the window, grazing her arm. "There was a poultry yard where all the animals were kept." He moved closer, and there was a tingling in the pit of her stomach. "Soldiers, skilled workers, servants and their families—everyone made their home within the castle walls."

Suddenly she felt giddy. "Tell me more," she begged. His words weren't going in one ear and out the other, not quite, but she was having a hard time concentrating.

"The portcullis, that wooden iron-banded gate at the barbican over there, would be down all the time, not just at night like it is now. The drawbridge would be raised unless someone needed to leave or enter."

When Colin paused, she turned to look at him. He captured her eyes with his. "This would have been the lord's bedchamber."

"Oh." She blushed furiously.

" 'Twould have been decorated with beautiful tapestries, and the beds would have been draped with yards and yards of fabric that could be pulled together to keep in the warmth. Huge beds, so that on cold nights they could all get in, the whole family together, and cuddle to keep warm."

Colin's words were naught but informative, yet his voice was deep and husky, as though . . . no, 'twas all her imagination. He'd not asked how she was, or anything else of a personal nature; he had obviously come only to fetch her for supper.

And to take her away.

"Is supper waiting?" she asked, before she could dwell any longer on the subject.

Colin blinked before answering, and when he did, his words were clipped. "I reckon it is. We should go."

Amy followed him down the twisting staircase, but when he headed toward the courtyard, she slowed on the bottom floor. Despite everything, she felt not quite ready to share him with his family.

"What was this room for?"

He hesitated, then turned back. "This would have been the main living quarters for the lord and his family." He was the tour guide again, his voice instructive, nothing more. "They would have eaten here, food brought to them by servants from the castle kitchens. The lord's children would have had their lessons here, and the family would have played games and received visitors here. There would have been lots of food and supplies in the storeroom underneath, in case of a siege."

Amy ran her fingers down the ancient wall. "You've a lovely home, my lord."

He shrugged. " 'Tis Jason's, really."

She walked around the circular chamber, trailing one hand along the rough stone. "I can picture your lord and his family living here. Were they happy, do you think?"

"I imagine so." Colin chuckled. "The Chases were always a boisterous lot, I'm told."

Amy halted, startled. Of course it had been his family living here these past four hundred years, but it had not occurred to her before. Nobility, for all that long. Just as her own family had been jewelers for an untold number of years. 'Twas an intriguing thought, and a sad one, emphasizing the many reasons they could never be together.

"They're surely waiting for us by now," Colin said, breaking her reverie. "Shall we?"

He hurried across the quadrangle; she struggled to keep up with his long strides. When they reached the dining room, they found the family arranged the same way they'd been seated the night before Colin left, forcing Colin and Amy to sit beside one another again.

He would have been surprised had they done otherwise, Colin thought, pushing Amy's chair in for her. He took his seat. Supper was served, and conversation swirled as usual, but tonight he was the one not participating. He was so aware of Amy, he could swear he felt heat emanating from her direction. It had taken all his willpower not to touch her in the keep.

She seemed different tonight. She wore a different gown, a hunter green he remembered Kendra wearing at a house party last year. Her hair was in curls again . . . 'Twas her eyes, he decided suddenly. The amethyst sparkle was back.

No one would think of describing this self-assured woman as "a wreck" now. She laughed and joked with his sister and brothers, kept up with the best of their repartee as though born to a large, noisy family.

This large, noisy family, in fact. Colin was stunned. She was everything he'd imagined her to be: beautiful, animated, talented, intelligent, witty . . . and entirely too comfortable with his family.

She laughed again, and his fists clenched under the table as he forced himself to look at his plate instead of her. She was enough to drive a man to the asylum. Or, even worse, to a life of debauchery. And he was not that kind of man.

He would deliver her to a ship bound for France—tomorrow. 'Twas obvious that Jason and Ford had no intention of doing so any time soon, and it must be done—the sooner, the better.

"What do you think, Colin?" Amy asked, startling him out of his trance.

"Pardon me?" Colin hadn't followed the conversation in the slightest.

"Amy has challenged you to a game of piquet after supper," Ford explained.

"I just taught her last month," Kendra pouted, "and already she puts me to shame."

"I'm weary tonight." Colin had no desire to match wits at a card game, most especially not with Amy. Besides, he had his plan to carry out. "I was looking forward to relaxing and listening to you play the harpsichord, Kendra."

"I played last night."

"Not for me. Please," he pleaded, "I've been locked up in my godforsaken stronghold for weeks, with no civilized entertainment . . ."

"Oh, very well. You've no need to act so miserable." Kendra sounded irritated, but her eyes danced. She dearly loved being appreciated.

The first wrong note slipped by practically unnoticed, what with everyone's voices raised in rousing song and Kendra's nimble fingers flying fast. But then she hit another sour note, and another . . . She paused momentarily, then resumed the tune.

Kendra rarely made mistakes. She'd been an apt pupil, training for hours upon hours while in exile, an eager student for the bored ladies looking for ways to pass the time. Just as the men had taken Colin and his brothers under their wings, putting them through fencing maneuvers until they could parry and thrust to perfection, so had the ladies put Kendra through her paces. As a result, she was quite an accomplished musician, making this night's trouble particularly frustrating.

When three more notes proved off key in less than a minute, Kendra stopped abruptly and shook her head as though trying to clear it.

"What's wrong?" Ford teased. "Too much Rhenish tonight?"

"I never drink too much, Ford, and you know it."

"Oh, yes, I forgot. That's Amy's problem. Half a glass and she's on the floor."

Amy giggled.

Colin looked at her sharply, then back to his younger brother. God's blood, his family knew more about her than he ever would have guessed. She'd really been worming her way in, the little witch. He hardened his resolve to remove her tomorrow, before she insinuated herself even deeper.

"Are you tired, Kendra?" Jason inquired.

"No, I'm not tired." Kendra was clearly irritated. "I'll just start over."

Start over she did, and proceeded to hit the same sour notes. She slammed her fists down on the keyboard, exasperated.

"Are your eyes bothering you?" Amy asked.

"No, my eyes aren't bothering me. I could play this with them closed, at any rate."

"Why do we not just talk tonight?" Jason suggested. "We've not all been together in a long while."

Kendra heaved an impatient sigh. "No. I know I can play this—I've done it hundreds of times."

She attacked the keyboard with a new vigor and hit the same wrong notes again. *The same wrong notes.*

She leapt off her bench seat and lifted the lid of the wooden instrument. Half a second later, she slammed it shut and whirled about, pointing an accusing finger at Colin.

"You! You and your damned practical jokes. Have you any idea how long it will take me to retune this?"

"However long it takes, you deserve it, little sister. 'You should marry her,' indeed."

"Marry who?" asked Amy.

"Never mind." Colin waved her off, his attention on Kendra. "Got you good, did I not?"

"I reckon you did," she admitted with a wry smile.

Ford walked over to the harpsichord. "What's going on here?" He peered inside, then convulsed in mirth.

"What? What is it?" Amy asked.

"He—he—loosened some strings," Ford managed to choke out between gales of laughter. "Look."

Amy wandered over to survey the instrument. Though she knew nothing of music, 'twas obvious what Colin had done: A half-dozen random strings were markedly less taut than the others.

"See?" Ford pressed a key causing a plectrum to pluck a tight string, followed by a key to a loose one. The resulting sound was so discordant that Amy burst into helpless giggles.

They felt so good, those unconstrained giggles. She couldn't help herself; the giggles led into peals of uncontrollable laughter.

'Twas infectious. Colin joined in, and Ford and Jason, and finally Kendra, until they were all laughing simply because everyone else was laughing. One by one, they stopped, their laughter dwindling into occasional chuckles, all except Amy. She held onto the harpsichord to keep from doubling over as she laughed and laughed; she knew not even why, anymore. Her sides hurt, and tears ran down her face.

Ford put a hand on her shoulder. "She thinks you're funny, Colin."

Amy blushed, but Colin just grinned. "I appreciate a woman who appreciates my jokes."

Amy's face heated even more. "I'll—I'll be right

back," she hiccuped between bursts of giggles. She had to gain control of herself.

She wove her way through the corridor, laughing, and down the stairs, leaning against the wall at intervals. To look at her, one would think she *was* drunk, but she was merely giddy from her proximity to Colin, intensified by a feeling of well-being, surrounded by laughing people who loved one another. Her family hadn't shouted, but they hadn't laughed together much either.

The laughter made her feel slightly sick, and she hugged her stomach and aching ribs. At the foot of the staircase, she gazed through tear-blurred eyes at the tall wooden front doors. The quadrangle beyond enticed her, the crisp night air exactly what she needed. She stumbled through the Stone Hall and out the doors, laughing all the way, almost tripped down the steps outside, and fell into a heap on the damp grass.

Her giggles diminished, and she took delicious breaths of cold air deep into her lungs. Finally she sat up, wiping the tears from her cheeks between hiccups. She placed her hands behind her on the grass and leaned back, staring up into the sky, enjoying the feel of the frigid air on her hot face.

Colin came into the quadrangle and crouched down beside her.

"The family elected me to check on you," he said wryly. "Better now?"

"Uh-huh." She watched a dark cloud creep slowly across the moon. "I'm sorry. I guess I made a fool of myself." She hiccuped, more loudly than she would have liked. "Excuse me."

"No excuses necessary," Colin declared chivalrously. "And you made no fool of yourself, either. To the contrary, we are all pleased to see you've recovered your spirits."

Silent, Amy continued watching the clouds gather, dark shapes against the starlit sky. She hiccuped again.

"I'll take you to Dover tomorrow," Colin said quietly

beside her. "I'm sorry Jason and Ford have not found the time to do it."

Suddenly, the air seemed cold instead of refreshing. She shivered and sat up straight, folding her legs beneath her. " 'Twas not a problem. I've been fine here."

His family's faint laughter sounded in the background. She felt a stab of pain at the thought of leaving them all; she was even growing used to their inevitable arguments. But 'twas only by chance that she'd been afforded the luxury of being a part of them for a while, and her time was up. She shivered again.

"Are you cold?" he asked.

"A little bit."

"We should go back inside. You'll catch your death out here." In opposition to his words, he moved closer and put an arm around her shoulders, pulling her tight against him.

Amy would have moved not an inch for the world. "In a minute," she stalled. His heat penetrated the side of her body, warming her all over.

"How is your hand?" he asked abruptly.

"Fine." Her words came quietly, as though if she spoke loudly, he might pull away. "It healed weeks ago."

Colin took her hand to examine it in the moonlight. "Mmmm." He rubbed his warm palm over the back, then suddenly his fingers came around and laced through hers. With a sharp movement, he brought their joined hands to his lips and held them there.

Amy bit her lip and closed her eyes. She felt Colin move around to kneel in front of her, and opened her eyes to find his just inches away.

"How are *you*, Amy?" he asked in hushed tones, searching her face for the answer.

"I'm better," she whispered, overwhelmed by his intensity. "Much, much better."

" 'Tis good," he replied, then swiftly, before either of them could think about it, his arms came around her, and he pulled her hard against him and brought his lips to hers. Her own arms wound over his shoulders and around his neck; her fingers meshed themselves in his thick, silky hair.

She was shocked at her surge of response to the touch of his mouth. Inexperienced though she was, her lips opened, inviting him in.

He eased her backward onto the damp, fragrant grass, and pulled his mouth from hers. His warm, moist breath trailed down, and she felt the heady sensation of his lips against her arched neck. He stretched out, half on top of her. She'd slept next to him at the inn, but this was different, and her body felt on fire in a hundred places where it made contact with his.

Her senses spun, and she thought that if he let go of her, she would die. He raised his head to choke out her name in a strangled voice, then his lips recaptured hers, more urgent this time. He tasted of Rhenish, but, underneath, he tasted of Colin. A unique, delicious flavor she knew she would search for the rest of her life.

His mouth felt hot and demanding, his kisses wet on her chin and her throat and finally between her breasts framed in the low neckline of her borrowed gown. She smelled his hair, his scent, not smoky this time, but warm and clean and masculine. His tongue traced a shivery line from her cleavage back up her neck, and she called out his name in a breathy cry.

He pulled away and sat up, muttering a soft oath. "I'm sorry," he sighed, running a hand raggedly through his tangled hair.

Of course he was sorry. He didn't like her; he wanted to get rid of her. What she couldn't understand was how he could kiss her like that, feeling as he did.

She didn't trust herself to speak. Instead, she sat up and put her head in her hands. But she didn't cry. She felt too dead inside to cry.

"I'm betrothed, you know," he said suddenly. Amy looked up, startled. She'd not known—nobody had thought to inform her.

"Her name is Priscilla Hobbs," he continued. "*Lady* Priscilla Hobbs. Her father's an earl—she'll make a perfect mother for my children. Oh, and she's very nice," he added unconvincingly.

"Why are you telling me all this?" she asked, confused.

"I'm just trying to explain why I cannot . . . pay court to you."

Humiliated, she lashed out at him. "Pay court to me? Because of a little kiss? What an absurd notion!" Her voice rose an octave in her agitation. "I'd never expect you to marry me—you've tried to get rid of me at every turn."

"That's not true," he protested.

"It is so true," she contradicted, but the anger was seeping out of her already. Things were as they were; she wasn't suited to him, and there was nothing she could do about it.

"Amy," he started, rising on his knees to face her. She instinctively scooted backward, and a flash of disappointment crossed his face. She looked down, picking at an imaginary piece of lint on her skirt.

"I'm sorry," he finally muttered.

They were silent for a long minute. Then Amy looked up and locked her gaze on his.

"When you touch me," she confessed softly, "I feel things I never thought to feel. I know not if you might feel them, too. What I do know is that it matters not. You belong here, with lords and ladies and the King, and I belong in France, working at a jeweler's bench."

An inscrutable mask settled on Colin's features. He hesitated, then slowly stood and brushed the grass off his breeches.

"We'd better get some sleep," he said in a voice devoid of any emotion. "I mean to get an early start."

His long legs carried him up the steps and through the door without hesitation. Amy took a deep breath and raised herself up, wondering if her own legs would carry her.

Chapter Ten

Colin cursed fluently, aiming a boot at the side of the coach for emphasis.

"My lord, we'll have to stop here," Benchley concluded.

"Oh, is that right?" Colin's voice dripped with sarcasm. "I imagined we could drag along to Dover on three wheels."

Benchley usually stood as tall as possible to compensate for his deficient height, but now his shoulders hunched over, and he positively drooped.

"Sorry, Benchley," Colin hastened to apologize. Though he would be hiring more servants in the near future, as soon as there was lodging available for them at Greystone, at this point Benchley was his valet, butler, coachman, cook, and serving-maid all rolled into one. He did not deserve Colin's misplaced wrath. "Damn me, but I'm vexed, is all."

"I quite understand, my lord. I'll just take one of the horses and return with a wheel and a wright to install it. You two sit tight and eat the dinner Lady Kendra sent. I'll be back in no time."

"The hell you will." Colin gestured angrily at the sky. "This storm is due to kick up any minute." As if on cue, a few snowflakes drifted down from the clouds.

Benchley brushed a flake off his beak of a nose. "You're right, my lord. I'm not certain I'll be able to find a wheelwright to come out in this weather."

The clouds that had begun gathering last night looked unequivocally threatening now. The family had tried to talk Colin into postponing this trip, but he had been adamant. He meant to deliver Amy to a France-bound ship, and he meant to do it today. Damn the broken wheel.

The thought of spending extra time with Amy, in a freezing carriage going nowhere, was daunting. The only thing colder than the weather was Amy's attitude. They'd spent the first short part of their journey in total silence, in diagonal corners on opposite seats, each with their nose buried in a book. No, spending the afternoon in this carriage was unthinkable.

"Pay the wheelwright whatever it takes." He dug in his pouch, slapped some coins into Benchley's hand. "I'll take Mrs. Goldsmith to Greystone on the other horse. When the wheel is fixed, ride on over and we'll be on our way."

Colin helped Benchley unhitch one of the matched bays and sent him off with a smack on the horse's rump. Then he climbed into the coach and sat down opposite Amy, shutting the door against the frigid air.

Amy looked up from the book she'd been struggling to read in the failing light. "Yes?" she asked in a frosty tone.

Colin stared at her. "The wheel is broken," he began.

"I surmised as much." Amy shut her book. "I heard every word you uttered, foul and otherwise."

"Benchley has ridden off for help," Colin explained anyway. "We'll ride the other bay to Greystone and wait for him there."

"How far is Greystone?"

"A mile and a half, perhaps."

"I'll walk."

"You will not walk," Colin declared.

"I'm not riding any horse."

He knew she was unhappy with him, but that was no reason to contradict him at every turn. He reckoned he could outstubborn her any day of the week.

"You will not walk," he repeated. " 'Tis snowing, and

you've no cloak. You'd freeze to death before you made it halfway."

" 'Tis snowing?" Shooting him a skeptical glance, she rubbed a circle of condensation off the window with her fist. She peered outside, wrapped the blanket tighter about herself, and leaned back into the corner. " 'Tis snowing."

Colin looked out the viewhole she'd created.

"Damn, 'tis getting worse than I expected." Her mocking expression made him bristle. " 'Tis not my fault we're surprised with a November snow. For God's sake, we've not seen snow this far south in three years. How the hell was I supposed to predict such an occurrence?"

" 'Twas cold regardless. You could have waited for decent weather before insisting—"

He set his jaw. "I have my reasons for needing to get on with this."

"Why? So you can get rid of me once and for all?"

"No." He'd said it too fast; she'd hit too close to home. He took a deep breath. "I'm sorry this happened."

Her response was a stony stare.

"I've already said I'm sorry for the way I've treated you."

She remained tight lipped. His hands fisted on his knees as he fought to control his tone. "We need to get to Greystone, and at the rate you're moving this will be a full-blown blizzard before we even get out of the coach."

Her icy mask fell, and she shrank further into the corner. "I cannot ride a horse."

"What?" His hands relaxed, and he rubbed them on his thighs. "Whyever not?"

"I've never ridden a horse," she confessed in a choked voice. "I cannot do it, I just cannot."

"People ride horses all the time."

"Other people."

"You've never been on a horse. What makes you think you'll not like it?"

"I didn't say I've never been *on* a horse. I said I've never *ridden* a horse. Papa put me on one once, in Hyde Park, when I was eight. I was up so high, and this thing under me moved, and I screamed until he pulled me off. I swore I'd never get on a horse again."

Colin couldn't believe what he was hearing. They needed to be on their way, and now. "You're not eight anymore, Amy."

"I cannot. I just cannot. The animal is ten times my weight, it has a brain all its own—why, it could buck me off, or run under a tree and make me hit my head on a branch, or—"

"Now you're babbling." He reached for her hand, to pull her out.

Snatching it back, she burrowed even further into the corner and tucked the blanket in tighter. "I'm sorry. If I cannot walk, then I'll just wait here. I have a blanket, a book, and food. I'm prepared to wait until Benchley returns."

"This storm could last until morning," Colin argued, though he hoped to hell 'twould not. "You're coming with me, and you're coming on the horse. I'll hold on to you. You'll be fine." He flung open the door, grabbed her hand from beneath the blanket, and pulled her up and out of the carriage in one smooth motion.

Glaring, she shivered in her blanket while Colin unhitched the horse. He watched her surreptitiously, his earlier annoyance rapidly turning to amusement. Imagine, a grown woman being scared of a docile animal. Surely once she was riding, she would see 'twas not frightening.

When the horse was free, he motioned her over. "I suggest you ride astride—'twill feel a lot more secure than sidesaddle."

"Sidesaddle?" She shot him an accusatory glare. "There's *no* saddle."

"Up you go," he said cheerfully, his laced fingers providing a foothold to boost her.

"You go first."

"Amy," he said with an exasperated sigh, "if I get on first, I'll not be able to help you up."

She huffed, then clenched her jaw and stepped onto his hands, swinging her leg over awkwardly.

She almost fell off the other side.

Her screech pierced Colin's ears even as he leapt to help her. Seated at last, her eyes wide with fear, she wrinkled her nose. "He smells terrible." Her skirts were hitched up in disarray, the look on her face so comical Colin had to bite his tongue to keep from laughing.

"He feels warm," she said. "And scratchy. And very *alive*." The animal took a small step backward, and she let out a shriek.

" 'Tis all right. He's not going anywhere," Colin soothed, then turned back to the carriage, muttering to himself.

"Wh-where are you going?" Amy yelled after him. "Come back! You cannot leave me alone on a live beast!"

Colin leaned into the coach to fetch Kendra's basket of food. "I was just getting our dinner." He swung up easily behind her, held the basket in one hand, Amy firmly against himself with the other. His arm reached almost all the way around her waist. "Better?"

She nodded. He waited until she relaxed back against him, then urged the horse at a slow walk toward Greystone. They moved—an entire twenty feet.

"Stop!"

Colin didn't. "You're doing fine, Amy."

"No! I mean, we have to go back!" She twisted, trying to face him. "We left my trunk!"

He reined in, swearing under his breath. "Oh, no. We're not lugging that damned trunk to Greystone. It will be here when we get back."

"No—it must come with me," she insisted in a panicked voice. She looked up and back at him, bumping her head on his chin in the process. "I'll get it myself if I have to." To emphasize her threat, she leaned to the side as though she were determined to slide off the horse there and then.

Colin clutched at her. "What the hell's in that blasted trunk that makes it so important?"

She gritted her teeth. "Everything I own."

The same answer she'd given before. He was certain she was hiding something from him, but then tears filled her eyes and he found himself climbing off the horse. He set the basket on the ground and headed for the trunk.

"Thank you so much," she called to his back.

'Twas the first civil thing she had uttered to him all morning. He wondered how he would manage to carry Amy, the trunk, and their dinner on one horse, but he supposed 'twould be worth the effort, if she would act pleasant as a result.

Another shriek rang out as he stepped into the carriage. " 'Tis moving! The beast is about to run away!"

"Pull back on the reins," he shouted through the door.

"The what? Oh, God in heaven, he's leaning down! He's going to roll over on top of me and crush me, I just know it!"

Alarmed, Colin backed out of the carriage. The horse had moved, all right—all of three feet. His head was lowered as he munched contentedly on a clump of grass by the roadside. "God in heaven is right." Colin hefted the trunk and made his way toward her. "Save me, please."

"What did you say?"

"I hope you're pleased I'm saving your trunk." He scooped up Kendra's basket. "Here, you'll have to carry this."

She gazed at him dubiously, but took it and wisely kept quiet. When he heaved the small but heavy trunk onto the horse's back, the poor animal turned its head to look at him dolefully. Colin sighed. He found it hard to believe the lengths he would go to in order to placate Amethyst Goldsmith.

"Now move back so I can ride in front of you."

"In front of me? How will you hold on to me?"

"I cannot hold on to you and balance the trunk, Amy."

"I'll balance the trunk." She tightened her knees around the horse's middle, as if she expected Colin to haul her off.

He looked at the heavy trunk and back to Amy, drumming his free fingers against his thigh. "I think not. Of course, we can leave the trunk here . . ."

"No," she capitulated. "I'll move."

She inched back until Colin nodded. Still balancing the trunk with one hand, he managed to mount the horse without kicking her in the face, a feat he felt deserved her undying admiration. She seemed not to notice, however.

"I cannot see ahead," she complained. "I can only see down. 'T-tis a *long* way down."

"We can leave the trunk here," he suggested pleasantly.

"No, no . . . I'll be fine. Wait a minute, though." She pushed the handle of the basket up over her wrist so she could place both arms around him. "I'm ready," she announced.

"Wonders will never cease," Colin muttered to himself. He urged the horse forward, torn between going slowly and freezing, and moving quickly and frightening Amy half to death.

Mercifully, he chose to freeze.

Her hands were clasped together about his waist, white knuckled with strain. "God's blood," he said, "you have me in a death grip. The basket handle is digging into my side."

"Sorry." Her arms loosened a good half inch, then tightened again when the horse gave a snort. He would swear he felt Amy's heart pounding against his back, even though he was insulated by his cloak, her blanket, and both their layers of clothing.

"Are you all right back there?" He'd not the slightest idea what he would do if she weren't.

"Mmm-hmm," Amy ground out between gritted teeth.

She wondered how long it would take to ride a mile and a half. It felt like forever already. "But snowflakes are tickling my nose."

"Well, for God's sake, can you not let go of me long enough to brush them off?"

She shook her head violently.

"Does it still seem a long way down?"

"My eyes are closed." 'Twas the only way she could bear it. Even pressed against Colin's warm back, she felt unsafe. Her heart skittered, and her legs were getting numb from squeezing tight around the beast's prickly body. 'Twas ridiculous, and she knew it—even country bumpkins were comfortable sitting a horse. But telling herself that didn't keep her from trembling.

"Cold?" Colin asked, obviously feeling her body quake.

"Yes." Better to let him think that was the reason.

"I warned you we needed to go quickly."

When the horse sped up, she yelped, and Colin scrambled to right the trunk, swearing under his breath. If she'd needed any more confirmation that she fit poorly in his world, she had it now. She resolved to stay calm until this torture was over, no matter what.

She squeezed her eyes shut tighter and started singing to herself. Perhaps by the time her song was finished, they'd be at Greystone.

" 'I tell thee, Dick, where I have been; Where I the rarest things have seen; Oh, things without compare! Such sights again cannot be found; In any place on English ground; Be it at wake or fair.' "

"You've a sweet voice," Colin called back, amusement lacing his words. She ignored him and continued singing.

" 'At Charing Cross, hard by the way; Where we, thou know'st, do sell our hay; There is a house with stairs. And there did I see coming down; Such folk as are not in our town; Forty at least, in pairs.' "

"Ballad Upon a Wedding," Colin remarked with a chuckle. " 'Twas written by Sir John Suckling, you know. He fought beside my father in the War." He chuckled

again. He was laughing at her. If she could get past her fear and let go of him, she might be tempted to shove him off.

" 'Amongst the rest, one pest'lent fine; His beard no bigger though than thine; Walk'd on before the rest. Our landlord looks like nothing to him; The King, God bless him, 'twould undo him; Should he go still so dress'd.' "

"That's the groom, who is said to be Lord Broyhill. And the bride was Lady Margaret—"

"If you know the song," she interrupted, finally addressing him, "the least you could do is sing along with me."

But he didn't. There were fifteen verses to *Ballad Upon a Wedding,* and Amy sang them five times through before the horse finally stopped. Her heart lurched, but she managed to stifle her cry of surprise.

"We're here," Colin said with an exaggerated sigh of relief. "I believe the basket handle has impressed a permanent indentation between my ribs."

"Thank heavens." Amy's eyes flew open, and she blinked against the daylight. She wiggled her jaw to soothe the ache from clenching her teeth. "I meant thank heavens we're here, not about your ribs."

A low chortle floated back. He unwound her arms from his waist and reached back a hand. "Here, let me help you down." When she landed on solid ground, her knees almost buckled under her.

She took a deep breath and looked around, consciously relaxing her shaky limbs. She found herself on a circular drive in a modest courtyard, enclosed on three sides by a crenelated curtain wall. The living quarters of the small castle made up the fourth side. The entire structure would fit into a corner of Cainewood.

She was enchanted.

Colin hopped down off the horse and slid her trunk to the snowy ground, fighting a grin. Obviously he found her fear amusing. He gestured at his home. " 'Tis not like Cainewood, is it?"

"No, not at all," she said seriously. " 'Tis much nicer."

That wiped the grin off his face. *"Nicer?"* he asked in apparent disbelief. She watched as his gaze wandered over the ruined portions of the wall and a huge roofless chamber that dominated the edifice.

Her gaze followed his, but she saw ancient weathered stones with stories to tell, a courtyard and rooms just perfect for one happy family. "Yes, 'tis much cozier. Cainewood is beautiful, but I cannot imagine why anyone would actually want to live there."

"Try explaining that to the woman I'm betrothed to," Colin muttered, leading the horse to one of the posts set around the drive.

Still carrying the basket, Amy wandered back to the entrance and stared up in wonder at the massive oak portcullis gate. Outside the walls, she could see the moat was dry and had been for some time. A mosslike grass grew in its bottom, lightly covered with snow.

"Once upon a time, 'twas filled by the River Caine," Colin's voice startled her, nearby. He pointed out the river in the distance. "It runs all the way from the coast past Cainewood to here. In fact, the license to crenelate was granted by King Richard II to protect Greystone from pirates who sailed up the River Caine from the sea. 'Twas originally built by a bishop."

Amy felt her beloved history books coming alive within these walls. "How long has it been in your family?"

"Not at all, 'til recently. Its Royalist owners perished with no issue. Charles awarded it to me after the Restoration."

A ruined tower sat adjacent to the entrance, and she looked down inside it—a long way down. Her gaze came back up to Colin's, questioning.

"The oubliette," he explained. " 'Twas secured with a heavy iron grille. Miscreants would be cast inside . . . and sometimes forgotten." His voice sounded mysterious and deep as the pit, and she shivered and pulled the blanket around her body.

"Come inside." Colin shouldered her trunk and motioned for her to follow him. They walked down a short passageway with an unassuming oak door at its end. He unlocked the door and entered, then bent to set down her trunk. She followed in time to see him shove it against the wall with one booted foot.

"There." He glared at her accusingly. "I'm not looking forward to our riding back with it, I'll warrant you."

"I'm not riding a horse back." Her legs were still shaking, though she'd never admit it. She set the basket on the floor.

"Benchley cannot drive the carriage here with one horse."

"Then you'll ride out with him and come back with the carriage. That way you'll not have to carry the trunk on horseback," she pointed out.

"That's true," Colin conceded, rather crossly. Averting his face, he turned to lay a fire in the fireplace on the right.

The vestibule was small and square, with an open-beam ceiling of oak. An oak staircase marched up the wall opposite the entrance. To the left, Amy saw an arched door. She walked over and tried the handle.

" 'Tis locked," Colin said, standing up. "The Great Hall is beyond, lacking half a roof at present."

Amy nodded and turned to him. The fire burned brightly behind him, illuminating the dim room. Shadows danced on the whitewashed, unadorned stone walls. The stone floor was polished smooth from centuries of use, and a fringed Oriental carpet rested in the center.

"Is this where you sleep?" Amy asked. She knew his home was mostly unrestored, and many families lived in a room this size or smaller. Perhaps he had a pallet that he put in here at night.

"Heavens, no." He laughed, picking up the basket. "I'm not that badly off. Come this way."

She followed him through an open archway and down a corridor. He paused at a doorway on the left.

"This is my temporary bedchamber," he explained.

"As soon as the roof is finished on the Great Hall, the rest of the living quarters will be restored."

Amy poked her head into the austere room. There were a wooden washstand, a dressing table with a mirror, and a large bed with a small table beside it and a chest at its foot. Carved in a twisted design, the bedposts supported a cream-colored canopy that matched the bedclothes and plastered walls. A gray stone fireplace and hearth echoed the gray stone that framed the three windows. She wandered to a window and drew in her breath in surprise.

"You're looking behind the Great Hall." Colin's amused voice came across the room from where he lounged against the doorjamb. " 'Tis officially called Upper Court, and the main courtyard where we entered is called Lower Court."

Amy gazed into the secret space, partially concealed by a light blanket of freshly fallen snow. 'Twould contain a beautiful garden come springtime, when the winter cold subsided. Placing her elbows on the wide stone windowsill, she leaned over, rested her chin in her hands, and stared out dreamily. Having grown up in crowded London, the thought of a private walled garden was heavenly. "I would call it Hidden Court," she said softly.

A low chuckle came from the doorway. "That's exactly what I do call it, to myself."

Amy was not surprised. 'Twas the perfect name for this most perfect place. "How do you get to it?"

"Through my study, next door."

She left the window and followed him down the corridor. His study contained a large scarred wooden desk with a comfortable chair; a long, plain, upholstered couch with a low table before it; and some rough shelving stuffed with a few books and a lot of ledgers and piles of paper.

"Benchley sleeps here," he said, indicating the couch.

But Amy had eyes only for the glass-inset double doors in the exact center of the back wall. She went straight to them, threw them open and stepped out into the courtyard beyond, heedless of the frosty air and falling snow.

Colin laughed and turned to start a fire. In his peripheral vision, he saw her brush snow off the plants to see what lay beneath. What a marvelous creature she was, quick to anger, but even more easily pleased. Now that she'd emerged from the cocoon of her grief, she was like a beautiful butterfly, and his heart ached with the knowledge that he could never capture her.

Finished with the fire, he turned to warm his back near the flames, watching Amy flit around his private courtyard . . . the courtyard Priscilla had failed to even notice on her one visit to her future home.

He shook himself. Priscilla embodied everything he required in a wife. He wasn't a man to let physical attraction rule his life—he never had, and he'd no intention of starting now. 'Twas not logical.

His betrothal was an ideal, rational arrangement. And not only was he bound by a promise, but he'd spent part of Priscilla's dowry on the restorations. He saw no way out of it, and he was a fool for considering it at all.

Amy was right; the two of them were unsuited, and 'twas no more simple or complicated than that.

He poked his head out the door to let Amy know he was going to take care of the horse and would be right back. By the time she brushed off the snow and came in from the courtyard, red cheeked and shivering, he had not only returned, but emptied Kendra's basket and laid out their dinner—cold chicken, bread, cheese, and a bottle of wine. Everything was neatly divided and set on cloth napkins, his on his desk, hers on the low table in front of the couch. He closed the doors behind Amy and took his place behind the desk.

"Hungry?" he asked.

"Yes, famished, although it must be early still." Amy picked up her food and carried it to the carpet bordering the hearth. She looked over at Colin, up through her thick eyelashes, where drops of melted snow sparkled in the firelight. " 'Tis much warmer here. Will you not join me in a picnic?"

Colin knew that if he joined her, 'twould be for more than a simple picnic. He felt much safer behind the desk. "No, I'm accustomed to dining here, and Benchley there," he answered, waving toward the table.

"I'm not Benchley," she pointed out.

He gave her a considered look. "I've noticed."

A blush crept into her cheeks, and his whole being was aware of how pretty she looked framed by the light of his fire, magical in the flickering hues. His body tensed.

"Do you suppose he'll return soon?" she asked.

"Who?"

Her eyes narrowed, regarding him uncertainly. "Benchley."

"Oh, him. I certainly hope so." He glanced out the window. The storm was building, damn it. God help him, Benchley had better return soon. He wanted this chapter in his life finished, without further incident. "I'm miserable at preparing anything to eat. I suppose you can cook?"

"I've never tried. We always had a housekeeper who cooked. You *do* have food?"

"Of course," he answered crossly. "I live here, you know."

"Of course."

Amy grinned, suddenly realizing how happy she was. Colin's plan to deliver her to Dover was foiled, and despite his wish that Benchley return soon, 'twas not likely to be so, judging by the weather. She'd survived the ride on horseback, and now she was alone with Colin in his enchanting castle, possibly overnight . . . she felt like she'd just received a stay of execution.

Maybe he'd even kiss her again.

"What's the verdict?" Colin asked dryly, unwinding himself from his cross-legged position on the floor, where he'd faced Amy across the low table and whiled away the past hours playing piquet.

Amy scribbled for a few seconds more, then looked up at him. "I won . . . but by less than a hundred points."

"That's supposed to make me feel better?" He smiled at the concerned look on her face. "You won all three parties."

"You won five hands."

There were six hands in each partie. Five hands out of eighteen . . . well, at least he'd not been completely humiliated. He'd proven himself a sharp cardplayer in the past. He was out of practice; he had not the time to spend hours—not to mention money—playing cards like many courtiers.

He was *not* distracted by her close proximity, her quick intelligence, her joyous laugh, the sweet curves that weren't hidden by that modest old lavender gown.

No. He was tired. He was unlucky. He was hungry.

Damn, he was hungry. Where the hell was Benchley?

He reached for his cloak.

"I've been playing a lot," she said, continuing her efforts to salve his ego.

"I thought you just learned?"

"Well, I learned recently, but I've been playing a lot."

He shrugged into the cloak. "I see." Actually, he saw plenty. For one thing, he saw Amy was not the sort of woman who would let him win just to make him feel good. He liked that.

"Bundle up, now," he said, holding out the blanket. She stood, and he wrapped it around her shoulders, vexed at himself when he noticed the enticing rose scent that seemed to waft from her whenever she moved.

He turned away, took an oil lamp off the mantel, and lit it.

"We're going outside?" she asked, trailing after him down the corridor.

"In a manner of speaking."

He stopped to unlock the door to the Great Hall, and she followed him inside. Lighting the way, he led her along the wall, moving beneath the overhang created by the partial new roof. She lifted her skirts to step over a rusted cannonball.

"I was hoping to have this roof finished before the cold set in," he called back to her. The wind was picking up, and 'twas noisy inside. "Now, if it proves to be a snowy winter, I may as well stay at Cainewood much of the time. I'll not see much progress in this kind of weather." He glanced through the open roof at the threatening clouds, shaking his head. "Bloody hell."

They were forced to brave the snow to get to another door in the center of the end wall. It led to a short corridor with a room on either side, which opened on the other end into a very large, impeccably restored kitchen.

"It projects outside the curtain wall," Colin pointed out. "I suppose it made the castle somewhat vulnerable at the time it was first built, but 'twas a sound decision as a precaution against fire damage."

Understandably proud of all his improvements, Colin showed her the ovens, spitted fireplaces, and amazing wash basins with bronze taps and spouts. After Amy had expressed suitable admiration for the kitchen, he took her down a long, unused passage to the left.

"This was the original garderobe," he explained. "It hung over the moat, a nice innovation at the time. Owing to the location, though, everyone had to go through the Great Hall and kitchen to use it."

Amy peeked into the rough wooden latrines, glad she was visiting now instead of then. She'd already made use of Colin's new garderobe, twin latrines with all the modern comforts, and thought they were the most luxurious cubbyholes she'd ever seen. They had water closets, newly imported from France, and pipes all the way to the River Caine.

"I'll stick with the one next to your study, thank you," she said. " 'Tis cold over here."

"It is, is it not? Let us take our supper and head back."

Backtracking through the kitchen and toward the Great Hall, Amy followed Colin into the room on the corridor's left, which turned out to be a pantry stocked with plenty of food, although not a great variety. Handing the lamp to her, Colin grabbed a basket and filled it with a small wheel of cheese, some carrots, apples, and a jar of something . . . brown.

"What is that?" Amy couldn't imagine.

"Pickled snails."

Pickled *snails*? The gentry certainly ate some strange things. Well, perhaps they would be good. Following him into the room across the corridor, she decided to try them, even if they did look and sound disgusting.

Walls lined with racks held but a few bottles of wine, one of which Colin hastily selected. Great empty barrels were scattered about, and two long, ancient wooden tables ran down the center of the arched chamber.

"Let me guess," Amy suggested, "the taproom?"

"The buttery."

"A butter room?"

"Well, 'tis not where they kept the butter, although that's what it was called. Your first guess was close—this room was dedicated to brewing and serving beverages. 'Butt' is an old word for bottle."

"How do you come to know so much about old castles?" Amy followed him out of the buttery and back toward the Great Hall.

Colin shrugged. "They always interested me. I spent my early years at Cainewood and the rest of my childhood in a succession of old, drafty castles on the Continent. I asked a lot of questions, read a lot of books."

He motioned with his head for her to open the door; she got a blast of cold snow in her face for her trouble. He ushered her ahead, and she held up the lamp to light their way back.

"Most men, given this land, would simply build a new house and keep the ruined castle as a relic for their children to play in," he shouted from the swirling snow behind her. " 'Twould probably cost less and certainly be easier to heat."

They reached the other end. Amy gratefully opened the door and stepped into the welcoming entry hall, warmed by the dancing fire. Colin shut the door against the wind, and the room went suddenly quiet.

With a small *clink*, he set the bottle of wine on the stone floor and turned to lock the door. "God knows why I'm restoring this place; it makes little sense." He turned to face her. "But 'tis three hundred years old, and it seems a shame to just let it crumble into ruin. The walls are thick and solid—'tis a good home . . ." He shrugged, lifted one eyebrow and smiled at her, his teeth as white as the snow outside. "I like living here."

" 'Tis the romantic in you, Lord Greystone," she said softly.

Romantic? No one had ever accused Colin Chase of being romantic. Handsome, yes, he'd have to be deaf not to have heard the ladies extolling his physical virtues. He liked to think he was a good lover and he embodied many other worthy traits. But romantic? Never.

He searched her amethyst eyes, scarcely believing she could be serious. But he could see she was sincere. She obviously didn't know him very well.

He cleared his throat, breaking the silence and tension between them. "Insane, is more like it."

She shook her head, smiling. Colin's gaze moved to her cheeks, pink from the cold, and her lips, red and slightly wind-chapped. Her curls, arranged so carefully by Kendra's maid that morning, were blown loose around her face . . .

God help him, he wanted to kiss her. He stepped forward.

She licked her lips. "Are those pickled snails really edible?"

He shook his head to clear those preposterous thoughts. "They're the best. Although I've just realized I forgot to pick up spoons in the kitchen."

"You needn't brave the cold. I'm perfectly willing to

share your knife with you." A gleam came into her eyes. "After all, I'm naught but a simple merchant's daughter."

Having delivered her jab, Amy leaned down to pick up the wine bottle. Colin frowned at her back. How did she know he thought of her that way? Kendra, most likely—the meddler in the family.

'Twas as well that Amy had reminded him, he decided firmly, for with all this talk of romance, he was on the edge of forgetting just who and what she was.

Clutching their supper to his chest, he turned and hurried down the corridor, back to the relative safety of his desk.

Chapter Eleven

The keep was built of lavender stone, cut in perfect rectangular bricks, set together seamlessly to form the tallest tower in the world. Arched windows graced each landing, and as Amy wound up the spiral staircase she paused to look out.

Ferocious, fire-breathing, terrifying . . . the dragon lumbered relentlessly closer, its heavy tread making the earth shudder. She ran up and up, a burning stitch in her side, but came no nearer the top.

Papa was up there. She had to get to him.

The dragon let out an earsplitting roar, breathing its red and yellow and blue fire through a window. She pressed herself against the wall as flames raced past her up the winding steps, in a thick burning line toward the top where Papa waited.

When it seemed as though neither her legs nor her lungs would hold out for one more step, she finally reached the top—but Papa was already on fire. A skeleton he was, reclining in a chair, holding an oval-framed picture, his feet bones resting on a bolster. Flames shot from his skeleton eye sockets and between his bare skeleton ribs. Black smoke rose in a column from the bony structure to the sky.

Gray ash rained down on the lavender stone. The dragon's roar shook the tower. Its glittering eyes looked straight into hers, then it bent its head and breathed fire into the stairwell. Red and yellow and orange flames rushed up the steps straight at her, burning a path all the way to her right hand. Her hand was on fire, burning brightly, and flames started up her arm . . .

She screamed for help, but nobody came.

Her hand had turned into a skeleton hand; the flesh was burning off her arm, the flames working their way to her shoulder. She screamed at the top of her lungs . . .

It sounded as if someone were in the castle, attacking Amy in the bedchamber next door.

His heart pounding, Colin leapt from the bed, threw his breeches over one arm, grabbed his knife from the desk and his rapier off the floor. Blades at the ready, he burst into the bedchamber. Amy thrashed wildly in his bed.

Alone. He could scarcely imagine what demons could cause such a nightmare.

He tossed the weapons into the corner and pulled on his breeches, hopping on one foot and then the other as he made his way across the room. Tugging on the laces, he launched himself onto the bed with a force that nearly sent Amy over the other side.

"Amy, wake up!" He shook her frantically. " 'Tis naught but a dream. Wake up."

A concerned voice floated up the winding staircase. Someone was coming to rescue her. Someone was coming, after all.

"Wake up! You're all right."

The voice was closer, right in her ear. Someone's hand was on her burning shoulder—no, 'twas not burning . . .

She heard her own cries and came down through her fog into reality, the screams turning into deep, wrenching sobs.

"Shh, 'tis over." Colin pulled her up into his arms. The quilt, which she'd thrown off during her nightmare, slid to the floor. She wrapped her arms around him, pressed her wet face into his bare chest. He rubbed her back through her thin chemise in a slow, soothing rhythm, murmuring to her all the while.

At last she quieted and pulled away to sit up, took a

deep, shuddering breath. She stared at her right hand in disbelief.

" 'Twas burning . . ."

"Does it hurt?"

She shook her head, remembering both the real pain from her old injury and the many-times-magnified pain of the dream. But the sensation now was just the fading tingle of memory, and the hand was fine, not the skeleton fingers she'd been half-expecting to see.

"No, it hurts not at all." She dropped her hand to the bed, still staring at it by the light of the dying fire. "I'm sorry I woke you."

"I thought you were being attacked." He laughed shakily and stood up. "I ran in here with my knife, ready to defend you, wearing absolutely nothing. I'm not sure I'd have been a very effective warrior."

"Oh." She looked up. Her gaze roamed past his chest, bronze in the shimmering firelight, to his compelling emerald eyes. Her own eyes widened as she suddenly realized he was wearing not much more than nothing now.

Her mouth gaped open in a little O as her gaze trailed back down. His tanned upper body was clad in naught but a thin white scar, long since healed, a diagonal slash across his left upper arm. She wondered fleetingly what had caused it, but was too distracted to give it much thought. Her eyes resumed their survey, all the way down to his bare feet. Why, he wore nothing at all, it seemed, other than a pair of unfashionably tight breeches, and those—she couldn't help noticing—only partially laced.

In an instant, she forgot her dream. Her cheeks flushed, and she tugged down the hem of her chemise, which had ridden up as she'd thrashed about. At best, 'twas an ineffective attempt, serving mainly to make Colin more aware of her dishabille.

She shifted as his gaze wandered from her face to her bare limbs. He swallowed hard.

"Cold?" he asked. He walked around the bed to retrieve the quilt, made a great show of shaking it out, then let it drift down upon her. The blanket seemed to caress her as it settled, and she wished it were Colin's hands, instead.

He sat on the edge of the bed. "Do you want to tell me about it?"

"About what?"

"Your dream."

She shook her head vehemently. "No. I want not to think on it at all." She scooted down to lie flat and cuddled into the covers. "Would you stay with me for a spell, though? We could talk of something else."

"I'll stay as long as you like," he assured her, taking her hand. "What would you like to talk about?"

His hand felt warm and comforting. She shrugged gracefully. "I don't know."

"Would you like to talk about how much you like pickled snails?" he suggested with a teasing grin.

"I *did* like them," she protested, although they both knew 'twas not true. She'd tasted one bravely, even swallowed it without gagging, but her appetite had fallen off afterward. Her stomach was grumbling now. "Are there any apples left?" she asked.

Colin chuckled. "I believe there are."

He left, but returned momentarily with a shiny, red apple from the study. When she sat up and reached for it, he pulled it back playfully. "Hungry, are you?" he asked with a knowing look. Grinning, he handed it to her and stepped over to the windows.

Amy took a bite and slowly chewed. She watched him peer out into the night, his legs spread, hands linked behind his back.

" 'Tis still snowing hard," he told her. "I reckon we may be stuck here through tomorrow."

"Mmm-hmm," she replied around a mouthful of juicy apple. The fruit was sweet, she was cozy, and she could think of worse fates than being stuck with Colin Chase another day and night.

"I should do bookwork tomorrow, so long as I'm here," he said.

"Mmm-hmm." She took another crunching bite.

"What will you do?" He turned from the windows to face her.

Amy chewed and swallowed before answering. "I can read. Prepare some dinner. Help you." She took another big bite.

"I need no help."

She shrugged. "I'll explore your castle, then."

"I'm afraid there's not much to discover." He walked over to the fire, added a log from the basket, and stirred up the embers with a wooden-handled poker. " 'Tis small. And cold and damp."

"That will not stop me."

Colin crossed back to her bedside and stood looking down at her with a wry smile. "No, I suppose a bit of cold and damp are unlikely to deter the likes of you. So long as there's not a horse involved." His mouth twitched with amusement.

Grinning back, she held out the apple core and slid down under the covers.

He put the core on the table next to the bed. "Better?"

"Much." She wiggled under the quilt, getting comfortable.

"Good." Offering her a distracted nod, he turned to the door.

"No, don't leave yet." She patted the bed beside her. "You said you'd stay as long as I liked."

With seeming reluctance, he turned back and slowly sat down. Amy reached over and took his hand. He tensed; she saw the muscles go rigid beneath his bronzed skin.

The nightmare had left her completely. The apple rested comfortably in her stomach, the room was warm, the bed was soft, and her hand tingled in Colin's. She gazed at his profile in the wavering firelight, and she wanted him to kiss her in the worst way. Just one more time. Just one more time before he put her on a ship and she sailed out of his life forever.

She squeezed his hand, and he turned to her.

Her heart beat faster. He was going to kiss her, she knew it. His eyes searched her face, and his free hand came up to wipe a bit of apple juice from the corner of her mouth. His hand lingered; his knuckles grazed her cheek.

"Holy Christ," Colin murmured. Amy's skin was petal soft, her eyes dark liquid pools of desire. He couldn't help himself. He'd kiss her just once, a goodnight kiss, and then he'd leave.

When she closed her eyes, he brushed her lips with his, naught more than a whisper. A little sound escaped her throat, and her arms came up and around his neck, dragging his mouth back to hers. She twined her fingers in his hair, her lips sweet and urgent.

"Amy," he moaned, giving in, his mouth demanding a response she seemed only too happy to give. His tongue traced the soft fullness of her lips, seeking entry. When she acquiesced, his blood surged in response to her sweet, velvety mouth. He would swear she stopped breathing.

He broke contact. Her eyes fluttered open, deep purple now, and she drew a long, shuddering breath. Using every ounce of his willpower, he pulled back. "I cannot do this," he grated out.

She ran her hands over the muscles of his back and lifted herself to place a warm, moist kiss in the hollow of his neck. She fell back to the pillows, her eyes questioning.

She was seducing him, the little witch!

"Amy," he said, sitting up fully, "this isn't right."

"Is it not?" Amy asked dizzily. Her senses still swirling, she came up on an elbow and impulsively ran a hand down his chest, surprising herself. She'd never before touched a man's bare chest. Colin's was warm and firm, with a light sprinkling of crisp black hair. Defined muscles twitched under her questing fingers. "I *like* kissing you. What is wrong with that?"

"I cannot just kiss you." He pushed her hand away.

She saw his jaw tense. "You're half-naked in my bed, for God's sake. I want you, all of you."

Shocked to the tips of her toes, she stared at him, tongue-tied. Never, in all her musings on the subject, had she imagined that Colin wanted to make love to her. He hated her, did he not? Or at least he didn't like her—she was naught but a bother to him. He seemed to enjoy kissing her, for some inexplicable reason, but . . .

"I'm sorry, Amy."

That loosened her tongue. "Would you *please* stop saying you're sorry every time you kiss me!"

"I'm sorry." He smiled innocently, and she burst into helpless giggles.

Seconds later, his smile reversed to a frown. "Amy?"

She sobered instantly. "What?"

"You understand what I'm telling you?"

Relieved that the semidarkness hid her blush, she nodded.

"And you agree 'twould be wrong?"

She hesitated, then hoped he'd not noticed. She knew what he wanted to hear, knew also what she was raised to believe. "Yes, 'twould be wrong."

Colin noticed, all right. He shook his head, amazed at her reluctance. "Then you'll understand why I cannot kiss you again," he said, intending to clarify his position once and for all. The sparkle left her eyes, and he rushed to reassure her. "Though 'tis God's own truth, I was never once really sorry I did."

Once more she nodded, and her head fell back to the pillows. He rose and tucked the blanket about her in a businesslike way. "Good night, then," he said, turning to leave.

"Stay. Please." Something in her voice made him turn around. "I'll not even touch you, I promise. Just sleep here tonight. I-I'm afraid I'll have the nightmare again."

Colin wasn't sure he could stand another night sleeping next to Amethyst Goldsmith. Or rather, he was sure he couldn't.

"I'll be right next door. You'll not dream it again, Amy."

"You cannot know that! I will, I'm sure of it. *Please.*"

She seemed genuinely frightened; her pleading went straight to his heart. Damn. Perhaps he could lie next to her until she fell asleep, and then leave. She'd never know the difference.

"Very well. Just don't touch me," he warned with a teasing glare.

"I promise," she said with a sweet smile—so sweet he immediately had second thoughts. Against his better judgment, he walked around the bed and slipped in on the other side, as close to the edge as he could manage without falling off, his back turned to her.

"Good night," she called out agreeably.

"Good night," he returned on a sigh.

Colin must be asleep, Amy thought half an hour later. He'd not budged in all that time. She could move over, not enough to touch him—she'd not break her promise—but just a little closer, and then maybe she could fall asleep.

She eased to the middle of the bed, and Colin didn't stir. His breath came deep and even. A warmth emanated from his body, and a ripple of excitement flowed through her at the thought of touching him. He was sleeping; he'd never know, and 'twould feel so comforting.

She rolled over, a smidgen at a time, until finally she brushed against his motionless form. His skin felt hotter than she'd imagined. His nearness was not as comforting as she'd thought it would be—it made the little hairs raise on her arms, instead. 'Twas not enough—she couldn't resist molding the front of her body to the back of his. He felt so very good.

He still didn't move, and her arm slowly sneaked up and around his middle.

She felt his sharp intake of breath.

"Ammmmy . . ." he growled in warning.

Oh, God, he was awake. She snapped her arm away and flipped onto her back. The side of her body still grazed his, but he voiced no protest. The firelight made patterns dance beneath her tightly closed lids as she lay rigid beside him, wishing he would say something, or do something . . .

She wished he would roll over and kiss her.

He'd cautioned that kisses were likely to lead to more, but while half an hour ago she'd been shocked, now, fiercely aware of him next to her, she found herself intrigued.

What would it be like? The French novels she'd read made it sound mysterious and wonderful, and if 'twould make her feel anything like Colin's kisses did, she was inclined to want to experience it. Who would she be hurting? Who would ever know? She would never see Colin again, and if losing her virginity was the price she had to pay for stealing a few more of his luscious kisses, perhaps she was willing to bear the cost.

Besides, she didn't really believe he couldn't kiss her without going further. The mere thought was absurd. Gentlemen flirted with and kissed ladies all the time, without anything more ever happening.

Maybe he really did hate her. Maybe this was his way of politely refusing to kiss her without hurting her feelings. Maybe he found her so repugnant he couldn't bear to touch her at all . . . after all, he had made her promise not to lay a finger on him, and growled at her when she did.

She had to know. And there was only one way to find out.

She waited a few more minutes and then rolled against him again, lazily, as though she were doing it in her sleep. Her arm crept up and around . . .

He flipped over, landing half on top of her, his lips searching for hers and finding their target. A harsh sound came from deep in his throat. His kiss felt punishing and angry, but she responded all the same, and after a minute he lifted his head. She opened her eyes to find his glaring fiercely back.

"I warned you, Amy," he said.

With a quick nod of acknowledgment, she pulled him back down to her. Lips parted, she raised herself to meet his kiss.

A curious quiver of wanting ran through her when his mouth came down on hers, and she lost all train of thought. One moment she thought that of course he could stop; the next moment she cared not. She wanted him to kiss her forever—damn the consequences. Then she ceased to think at all. It seemed she was capable only of feeling—feeling the demanding caress of his lips; feeling his tongue invading her mouth, soft and teasing; feeling his body, hard along the length of hers.

She inhaled, and his distinctive scent made her dizzy. The crackling sound from the fireplace receded, replaced by a rushing sound deep in her head. His gentle, damp kisses trailed her eyes and nose and cheeks, then he nibbled at her earlobe, making a shivery thrill race through her veins.

He pulled away, his darkened eyes questioning. "Are you sure?" he asked in a suffocated whisper.

Her heart lurched in her chest. Oh, no, he couldn't change his mind, couldn't leave her now. Unable to say it out loud, she grasped his shoulders, clutched him roughly, wordlessly.

He dropped his head, but not before she saw the raw hunger in his eyes. His lips claimed hers once again, sending the pit of her stomach into a wild swirl. His heart thudded against her breasts, and she knew he was experiencing similar sensations. She had asked for this. She had wanted to know how he really felt about her.

She had her answer. Yet she didn't want him to stop.

Inching down a hand, he lightly brushed one breast through the thin fabric of her chemise, and the peak tightened into hard tenderness. Her body arched toward him involuntarily, and she whimpered, her breath becoming strangely ragged.

"Like that, hmmm?" he murmured against her mouth.

Her cheeks flamed, and "Mmmm" was the only answer she could manage. Her fingers tangled in the thick hair on his neck as she kissed him frantically, pressing up against his hand, her body yearning for something she couldn't put a name to.

With whisper-soft caresses, his hand moved lower, skimming leisurely over her taut stomach. She tensed when his fingers traced the curve of her hip.

His voice soothed, a husky whisper. "Ah, sweet Amy." He brushed her mouth with his as his hand teased lightly through the fabric, then more firmly, tracing the line where her thighs met. A heat spread from his fingers, bathing her entire body in warmth. Her body was humming, or maybe she was humming; she wasn't sure which. Or maybe 'twas neither, maybe 'twas all in her head. Her head was swimming.

"Sweet," he repeated, his breath warm in her ear. "Has no man touched you here before?"

Her face flushed, and the rest of her too—her skin tingled. "N-no," she whispered back.

" 'Tis good, is it not?"

She moaned softly and felt Colin smile against her lips. Before she knew what was happening he'd tugged down her chemise and fastened his hot mouth on her bare breast, suckling gently, laving his textured tongue over the sensitive tip.

It felt wonderfully scandalous. Did all men do this? She'd thought of lovemaking as kissing and hugging and mating, not . . . consuming. God in heaven, 'twas indescribable.

He wandered to her other breast, his mouth hot there, the air cooling the wetness he'd left behind. Driven to distraction with new sensations, she writhed against him. Her breath came in short gasps; her hands roamed the hard planes of his back. She could scarcely believe she was acting so wanton, but she couldn't seem to help herself.

She didn't *want* to help herself.

He dropped damp, teasing kisses on her shoulders and neck, then everywhere near but not on her lips, until she grabbed his head in demand. He laughed triumphantly into her mouth, a deep, rich sound of pleasure.

Suddenly he was in motion, sitting up, the blanket tented on his shoulders. He swept off her chemise, and when she felt the shock of cold air on her unclothed body, her eyes flew open. She shivered, though whether from cold or the astounding reality of him gazing hungrily upon her, she wasn't certain.

Colin drew in his breath. "You," he said slowly, worshiping her with his eyes, "are the most beautiful creature I've ever seen." Leaning over, he ran gentle hands on her skin, skimmed her breasts and hips, raising goose bumps on her flesh. Her heart pounded almost painfully, but when she tried to look away, he caught her face in his hands and captured her eyes with his.

Bringing the blanket with him, he lowered himself, reclaiming her mouth in a devouring caress while he slipped his hand between her legs, parting them gently, his fingertips trailing sensuously on her inner thighs. She began to tremble, and when he brushed against the curls that guarded her most secret self, she gasped in shock and wonder.

"Shh," he whispered into her open mouth. Concentrating on one long, deep kiss, he slipped a finger inside her tight passageway.

Somewhere in the back of her passion-hazed mind, Amy was scandalized. She could scarcely believe she was permitting a man to touch her there, let alone move his finger in and out of her body, as he was slowly doing now. It couldn't be right . . . or could it? She wondered foggily where the slickness was coming from, but the slippery feeling was so delicious she couldn't possibly care.

Colin's thumb found her swollen jewel of pleasure, and waves of desire swept through her body, taking her unawares. She clutched him tighter, feeling as though her heart would burst if something, she knew not what, did not happen soon. She thought she would go insane with the pleasure of it.

He left her and she felt abandoned, holding her breath as he slipped off his breeches. When he rolled back to her, she threw her arms around him and held him tight, silently daring him ever to leave her again. He laughed deep in his throat, a husky, choked sound, then reached back blindly for her hand, guiding it to his rigid flesh. Overwhelmed by wondrous new sensations, Amy was beyond shock. Her fingers closed around him, and her eyes opened wide.

" 'Twill work, Amy," he whispered, kissing her eyes closed, one and then the other. Amazed at her own boldness, she moved her hand a bit, learning him. Warm, velvety . . .

With an audible breath, Colin wedged a knee between hers, and her legs came up instinctively to cradle him. God in heaven, he felt so right covering her body. He pressed himself against her, and she held her breath, but he stayed poised there, waiting . . . for what? A whimper sounded deep in her throat, surprising her, then she involuntarily rose to meet him.

He groaned softly. "I mean not to hurt you, love," he forced between gritted teeth. "But this once—"

She moaned in response, but she'd not really processed his words, only the "love." She knew it didn't mean anything, couldn't mean anything—'twas just the type of thing men said to women in the throes of passion—but it made her blood sing anyway, just to hear it.

Still thinking of that, she stiffened in shock when he thrust home. Her breath caught in her chest.

He stilled and came up on his forearms, murmuring wordless sounds of comfort. He kissed her gently on the forehead, ran his fingers up her scalp and through her tumbled curls, arranging them on the pillow. Slowly the pain subsided, replaced with a growing sense of wonder at the throbbing fullness within her.

She felt an incredible urgency radiating from where Colin met her core.

His lips traced a path from her forehead down her nose, settled tender and soft on her mouth. His tongue plunged inside as his hips began a slow rhythm below.

Amy's blood rushed faster and faster. She was climbing higher and higher, to the top of a tower. Only this time there was no dragon, no fire, except when she suddenly reached the top and burst into the flame of a million glowing stars. They shot from her core like the most dazzling fireworks, throughout her straining body, to the tips of her fingers and toes, glowing streaks of sensation that raced through her veins in long, flickering bursts of pleasure beyond her wildest imaginings.

She felt Colin pulsing within her, the warm flood of his release. He collapsed against her, his chest hot and slick against hers, his back straining as he gulped for air. Her hands were everywhere, trying to feel him all at once as her breath came in long, shuddering sighs. "I didn't know," she gasped in wonder. "*I didn't know.*"

He struggled up on his elbows. "How could you know?" His smile, proud, contented, and erotic all at the same time, made her pulse flutter anew.

Taking her with him, he rolled over and hugged her tight against his chest. Then his smile faded. " 'Twas wrong," he said strong and clear, and then, in a whisper so low she had to strain to hear it, "but I'll not say I'm sorry."

"No. No apologies." Her senses were still spinning, and she felt strangely quivery, as if a mere attempt at standing would cause her knees to buckle. But the aftermath of dizziness was a small price to pay for that heady sweetness of buildup and release, the incredible wonder of sharing her body with Colin's.

She struggled to find words. " 'Twas . . . do you remember the fireworks, the night of the coronation procession?"

"Yes . . ." She could see him pondering her question; a small frown appeared between his eyebrows. He didn't understand.

"Oh, 'twas like that, Colin—'twas just like that. Great fiery streaks . . ."

His face cleared and he said gently, "I know."

"Can we do it again?" she asked enthusiastically.

He laughed then, a great booming laugh that nearly bounced her off his chest. She dropped her head to his shoulder, her face burning. Did he think her wanton? After all, she had practically seduced him and followed it up by asking for more.

"No, love, I think not. Even were I able, I imagine you're too sore to attempt any such thing for a day or two."

She relaxed a little. She didn't quite understand everything he meant, but he didn't sound disapproving. Besides, he'd called her "love" again, and that was enough to cause all her worries to flee her mind, even sure as she was that he meant nothing by it.

Cursing silently at himself, Colin stroked her hair. "Love," he'd called her. Bloody hell. What had he been thinking?

He'd not, obviously. He'd not been thinking at all. The endearment had escaped his lips thoughtlessly.

He had never been "in love," and though no one else made him feel like this slip of a girl, that did not mean he loved her. He hardly knew her, despite their weeks of acquaintance. Besides, love wasn't part of his plan. Love was dangerous. It made one too vulnerable, too open to the pain of loss and betrayal.

Luckily, she'd seemed not to notice, let alone react to, his slip of the tongue. Still, he must be more careful in the future.

She snuggled closer, and he breathed her clean, sweet scent, tinged with rose oil from her bath at Cainewood that morning. Rose oil and something else . . . the heady musk of their encounter.

His heart clenched at the still-fresh memory of her quivering in his arms. Her quick breath, her pounding heart, her passionate cries. All for him. She'd not been grieving or trying to escape—she'd wanted him. Blood coursed through his veins at the thought of it—at the thought of them together.

But deep inside he knew 'twas naught but a fluke. A unique combination of fear, curiosity, and attraction had driven Amy into his arms this one precious time. She was not the sort of woman who would accept life as a man's mistress, beloved or not.

Running his fingers through the ebony curls that tumbled over his chest, he sighed, recalling the first time he'd seen her, how he'd yearned to see her hair unbound, itched to play with it just like this. Brushing a few stray strands off her forehead, he lifted his head to place a reverent kiss there.

She was sleeping, her breathing even and untroubled. He smiled gently, eased her off himself and onto her side, curling his body around hers protectively. His plan to leave her once she fell asleep was abandoned, forgotten.

He hoped it would still be snowing hard in the morning.

Chapter Twelve

Amy peered into the mirror, surprised when her old face stared back. After last night, should something not have changed?

Self-conscious, she glanced about to make sure she was alone, then dropped the sheet she was wrapped in and cast a critical eye on her body . . . nothing had changed there. Colin had brought her breakfast in bed this morning, then refused her offer of help again before disappearing into his study.

She sighed. Nothing had changed there, either.

She quickly bathed from the washstand, taking a mental inventory as she rinsed away all evidence of last night. In spite of a nagging feeling that something should be different, she felt just the same. Her only souvenir seemed to be a slight but persistent soreness between her legs.

A delicious soreness . . . it started to tingle, radiating throughout her body. Her heart skipped a beat as she remembered exactly how Colin had touched her last night, every little thing he had done to make her feel so wonderful. She felt her face heat, though no one was there to see it. She shook herself, then dug under the bedclothes for her chemise.

The sheets were stained. God in heaven, she couldn't just leave them like that. Slipping the chemise on over her head, she looked around for where bedclothes might be stored. The chamber held no cupboard, only the chest at the foot of the bed. She lifted its heavy wooden lid.

Colin's scent wafted out, and she breathed deep, a

smile teasing at her lips. Inside, his clothes were neatly folded. The suits were darker colors than were currently in fashion—hunter green, deep blue, rich brown—the fabrics fine, the decorations tasteful. One was black velvet with glinting gold braid . . . was it the same one he'd worn for the coronation procession? His shirts were very white, sewn of gossamer cambric that felt smooth and expensive beneath her fingertips. She shook one out and held it up to herself, giggling when it fell well below her knees.

Carefully she folded and replaced it, then delved beneath lace-edged cravats, tall boot stockings, and more handkerchiefs than a man could possibly use in a lifetime. There were extra sheets in the bottom, she saw with relief. And atop them, a small leather-bound book.

Gold lettering on the red cover identified it as *Hesperides, or The Works Both Human and Divine of Robert Herrick, Esq.* Inside 'twas inscribed in beautiful, flowing script. "March, 1649. Poetry, for my son the dreamer. Your loving Mother."

Colin, a dreamer? Her lips curved at the thought.

She opened it to a random page. "To the Virgins, to Make Much of Time." Well, the title wasn't fitting after last night—she blushed to think it—but . . .

Gather ye rosebuds while ye may,
Old Times is still a-flying:
And this same flower that smiles today,
Tomorrow will be dying.

Words to live by, were they not? Smiling, she replaced the book and changed the sheets, folding the stained ones and leaving them atop the chest. Anxious to explore the castle, she hurried to finish dressing.

A survey of the ground floor revealed nothing of interest. Narrow slits through the curtain wall let in little light, rendering the unrestored chambers dank and dark. What was left of the furniture was draped in cloth, encrusted with layers of dust sufficient to discourage her from peeking underneath.

She paused at the closed door to Colin's study, picturing him inside hacking away at his ledgers. She hoped he was suffering mightily, although in truth she had no idea whether he'd an aptitude for such work. There was a lot she didn't know about him, she admitted to herself. And a lot she *did* know. Weak-kneed at that thought, she leaned against the door, half-embarrassed, half-brazen for thinking such things. 'Twas shocking and wicked and wonderful, all at the same time.

Squaring her shoulders, she made her way to the entry, where the beautifully restored oak staircase renewed her hope of finding something more intriguing upstairs. As she trudged slowly up, her muscles ached in places she'd not known she had. Whether they protested at being forced to ride a horse or from unaccustomed exertion in Colin's bed, she knew not. But she blushed again as her sore body bade her to recall the latter—as she had done a hundred times this day already. And 'twas not even noon yet.

She sat abruptly on the top step. 'Twas a good thing Colin had refused her help today, because she seemed wholly unable to concentrate on anything for more than a few seconds before she started remembering again. Before she started wanting him again, if the truth be told.

Her gaze lit on her trunk downstairs, still sitting against the wall where Colin had shoved it. What was left of her family lay locked inside. She closed her eyes, rubbing her temples. God in heaven, what would they think of her after last night? If they were here today and she confessed her wanton ways, would they turn disapproving eyes on her? Or enfold her in their arms and say they loved her . . . even though she wasn't one bit sorry for what she had done . . .

"Oh, Papa!" Her hoarse whisper filled the entry as she lifted her skirts and bolted downstairs for the trunk, dragged it scraping along the stone floor to the bedchamber. She reached to pull the key from her hem even as she shut the door behind her.

Falling to her knees, she worked the lock with unsteady fingers, then threw open the lid. The tray on top was lifted and dropped to the floor, the box of loose gemstones discarded without a thought. For underneath lay the real treasure: bits of her father wrapped in small squares of white flannel, pieces of his soul etched forever in his exquisite works of art.

She thrust her hands into the trunk, filled both fists with jewelry, then moved to the bed and allowed the pieces to sift through her open fingers . . . remembering.

With a heavy sigh, Colin dropped his head into his hands. His desk was piled high with receipts, his ledgers lined with numbers he'd spent the morning staring at with unfocused eyes. In fact, he'd found himself unable to focus on anything this morning—anything except Amethyst Goldsmith.

'Twas obvious he was not going to accomplish anything today, he thought, twisting the heavy gold ring on his finger distractedly. A glance out the window convinced him he'd not be delivering his distraction to the docks today, either. The storm was waning, but the snow still fell steadily and the drifts were deep. His rumbling stomach reminded him 'twas past noon and Amy had promised to prepare dinner.

Leaving the study without bothering to don a cloak, Colin briefly poked his head into each of the empty downstairs chambers, then dashed through the freezing Great Hall and into the kitchen. He'd laid a fire for her earlier, hoping she'd be inspired to prepare something hot. She was nowhere to be found, however; neither was there anything bubbling in the stew pot nor any other evidence she'd been at work. Quick glances into the pantry and buttery also failed to reveal her presence.

Was she lost? No, Greystone was too small to be confusing. Hurt, perhaps? That was a possibility. Despite years and money spent on restorations, the structure was still in bad shape; she could have tripped and twisted her ankle, or even worse. He set out grimly to find her, back through the Great Hall and the ceaseless snow.

Once in the entry, his gaze swept up the stairs, and he remembered the library. Of course, he thought, relieved. Ford had told him of the countless hours she'd spent in Cainewood's library. She must have discovered his library and lost track of the time, forgetting about dinner altogether.

He took the steps two at a time, ran to the back of the upper level, and burst through the library door.

No—she was not here. Nor had she been here. Not a speck of the considerable dust was displaced; the titles on the neatly rowed books were as obscured by grime as ever. Amy could not have found this room and left it undisturbed. 'Twas completely against her nature to ignore a room full of books, regardless of its filth and neglect.

She wasn't in any of the other upstairs chambers, either. His heart started pounding as he once again imagined her stuck somewhere, arms or legs broken, perhaps lying in the freezing snow or at the bottom of the oubliette. He should have toured her around the castle and offered to help her prepare dinner. What had he been thinking?

He'd been thinking about getting away from her for a while, that was what. He'd been pretending she had no effect on his life, that he could set to work as usual regardless of her presence. He'd been hoping that a few hours of separation would break the spell she'd woven so expertly around him.

'Twas all for naught—he was as spellbound as ever, and now she might be hurt, thanks to his negligence. He cursed at himself. She was in his care, and at the very least he should have asked her to stay in the bedchamber with a book while he worked.

The bedchamber. He'd not even looked there. Maybe she *was* in the bedchamber with a book. As he hurried down the stairs, he pictured her curled on the bed, lost in the world of literature or perhaps even napping—it had been a short night for them both. He could hardly blame her for losing track of time.

He knocked softly on the door, half afraid he'd wake her up, half afraid she'd not be there at all. No answer.

"Amy?" he called, his voice muffled by the thick oak. "Amy? Are you in there?"

He knocked louder. "Amy?"

On the faint hope she was inside, sound asleep, he eased open the door. His jaw went slack at the sight that greeted him.

Glittering jewels were strewn around the room. She knelt on the floor beside her trunk—that damned heavy trunk that she'd insisted go with her everywhere. And no wonder. The bloody thing was heaped with gold and gems and God knew what else.

He swore under his breath. "Why did you not answer me?"

"I—I don't know. You surprised me."

"I was worried sick about you, Amy. You were supposed to be preparing dinner, and I couldn't find you."

"I'm sorry. I . . . forgot." She glanced out the window, but the sun was hidden behind snow clouds and gave no indication of the time. "Is it very late?"

"It doesn't signify," he muttered, his anger beginning to ebb as the shock wore off and the implications of her deception dawned on him. "God's blood, I suggested you leave that trunk on coaches overnight. Why did you not tell me what was in there?"

"I . . . was taught never to trust anyone." She hung her head as tears filled her eyes. "I'm sorry. I should have told you. I've treated you badly when you've always been honest with me . . ."

Colin knelt beside her, wracked with guilt for being the cause of yet more distress, knowing he'd been much less than honest with her—hell, he wasn't even honest with himself where she was concerned. "I understand," he said softly.

She looked up at him, her amethyst eyes bright with

hope and unshed tears, and his heart turned over. She was still fragile emotionally, in a way that made him want to gather her into his arms and protect her from the world. He touched her instead, just lightly on the arm, and smiled at her, a smile of forgiveness that widened as they reached a silent understanding and he saw her eyes clear.

He ran his fingers down her arm, and her cheeks flushed pink. She looked away, flustered, and began gathering the jewelry.

He grasped her hand, halting her frenzied clean-up effort. "May I see some of your things?"

She glanced at him in surprise. "Of course." Her face lit with pleasure as she gave him the piece in her hands, a large diamond stomacher brooch.

"This is breathtaking." An enormous, rectangular step-cut diamond rested in the center, surrounded by round diamonds set into a spray of gold leaves. He turned his hand to admire how the gems caught the light.

"Papa bought the center stone from an Antwerp dealer, then saved it for almost a decade before mounting it." She wasn't flustered now; her words flowed easily. She missed her craft, Colin realized. "He rarely showed it to anyone. I don't think he really wanted to part with it."

" 'Tis a shame that it has never been worn and enjoyed."

"I made some bodkins to go with it." She rummaged in the trunk for a few seconds and came up with a half-dozen long gold pins, each topped with a gold leaf set with a rose-cut diamond. She dropped them into his other palm. "They would have been so pretty in a lady's hair, with the matching brooch. I always thought that someday, someone very important would own them."

"Someone important owns them now," Colin said, half-teasing, but her heart leapt into her eyes.

He'd best be more careful.

Mindful not to stick her with the pins, he handed the jewelry back to her and watched her wrap it up in two of the pieces of flannel that were scattered about. She'd gone quiet again.

He moved to sit on the bed, where a pile of trinkets glittered. "Is there anything here that you made?"

"Oh, many things." She jumped up to sit beside him, sifting through the jewels until she found an oval, coral-colored cameo and handed it to him shyly.

He smiled down at it. Set into a braided gold bezel, the intricate carving was a profile of a beautiful young woman. She wore a little necklace of twisted gold wire with a tiny diamond pendant attached, as if it were dangling in her cleavage. Suddenly, Colin narrowed his eyes and looked more closely. "She looks like you," he said in surprise, and she giggled a little.

"Papa said the same thing. I didn't hold with that at the time, but then Mama agreed, and others, and I finally decided she must be me after all. Although I swear I'd not intended to carve a likeness of myself. See, her hair is loose, and I never used to wear my hair that way."

He looked up at her sharply. "Yet you've worn it loose since the fire. Why did you change it?"

"I never had learned how to braid it myself." She thought a minute, frowning. "It seems to fit my life now; I feel like a different person." She shrugged. "I wore it braided for practical reasons—I couldn't work with it billowing about, getting in the way. And I've not made much jewelry the last few months, have I?"

"No, you surely haven't," he agreed with a wry smile. "I fancy it loose, anyway. At your shop . . . I wished I could unplait it."

"Did you really?"

Colin cleared his throat. Now, why had he let that slip? "She truly looks like you now, at any rate," he rushed to say, hoping to gloss over the thoughtless remark. He held the cameo between one finger and thumb, glancing back and forth between Amy and her likeness. The resemblance was unmistakable. "May I have it?" he asked, surprising himself.

Amy flushed with pleasure. "Oh, yes, I would love for you to have it. And anything else you want," she added, gesturing at the pile on the bed.

He laughed at that, pleased with her generosity, for he knew not what he'd have said had she refused him. He really wanted the cameo. "No, this will do nicely. I thank you."

"My pleasure." The underlying warmth in her voice captivated him. She seemed genuinely happy to give him the trinket. He wondered if she had any idea how much it meant to him.

The cameo was but one piece from a virtual treasure trove of jewelry. Looking over the pile on the bed, mentally adding it to the amount littering the floor and left in the trunk, he came to the conclusion the trunk had been nearly full. Why, 'twas a cache any pirate wouldn't hesitate to kill for.

He shook his head, berating himself for not realizing the contents of the trunk, and at the same time amazed at her skill in hiding it. The more he learned about her, the more he admired her. She had a streak of self-preservation that ran deep.

He set aside the cameo and sifted through the jewelry on the bed until something caught his eye—a brooch in the shape of a bow, encrusted with tiny rubies, sapphires, emeralds, and diamonds. "This is a pretty piece. Did you make it also?"

Amy nodded. "There are many similar pieces here. Galants, they're called, and very popular. I think we could all make them in our sleep." She smiled at the memory. "Shall I give it to Kendra, do you think? And we should choose something for Jason and Ford, too." Her face lit up at the idea. "Everyone was so kind to me—why did I not think of this before?"

"Because you would have shocked the hell out of us." She laughed, and Colin joined in. "Regardless, 'tis not necessary," he assured her. Chances were Amy would be living off this jewelry in the months and years to come; she shouldn't be giving things away.

"I want to do it." She dropped to the floor, already delving into the trunk for the perfect gifts.

"No, Amy." He put a hand on her arm.

She shook it off. "I insist." Gems flashed as she rummaged around, her attention wholly focused on the jewelry. " 'Twas a terrible lack of manners on my part; I must thank them for their hospitality."

He gave up. She rivaled the Chases for stubbornness; he'd give her that.

After much searching and good-natured bickering, they settled on an aigrette for Ford. Of all the brothers, he liked to dandy-up a bit, and the fancy pin would make a smart statement on his hat.

Jason was another story. Amy insisted on giving him a large pocket watch with an enamelled face and an open-work lid set with one enormous oval cabochon sapphire and eight smaller ones.

" 'Tis too much," Colin protested. "Besides, he has a pocket watch."

"I've seen it. 'Tis small and has no lid. The Marquess of Cainewood should pull out an impressive watch to check the time. Papa had someone just like Jason in mind when he made this."

"Here's a nice, large watch." Colin pointed out a likely specimen with a solid, simply engraved lid.

"No. I want him to have this one. He opened up his home to me, Colin—"

"I left him not much of a choice," he interrupted wryly.

"It doesn't signify. He was perfectly wonderful to me, and this is the least I can do. Besides, Robert made that one. I want him to have one my father made."

"Robert?"

"Robert Stanley. Our apprentice."

"Your apprentice?" Twisting his ring, he had a sudden vision of an insolent blunt-featured man leaning against the archway to Goldsmith & Son's back room. "You mean that red-haired fellow?"

She shot him an appraising glance. "You remember him?"

Distrustful light blue eyes. He remembered, all right.

That settled it. Not only was Amy intractable, but Colin didn't want anyone in his family to own anything made by that apprentice. He felt uneasy just thinking about the man.

Amy was already wrapping up the remaining jewelry. He set the pocket watch with their other choices and began to help her. "Whatever happened to him? Do you know?"

"Who?"

"The apprentice. Robert." He disliked even saying his name.

Her hands stilled for a moment. "I know not. He went off to fight the fire, and I never saw him again." She toyed with a flannel square. "I was supposed to marry him."

"Were you, now?" No wonder Robert had acted so hostile. An imagined scenario popped into Colin's mind, of Amy kissing the freckled, carrot-topped man. It made him sick in his gut, and the question came out of his mouth before he could catch himself. "Do you love him?"

"No." Amy tensed visibly as she folded the flannel around a bracelet. "Marrying him was my father's idea. Lacking a son, he needed someone to run the shop, and he'd known the Stanleys forever." She moved to the trunk to set the bracelet inside, then returned to the bed. "My betrothal papers burned in the fire. 'Twas the only good thing that came of it."

Colin let out his breath, which he'd not realized he'd been holding. Just because he couldn't have Amy didn't mean he wanted some dolt like Robert to get her.

Yet, she had to marry . . . a woman had to marry. "Is he not still expecting you to wed him?"

"It doesn't signify." She slipped a topaz ring on her finger, pulled it off again. "I would never have wed him of my own free will."

"What of the church records?" he reminded her. "He may think to use those to hold you to the betrothal."

She shrugged, still staring at the ring. "We were betrothed during the Commonwealth."

Colin nodded. The Puritans considered marriage solely a matter between the couple and the state, not involving God. During Cromwell's rule, weddings had been performed by a Justice of the Peace, and betrothals had taken place without ceremony.

He lifted a torsade of pearls. "Still, you must wed, Amy. With these jewels you could buy a title—"

"And marry a nobleman?" The topaz ring fell from her hand to the bed, and her eyes burned into his. "No. I'd never be able to reestablish Goldsmith & Sons."

"No, of course you would not." Absently, he fingered the heavy twisted ropes of pearls. "But you'll be in France, not London."

"I'll open a shop there. Not right away, but eventually."

"But—"

"No 'buts,' Colin." She smiled at her use of his words, then turned serious. "Yes, I'm a woman. And a jeweler. I promised my father I'd not let Goldsmith & Sons die with me. No, 'twas more than a promise—a vow. And our last real conversation."

'Twas a ridiculous plan. 'Twas . . . none of his business.

Consumed by disturbing thoughts, he toyed with the necklace, admiring the way the creamy colors matched and the pearl sizes graduated along the strands. The little clicks of the pearls sounded loud in the silence. "This must be worth a fortune," he said finally.

She nodded her head. "Pearls have doubled in price in my lifetime, and they're still rising. Would you like it? The clasp is beautiful, but I know not who made it, so it has no particular value to me."

Colin glanced at the clasp, delicate filigree encrusted with sapphires and diamonds. He wanted nothing except the cameo. "I'd not dream of taking this from you. I know King Charles and his cronies drape themselves in such jewels, but no man in my family would be caught dead wearing ropes of pearls." He couldn't give it to Priscilla. He would never feel right giving her anything he'd taken from Amy. "Besides . . ." He couldn't believe he was about to say this—to lend credence to her ludicrous plans. "You'll need to sell it to open your shop. 'Twill be expensive—"

She shrugged. "I have the gold."

"The gold?"

"In the bottom." She waved at the trunk. "My family has been accumulating coins forever. 'Twas"—she hesitated—"a secret. There. Now you know." Her sudden disarming smile enchanted him. " 'Tis why my father never worried when business fell off during the Commonwealth. There are a few gold bars as well—for fabrication, you understand. We never melted coins."

Surreptitiously, he hoped, Colin nudged aside some of the jewelry in the trunk, revealing a pile of gold coins, many of them old and pitted; he glimpsed one dated 1537. Gauging the thickness of the trunk's walls, he came to the conclusion there was a fortune in gold coins there. A vast, unbelievable fortune.

He was shocked speechless. Why, Amy was rich! Richer even than Priscilla, or at the very least, richer than Priscilla would be until the death of her very healthy father.

His gaze swept to Amy wrapping her jewelry, calmly making a pile of white-blanketed bundles, surrounded by gold, diamonds . . . riches beyond his comprehension. But what he felt for her had nothing to do with wealth or position, and everything to do with the way just looking at her made the blood course through his veins. His need for her was illogical, emotional . . . dangerous.

It didn't bear thinking about.

He resumed helping her, full speed. The trunk should be locked and hidden. From whom, he knew not. But although he'd been raised surrounded by beautiful, expensive things, after the War started his family had never had much in the way of liquid assets. This much gold, exposed, made him uncomfortable.

They placed the last pieces on top, and Amy retrieved the fitted tray and set it in place with a flourish. Then she reached for a long, black leather box, halfway under the bed.

"The stones," she said, in answer to his unasked question. She flipped open a flap cover to reveal a single neat row of paper packets. Pulling one out, she opened the precisely folded paper and placed the contents in his hand.

He marveled at the two loose, matched gems. "Diamonds?" he guessed.

"Yes. Waiting to be made into something wonderful. Earrings, perhaps." She took back the diamonds, her fingers flying as she refolded the paper in a complicated pattern. Even having seen her do it, Colin doubted he could make such a packet from a plain rectangle of paper.

Amy slipped the packet back and pulled out another, opening it to reveal hundreds of tiny diamonds. "Melee, they're called," she explained. "About five carats worth, averaging fifty stones to the carat." The pile of stones glimmered in their paper, and Colin leaned forward to look. Instead of handing them to him, though, she refolded the packet. "If they spilled, we'd never find them all in this carpet," she explained apologetically.

She replaced the packet and flipped through a dozen or more. On the fronts, Colin glimpsed nonsensical numbers in tiny, precise printing. With a smile and a nod, she finally pulled out one and unfolded it, revealing an enormous blood-red ruby.

Mesmerizing, it shone with a life of its own. Colin was no gem connoisseur, but he was certain he had never beheld such perfection before. He reached for it.

"My father was working on a design for this when he"—she swallowed hard—"when he died. 'Twas to be a necklace. There are twenty carats of matched diamonds in here that he'd planned to set with it."

" 'Tis beautiful," Colin responded gently. He examined the ruby, holding it up to the light, then set it back on the paper in her palm. "These gems must be worth an enormous amount." His vision clouded as he tried to imagine how one young woman could have so much in her possession.

"I'll warrant they're valuable," she admitted, "although I never think about it, really. You cannot easily use them to buy anything, like the gold." She folded the paper and returned it to the box. "They were always just there. Some of them have been in my family, waiting for the perfect mounting, for over a hundred years." She removed another packet and spilled the contents into Colin's open hand.

He walked to the window, moving his palm so the twenty-odd diamonds shimmered in the light reflected off the snow outside. "They sparkle so . . ." he murmured. A myriad of subtly different colors, they ranged from a pure, clear white to a light but distinct yellow.

"About half a carat each. Not well-matched. They'd end up in different pieces."

He closed his fist around the glittering stones. "They're beautiful. I can hardly credit . . . Amy, there's so much here." He frowned in puzzlement. "Your family . . . you had so much. Yet you lived above your shop . . ."

She came up next to him and held out the paper. He tipped the diamonds into it, a dazzling waterfall of costly gems. "We were not—I *am* not—nobility. No one expected us to live lavishly. If people had known what we had, 'twould have been stolen." She folded the packet and returned it to the box, closing the flap.

"But—"

"We lived very nicely." She smiled at his confusion. "I had the best clothes, and we always had a maid and housekeeper. We ate well, and we never had to prepare meals or clean up after ourselves. Mama collected things—pretty, useless things, figurines and vases that made her smile. We had books, we went to the theater—

the gold was security, so we never had to worry. 'Twas collected over so many generations that I feel as though 'tis not mine, really . . . almost like I hold it in safekeeping for someone else." She walked to the trunk, set the box inside.

"But it *is* yours, Amy. 'Tis all yours."

Silently she knelt by the trunk to close and lock it, then joined him at the window. They both gazed at the snow drifting down. The storm was dwindling, and this would probably be their last night together.

"You're right," she said softly. "It is all mine. But in the last two years I've learned that what counts are the people you have around you. Money is not important."

"It is if you don't have it," he returned bitterly, thinking about the years he'd spent struggling to get the estate into shape and restore his home, delaying his marriage and family plans.

"I'd trade it all—every bit of it—to have my parents back," she whispered.

He felt his heart tug in his chest. She was right, of course. He turned to her, took her face between his palms, gently tilted it to look into her eyes. "I know," he whispered back. "I know you would."

The chamber was quiet. The snow fell inaudibly outside the window; the crackling fire and their breathing were the only sounds. Her eyes deepened in color as he gazed into them, and he bent his head to capture her lips.

Amy felt her torn spirits mending in his embrace. His kiss was slow and caressing. His hands crept from her cheeks down the sides of her neck, to her shoulders and around to her back, where she felt their warm imprints pressing her against his powerful body.

A long, dreamy, melting time later their mouths broke apart, and Amy laid her head on his chest. Beneath her ear, his heart beat strong and steady. He stroked her hair with unhurried, gentle movements and twisted it in his fingers, almost as though he liked it, she thought lazily.

Her gaze drifted to the jewelry that sparkled on the bed. The galant, the aigrette, the pocket watch . . . the cameo. The thought of him owning it made her feel warm all over. Would he treasure it like she hoped he would? Years from now, would he look at it and remember the passion they'd shared? She hoped so. If he felt even a shred of the emotion she did, she suspected he would remember it all his life, for she was certain she would.

When she finally pulled away, she was surprised and relieved to find that, somewhere between his discovery of her secret and their shared, healing kiss, her uneasiness with him had vanished.

"I owe you a dinner," she reminded him with a grin. "Are you willing to try my very first stew?"

"With a side dish of pickled snails?" he asked, grinning back devilishly.

She groaned, heading out of the bedchamber.

Chapter Thirteen

With a hum of satisfaction, Amy moved her bishop diagonally across the chessboard toward Colin's king. "Check," she announced.

Colin was hard put to keep a smile off his face. After two complete games, 'twas clear Amy was the thoughtful tactician, while his style was fast and aggressive. But he'd put his mind to this match, planning his moves far in advance. He knew exactly what would happen from here on out.

He moved his king one space; then, the game well in hand, he turned his thoughts to something much more interesting: plotting the perfect practical joke.

Amy's gray marble knight made a decisive click against the black and white board. "Check."

Colin's hand shot out to rescue his king. He decided he would offer to prepare supper. Alone in the pantry, he ought to be able to dream up a clever prank. Ahh . . . yes.

She grinned, oozing confidence, and slid her bishop into place. "Check."

He managed to respond with no more than a speculative glance and a raise of one arched eyebrow. Though he was relieved to find them much more evenly matched in chess than they'd been in piquet, there was no reason to rub his impending victory in her beautiful face.

He tapped his king into place, threatening her knight.

Amy frowned at the board, then slowly withdrew the knight, relieving the pressure on his king.

Colin rubbed his hands together in glee. Now he controlled the events of the board, and he quickly moved one of his jade-green rooks across to threaten Amy's gray one.

She had no choice—either move her rook or lose it. Colin saw her freeze—she could see the inevitable. No matter which way she went, she would be dead in two moves—checkmated by his bishop.

She looked up, a surprised, wry smile on her face, then her hand moved to her king and gently laid it down.

Colin reached across the table to offer the obligatory victor's handshake, though he thought a kiss would be a much more interesting forfeit. "Good game."

"Shall we make it three out of five?"

"I believe two out of three was the agreement." He grinned. The slim margin of one game made victory all the sweeter. "Shall I collect supper?" Standing up, he glanced at the clock on the mantel. "A midnight supper, as it turns out."

"I'll help," Amy offered.

"No, 'tis my turn." He shrugged into his cloak before she could offer again. "See if you can finish that book. You said you cannot bear to let me return it to Jason's library without seeing how it ends."

Reaching for the book, the tenth volume of Madeleine de Scudéry's *Clélie*, she smiled and settled back. Apparently she wasn't suspicious. He ducked out the door before she could change her mind.

When Colin came in whistling, Amy was jarred out of Clélie's adventures. She'd never heard him whistle before. He did it quite well, although he sounded a bit too cheerful, even for a man who had just won a chess match.

"What might you be so happy about?"

"Oh, nothing." Still whistling, he moved the chess set off the table and laid out their light supper. "Sorry, but I've no bread," he said, apologizing for the unusual offering. Wine, oranges, smoked salmon, small dried biscuits, and another jar of those disgusting pickled snails.

Amy frowned at the jar. "Have you not had enough of those?"

"Never," he said, and went back to whistling. Amy's book lay open and ignored as he poured wine into two goblets.

He was happy about something, she thought—probably that he would finally be able to get rid of her tomorrow. It had stopped snowing a couple of hours earlier.

Handing her a goblet, he leaned down to kiss the top of her head. She sipped, watching him through her eyelashes. He was hardly acting like a man who couldn't stand her presence—'twas confusing, to say the least.

"Like it?" he asked.

"Mmm." Accepting a biscuit layered with fish, she popped it into her mouth, closed her book and set it on the table.

" 'Tis Madeira." He took a swallow of his own wine, raised the goblet in salute. "King Charles's favorite."

Chewing slowly, she watched him out of the corner of her eye. 'Twas light, meaningless conversation he made, but underneath she sensed a glee he could scarcely contain. Something was up. On the other hand, she reminded herself, she knew him not very well.

She knew his body, though. Her gaze traveled his snug buff breeches and white shirt, casually unlaced to reveal the top of his tanned chest. And under that shirt, she remembered . . .

"Where did you get the scar?" she asked suddenly.

"The scar?"

"On your arm. The long, white—"

"Oh. That scar." He sat beside her and placed salmon on a biscuit. "I seldom notice it anymore." As if the injury were of no consequence, he waved the hand with the biscuit airily. " 'Tis an old fencing practice wound—I was sixteen or so."

"Did it not hurt?"

"Hell, yes." He bit off half the biscuit, washed it down with a gulp of wine. "Someone poured brandy on it—that was the worst part—and then even more brandy down my throat. Then they stitched it up with a needle and thread."

"Lord! I cannot even imagine . . ." Amy took a deliberate sip of her own wine, to fortify herself or wash away the image—she wasn't sure which. "And 'twas only a practice . . . did that not make you angry?"

Colin stuck the rest of the biscuit in his mouth and chewed it slowly, considering. "No," he said finally, a wry smile on his lips, "it made me the best bloody swordsman in all of Europe. I made damn sure it would never happen again."

Amy thought about that: How Colin seemed determined to turn every disadvantage life dealt him into a benefit. He'd done it with his disappointing childhood, determining to do much better with his own family. He'd done it with his dilapidated estate, toiling tirelessly to turn it into something of value. He believed hard work and dedication—whether countless hours of swordplay or working the land with his own hands—were the best means to a happy ending. And he did not expect the good things in life to be handed to him on a silver platter. There was much to admire in such an attitude, she thought.

For Colin's part, he'd ceased thinking about it at all. The jar of snails on the table had reclaimed one hundred percent of his attention. Those snails beckoned, practically begging to be opened and play their part in this evening's performance.

A veritable model of patience, Colin considered himself, as he waited until he'd polished off his fifth biscuit before reaching for the jar and removing the lid. "Ready for one of these?" he asked innocently.

"Not yet," she said through a mouthful of fish. She held up a half-eaten biscuit to demonstrate her unreadiness. With a shrug, Colin nonchalantly dipped his spoon into the jar, scooped a snail, and placed it in his mouth.

Even the foreknowledge left him vastly unprepared for the taste of his concoction. Struggling to keep his face straight, he washed down the snail with a large gulp of wine as quickly as he could. If Amy succeeded in pretending she liked *these* snails, she was undoubtedly the best actress he'd ever met.

She finished her biscuit and put together another, and then another. At last, when he doubted she could cram in another bite, she announced, "I'm ready."

"For what?" He fixed her with a puzzled, innocent look.

"For a snail, of course," she snapped.

"Oh, you want one?" Quelling a smile, he stuck in his spoon and lifted a snail, tipped it and watched the liquid dribble back into the jar. The massive quantities of salt and sugar were undetectable. He licked his lips.

"Here," he offered, moving his spoon toward her mouth with the mock generosity of a man reluctant to part with his favorite morsel of food.

She opened her mouth, and he delicately placed it inside. Her face scrunched up in a look of dismay, but she did manage to swallow it. She rushed to wash it down, draining her goblet of wine in the process.

Refilling the goblet with pretended indifference, Colin struggled to contain his mirth. "Is something wrong?" he asked, knitting his eyebrows in feigned concern.

"It—it tasted a bit different. Do you suppose it might be a bad jar?"

Colin was enjoying himself immensely. "No, they all came from the same batch. Perhaps you simply care not for pickled snails."

"No, no, I like them," Amy insisted. "But this one tasted different. Try one, you'll see."

"I already had one," he reminded her. " 'Twas fine. Try another."

She put a hand on her stomach. "Please, I'd feel better if you have another one first."

There was nothing for it. He had to eat another snail or give up the game, and he was having too much fun to admit to his trickery, just yet. He took a deep breath and popped another one in his mouth, swallowing without even chewing.

" 'Tis fine," he declared. "Delicious, in fact. Perhaps there was one bad snail in the batch." He fished out a snail and handed Amy the spoon. "Here, try another."

Moving at the speed of a snail herself, Amy took the spoon and brought it to her lips. In the meantime, Colin took a long sip of wine, swishing it around his mouth to remove the foul taste. Relieved, he turned to her expectantly.

Her face was slowly turning red. When she gagged, he burst out laughing.

Amy's eyes opened wide as she finally realized what was happening. She spit the snail into her napkin. "Colin Chase," she demanded. "What have you done to these?"

Wiping tears from his eyes, Colin sputtered, "S-salt. And sugar."

A smile dawned on Amy's face as she reflected that she'd been well and truly duped. She deserved it, she decided, chuckling a bit.

"What else? What else was in there?"

"Nothing, I swear. You cared not for them to begin with, remember?" His eyes glittered again, devilishly. "Oh, I forgot, you'd never admit to that."

"I admit it, I admit it. I hate pickled snails. I'll never eat another of those vile creatures so long as I live," she choked out, laughing. "With or without your special recipe." She laughed again, partially because his joke *was* funny, given the circumstances, and partially in relief, because she felt as though he'd just given her a test which she'd passed with flying colors. One was not allowed to be close to Colin Chase if he or she couldn't take a joke.

And yet . . . he was really not trying to get closer to her, was he? She was leaving tomorrow, after all. His pleasure at her reaction, and the motive she'd credited him with, must be a figment of her imagination.

"Having coerced that admission from you," he declared now, "I proclaim my practical joke an unqualified success."

"Just a minute, Lord Greystone. You were forced to

eat two of those putrid snails, the same as I was. Surely a superior practical joke would not require its perpetrator to suffer the same consequences."

"You would dare to criticize the quality of my joke?" Colin's eyes went wide with pretended outrage. In truth, he couldn't have been more pleased with Amy than he was at the moment. He was pleased with her good-humored response to his joke, pleased with her rediscovered ease in his presence, pleased with her quick wit, pleased with her high color and those incredible sparkling amethyst eyes . . . all in all, he was very pleased. Dangerously pleased. "Mrs. Goldsmith, what qualifications do you have to recommend you as a joke judge?"

"My qualifications are beside the point entirely. The fact is, I saw the joke you played on Kendra a few days ago, and she told me about Benchley's fake murder and other tricks you've played over the years." Amy raised her chin. "The fact is, this joke was just not up to your usual standards."

"Is that so?" Colin lifted one eyebrow and brought his nose to within an inch of hers.

Amy inhaled his distinctive scent, and her heart beat a little faster at his nearness. "Absolutely. Without a doubt—" She broke off as his mouth came down on hers, cutting off any further aspersions on his joke, not to mention her air supply.

Their good-natured argument was forgotten as his lips covered hers with demanding finality. Her senses reeled with now-familiar feelings of pleasure, and she instinctively moved closer to the source, parting her lips in invitation. Slick and warm in her mouth, his tongue sent new spirals of delight through her awakened body.

Urgently, Colin eased her back onto the couch. He knew he was acting irrationally; he'd been irrational since the day he'd walked into her shop. But she would be gone tomorrow, and he could be rational for the rest of his life. Tonight . . .

His fingers worked feverishly to detach the embroidered stomacher from her bodice. The two of them couldn't be as good together as he remembered. 'Twas not possible.

It *is* possible, his inner voice told him. 'Tis possible and true, and she's beautiful and sweet and intelligent and . . . *You're a fool, Colin Chase*, the voice said, *a fool if you let her get away.*

But a louder voice was there, too. 'Twas the voice that Colin considered his honor and his logic, and it drowned out the other one, telling him he was committed to a lady who fit his every requirement. Unbreakably committed.

He should be committed to Bedlam, he thought briefly. Then he bent his head to capture her lips once more, and the voices were quieted for good.

Caught up in her feelings, Amy barely noticed her stomacher drop to the floor, and the next thing she knew, her bodice had been magically unlaced and her breasts sprang free between the parted front, veiled by her loose chemise.

Colin's fingers teased through the thin fabric, and her nipples swelled and tightened under his expert touch. A delicious shudder rippled through her as she ran her hands up and down his back. Lightheaded, she pulled his shirt from the waistband of his breeches and slipped her hands inside to feel the warm skin beneath.

He sat up and tugged off one of his boots. Bereft of his mouth and body, Amy marshaled her senses and realized what he was doing. "Colin—not here!"

He reached for his other boot. "Yes, here," he said, his voice husky. "Whyever not?" His stockings followed his boots, thrown to the floor in an untidy heap.

" 'Tis not . . . there's no bed!" Hot color stained Amy's cheeks. One was supposed to make love in the bedchamber, was one not? Her parents, had they done so at all—and she admitted to herself that she was living proof of the deed—had certainly never made love in the study. Of course, they'd not had a study, but that was beside the point.

While Amy worried about their circumstances, Colin

pulled her feet into his lap and slipped off her shoes, adding them to the pile of assorted clothing on the floor. With a devilish grin, he plucked off her garters and sensuously rolled down one stocking, his fingers brushing feathery paths along the length of her leg. Lifting her foot, he removed the stocking and pressed a spine-tingling kiss to her sole. Her toes curled as the sensation shot all the way up her leg and further, straight to the part of her he'd awakened the night before. She shivered, and Colin chuckled.

"We need no bed, love," he murmured in a low, passion-roughened voice, while removing her second stocking in a manner similar to the first. "This couch will do fine. Or the floor, or the desk, for that matter."

At her sharp indrawn breath of shock, he chuckled again. "The grass is nice," he continued, slowly sliding up her body to lie atop her, "but 'tis a bit cold out there right now. The bath is wonderful. I've not tried the stairs . . . yet." He bent his head to kiss her throat, his warm mouth caressing the hollows there. She shivered again. His lips trailed up to her ear, and she could feel his heated breath as he whispered, "No . . . I think the stairs would be uncomfortable . . ."

Burning all over, from both his touch and the sensual images his words were causing her to envision, she turned her head and caught his lips with hers.

His kiss was unhurried, his mouth exploring hers as though he were trying to memorize every nook and cranny. She felt drugged, and time slowed until nothing else mattered but his taste, his scent, his touch.

With shaking fingers, she unlaced the top of his shirt and slipped her hands inside to grasp his shoulders. Her palms swept over the corded muscles, then traveled over his chest. She felt and heard his breathing become uneven, matching hers.

Muttering a soft curse, Colin leapt up and drew the shirt over his head and off in one smooth motion. Reaching down, he pulled her to her feet and pushed her gown off her shoulders and down past her hips, until the worn lavender fabric pooled at her feet. He stepped back to look at her.

"The light," she protested weakly, gesturing with a sweep of one arm at the oil lamps she'd been reading by such a short time ago. Making love half-cloaked by flickering firelight was one thing, but surely he didn't intend to unclothe her in the bright lamplight?

"You're beautiful in it," he responded huskily. His hungry, seductive gaze roamed her body. "Like a painting by Sir Peter Lely." Amy's gaze shot down to her diaphanous chemise, and a blush heated her face. Lely was famed for his paintings of Court ladies—nude Court ladies.

Resigned to the fact that he had no intention of dousing the revealing lamps, Amy shyly perused him in return. Though the room was not overly warm, his broad shoulders were glazed with a thin sheen of perspiration. The light sprinkling of crisp black hair on his tanned chest tapered in toward his waist, disappearing into the waistband of his breeches, where his long fingers worked to loosen the laces. He impatiently tugged the tight breeches down and off.

Her eyes widened at the sight of him, large and ready. Surely that wasn't the same part of him that had slid inside her last night, was it? But though her cheeks flushed at the mere thought, her body moved toward him of its own volition, leaning against his solid chest as one hand closed around his velvet warmth.

Colin gasped. He reached for the hem of her chemise, pulled it up and over her head and tossed it away, even as he guided her back to the couch and came down on top of her.

The fabric was rough under her bare skin, but Amy's senses careened, and she could have been atop the finest linen sheets for all she was aware of it. Her awareness was for Colin only: his warm weight; his hot, wet mouth; his already familiar spicy scent.

His lips played over her face and neck, while his fingers roamed her body, grazing her arms, her legs, her breasts, her belly. Wherever he touched, tendrils of desire raced from his fingertips to the core of her womanhood, until she thought she would faint from anticipation unless he touched her there.

Finally, *finally*, his strong fingers urged her thighs apart, and when she felt his intimate caress, warm against her slickness, she thought she would explode with relief. Her nails dug into his shoulders. "Oh, Colin," she said in a tremulous whisper.

"Oh, Christ," he grated out. In one lithe motion, he came over her and buried himself in her taut sheath, and a moan of ecstasy escaped her lips.

He froze.

"Oh, love," he whispered in an agony of concern mixed with desire, "is it too soon? Are you too sore?"

"No," she whispered on a sigh. "God in heaven, no."

For one second her face flamed at the intimacy of his question, for the next second she was astonished that her soreness had indeed disappeared, was forgotten completely, and then she felt him move inside her and all thoughts fled. She arched against him, abandoning herself to the whirl of sensation.

At first Colin shifted slowly, until she squirmed beneath him in a frenzy of passion. Then he moved faster, matching every arching motion of her straining body, until waves of burning sweetness overcame her. Her arms tightened around him, her breath came in long, shuddering moans, and when she heard his cry of release she was flooded with an amazing sense of completeness.

Lying beneath his welcome weight, Amy filled her lungs with great gulps of air, more satisfying than the most splendid meal. Colin showered her face and neck with small, wet kisses, and she marveled at her feelings of attachment, so new, so perfect.

"Sweet love," Colin murmured. He couldn't make himself cease kissing her, stop and collect himself. For such would bring thoughts—thoughts that would confirm their impossible perfection together, thoughts that would tell him he'd be making the worst mistake of his life if he let her go. He couldn't afford such thoughts. They were the thoughts of an emotional man, and he was a rational man.

Still, he could not stay on top of her forever.

When he finally eased himself off her, molding himself against her side on the narrow couch, Amy made a small sound of loss. She turned to him, wrapped an arm around his middle, pressed her satin breasts against his chest, entwined her legs with his.

He groaned in contentment. "Are you cold?" he asked softly.

She shook her head and wiggled against him, attempting to get closer still, and he nearly fell off the edge. He caught himself just in time.

"We do not really fit here, you know," he teased, raising his eyebrows a fraction.

The moment was shattered. Amy came up on an elbow. "I told you so," she retorted good-naturedly, "before . . . before . . ."

"And so you did," Colin interjected, saving her from the dilemma of deciding how to describe what had just taken place between them. Standing, he took Amy's hand and pulled her up beside him. "Shall we?" he asked, gesturing to the bedchamber next door. Still holding her by the hand, he headed out to the corridor.

She blushed prettily at finding herself casually walking beside a man, the both of them stark naked. He left her not much time to dwell on the strangeness of it, however, as he seemed unable to resist stopping every few steps to draw her into his arms for a long, lingering kiss. When they reached the chamber, she broke away and ran for the bed, diving under the quilts.

"Brrr!" she said with an expressive shiver, pretending she'd run for cover because of the cold, and not fooling Colin for a second.

He stirred up the fire and added a couple of logs. 'Twas a shame they'd not be together long enough for her to become truly comfortable with him, for him to take pleasure in watching her come to terms with her sensuality. The thought of her freely giving herself to another man, without embarrassment or artifice, made his insides clench, but he knew, given her passionate nature, 'twas inevitable. He would have to content himself with the memory of awakening her passion in the first place.

From the safety of the bed, Amy watched him boldly, enjoying the view more than she would ever have thought possible. She felt like a whole new person, an entirely different Amy. *Amethyst.* She pronounced it in her head, drawn-out and elegant. *Amethyst Chase. Lady Greystone.* No, she decided, she was still Amy. "Lady Greystone" would never design and create jewelry, never own and run a shop. She wouldn't—couldn't—let herself contemplate the possibility of anything permanent with Colin. Lucky circumstances had resulted in these short hours of bliss, and 'twas almost time to return to the real world.

But must she be wrenched from his side so soon? She knew full well it couldn't last, but they had scarcely discovered each other. She cast around wildly for an idea, any idea, and just as he crawled into bed beside her, she came up with one. "Colin?"

He turned toward her expectantly. "Yes?"

The idea suddenly seemed stupid. 'Twas impossible to believe he would agree to it. Still . . . 'twas worth a try. "I—I know we have to leave tomorrow, but . . ."

"But, what?"

"Do you think you could take me to London?" she asked in a rush, before she lost her nerve. "I have no clothes at all, not anything, you know, and—well, 'twould take me naught but a couple of days to purchase everything I need, and then—"

"I'd be happy to take you to London first for a few days. We'll find you a chaperone there, and—"

"—I would just prefer not to arrive in France with nothing—"

"Amy." Colin leaned forward, planted a warm kiss on her forehead. "I said I'd be happy to take you."

"Oh." It had worked. She could hardly believe it. A few more days with Colin—'twas a dream come true.

For his part, Colin was just as relieved. Of course the whole idea was nothing more than a ploy to stay with him longer, but, hell, he wasn't ready to part with her, either. "We'll stay at the family town house," he found himself saying.

A mistake—he knew it was a mistake the moment it came out of his mouth. Alone together at the town house. Alone, but surrounded by all of Charles's gossipy, meddlesome Court. Damn, but this was a bad idea. He regretted his agreement already.

But Amy's eyes glittered violet with excitement. "Thank you," she breathed.

"My pleasure, love." He lifted her chin to lock his lips on hers. She melted into his arms. They had a long night ahead of them—there would be time for regrets tomorrow.

Chapter Fourteen

Retrieving her book from the study, Amy dragged her trunk to the front door and sat on it to watch through the narrow window. She unfolded the note and read it again. *Amy*, it said in Colin's bold printing,

> *I have gone with Benchley to retrieve the coach. Please ready yourself to leave. We will breakfast on the way to London.*
> *Greystone*

That was it. No "Dear Amy." No "Love, Colin." Amy told herself nothing was wrong—Colin simply wasn't demonstrative on paper—but she knew she was fooling herself. The Colin who had made love to her three times during the long night had vanished.

She looked up from the note to see the coach pass under the portcullis and onto the little circular drive in the courtyard. When Colin opened the door, she was standing by her trunk, book in hand, the note tucked safely away.

"Good morning, my lord," she said as cheerfully as possible.

Colin winced at the formal address. "Good morning," he muttered back, avoiding her gaze. He lifted the trunk—more carefully than he had before he'd known what it contained—and carried it to the coach. Amy trailed slowly. Colin waved her inside and went back to lock the door, then climbed in opposite her, and they were off.

He pulled Kendra's basket from under his seat and set it on the floor between them. "Breakfast?" He reached in, selected an apple and polished it on his shirt before taking a bite.

Amy dug out another apple. Any minute now, she expected him to smile and tease her or start pointing out the features of his estate, but as time crept slowly by she realized 'twas less and less likely.

They drove a mile or so in wary silence, the only sounds those of the wheels on the rutted, slushy road, the steady clip-clop of the horse's hooves, and the juicy crunch of apples being chewed and swallowed. Colin fetched a napkin from the basket and deposited his apple core in it, then held it out for Amy to do the same. Their eyes met, Amy's questioning, Colin's hooded and indecisive.

The core-filled napkin dropped from his hand to the basket. "This changes nothing," he blurted out. "I'm still betrothed to Priscilla."

Amy stared at him sitting stone-faced across from her. Unbidden tears threatened to spill from her eyes.

He hunched over, his elbows resting on his spread knees, his head in his hands. "Don't cry, Amy," he said to the floor. "I don't think I could stand it."

She blinked back the tears. "I know you're betrothed. I've not been thinking anything had changed, my lord. Have I said something to make you think I have?"

"Well, no . . ." He hesitated, then moved over to her side and placed an arm around her shoulders. "No, you said nothing." He stared out the window. "But as much as I wish to spend every minute with you in London, there are those who would take note of it and make both our lives miserable."

"I know no one important in London."

"What about your former clientele?"

Amy bit her lip. He had a point. They may not have been her friends, but the fact remained she was acquainted with many of London's elite.

Could he possibly be suggesting they share the town

house but not the same bed? Having already surrendered her innocence to Colin, she couldn't imagine living in celibacy with him, even for only a few days. Why should she, anyway? People would assume they were sleeping together whether they were or not.

" 'Twould be worth it," she said, turning in his arms, her eyes sending the message she was too shy to put into words. "I'll be in Paris the rest of my life, in all probability. What London thinks of me couldn't possibly matter."

Colin scooted as far away as the bench would allow, his hands resting on her shoulders as he looked into her eyes. "You know not what course your life will take, Amy." He dropped his hands to his lap, and his voice took on a flat, emotionless tone. "I'll set you up at the town house, but I'll not be spending nights there myself. A coach and driver will be at your disposal. I'll let you know where you can reach me so you can send word when your shopping is complete."

"Where will you stay?"

"That depends upon who is in town. But I'll make sure everyone knows we're not sharing the town house." Distancing himself from her already, he moved back to the opposite bench.

The implication was obvious. He would not risk anyone finding out they'd been intimate, period. Not for a second did she believe he was protecting her reputation.

Colin stretched his legs and crossed them, then retreated behind his book. Miserable, Amy withdrew into one protective corner of the carriage. There was no point continuing the discussion. He had made his intentions clear, and he'd not asked for her opinion, anyway. He was so unfair! She'd never asked to stay with him, or even hinted at it—she knew plain Amy Goldsmith didn't belong with the Earl of Greystone. She had her own life—obligations to fulfill. All she wanted was a few more days with him, a few more days of happiness, a few more days when she could pretend she wasn't alone in the world.

Even now, aloof as he was, she wanted nothing more than to reach out and touch him, to lose herself in his arms. As hard as he was trying to be cold and demanding, he'd melted when her tears had threatened. She should take comfort from that, she told herself. The real Colin was in there somewhere, obviously just as confused as she was—if not more.

She opened her book and held it in front of her face, staring blindly at a page while she composed herself. If she had any hope of regaining their intimacy for a day or two, she'd not accomplish it by weeping and begging.

She took a deep breath and forced herself to focus on the words, until she was caught up in the exciting end of Clélie's long tale. Three hours of silence later, just as they crossed London Bridge, she finished and, with a sigh of satisfaction, laid it down on the seat beside her.

Gazing out the carriage window, she marveled at the changes the fire had wrought in her hometown. Blocks and blocks were naught but charred vacant lots; the odd chimney or blackened stone oven stood like gravestones among the debris. 'Twas hauntingly quiet, with no noise other than the clip-clop of horses and the creaking and crunching of wheels passing through. As Amy moved closer to the window, a small sound of distress escaped her lips.

Colin looked up from his book. " 'Twill not be like this forever," he said gently.

She listened carefully. Here and there came rare, banging sounds of construction. "Some are rebuilding," she observed.

"Yes, but 'tis forbidden until owners clear the rubble and establish their claims to the land. 'Twill take time."

Driving along Fleet Street toward Chancery Lane, they passed into the unburned area at last. Amy breathed a deep sigh of relief as the familiar smells of London hit her. Odors of tar, smoke from incessant coal fires, and the stench of tanneries were overlaid with a pervasive reek from the open sewer that the Fleet River, commonly called the Ditch, had become over the centuries. Though rank and foul, the stench was a comforting memory of another life.

And the traffic! Carriages, hackney coaches, carts, mounted riders, sedan chairs, pedestrians, and animals jostled one another in the noisy, crowded streets. After months in the quiet countryside, Amy's ears seemed assaulted with the cacophony of hawkers peddling their wares in pushcarts, wheelbarrows, and simple baskets, crying out in singsong rhyme of the superiority of their goods. One man called out, "Rats or mice to kill!" and Amy chuckled and smiled.

"The rats," she mused. "How could I have forgotten the rats?" Colin smiled in return.

Thieves, pickpockets, and beggars were everywhere, but so were street singers ballading for pence. Amy caught sight of a familiar face and turned excitedly. "Oh, 'tis Richardson the fire-eater! May we stop and watch?"

Colin shrugged and knocked on the roof for Benchley to halt. Amy hung out the window, wide-eyed, as Richardson chewed and swallowed hot coals, then melted glass and, as a finale, put a hot coal on his tongue, heated it with bellows until it flamed, cooked an oyster on it and swallowed the lot. The audience burst into wild applause, and Colin dug in his pouch and handed Amy a coin to toss out the window before they moved on.

They finally reached Lincoln's Inn Fields, a fashionable residential neighborhood bordering a large, grassy square. 'Twas quieter here, but only in comparison to other parts of London; Lincoln's Inn Fields Theatre was here, known for spectacular moving scenery, and the square was often the scene of fights and robberies, as well as a place for public executions.

The coach stopped in front of the Chases' town house, a four-story brick building on the west side of the square. Amy climbed out and gazed up at the distinguished facade. Giant Ionic columns held up a boldly projecting cornice and balcony. Triangular decorations crowned tall, rectangular windows.

Colin came out after her and stretched, yawning.

" 'Tis Palladian," Amy breathed in an awed tone. "Was it designed by Inigo Jones?"

"Yes." He took off toward the front door.

Following him, Amy frowned, her exhilaration at being back in the City dampened by his attitude. Where were his usual chatty explanations? Colin loved showing his family's homes and recounting their histories. Was he that unhappy with her, then?

The interior was every bit as impressive as the outside. The few aristocratic residences Amy had seen were paneled in heavy, dark, traditional Jacobean wood. Not so this home; the comparison was like coal to diamonds. Her gaze swept up a wide, graceful curving staircase, over light, cheerful painted walls, ornamented with classical motifs and festooned with a riot of carvings: flowers, fruit, ribbons, palms, and masks. She couldn't wait to get a tour of this magnificent house.

Colin prodded her forward, toward the lined-up servants.

"This is Mrs. Amethyst Goldsmith," he said, pleasantly enough. "She'll be staying here for a few days. Ida?"

A slight, blue-eyed girl stepped forward, perhaps sixteen or so. "Yes, my lord?"

"Please see to Mrs. Goldsmith's comfort." The maid's blond curls bounced as she nodded, eagerly accepting the responsibility. Colin turned to Amy. "I'm taking a nap. I suggest you do the same."

With that, he was off, his long legs taking the stairs two at a time. Ida showed Amy to a chamber and pulled back the covers on the bed. Amy still wondered about the house, but she'd not been anticipating a self-guided tour; she wanted Colin beside her, telling her all about it.

She lay down, and when she awakened from her fitful sleep, Colin was gone. On her way down to supper, Ida said something about him dining with Priscilla before making an appearance at some ball or other, but Amy listened with half an ear. Although she'd had most of the day to get used to the idea, she still couldn't believe that Colin had left her alone.

As the dance prescribed, Priscilla performed a graceful bow and pointed one square-toed shoe, chattering over the subdued music of the slow minuet. Growing more impatient by the minute, Colin wondered what on earth had possessed him to squire her to Lady Carson's ball. He hated these affairs. And why had he never noticed before what a gossip she was?

Her mouth was as mincing as the minuet. Perhaps if he backed her into that matron over there, who rather resembled the stuffed peacock on the buffet table, Priscilla might shut up.

"Excusez-moi!" The matron pinned him with accusing eyes.

"My apologies, madame." He wrinkled his nose against the cloying perfume that wafted from the woman's unwashed body. But his ploy had worked. Priscilla ceased babbling about Lady So-and-So and Lord Such-and-Such, and turned her attention to him instead.

"Really, Colin. You must be more careful."

He flashed her an innocent smile. "Od's fish, my dear, but you are looking well this evening." 'Twas true. Her shoulder-length silver-blonde hair gleamed in the candlelight from the blazing chandeliers. Her figure was tall and willowy rather than curvy, but she carried herself regally, and her ivory satin gown accentuated her pale beauty. The complete opposite of Amy's coloring.

He shook himself. Whatever made that pop into his head?

"Thank you." Priscilla smiled back at the compliment, but no blush marred her complexion. Sedate and proper at all times, she never blushed. Unlike Amy, who—

"Colin, did you hear me?"

"I was admiring your complexion. You're as beautiful and flawless as a porcelain doll."

"Oh." She concentrated on the next dance step. "I was saying that Lady Beauchamp—"

"Shh." His long, tanned fingers skimmed up her perfect chin and along her jaw. When she flinched and pulled back, he frowned and mentally revised his list: She was as cold and hard as a porcelain doll as well. He would have to work on that.

They both balanced forward in three-quarter rhythm. "As I was saying, Lady Beauchamp—"

"Do you think we might discuss something relevant?"

"Relevant?" Her toe traced a half-circle.

"Relevant. Morals or values—but not in the context of the latest scandal. Politics. Literature. Art." The peacock matron shot him another dirty glare, and he edged Priscilla farther into the glittering jeweled throng of dancers. "What did you think of the play tonight?"

"Lady Scarsdale's gown was horrendous. The orange girls were better dressed. And did you see the earl's periwig? It had lice. I cannot believe we were forced to share a box with them."

The music ended and Priscilla glanced around. "Lady Whitmore has arrived. I have something to tell her."

"By all means." With a great sigh of relief, he sent her sailing from the dance floor. He must find a way to stop this habit of perpetual gossip before it drove him mad. Perhaps an instructive practical joke—

Ah . . . yes. He smiled as he caught the eye of an old friend across the ballroom. Barbara Palmer, the Countess of Castlemaine. King Charles's mistress these past six years, Barbara had a passionate nature both in and out of the bedchamber. A perfect coconspirator, she would undoubtedly enjoy a prank as much as he.

As he approached Barbara, he couldn't help but admire the auburn hair and deep blue eyes that had helped make her Charles's favorite.

"My Lady Castlemaine." With a little bow, he took her arm and drew her away from the group surrounding her. Everyone was well aware she had the King's ear and, even more important, was not opposed to dabbling in politics. For a price, of course.

"Greystone!" Barbara's eyes danced. "You have my

thanks for rescuing me. Where have you been hiding these weeks past?"

"Some of us have to work, you know," Colin teased. Pulling her farther away from the masses of people, he dropped his voice. "I was wondering . . . Might you be willing to help me play a little trick on Priscilla?"

"One of your practical jokes? On Priscilla?" Barbara's musical laughter tinkled through the ballroom. "I'd love to! What have you in mind?"

"Well . . ." His ideas were half-baked. Suddenly, though, inspiration hit. "Would you mind pretending you're with child?"

"How would that help?"

"I've discovered Priscilla is a devil of a gossip—"

"You're just finding out? For the love of God, I've known that for years."

"Well, I was thinking to tell her you're expecting again—Charles's babe, naturally—but not to tell anyone. She'll tell *everyone*, of course, and eventually someone will congratulate you. Then—here's the part you may not like—then you'll burst into tears, saying you lost the babe, and Priscilla will be mortified that she started this rumor."

"I love it!" Barbara exclaimed. " 'Tis *so* mean!"

"Do you think so?" Colin frowned. 'Twould not do to humiliate Priscilla; he just wanted to teach her a lesson.

"No, not really," Barbara recanted. He looked at her sharply. "Most any lady here would spread the rumor," she rushed to reassure him. "Priscilla will not be thought of unkindly. Besides, no one will know where it started. One request, though. Afterward, we must tell the poor soul I break down in front of—and Priscilla, of course—that I was never actually with child. I've never lost a child, you know." She put a preening hand to her auburn locks.

"Of course. And we'll make sure everyone else knows, too."

"Oh, that will not be necessary. 'Twill do my reputation good for people to think Charles has come back to me again. He will, you know."

"Of course he will," Colin assured her. "He always has."

"He's made such a fool of himself over Frances Stewart."

That wasn't news to Colin. A tall, beautifully proportioned girl some eight years younger than Barbara, Frances had arrived at Court almost four years ago, and King Charles had been head over heels for her ever since. His love was unrequited, however, since Frances was that rarest of creatures: a chaste courtier.

"I cannot stand her," Barbara said. "She prances around in that man's dress made fashionable by the Queen—as if I could wear such garb after bearing five of His Majesty's children!"

"Come now, such dress is ridiculous anyway. And no one could rival you in that gown." He conspicuously eyed her low decolletage.

"Thank you," she said, as though such compliments were her due. "Charles wrote a poem about her, you know. 'Oh, then 'tis I think there's no Hell, Like loving too well,' " Barbara quoted in a sickly sweet voice. She rolled her eyes. "And still she'd not share his bed."

"There are those who think Frances must be simple-minded to persist in such virtue," Colin consoled her.

"Oh, she's a dunderhead, all right. Her favorite pastimes are playing blind-man's buff and building castles out of playing cards. Grammont said 'tis hardly possible for a woman to have less wit or more beauty."

"Then she's no true rival to you," Colin assured her. He spotted his intended making her way across the ballroom. "Priscilla is headed this way. You agree to my plan?"

"Yes, it shall be great fun. I will dazzle you with my performance."

"Very well, then. I look forward to it." He walked toward Priscilla nonchalantly, hoping she'd not noticed the long time he'd spent talking with Barbara.

After mingling a bit, he danced again with Priscilla, enjoying the jealous glances of the other men present. She was tall and graceful in his arms, and she wasn't gossiping, for once. At the end of the dance, he realized he'd not thought about Amy for quite a few minutes, and was pleased with himself.

Coming off the dance floor, he said casually, "I've heard tonight that Barbara is expecting His Majesty's sixth child."

"She told you so?" Priscilla was more animated than usual, her interest piqued by the opportunity to be in on a juicy bit of gossip.

"No, 'twas someone else. You mustn't tell anyone, though, for she's not even told Charles yet."

"Oh, I wouldn't," Priscilla said, much too quickly. "Who told you, though?"

"I've been sworn to secrecy. I chatted a bit with Barbara to see if she'd let it slip, but she said not a word."

"She doesn't look *enceinte*." Priscilla slanted a dubious glance to where Barbara was surrounded by a new group of hangers-on.

"She's only just had it confirmed, according to my source. She'd not be showing yet."

"Of course. I'm not well versed in such matters, since I've not had children myself—yet." Priscilla knew Colin wanted several children; he'd made no secret of the importance he placed on family life. And she'd offered no arguments, he reminded himself now, seeking further reasons to be satisfied with his choice of mates.

"Would you care for some spiced wine?" he asked, knowing 'twould be out of character for him to discuss such a gossipy subject too long.

"No, thank you," Priscilla declined prettily. "I'm not thirsty." Colin saw right through her excuse: She couldn't wait to get back to her friends. However, he enjoyed his jokes tremendously, especially the anticipation, and wasn't quite ready to let her get started.

"No, I insist." He drew her over to the refreshment table and handed her a cup of wine. Taking one himself, he grasped her firmly by the elbow. "Shall we enjoy the garden for a while?"

" 'Tis freezing out there," Priscilla protested, clearly impatient.

Colin smiled to himself. "Just for a minute. 'Tis beastly hot in here." She could find no argument with that. Between the blazing fires on either end of the ballroom, the hundreds of candles burning in the chandeliers above, and the guests packed in elbow-to-elbow, 'twas difficult to breathe. Priscilla reluctantly went with him, in no small part because he dragged her along physically, and he guided her through the crowd and outdoors.

"Ahhh." Colin inhaled deeply of the fresh air. " 'Tis pleasant out here, is it not?"

Priscilla drained her cup and crossed her arms in a most unladylike fashion. 'Twas quite unlike her, and Colin was pleased; perhaps she was becoming more human. "I'm finished. May I go back inside now?"

"Not just yet." Colin drew her further into the formal garden, over to a low brick wall. He set down both their cups and leaned back against it, wrapped his arms around Priscilla's waist and pulled her close. Ignoring the startled look in her eyes, he brought his lips down to hers—just a little bit down, he realized, momentarily surprised at the reminder of her height. But her mouth was warm in the cold night, and he was pleased that this statuesque heiress was his, so 'twas a few moments before he realized she wasn't kissing him back, and in fact was pushing away from him, her palms flat against his chest.

"Colin—not here."

"Why? No one is here to see."

" 'Tis not proper. And there's no one to see because no one else is fool enough to come out in this weather."

"I'll keep you warm." Though taken aback by her reaction, Colin offered her a smile as he pulled her back against himself. Although not the most passionate of women, she'd never resisted his advances before. She had even been willing to share his bed; after all, no one at Court—barring an aberration like Frances Stewart—was celibate.

But Priscilla was ever well mannered and proper, and Colin realized with surprise that he'd never tried to steal a sensual moment with her before, that every action had had its time and place. And he had no doubt that, with time, she would learn to enjoy a stolen kiss or two.

Priscilla went limp in his arms now, not resisting but not participating either, and Colin decided her first lesson in sensuality was over. He swung her about and walked her back to the ball, his arm lightly around her shoulders. When Priscilla's own arm stole around his waist as they crossed the threshold, he was pleased.

A second later she was gone. She'd spotted Lady Crowhurst across the room and said she just *had* to talk to her, and Colin let her go. He chuckled to himself when he saw her lips mouth the word "Barbara."

Not five minutes later, Colin would swear there was a new buzz in the room as gossiping ladies rushed to be the ones to spread the delicious rumor. And in the end, 'twas Priscilla herself who couldn't resist approaching Barbara.

She waited politely until Barbara was free. "My Lady Castlemaine," she said, pulling her aside, "I hear congratulations are in order."

Colin sidled closer and concealed himself behind a post. Barbara played her part to perfection. "Is that so?"

"I have heard in the strictest of confidence that you will be presenting His Majesty with another child soon."

Barbara's face fell.

"Is something wrong, my lady? Am I mistaken?" At the sight of Priscilla panicking already, Colin had to choke back laughter or risk revealing his hiding place.

Slow tears leaked from Barbara's blue eyes—what an actress she was! Desperate, Priscilla grasped her by the shoulders. "Oh, my lady, are you all right? Do you not *want* the babe?"

"I lost it last week," Barbara wailed, the tears pouring in earnest now. "A tiny babe, perfectly formed . . . oh, my heart breaks to think of it . . ." She clutched her chest and let out a great sob, then ran from the ballroom and up the wide staircase, weeping all the way.

Priscilla followed her out into the hall and watched her flight. She was still gazing up the sweeping stairs when Colin came up behind her.

"Is something wrong, Priscilla?"

She turned to him immediately, a frown of dismay creasing her beautiful forehead. "Oh, Colin, I've made the most dreadful error. I thought to congratulate my Lady Castlemaine, only to discover that she has miscarried. Now she's horribly upset, and everyone thinks she's with child. What am I to do?"

"Whyever would everyone think Barbara is carrying?" he asked with a glint in his eye.

"I told them!" Priscilla wailed. "And they told each other."

"Priscilla! You promised!" he exclaimed in pretended disbelief.

"You mean to say you really meant it?" Priscilla protested. "Why would you tell me if it were a secret?"

"You mean to say I shouldn't trust you? I shouldn't tell you anything unless I want everyone to know?"

"Yes! I mean, no! Oh, Colin, I shouldn't be such a terrible gossip, should I?"

Colin grinned; he couldn't help himself. The scene was playing out even better than he had hoped.

"Why are you smiling?" Priscilla demanded. "I've ruined everything! She never really liked me—she only invited us to her parties because of my father, and now she'll hate me. We'll not be welcome anywhere."

"Now, Priscilla, you know that's not true. Barbara would never leave me off a guest list. We were in exile together—I'm one of her dearest friends. Besides, Charles is like a big brother to me. He'd never allow her to snub us." He was right, and Priscilla knew it. Colin's relationship with the King was her father's primary reason for promoting the match. Lord Hobbs had been a fence-sitter during the War, and consequently, though he'd not lost his lands, he held no favor with Charles, either.

"I suppose you're right," Priscilla sniffed.

Just then, Barbara came back down the stairs, dry eyed and grinning from ear to ear, and Colin took one look at her and broke out laughing. Priscilla stared at Colin, then at Barbara, and back to Colin before bursting out, "What is going on here?"

Colin's face was turning red under his tan. "I—we—I—"

Barbara rescued him—sort of. "What Colin means to say, dear, is that we set you up."

"Set me up?" Priscilla's pretty brows furrowed in confusion. "You mean you suffered no miscarriage?"

"I was never with child in the first place." Barbara chuckled. "Colin thought to demonstrate how gossip spreads." Priscilla glared at her, openmouthed. " 'Twas a joke," Barbara finished weakly.

"A practical joke," Colin put in.

"A practical joke?" Priscilla repeated in disbelief. "On *me*?" She snapped him on the arm with her folded fan. "How dare you play a practical joke on me."

Colin rubbed his arm out of reflex, though it didn't really hurt. Priscilla had put as little enthusiasm into the blow as she gave to everything else. "I play practical jokes on everyone," he reminded her.

"You'll not play them on me, Colin Chase. They're stupid and childish, and I'll not stand for it."

"Do you not think it funny?" Colin's laughter died. "Do you not find it amusing that I know you well enough to devise a trap you would fall into perfectly?"

"No. I find it not in the least amusing." Priscilla turned on Barbara. "How about you? I find it difficult to imagine why you would play along with his trickery—now everyone thinks you're with child."

"It doesn't signify." Barbara waved a hand airily. "I probably *will* be with child by the time anyone could find out otherwise. I always am, it seems," she lamented.

Colin laughed. "You're a good sport, Barbara."

"There are those who would disagree," Barbara pointed out archly. Colin nodded, a knowing smile on his lips. More than one man had met his downfall at the hands of Barbara Palmer. Luckily, they'd been friends too long, and he knew her too well to make the sort of blunder that would turn her against him.

The wind blew out of Priscilla's sails when she realized neither Colin nor Barbara were the least bit sorry they'd used her as the butt of their joke. "Please call for the coach, Colin," she requested calmly.

"What?" The evening was still young.

"We will forget this ever happened. I trust it won't again. I wish to return home now."

"Lost your taste for gossip, Lady Priscilla?" Barbara asked sweetly.

The barb went right over Priscilla's head. "I merely find myself fatigued. Colin?" She took his arm and led him away.

Colin looked back at Barbara, raising his eyebrows and shrugging his shoulders helplessly. She laughed and waved him on before gliding back into the ballroom. For the life of her, Barbara couldn't imagine what Colin saw in Priscilla, though she supposed it mattered not. Priscilla was wealthy, and that was enough. One was not required to like one's spouse, and God knew Barbara despised hers. Marriage alliances were arranged for the benefit of both parties, and one could always take a lover. Or two or three.

Chapter Fifteen

"I have a headache." Priscilla lifted her elegant chin and calmly shut her door in Colin's face.

Now what? Distracted by his prank, he'd neglected to approach anyone at the ball to arrange lodging. At a loss, he wandered back to his carriage.

He wasn't about to drop in on a friend unannounced. None would be home at this hour, regardless; 'twas much too early for any self-respecting man-about-town to make his way home. Opening the coach door, he sighed. He could visit Whitehall Palace, where the Court stayed up until the wee hours gambling and playing billiards, but he wasn't in the mood.

"Bloody hell," he said aloud, and gave Benchley instructions to return to the town house. No one even knew Amy was there, he rationalized, shoving aside the concerns he'd voiced earlier in the day.

As he settled back, his thoughts turned to the amethyst-eyed witch who had wormed her way into his bed and heart. Now, *there* was someone who appreciated his efforts at humor. A vision popped into his head, of Amy laughing the loudest when the joke was on her. Her color high, her rosy lips parted . . .

He shook his head to clear the image. Amy would be asleep by now. He hoped to sneak in, get a good night's rest, and be out again before she awakened. Where he would go, in the early hours when most of his class were abed sleeping off their overindulgences of the prior evening, he knew not. But he trusted he could find some way to amuse himself. Perhaps he would breakfast with

Priscilla—she'd turned in early enough to be ready for company come morning.

Entering the house quietly, he ducked into the study to pour himself a brandy before stealing upstairs. No need to wake the servants—he was perfectly capable of putting himself to bed. And he certainly didn't want to take the chance of waking Amy.

He sneaked past her door and almost choked on a mouthful of brandy when he heard the unmistakable sounds of a heartbroken woman crying herself to sleep. Damn, she was still awake. He paused, his fingers drumming on one thigh while he listened.

He reached for the door latch, then jerked back, almost as though it had burned his fingers.

He knew all too well what form any attempts at comfort would ultimately take. Better to let her get this out of her system once and for all, he decided firmly. There was no sense prolonging the agony, or giving her any ideas that things between them might be different.

Colin gritted his teeth and passed by her chamber, then let himself into his own. He could still hear Amy through the adjoining wall. Easing the door shut failed to block the sound. He cursed at himself for allowing Ida to install Amy in the room next to his, but he'd thought he wouldn't be here tonight, so it hadn't occurred to him to interfere.

'Twas pointless to attempt sleeping until Amy nodded off. Her muffled sobs went straight to his heart, and he'd never fall asleep while listening to such a poignant reminder of his guilt. He unbuckled his sword belt and tossed it on the bed, started a fire as quietly as possible, then sat in the nearby chair and slowly sipped his brandy.

He had done this to her. Weak, despicable man that he was, he'd let his emotions rule his head—taken this poor, innocent girl, callously, with no honorable intentions whatsoever, and then abandoned her.

But it had felt so right . . . *she* had felt so good . . .

The brandy flowed in a warm path down Colin's

throat, but it failed to melt the knot in his heart. Draining the glass, he set it on the small table by his chair and stared into the fire, twisting his ring. He wondered how long she'd been crying her eyes out. He tried to picture her: hair a tangled mess, eyes red-rimmed and bloodshot, face puffy and swollen, creased from where she'd pressed it into the sheets to muffle those heart-rending sobs. 'Twas not a pretty picture.

Perhaps he could go to her, soothe her, apologize. She wasn't likely to be attractive to him at the moment, looking so pathetic, nor would she be in an amorous mood. He stood up, shrugged out of his surcoat and removed his waistcoat, the better to put his arms around her—then stopped short.

Who was he fooling?

Telling himself he needed a distraction, he silently finished undressing, slipped into a robe and padded softly out of his bedchamber, intending to head for the library.

When he passed by her door the moaning started. Soft and resonant, the sound snapped his battered heart in two. He was into her chamber before he even thought about it.

She was a long lump under the heavy quilt, her head buried under the covers. He knelt by the bed. "Amy?"

"Colin?" The moaning ceased at once, and she peeked out, then sat up. In the firelight, she looked beautiful—and not at all like he'd expected. Her face was pink and tear streaked, yes, but not even close to the puffy mess he'd imagined when he heard her through the wall.

"What—what are you doing here?" Amy looked over the edge of the bed, taking in Colin's state of undress. He stood up, belting his robe tighter, and her gaze slid down to his bare feet, then slowly back up to his face. She sniffled, dashing the tears from her cheeks with an impatient motion. "How long have you been back?"

"Long enough."

"You've been . . . ?"

"In the next room."

"*Oh, God.* You heard me, then."

She threw herself back to the mattress, ducking her rapidly reddening face under the covers. "Go away, please."

Her body shifted toward him as his weight dropped onto the edge of the bed.

"Go away!"

He didn't.

Amy lay rigid, apparently willing him to leave—or herself to magically vanish—until he folded the blanket back from her face. "I'm sorry," she squeaked out, the tears threatening again.

"*You're* sorry?" he asked, incredulous. He couldn't credit it. He had abandoned her, and she was sorry.

"I've been . . . wallowing in my misery, I guess you could call it. I've . . . not been alone before tonight. Since the fire, I mean. Not all alone, where I was sure no one could hear me. Since my father died." She sniffed and released a long breath. "I thought I was alone . . ."

Colin let out a sigh of relief and amusement at himself. Here he'd been, certain he was all-important in her life, wracked with guilt for hurting her, and she'd not been thinking of him at all.

" 'Tis nothing to be ashamed of." He gently wiped fresh tears away, his fingers an impossibly warm promise on her wet cheeks. "And here I thought you were heartbroken because I left you alone this eve," he teased. "The tears were probably just what you needed. I'm sorry I interrupted."

"I was just feeling sorry for myself," Amy said to her lap.

He believed her. Almost. But there was something in her voice . . . and she wouldn't look at him.

He lifted her chin, forcing her gaze to meet his. "Is that all?"

She nodded. "Though I did wish you were here with me," she admitted softly. Her eyes were wide and trusting, darkened in that compelling way that drew him to her, inexorably.

Without thinking, he leaned over to kiss her, his mouth moving gently on hers in a silent apology. It felt so . . . natural. When he pulled away, her voice dropped to a whisper. "Why did you come back?"

"I couldn't stay away," he confessed hoarsely, knowing 'twas true the moment he said it. "I never made any other plans. I couldn't bear to think of you in my very own house and me somewhere else entirely. But that means not—"

"Shh." Amy placed her hand upon his lips. "Say it not. I know you're promised, Colin Chase, and I've a destiny of my own. Just let me have you for one more night."

She was mirroring his thoughts. 'Twas impossible for him to stay away from her when she was so close by. Absolutely impossible. He'd never been able to resist her pull, *never*. "Four," he corrected. "The shops are closed tomorrow, but you'll order a few gowns on Monday, have them delivered Tuesday, and the next morning we'll leave. We'll have four nights. And no one will ever know."

"But will Priscilla not—"

"Shh," he admonished, borrowing her gesture and placing his fingers on her lips. "I'll take care of it. Don't you worry." In truth, he had no idea how he would keep their liaison secret from Priscilla or anyone else, but he would find a way. "Four nights."

"Four nights," Amy agreed solemnly. Four nights. Four nights more than she had any right to hope for or deserve.

As though to seal their secret pact, Colin lifted her hand and kissed the back, then, his emerald eyes locked on hers, turned it over and kissed the palm, his lips warm and tender. His eyes glittered suggestively, and his tongue came out and teased at the sensitive skin. Amy closed her eyes as glimmering tendrils of feeling swept up her arm and all through her body.

Colin slipped under the quilt and stretched out beside

her, gathered her into his arms, held her close while his head slowly descended to meet hers.

Amy felt like she floated on a puffy, comforting cloud, lulled by the gentle, even pressure of his mouth. Her hand slipped under his robe and explored across his broad back and down his arm. There was that scar; her fingers traced the mark as though they could heal it, along with all his other childhood hurts. Enjoying the warm, smooth expanse of skin, her palm brushed down his side to his hip, and she startled when she realized he wore nothing underneath. Boldly—of its own volition, it seemed—her hand edged around to find him, hard and ready.

Tensing at her intimate touch, he breathed heavily into her mouth, and she tasted warmed, rich brandy as his tongue fenced skillfully with hers. His kiss became fiery and possessive, and her breathing quickened to match his.

For long, sweet minutes he played her body, making her senses spin with the consummate deftness of a master. Somehow her chemise magically disappeared. Every intimate stroke of his fingers, every burning trail of his lips sent currents of desire pulsing through her, imprinting the memory of him so deep in her heart that she knew she'd always carry a part of him with her, though they be parted by a continent and the impossible gulf of lives that were never meant to cross.

Her breath came in little shuddering gasps, and her hands reached for his hips, wordlessly begging him to come inside her and make her complete.

But he complied not with her desperate plea. Instead, he rolled over, bringing her with him, and she lay on top of him, trembling with anticipation as he ran warm, soothing palms over her back and bottom.

When his hands reached down to rearrange her knees, causing her to straddle him in the most strangely intimate manner, Amy's eyes flew open. "Colin?" she whispered, not even knowing what to ask.

"Shh, love," he murmured. "There are many, many

ways, and all are exquisite." And he lifted her hips, guiding himself into her.

As she settled around him, a delicious shudder flowed through her body, and a small part of her marveled at her ability to accommodate his hard, deep penetration. With a bit of incitement and direction from his encouraging hands on her hips, she moved experimentally against him.

She shifted tentatively at first, then faster as she discovered and reveled in her freedom of mobility. Her tumbled tresses played over his chest, a whisper of sensuous silk against his straining body. He pulled her down to him, bringing her lips to his for a slow, deep kiss. But she wanted swift, not slow, this time; she felt wild, and her mouth wandered his raspy cheeks, her teeth nipped at his shoulder.

With a throaty laugh, he pushed her away, so that his questing hands had access all over her inflamed body, caressing her tingling breasts and wandering the length of her back, a hot swath of sensation.

Blood pounded through her veins as he drove himself into her and she met his moves again and again. Through unfocused eyes she saw his face, slick and dark in the wavering firelight, a mask of ecstasy that sent her nerves skittering with pleasure. Then she felt him begin pulsing inside her, and her vision blurred as she exploded in uncontrollable, joyous passion. She soared higher and higher, until she felt her heart burst in a fierce combination of love and agony. His hands slipped up her arms, pulling her close, and she fused her mouth to his and collapsed against him.

Colin kissed her for a long minute, then pressed her cheek to his shoulder. He lay motionless, enjoying her light rose fragrance, listening to her ragged breathing, matched by his own. In the stillness, he could feel her heart thudding, *for him*. And he was seized momentarily by a profound sense of sadness, for what was, and what could not be.

At last she lifted her head, raised a languid hand to

shove the long, tangled ebony strands from her face, and gazed at him wordlessly. Her eyes were deep purple, brimming over with a complicated blend of passion, disbelief, and pain.

Incredible, incredible pain.

He pushed her head back down to his chest, unwilling to look into those anguished eyes just now. "Shh, love," he whispered into her hair. "Think not of it. We've three more nights. 'Tis a lifetime."

'Tis not, she thought. But it had to be. 'Twas all she would ever have.

Colin moved inside her then, an exquisite promise where their two bodies joined. "Think not of it," he repeated, and then he proceeded to make sure she couldn't, with his hands and his mouth and his body and the incredible power he had at his disposal—the power of two souls that were made to be one.

Voices sounded in the corridor. Colin cracked open one eye. The full light of day streamed through the window. Damn, he'd overslept.

Now the servants were up and about, and he'd be hard put to return to his chamber unnoticed, which was imperative if he wished to keep the gossips at bay. The servants' grapevine was well established in London; should he be caught in here with Amy, the news would be common knowledge before the day was out.

He lay still, listening, waiting for the best time to jump out of bed and make a run for it.

Wait. He groaned and rubbed his aching head. Those were not servants' voices, chatting in passing as they went about their daily chores. The voices were louder and much more familiar. Jason's voice, and Ford's and Kendra's. *Bloody hell.* Of all the rotten luck. He'd thought he could spend his days and evenings with Priscilla, his nights with Amy. But 'twould be harder now, perhaps even impossible, to keep her presence a public secret.

Or maybe . . . ah, yes. His mind raced as he slowly

released the breath he'd held since recognizing the voices. His family liked Amy. They'd no knowledge that he'd slept with her at Greystone. They could even act as his cover—*yes*, she'd stayed at Cainewood, after all, and they considered her their friend. 'Twould work—so long as he wasn't discovered sneaking into her chamber at night. They would never approve of that.

The voices faded. Colin slipped out of bed and soundlessly into his robe, watching Amy sleep. The witch looked angelic now, her cheeks a delicate pink, her ebony hair a tangled halo around her head.

He leaned down and brushed a gentle kiss across her lips, then padded to the door and pressed his ear against it.

All clear.

He opened the door a crack, smiling when it didn't creak. Poised to run next door to safety, he took a deep breath and flung it open—to be greeted by Kendra's startled face.

He backed up and slammed the door shut.

"Colin?" Kendra's muffled voice came through the wood. "Is that you?"

He cursed at himself. In one split second, he'd made a complete mess of everything. Why the hell had he not just walked brazenly into the corridor as though nothing were amiss? He could have come up with some plausible excuse for being in Amy's chamber. Now he looked every bit as guilty as he was, no doubt about it.

Kendra hammered on the door. "Colin? What are you doing in there?"

One hand on the door latch, Colin stood rooted to the spot, his gaze riveted on Amy as she moved restlessly under the covers, fighting her way toward consciousness.

Footsteps approached. "What the devil?"

He sagged against the door. Damn, Jason was there now, too.

"Colin is in there." Hearing Kendra's smug tone,

Colin could cheerfully wring her neck. "Hiding. With Amy."

There was nothing for it. With a last, lingering glance at Amy, he opened the door and slipped through, closed it behind him and leaned against it protectively. "Shh!" he said in an exaggerated whisper.

"What were you doing in there?" Kendra hissed back.

He mustered his most convincing whisper. "Amy was having a nightmare. I was just checking on her."

"Is that so?" Kendra crossed her arms. "Then why did you run back into the room when you saw me?"

He wrinkled his brow in what he hoped was a puzzled expression. "Were you there? Amy was calling out again, so I went back inside."

"Poppycock! You think I'd fall for such an old chestnut? I heard not a thing. This looks mighty suspicious."

"What business is it of yours?" Colin spat defensively. "I needn't answer to you, little sister!"

"Amy is my friend, and if you've taken advantage of her, 'tis my duty to see you do right by her, Colin Chase!"

Both of them had long since abandoned whispering. Jason stepped between them and faced Kendra. "If Colin says he was just checking on her, we'll have to take his word for it." Ah! Some male loyalty. Colin smiled.

Until Jason swung around to confront him. "What is she doing here? I thought you were taking her to Dover."

"She wanted to buy some gowns before she left."

"Is that all?"

"Yes, damn it! I spent last evening with Priscilla, at Lady Carson's boring ball." Colin yanked the belt of his robe tighter. "This is ridiculous. I needn't explain myself to you two." He stalked toward his chamber and had his hand on the door latch when Amy's door opened.

"Colin?"

He whirled around. Amy was framed in the half-open doorway, dressed in nothing but a sheet, her hair tangled, her lips still rosy and swollen from his kisses, her expression sleepy and confused. She looked adorable.

Colin was horrified at the sight of her.

He gazed at her beseechingly, vainly hoping she would play along. "Amy! You weren't dreaming again, were you?"

"Dreaming?" Clutching the sheet with one hand, she shoved her hair from her eyes with the other. "What?"

Colin's heart sank as Kendra and Jason swung accusing eyes on him. But he was not yet ready to concede defeat. "The nightmare. The reason I came in to check on you."

"The nightmare?" Amy blinked.

Colin glared at her in exasperation, and she finally woke up enough to absorb his silent message. Her sleep-glazed eyes opened wider. "The nightmare. Oh, yes. I mean, no. 'Tis gone now . . . thank you for your concern." Her gaze dropped to the floor, and her cheeks turned pink. Her fists white knuckled, she tightened the sheet around her body and backed up, easing the door closed.

Kendra's hand shot out and stopped the door. She gave Jason a long, meaningful look before turning to Amy. "I'm surprised to find you here, Amy," she said brightly. "Colin said you needed some clothes?"

"Yes. What are *you* doing here?"

Kendra took Amy's arm, and Amy threw Colin an apologetic glance before turning to his sister.

"We came to London for Christmas shopping. We always do, this time of year." Kendra drew Amy back into the room. "May I come inside? Let me help you dress, and we'll talk." The door shut behind them.

Intending to make a quick escape, Colin opened the door to his chamber, but his older brother swung him around by the shoulder and leveled a stare at him. "Well?"

"Well, what?"

"Give up, Colin. You cannot fob me off that easily."

Jason's lips thinned beneath his mustache. "We all know what went on in that chamber. In that *bed*."

"What of it?" 'Twas pointless to pretend any longer. "We're both adults. Give me three days, and I'll have her delivered out of our lives forever. And talk not to her of it," he warned. "She'd die before she'd admit it, and I'll not have you putting her through that kind of hell."

"I'm too much a gentleman to do anything of the kind," Jason assured him coolly. "Unlike you."

"What the hell is that supposed to mean?"

"Only that you should do right by the lady, and marry her."

"We've been through this . . ." Colin growled in warning.

"Things were different then. 'Twas naught but a suggestion. Now I insist."

"To the devil with you." Colin paused for a deep, calming breath. "I have other plans. I know you expect the Chase name to be beyond reproach, and I'm sorry to disappoint you. I made a mistake, but I don't intend to pay for it the rest of my life."

"I take it you'll not be continuing to make the same '*mistake*' now that we're here?" Jason asked stiffly.

Colin's fists clenched. "That is none of your concern."

"I'm afraid it is," Jason argued. "She's under my roof, under my protection. And she's a wonderful girl who deserves not to be treated like this."

"Treated like *what*?" Colin exploded. "She's been treated very nicely, I'll have you know. Believe me, she's not complained." He dropped his voice, afraid Amy might overhear. "Unlike you, she never expected me to marry her. In case you've forgotten, I'm betrothed—and I've already spent part of Priscilla's dowry, for God's sake. I regret not living up to your standards, but my mind is made up. I hope you'll be able to forgive my besmirching our family."

"Of course. You're my brother."

"I'm glad you see it that way." His jaw set, Colin turned to the door.

"But we all love her . . ." Jason muttered under his breath.

Colin was seized with an unreasoning fury, and a hazy red mist exploded across his vision. Swiveling back, he glared straight into his brother's eyes. "Well, I do *not*." His voice was low and dangerous. "Since you all love her so much, why do you not all take care of her? Just see that she gets to France this time, will you? I'd prefer not to deal with her again." He backed into the chamber. "Do me a favor, and let Priscilla know I returned to Greystone. I have work to do."

He slammed the door and kicked it, then hopped around clutching at his aching, bare toes. Bloody hell, what was happening to him? He was never such a hothead before, banging doors and kicking things. And though his family had always been loud and argumentative, of late his exchanges with them were less good natured and more acrimonious.

And now, in a moment of unthinking anger, he'd thrown away his last three nights with Amy.

Damn.

He had to leave or risk looking like even more of a fool than he was. And he couldn't so much as tell her good-bye. One look at her face and he knew his heart would break, as well as his resolve.

He threw on his clothes and left, cursing himself a hundred times for the hothead, fool, and coward he'd become. No woman had ever had such an effect on him before, and he intended to make certain that no woman ever did again.

Chapter Sixteen

Kendra stood back, casting a discerning eye as Amy twirled around in the sapphire and cream gown. " 'Tis beautiful!"

Nothing like the day dresses Amy had planned to order, the shimmering satin gown's scooped neckline was set off with a wide vanilla lace collar, enriched with lustrous pearls. Matching lace spilled to her wrists from beneath tight three-quarter-length sleeves. The full cream overskirt split and gathered to the back to show off a pearl-embroidered sapphire petticoat. "It makes me feel pretty," Amy admitted, "though I still cannot believe I let you talk me into it. I haven't a clue where I'll wear it."

"Colin will take you to a ball—"

"No, he'll not." Though her initial reactions to Colin's disappearing act had been anger and hurt, in the past two weeks Amy had resigned herself to the facts. "Colin wants nothing to do with me; he's made that perfectly clear. And most certainly not in public."

"He'll come around. Trust me. I know my brother. He's stubborn, but he's not addlepated."

Amy's finger traced a row of embroidered pearls on her skirt. "Colin and I don't belong together, and we both know it, Kendra. I'm destined to be a jeweler in France. 'Tis not only what I want, 'tis what I have to do." She smoothed the slick satin, then turned to the seamstress with a rustling swish. "Unlace me, please, Madame Beaumont."

Amy had been distraught to find Mrs. Cholmley's

shop burned to the ground, the seamstress herself nowhere to be found. Owing to the King's passion for everything French, French dressmakers were all the rage. Kendra had insisted Amy order her wardrobe from Madame Beaumont, London's most sought-after *modiste*.

The seamstress's deft fingers loosened the gown, and Amy wiggled out of it. "The hem is fine. Will it be ready Monday?" She stepped into the butter-yellow gown she'd borrowed from Kendra and pulled it up.

"*Certainement.* Along with everything else." Madame Beaumont turned her around to lace her up in back.

"Thank you." Amy looked pointedly at Kendra. "Do you know if Jason is free Tuesday to take me to Dover?"

"I haven't the faintest idea, but it matters not anyway."

"What is that supposed to mean?" Amy peered into the looking glass, rearranging her long, untamed curls.

"You still have to buy stockings, gloves and ribbons, not to mention shoes for all these gowns," Kendra declared gaily. "Then I want help with my Christmas shopping . . . you'll not be ready to leave for weeks yet—perhaps not until after Christmas."

"Oh, no." Amy shook her head, remembering Colin's original plan to secure her wardrobe within a day or two. Madame Beaumont had taken a full twelve days to create her gowns, and that was after considerable begging and extra payments.

"Oh, yes. You had nothing whatsoever to wear; it takes time to outfit yourself properly. Besides, I'm having too much fun to send you on your way. Why, 'tis almost like having a sister."

"Colin would be furious."

"A pox on Colin! If he weren't so damned obstinate—"

"Marry come up, Kendra! Let us not start that again," Amy groaned.

"Only if you agree to stop talking about leaving so soon."

"Well . . . I did forget about stockings and shoes . . . maybe I'll stay an extra week." Amy stopped fussing with her hair and turned from the mirror to look Kendra in the eye. "But that's all. Colin and I will never happen. I mean it."

"Of course you do," Kendra agreed, if not quite sincerely.

A tinkling bell on the door announced another customer. Amy and Kendra prepared to leave as Madame Beaumont rushed out to greet the newcomer. Her melodious voice drifted back to the fitting salon. "*Bonjour*, Lady Priscilla."

"No, it cannot be . . . ," Kendra whispered under her breath.

"Your gown is ready for the final fitting." Madame's accented words grew louder as she made her way to the curtained salon. "I'll fetch it from the back room. The salon will be vacant in a moment." The curtain parted, and Madame slipped inside. "Mesdemoiselles? Is there aught else I can do for you?"

"We were just leaving," Amy assured her.

The dressmaker stuck her head back into the shop. "*Une minute*, Lady Priscilla, *s'il vous plaît*." She hurried through the salon and into the back, murmuring "*Merci*, mesdemoiselles" as she went.

"Please let it not be her," Kendra whispered, her hand on the curtain's opening.

"What are you talking about?" Amy whispered back.

Kendra froze and stared at her. "Lady Priscilla."

"Lady Priscilla?"

"*Colin's* Lady Priscilla."

"Oh . . ." Amy wasn't at all sure she wanted to meet the illustrious Priscilla, but she'd not much of a choice, as Kendra grabbed her by the arm and pulled her into the shop.

"Priscilla." Amy had never heard Kendra sound so sickly sweet, or seen such a false smile plastered on her face. "How nice to see you."

"Kendra." Priscilla's voice was cultured and emotionless, as though she ran into acquaintances everywhere and nothing ever surprised her. She leaned over and pecked Kendra on the cheek; a casual kiss between ladies was *de rigueur* upon meeting. "I didn't know you were in town. Is Colin back as well?"

"Oh, no. You know how he feels about the City," Kendra said significantly.

"Yes, but he was here barely a day last month."

"Perhaps you should visit him at Greystone." Amy knew that Kendra's suggestion was far from innocent, since she'd told her that Priscilla loathed Colin's rustic home.

"Goodness, not in the state it is in. Although I'd consider an invitation to Cainewood . . . Who do we have here?" Priscilla's eyes sought out Amy standing halfway behind Kendra, rooted to the spot and praying she'd not be noticed.

"Forgive me for failing to introduce you," Kendra said smoothly, stepping to the side and subjecting Amy to Priscilla's cool gray gaze. "This is Mrs. Amethyst Goldsmith. Lady Priscilla Hobbs."

Amy watched Priscilla look her over and instantly dismiss her as untitled and insignificant. "I'm glad of your acquaintance," Priscilla said with a small bored bow.

Amy opened her mouth to respond, but no words came out. The sight of Priscilla rendered her speechless. God in heaven, if Priscilla were Colin's idea of the perfect woman . . .

Titles aside, she was Amy's complete antithesis. Priscilla was tall where Amy was diminutive, fair where she was rosy, straight where she was curvy, and cool where she was emotional. Priscilla's hair was blond, short, and styled, where hers was dark, long, and unruly. And those were just the obvious differences.

Amy had not known 'twas possible to hate a virtual stranger. She felt like a sorry example of a human being, but she couldn't seem to help herself. If she believed in witchcraft, she'd surely be casting a spell forthwith.

Kendra nudged Amy with a discreet elbow. "I-I'm glad of your acquaintance," Amy managed to return.

"She's a friend of yours?" Priscilla's pretty arched brows drew together in puzzlement. She looked directly at Kendra, as though Amy were not there, which Amy wished were the case.

"She's been staying with us since the fire. She lost her family and their jewelry shop."

"Their shop?" Priscilla's expression showed just what she thought of the Chases befriending a merchant, but the look also radiated annoyed indulgence—as though the Chases were known to be rather eccentric.

"We've known Amy for some time," Kendra stated defensively. As her fingers moved to the center of her neckline, where she'd pinned the bow-shaped jeweled galant that was her gift from Amy, a glint came into her eyes. "Our family has acquired much jewelry from hers. Colin especially."

"Colin?" Priscilla frowned. "Colin has never given me any jewelry."

Though she wondered why her friend was deliberately misleading Priscilla—Kendra must know Colin had only bought her locket and the ring for himself—Amy decided to play along. "I can assure you that Colin has often purchased jewelry, since he always asks for my assistance."

"Well then, perhaps *Lord Greystone* is waiting until after we are wed to gift me with it," Priscilla sniffed.

"Perhaps."

The single word was a challenge, but apparently Priscilla chose not to see it that way, since she looked straight past Amy to where the seamstress waited between the parted curtains. "Madame Beaumont, you are ready?"

"*Certainement*, my lady."

" 'Twas nice seeing you, Kendra," Priscilla said on her way into the fitting salon. No such pleasantries were directed at Amy, who evidently was beneath common courtesy.

" 'Twas nice meeting you, Lady Priscilla," Amy called out pointedly, if insincerely. But the curtain closed before Priscilla could reply, assuming such was her intention. Somehow, Amy thought not.

"What a rude woman," she whispered to Kendra. "*That* is your brother's intended?"

"In all her glory." Kendra laughed, coming up to take Amy's arm as they headed into the street.

"I suppose this has been a bad day for her," Amy suggested, searching for a possible excuse for Priscilla's behavior.

"I doubt it. I call her Priscilla Snobs, you know." They shared a companionable giggle before Kendra continued, "It makes Colin furious."

"Whatever does he see in her, I wonder?"

"You're not the only one."

Seeing their approach, Jason's coachman rushed to open the door. "We'd like to visit the New Exchange now," Kendra informed him before climbing into her brother's wood and leather carriage.

"As you wish, my lady." The coachman took her by the elbow to help her in.

Amy followed slowly, still thinking about Priscilla. She'd not known what to expect, but Priscilla had turned out to be so perfectly upper class that any lingering unrealistic dreams Amy had harbored were swept away. No amount of heart-pounding attraction, she thought, could entice Colin Chase to trade such an aristocratic paragon for plain old Amy Goldsmith.

'Twas a depressing thought, even though she couldn't wed Colin whether he wanted her or not. As she ruminated on it, she almost missed the voice that called from down the street. The shocked, all-too-familiar voice.

"Amy? Amy! Can that be you?"

"I wish they'd hurry and rebuild the Royal Exchange," Kendra lamented from inside the coach. " 'Twas so much better than the New Exchange."

Amy hesitated only a moment before ducking inside to join her. Meeting Priscilla was enough excitement for one day, she told herself to assuage her guilt. She pulled the door shut before the startled coachman had a chance to close it.

Inside, Amy tugged the curtains over the windows, cursing the heavy traffic that perpetually clogged London's streets.

"What is happening, Amy?"

"Shh! Say not my name out loud." Amy bit her lip. "Oh, why can we not get going?"

The coach gave a small lurch as it started into the center of the busy street, but 'twas too late. *Bang! Bang!* A fist hit the door, and the driver reined in the horses.

"Amy! I know you're in there!"

"Hey!" The driver jumped to the street with an audible thump. "Keep your hands off Lord Cainewood's coach!"

Through a slit in the curtains, Amy glimpsed carrot-colored hair, but she needed no confirmation. Having worked with him for five years, she would have recognized Robert Stanley's voice anywhere.

"I give not a damn whose coach this is!" she heard him yell. "Amethyst Goldsmith is inside, and I must speak with her."

'Twas no use concealing herself any longer. The door opened and the driver asked, "Mrs. Goldsmith, know you this gentleman?"

Amy decided to pretend she was surprised. "Robert!" She jumped out and wrapped her arms around the freckled man in a hug that was halfhearted at best, but she hoped would be convincing since she'd never been overly affectionate with him. " 'I'm so glad to see you're fine—I've been wondering about you," she gushed. And 'twas true, in a way. Robert had been in her life a long time; she was relieved to see him whole and healthy.

"Your letter said not where you were," Robert said doubtfully, setting her away from himself. "Did you at least tell your Aunt Elizabeth? I wrote to her to find out, but haven't heard back yet."

"I wrote to her," Amy said slowly. God in heaven . . .

it hadn't occurred to her that Robert would contact her aunt. He would have found her even in Paris. She'd not credited him with being that resourceful.

No, she corrected herself, she'd known all along that Robert was intelligent, if a bit unimaginative. The truth was, she had done her best not to think of him and what he would do at all. "I'm sorry," she said now, meaning it. "I should have found you to discuss matters. I wasn't thinking straight. I was . . . mourning. Devastated." She took a deep breath. "Wh-what have you been doing?"

Robert shuffled his feet on the slushy ground. "Looking for you. Helping my father a little. Drinking with my old chums at the King's Arms, mostly." Not only drinking, Amy surmised, but eating his troubles away as well. He'd put on weight in the three months since she'd seen him.

Suddenly, he grabbed her by the shoulders. "I vow and swear, I cannot believe I've found you. I thought I'd never see you again."

When Amy didn't respond, he paused, considering. "Were you *ever* going to try to find me?" he finally asked in a slow, suspicious tone.

Amy looked down at the street. She wished he'd let go of her, but he had her shoulders in an iron grip. A faint, stale smell of ale washed over her; she could taste it in her mouth. "Of course. I—I just got to the City," she hedged. "I've been staying with friends. Out in the country."

"Friends? Friends I don't know about?"

She lifted her head and shot him a bold look. "There is much you don't know of me, Robert."

"I am coming to see that," he returned, dropping his arms to fold them across his chest. "Our wedding date passed, you know. We will have to reschedule."

Amy stared at him. "Did you not read my letter?"

"Wedding date?" Emerging from the shadowed corner of the coach, Kendra stuck out her head. "Amy?"

Amy turned to her gratefully; this talk of weddings

was making her ill. "Kendra, this is Robert Stanley. Robert, my friend Kendra."

He aimed a curt nod at Kendra. "This is your friend?" he asked Amy bluntly. "The one you've been staying with?"

"Yes."

"Fancy coach." He said it like it was a crime to own one.

"It belongs to my brother," Kendra explained.

"Lord Something-or-other?"

"The Marquess of Cainewood."

Robert blinked and frowned, as though he were trying to remember something, then gave a quick shake of his head. He turned back to Amy. "So . . . when do you want to get married?"

"I don't want to get married," she said quietly.

"You were promised to me." Robert's voice was low and deep and even more quiet than hers. Too quiet.

Though Amy looked at him defiantly, she was shaking inside. She didn't want to hurt him, but she had to make him understand she had no intention of becoming his wife. "My father is dead. Everything has changed for me. And—and I don't have to marry you."

"Damn it, Amy, you're supposed to be mine. I waited and waited. The shop was supposed to be mine, too, but now 'tis gone. The inventory . . ." His eyes lit up. "Where is the inventory?"

Amy swallowed hard. "I don't *want* to marry you, Robert."

"Where is the inventory?" Robert's jaw was set. His pale blue eyes flashed with menace.

"I don't have it." Her voice wavered, but 'twas not quite a lie. She didn't have it here.

"You know where it is, do you not?" He took a step closer. "I went back to look, but found not a trace. No molten metal, no diamonds in the ashes. And diamonds don't turn to ash. Where is it, Amy?"

"I don't have it," she repeated shakily. "I—I have to go now." She turned to enter the carriage.

He grabbed her by the upper arm, swung her around and dug his fingers in painfully. "The inventory is *mine.* I worked five years for it. Where is it?"

Amy winced and threw a worried glance at Kendra, spurring her friend into action. Kendra planted herself firmly in the doorway of the coach. "Leave her alone!" she yelled at the top of her lungs. "She doesn't have it!"

Visibly shocked at this outburst, Robert turned on Kendra. "You stay out of this! 'Tis not your concern."

Kendra's eyes narrowed recklessly. She came down from the carriage in a flash, curling one hand into a fist, which she propelled expertly into Robert's face. "Leave her alone, I tell you!"

Robert's pale eyes bugged out, and he dropped Amy's arm to grasp his rapidly reddening jaw.

With a triumphant grin, Kendra grabbed Amy's freed hand. "I haven't three brothers for nothing!" she informed nobody in particular, then jumped into the carriage, pulling Amy after her.

Amy stuck her head out and pinned Robert with a disdainful look. "Five years? My family worked five *centuries* for that jewelry. You learned your craft and were paid a fair wage, as well as room and board. I owe you no more, and you'll never have more, Robert Stanley!" She slammed and latched the coach door.

Robert beat on it with both fists. "You're mistaken, Amethyst Goldsmith! I'll have the jewelry yet, and you as well. You just wait!"

Inside the darkened carriage, Amy hunched over on the bench seat, covering her head with her hands so she'd not hear him. After what seemed an interminable wait, the coach jerked and started out into the middle of the street.

Amy sat up. "I'm sorry about that," she apologized, massaging her upper arm. She was certain to have marks from Robert's fingers.

" 'Tis not every day I get to practice my boxing." Kendra's laugh was shaky. She rubbed her bruised fist ruefully. "God's blood, was he ever surprised!" She pushed open the curtains, and sunlight flooded the cabin. "Are you all right?"

Amy nodded mournfully. Suddenly, she burst out, "I cannot believe what a perfect beast he was! And to think I almost married him." She shuddered.

"You never told me you were betrothed."

"I wanted to forget it. I never wanted to wed him in the first place—'twas all my father's doing."

"He's so . . . he doesn't fit with you." Kendra's face turned contemplative. "He looked as though he might have an engaging grin when he's not angry, but he's short, bulky . . . soft-looking. I cannot imagine you as his wife. Now, you and—"

"He always scared me a little," Amy interrupted Kendra's musings. "He lived with us as our apprentice for five years, but we were promised from the outset."

"Did you like him at all?"

"At first, until I got to know him. He had definite ideas of what he wanted in a wife, and they meshed not with mine. Still, I could have done worse, and my father was insistent." She shuddered again. "I'll *never* marry him, especially not after this," she declared vehemently. *"Never, never, never."*

Kendra frowned. "Your aunt won't expect you to marry him, will she?"

Amy thought a moment. Aunt Elizabeth was a warm, motherly type who wanted to see everyone around her happy. And she'd never been particularly fond of Robert. "No," she said at last. "No, I believe she will not. Or my uncle, either."

"Then you've nothing to worry about. Robert knows not where to find you while you're staying with us—"

"And I'll be gone soon. Very soon." The sooner the better, she thought morosely. Her time in England was really at an end.

Kendra leaned over to touch her hand, then suddenly grinned. "Five centuries?"

Amusement flickered in Amy's eyes. "Well . . . perhaps I exaggerated, just a little." Her eyes met Kendra's then, and they both burst out laughing.

Robert's alcohol-laden brain was trying to tell him something. Surrounded by his friends at the King's Arms, he was drinking too much and eating too little. He felt sick. Still, something in the back of his head was working its way out.

Kendra. Kendra. He took another swig. Was there not—*yes!* That bastard Greystone had a sister named Kendra. They'd come into the shop only once, but the way the man had looked at Amy, and Amy's flushed reaction, still burned in his memory. He'd not paid the sister any attention, but this could easily be the same woman.

He rubbed his aching jaw. This Kendra, with her iron fist, looked not much like Greystone. Her hair was dark red while Greystone's was black, and her eyes were a lighter green than his, too. She was petite, and the bastard was tall—so tall that Robert had felt intimidated, although Greystone had ignored him. Well, the sister intimidated him, too. Now.

Yes, she must be his sister. He squinted his bloodshot eyes, trying to better picture them both. They shared the same facial bone structure, he was sure of it, and the same shape eyes. And they both had the same cocky self-assurance.

And they were both "friends" of Amy's.

Amy. Beautiful, elusive Amy. She had promised to marry him. For five long years he had sat at her father's bench, with the promise of Amy and her riches in time.

The time had come. She was in London. If she'd not come with him willingly, he would have to force her. There were places he'd heard about, "privileged" churches where a man could marry a woman without posting banns, without taking out a license.

Without her consent.

He turned to the man next to him, one of the many who spent their evenings in this popular middle-class tavern. "Hey," he said, surprised to find his voice wavering, "have you knowledge of a privileged church? Not too far?"

"St. Trinity, in the Minories," the man answered.

"St. James in Duke's Place is another," a man sitting across the table put in. "They're the only two, I think. Claim they're outside the jurisdiction of the Bishop of London and can therefore make their own rules. M'sister was wed at St. James."

"Against her will?"

"Nah. She was just in a hurry. Got a predated certificate, too, so the babe wasn't early."

Robert nodded, digesting the information. Both Duke's Place and the Minories were nearby, just outside the old Roman wall. "I'll not need a license or anything?"

"Nah. Just two crowns for the curate and a couple of witnesses." Not a problem, thought Robert, imagining the stash of coins, gold, and gems that awaited him upon his marriage.

His stomach roiled, protesting another swig of ale. He was sorry it had come to this, sorry she wasn't wedding him of her own free will. But she was his due, and once the deed was done she'd get used to the idea. She'd come to his bed and bear his children. Eventually. She'd always been a cold one, anyway—he'd never expected much of her sexually.

And when she was his, everything she owned would be, too.

He looked up at his two drinking companions. "Either of you heard of Lord Greystone?"

"Nay, never heard of him," the man next to him muttered.

"Nah." The man across from him shook his head.

"Hey," he called out, his voice slurred. "Anyone here know a Lord Greystone? Colin Something-or-other?"

"Chase," someone called out. "Colin Chase." The man wore a long, crimped periwig and was dressed a tad more stylishly than the average patron of the King's

Arms; Robert believed he could be acquainted with Colin Chase, or at least know of him.

"He got a brother? The Marquess of something?"

"Cainewood. The Marquess of Cainewood. Jason Chase."

"Right." Pleased with his powers of deduction, Robert paused for another swallow and dragged his sleeve across his mouth. "Anyone know where he lives? I'll pay someone"—he burped loudly—"ten shillings to show me where he lives."

There was a scraping of benches as men rose, eager to collect ten shillings for such an easy job. Robert wasn't so sotted, however, that he didn't realize most of them probably didn't know Jason Chase's house from the London Bridge. "You," he said. He rose unsteadily and pointed at the man who had answered his questions. "You're the one. Come along."

Gesturing for the man to follow him, he stumbled through the door and out into the street. His companion pressed himself up against the wall as Robert paused to throw up in the gutter, his vomit barely adding to the refuse and filth already there. Robert stood up, swiped a sleeve across his mouth, and let loose a loud belch. "That's better. Let's go."

Shaking his head in disgust, the man led the way all the same. Ten shillings was ten shillings.

Chapter Seventeen

Amy jerked awake, struggling against a hand over her mouth—a grimy hand, smelling of ale and sweat and vomit. She gagged.

"Hush," came a hiss in her ear. "Make a sound and I'll kill you, I swear it. I've got a knife."

She froze at the sound of Robert's voice, not believing him for a second. Jeweler's tools were the closest thing to a weapon he ever touched. He'd not know what to do with a knife if someone walked up and put it in his hand.

She lashed out at him, scratching at his face and kicking her legs wildly. He fell awkwardly on top of her, pinning her legs beneath his heavier ones. Her arms came around, and she sank her fingernails into his fleshy back.

"Damn it, Amy, I didn't want it to be like this," Robert whispered fiercely. His body held her crushed to the bed as he groped with a hand in the darkened room. Something fell and rolled along the floor. "Hell." He came up on one elbow, then her head exploded in pain.

One second she was fighting for her life, and the next second the world went black.

Robert pulled himself off her, panting from unaccustomed exertion. The heavy candlestick thudded to the floor as he dropped to his knees and scrabbled under the bed for the candle. When his fingers closed around it, he ran to the fireplace to light it and rushed back to examine Amy.

A thin trail of blood ran from her scalp down her

forehead. For a minute Robert panicked, searching incompetently for a pulse. He pressed his ear to her chest, heard her heart beating, felt the rise and fall of her even breathing. *Thank God.* Dead, she was useless to him. He needed to marry her to get his hands on her fortune.

He ripped long strands of the sheet and tied one around her head as a crude bandage, used another as a gag, and a third to bind her hands together. Hoping she'd cooperate and walk when she awakened, he left her feet unbound.

Wrapping her awkwardly in one of the blankets, he grabbed her under the arms and tugged her limp form off the bed. He'd not counted on the dead weight. Petite Amy felt heavy as a horse. Pausing twice to rewrap the blanket around her, he dragged her to the open window, where a ladder waited.

With a mighty effort, he hefted her inert body over one shoulder and ducked out, feeling for the ladder with one unsteady foot. Balancing her precariously, he lurched down a rung at a time, more than relieved when the hackney driver met him halfway and took over his heavy burden.

The driver dumped Amy onto the bench seat, and Robert climbed inside. "You know where to go," he growled under his breath, sending the man up top with a wave of his hand. He wedged himself next to Amy and fought to catch his breath as the cab squeaked through the quiet streets.

The sidelamp threw light into the interior, casting a yellowish glow onto Amy's slack face. Thankfully, her wound was superficial, the bandage stained but the bleeding stopped. He tucked the errant blanket tighter around her, then slumped against the side of the coach, relieved and exhausted.

A bellman called the hour of midnight, the words resonating through the thick, clammy fog. Three-quarters of an hour later, the springless cab bumped through Aldgate and into Duke's Place, rattling to a stop in front of St. James.

The door was unlocked, it being a church, but no one was inside. Robert walked to the altar, his footsteps on the stone floor echoing in the deserted chamber. Votive candles were set about the sanctuary, flickering, contributing to the eerie atmosphere.

Robert had never been in an empty church before. The truth was, he'd not been in a church at all in recent memory. In his opinion, life was for living, and there would be ample time for regret and penance when he was older. He shivered.

"Anyone here?" he called, half-expecting the figure on the cross to look down and answer him. But it didn't, of course. 'Twas silent save for his own breathing, sounding louder and louder as he became more agitated. The place was giving him the creeps. Everyone knew that dead clergymen were buried under the floors of these churches, and suddenly Robert was certain one was about to pop up and grab him. He turned and ran down the aisle and out the door.

"No one's there," he yelled at the hackney driver, as though it were his fault.

The driver shrugged. " 'Tis Saturday evening."

'Twas actually Sunday morning by now, but Robert didn't bother arguing. Besides, what if someone needed a priest on a Saturday night? They must be available, somewhere. "Take me to St. Trinity, in the Minories," he ordered before jumping into the cab and kicking the half-door shut.

The driver shrugged again, then took a swig of the brandy he carried with him against the winter chill. He cared not if the gentleman wasted his time. Robert had promised him a full evening's pay, and he'd quoted double his usual night's take and demanded half in advance.

St. Trinity was a scant three blocks away, much too close for Robert, still unrecovered from the last stop. The deserted streets contributed to his unease. Londoners stayed inside at night, venturing outdoors only for necessary travel, and then generally with an escort of footmen and linkboys to light the way. The Act of 1661 required citizens to hang lamps outside their houses on dark nights, but no one complied; the unlit, foggy streets were spooky, and Robert felt nervous and shaky. He forced himself to get out of the cab and slowly walked up to the massive church doors.

Inside, St. Trinity looked much like St. James. His feet made a shuffling sound as he crossed the threshold, and his heart hammered in his chest as he scanned the flickering, shadowed walls. When a door at the other end opened, he jumped, letting out a little shriek.

A florid, balding man stuck his head into the sanctuary and smiled. "Feel free to pray here, my son. Problems seem smaller when you share them with Our Lord."

"I—I've come to get married, Father."

The curate stepped out into the sanctuary, and Robert saw that he was plump and healthy, evidently well fed and cared for, unlike most parish priests. Obviously, the curate of a privileged church enjoyed a highly lucrative position. The man did not look frightening in the least. The whole chamber seemed to lighten, and Robert heaved a sigh of relief.

The clergyman looked pleased. "Ahh, I see. Have you need of a—shall we say 'special'—certificate?"

"Nay, the date matters not. But the lady is . . . reluctant."

" 'Tis none of my concern. The price will be three crowns."

"I heard tell it was two." In truth, Robert would have paid ten crowns or more, and gladly, for securing Amy and her riches.

"Two and a half, then. Special, for you."

"Done." Robert half-turned toward the door, intending to fetch Amy posthaste and get it over with. He hoped mightily that she was awake, or that 'twould not matter either way to the curate.

"I'll see you Monday morning, then," the curate called out.

"Monday? I—can we not do it now?"

The clergyman smiled wider, showing large, uneven

teeth. "The Sabbath approaches, my son. There will be no weddings until Monday."

"But—"

"Bring with you two witnesses and a pistol—'twill make it go faster." He winked at Robert. "I have five other weddings Monday, so come early or expect to wait. Good evening." He disappeared, shutting the door behind him, leaving Robert standing openmouthed.

Where was he going to get a pistol? And even more important, whatever would he do with Amy until Monday? He cursed himself, loudly, for acting without planning first, then clapped a hand over his mouth. Surely cursing in a house of the Lord was much worse than cursing elsewhere. He bolted for the street.

His heart was pounding, but it took him no more than a few moments to notice the hackney's door was wide open and he could hear someone running down the street. Still, he wasted precious seconds before actually realizing Amy had escaped.

She ran as fast as she could, clutching the blanket in front where her hands were tied together. It flapped behind her, floating in the draft, not providing any warmth to speak of. But she held on to it for dear life, knowing it could save her from freezing to death later on, if she couldn't find shelter.

With every jarring step, pain burst in her throbbing head. Racing along the scum-lined street, she stumbled over rocks and debris. A sharp sliver sliced into one bare foot, but she scarcely noticed. She developed a stitch in her side as she turned the corner onto Whitechapel, but she scarcely noticed that, either. She was too preoccupied with the pounding feet she heard approaching—feet that were bound to be Robert's, since she'd seen no other soul in the gray, foggy night.

She ducked into a narrow space between two buildings and hunched over there, trying with little success to maneuver the blanket around her shivering shoulders. The nightgown she'd borrowed from Kendra was all but useless against the winter cold.

Robert ran past, panting heavily, a dark shadow against the foggy background. She held her breath and flattened herself against one of the walls, trying to make herself invisible.

As his echoing footsteps faded away, Amy let out her breath. The stench of rotting refuse permeated her nostrils, making her want to gag. Still, she forced herself to stay motionless, pressed against the rough, cold stone wall for what seemed like hours, but she knew was only minutes. As the chill seeped into her body, penetrating to her very bones, she listened. She heard a baby crying, a couple's raised, angry voices, her own heart thudding in her chest. The footsteps didn't return.

Minutes ticked by. She grew colder still; she would have to find shelter soon. Barefoot, clad in only a thin white nightgown and blanket, gagged, and with her wrists bound, she imagined herself to be quite a sight. Regardless, someone would doubtless help her, take her in for the night, if only she could get to their front door. The arguing couple was her best bet—not an attractive alternative, but she was in no position to be choosy.

She waited a few more agonizing minutes, while her heart slowed to its normal rhythm, her breathing became more regular, and her shivering escalated to new heights. Finally convinced she had escaped successfully, she decided to venture forth.

Her deep, fortifying breath created a cloud in the frigid air. She peeled herself away from the wall and limped to the edge of the buildings. Her eyes now adjusted to the unlit London streets, she stuck her head out and looked both ways, seeing nothing that alarmed her, although she could see not far through the fog.

She thought the bickering couple lived across the narrow street, down Whitechapel to the right. The hazy yellow of a lit window in approximately the right place confirmed her conclusions.

Steeling herself to leave her cramped, freezing cold haven of safety, she counted. One, two, three . . . *now.*

She bolted across the street, angling toward the comforting light of the window. Suddenly, a rickety noise sliced through the blanket of fog as a coach came barreling around the corner. Releasing a whimper of fright that was muffled by the gag in her mouth, she dropped her blanket in the middle of the street and, reaching the other side, took a sharp left, running the opposite direction of the coach's travel.

'Twas no use. Before the hackney even screeched to a halt, Robert jumped off and gained on her immediately.

A fierce tug on the back of her nightgown brought her stumbling to her knees, ineffectively breaking her fall with her elbows and bound fists. Numb with cold and shock, she scarcely registered the new scrapes. Moments later, Robert threw himself on top of her, forcing her facedown into the dirt and knocking the wind out of her lungs.

"Hell and furies!" he hollered. "Did you think you could actually escape me?"

Even had she not been gagged and breathless, she'd not have answered him. Darkness had closed in again.

Morning sun fought to illuminate the room through a small dirt-streaked window. Amy struggled toward consciousness, blinking in the dimness. Although she was alone and ungagged, her hands were still bound together. Beneath the dirty, threadbare blanket, her feet were tied to the bedposts.

She lay still, taking stock of herself. Her head ached, her knees and elbows burned, her body felt stiff and sore, bruised all over. She needed a chamber pot, but that would have to wait. Diminished but still whole, she was determined to fight Robert to her last breath.

Her scraped elbows were roughly crusted over with new scabs that cracked and opened when she moved. She licked her dry lips, tasting coppery blood in the corners where the gag had rubbed them raw. She tested the bonds on her wrists, twisting them experimentally. They chafed horribly, the skin red and abraded. But, with patience and her teeth, she was sure she could untie the cloth strips. This time, however, she would have a plan before she did anything.

The room gave no clue to her location. The window was so obliterated with dirt that she had no view of the outside. Dark shadows against the panes told her 'twas barred, anyway. The plain chamber contained nothing more than her flea-ridden bed, a rough table, and two chairs on a filthy, bare wooden floor. A paltry fire gave off little warmth and a fair amount of smoke, laid as it was in a blackened fireplace that had long been in need of cleaning.

She had no memory of her arrival here. She thought she had been in Whitechapel when she made the aborted attempt at freedom, but she could be a day's ride from there for all she was aware of the lapse of time. She would have to wait for Robert's return before she could begin to plot her escape.

She closed her eyes and prayed for the oblivion of sleep.

Chapter Eighteen

Colin leaned low over the saddle, his hands clenched on the reins, the paper crumpled in one fist. 'Twas not possible to read it while Ebony's pounding hooves ate up the miles of rutted road, but Ford's scribbled words were burned into his brain.

Amy is missing. Come immediately.

His heart had been hammering since he'd set eyes on the cryptic note. He'd wasted no time setting out for London, his fevered imagination conjuring up scenes featuring every possibility, from Amy deciding to leave on her own, to Amy lying dead in a ditch, a pistol wound in her chest.

The wind whipped past as he barreled along, praying to a God he rarely addressed, save in the questionable form of a favorite curse or two. He made the most outlandish promises, bargaining with the Almighty for Amy to be returned unharmed. He would attend church every Sunday (no one did). He would give all his riches to the needy (what riches?). He would somehow convince Priscilla to marry him immediately, and never spare a single thought for Amethyst Goldsmith again.

This last promise was the most unlikely of all.

He'd been fighting with himself for months now. 'Twas a losing battle. As he shot through the City gates, one spurred boot nicked a vegetable barrow. He turned in the saddle, watched lemons and artichokes plop to the muddy street, yelled an apology to the vendor . . . and finally admitted to himself that he couldn't be happy living without Amy.

The truth was it mattered little whether they were parted by his own choice or the actions of a faceless criminal. The thought of whiling away his years at Greystone without her—whether she was growing old with her aunt, married to another man, or cold in her grave—made him sick in his gut. She was meant to be his.

He loved her.

Bloody hell, when had that happened? The admission was wrenched from a realm beyond reason or logic. His head reeling, he fought for breath, swearing to God and himself that he would personally see to her safe return. After that, they would come to some kind of arrangement. Priscilla would have to understand.

Understand *what,* he knew not . . .

Ebony was lathered long before he reached Lincoln's Inn Fields, but he merely tossed the reins to a groom instead of rubbing the horse down personally as he normally would after a hard ride. He threw open the front door of the town house and raced into the marble entry, heedless of the mud on his boots.

"Jason! Ford! Kendra!"

"Colin, thank God you're here." Kendra appeared from around the corner and threw herself at him. "We've been beside ourselves with worry."

"Jason is not home." Ford bounded down the stairs. "He left early this morning, before we discovered—"

"Discovered what?" Colin pulled Kendra's arms from around his neck and set her away. "Tell me what you know, *now,*" he demanded.

She bit her lip. "Yesterday Amy and I visited Madame Beaumont. When we came out—"

"—Amy ran into a man named Robert, and they had a huge row," her twin finished for her.

Colin held up a hand. "Robert Stanley?"

"I cannot remember his surname," Kendra said, "but he was her father's apprentice, and he was planning to marry her."

"Robert Stanley," Colin forced through clenched teeth. "Go on."

Kendra took a deep breath and beckoned him up the stairs. "When she told him she'd no wish to marry him, he lost control. He seized her and threatened her—"

"—and Kendra punched him in the jaw." Ford paused on the landing. "Can you not just picture it?"

Kendra's eyes flashed green fire. "This is *serious*, Ford! And 'twas clearly a half-witted move on my part. Amy is gone."

"What happened then?" Colin snapped.

She turned down the corridor. "He was shocked—and gravely injured, I'm hoping. In any case, he let go of Amy, and we jumped into the coach and rode away."

"But not"—Ford stopped, his hand on the latch to Amy's door—"before he claimed he would have Amy's jewelry and Amy as well. It looks like he meant it." He pushed open the door.

Colin was struck by a blast of cold air.

Momentarily dazed, he walked to the open window and peered outside. Below, a ladder rested against the house. He swung back around. The fire had long since burned out, and judging by the frigid temperature of the chamber, the window had been open for some time. Bedclothes littered the floor, and the blanket was missing.

"We left it as we found it," Kendra whispered. "Look."

Colin followed her gesture to the bed. Spots of blood dotted the sheets.

He dropped onto the mattress. A rose scent—Amy's scent—wafted into the air. "You think he's made off with her?"

Kendra knelt at his feet and rested her head against his knee. " 'Tis the only explanation. Amy would never leave without telling us. And the blood . . . she might be dead. Oh, Colin."

One hand absently rubbed her bright curls while his other fingers traced the dark red spots on the sheet.

Blood. Amy's blood. His stomach knotted, and he couldn't think straight.

Ford paced the room. "As usual, Kendra, you're jumping to conclusions. There are but a few drops of blood here, and none trailing toward the window—I doubt she was seriously injured, let alone murdered. Why would this fellow want to kill her, anyway? You said he wanted to marry her."

"But she wasn't agreeable," Kendra wailed. "I'm telling you, he was furious."

"Look here." Ford pointed to Amy's trunk in the corner of the room. "He's not taken the jewelry, has he?"

"No . . ."

"Perhaps he means only to convince her to marry him."

"By wounding her? For God's sake, Ford, *think*. He's taken her. If she's not dead, he obviously intends to ransom her, for her own jewelry or our money."

With a violent shake of his head, Colin regained his senses. He rose and went to the window, shutting it with a resounding *bang*. "I doubt he intends to ransom her. He cannot be at all certain we'd pay—we're not even related." Colin's mind raced. In truth, he knew not whether to be relieved or alarmed that Amy's abductor seemed to be her ex-betrothed, rather than some crazed criminal. "Are you sure he knows where the jewelry is?"

"No." Kendra stood up slowly. "No. She didn't actually admit to having it."

"I assumed as much." Ford shot a meaningful look at the trunk. "Otherwise, he'd not have left it here."

Kendra stamped her foot. "All right, we bow to your scientific logic. What do *you* think this is about, then?"

"My guess is, he plans to compromise her, figuring she'll agree to wed him once the deed is done. Then he'll own her fortune outright."

"He'd not do that!"

"Grow up, Kendra. It happens all the time."

"She cannot be compromised; she's not even a vir—"

"This Robert doesn't know that, does he?" Ford shook his head, slanting her a condescending look.

Her face reddened. "But—"

"Ford is right." Colin's voice was a command. The twins turned and stared at him.

Under the circumstances, his imagined scenarios of violent death seemed improbable. On the other hand, Ford's conclusion of rape followed by coerced marriage seemed chillingly possible.

Colin took deep breaths to keep from retching at the thought. Hands fisted at his sides, he strode to the door, then whirled to face his brother and sister. "Stay here, in case we're wrong and a ransom note arrives. I'll be back. With Amy."

The screech of a key working a rusty lock brought Amy instantly alert. *Finally.*

Robert slunk in and shut the door behind him, taking pains to lock it before he turned to face her. His pale blue eyes impaled her as he slowly slipped the key into the pocket of his loose breeches. If only she could reach that key, she'd be halfway out of here. But 'twas impossible at the moment.

Patience, she reminded herself, forcing herself to breathe in a slow, measured rhythm.

He looked much the worse for wear. His shirt was torn, his fawn-colored breeches wrinkled and filthy. His hair hung in lanky strings, and the freckles on his face were obscured by a thin coat of grime. Then again, Amy told herself wryly, she was hardly in a position to pass judgment. Clad in nothing but a ripped nightgown, bruised and bloody, 'twas not likely she presented an appealing picture herself.

"How are you?" he finally asked.

Her answer was a scornful roll of her eyes. Regardless of her firm decision not to agitate him, she couldn't bring herself to engage in conversation as though her situation were ordinary.

"Very well then, are you ill?"

"No."

"Are you injured?"

"Not mortally."

"Good. I've some errands to run. I just wanted to make certain you were all right before I left." He turned to do so.

She couldn't let him go so fast. She knew nothing that could help her make plans. "Where am I?" she blurted out.

He hesitated, then turned back. "At an inn," he answered slowly.

"But where?"

"It doesn't signify. You'll be here only until tomorrow."

"And then?"

"I'll let you know later. When I'm prepared."

For what? The words stuck in her throat; 'twould be useless to ask. "Wait!" she called when he turned to leave again. "I have to . . . you know . . . use the chamber pot."

His lips puckered, but he strode to the bed and reached underneath, retrieving a dusty, chipped pot. When he lifted the edge of her blanket, Amy gasped; she'd rather lie in a wet bed than have him assist her in this matter.

She moved her bound wrists to press down on the coverlet. "Robert, no!"

"Did you honestly think I would untie you?"

"Just my hands, please. I promise I'll not try anything."

He stared at her, the sound of his heavy breathing filling her ears while she shifted on the bed. "Very well," he said finally. "But only your hands." He unbound them, newly abrading her wrists in the process, but she gritted her teeth and held her tongue. He slipped the chamber pot under the blanket and stepped away, turned his back and waited expectantly.

Mortified, Amy's eyes opened wide. "You have to leave."

He swung back around. "Oh, no . . . no, I don't."

"*Please.* You cannot do this to me, Robert." She thought quickly. "I'm sorry we quarreled yesterday," she lied. "I—I'm sure we can work something out. And—and we cannot really start this way if we're going to be happy together."

His eyes bore into hers. She met his gaze, willing him to believe her.

"I'll wait outside the door, but for only two minutes," he said at last. "Then I'm coming in, whether you're ready or not."

He pulled out a pocket watch, and Amy recognized the ruby-encrusted case that he'd labored hours over, back in the days when life was normal. With a meaningful glance in her direction, he flipped open the lid and stepped out into the corridor, banging the door closed behind him.

Inspired by his threat, she finished in record time. Leaning halfway off the bed to set the chamber pot on the floor, she was contemplating whether she had time enough left to untie her ankles, when he barged in. She bolted upright.

"Finished?"

She nodded mutely. He retied her wrists, yanking the knot tight in a silent show of domination, then peeked beneath the blanket near her feet. Her heart pounded at the thought that he might have discovered her duplicity.

When he reached the door, he turned back to face her. "You know, I am not nearly the simpleton that you think I am. But you'll learn that over time." And he turned and left, locking the door behind him.

Colin strode out the door of the town house, his stomach churning with anxiety and frustration. *Amy-Amy-Amy-Amy-Amy,* repeated over and over in his brain, accomplishing nothing but the beginnings of a massive headache.

He had to find her, but how? London was bursting at

the seams with buildings and humanity, and Robert could have taken her anywhere.

Assuming 'twas Robert who had taken her. And assuming they were still in London. The sheer number of possibilities was overwhelming.

Leaning against the stable wall while his horse was resaddled, Colin forced his pulse to slow and his head to clear.

He took slow, deep breaths, rubbing the white star on Ebony's forehead in a soothing rhythm. *Robert.* How could he find Robert? He must have family, somewhere. And that family would be jewelers, no doubt. Robert had been Hugh Goldsmith's apprentice, and if Colin understood how the guild system worked, apprenticeships were arranged between families well nigh at birth. He would lay odds that Robert's father was in the same business.

He just had to find him.

Robert returned several hours later, his freckled face scrubbed clean, his damp orange hair slightly curling at the ends. He was dressed in an immaculate brown suit, the jacket's wide cuffs trimmed in icy blue, the loose breeches beribboned with poufs of blue loops. As he entered, he unfastened his knee-length cloak and folded it over the back of a chair, revealing a starched, white, lace-bordered cravat tied neatly at his throat and secured with a diamond brooch. His wide-brimmed hat boasted a blue ostrich plume and a jeweled hatband. He swept it off his head and tossed it on the battered wooden table with a flourish.

"I'm ready," he announced.

Amy eyed him dubiously. 'Twas clear he was decked out for an important occasion—he almost looked handsome in his finery. She lifted her head to inspect him more closely. "Ready for what?"

"Our wedding."

Nonplussed, her head dropped back to the dirty pillow. A puff of dust whooshed out, clogging her nostrils and making her cough. How could he think she would agree to marry him now, after a forcible abduction? 'Twas beyond her comprehension. This was hardly her idea of courtship.

When she offered no comment, he continued, his cheerfulness unabated. "Of course, 'tis a Sunday, so we'll have to wait until tomorrow. But I decided to ready myself now, since I plan not to leave you again beforehand. It makes me nervous."

So now she was stuck with him. This turn of events was unlikely to facilitate her escape, which she was more determined than ever to achieve. In the course of the past twenty-four hours, she'd decided that besides harboring an unforetold capacity for violence, Robert was quite obviously insane.

A shadow of discomfort crossed his face. He flexed his shoulders restlessly before dropping into a chair. "Are you not going to say anything?"

"I'm not marrying you," she said bluntly.

In answer, he rose from the chair and reached behind his back, drew a pistol from the waistband of his breeches, and set it on the table. Softly, but she still heard a metallic thud. "Yes, you are marrying me."

Amy was fairly certain he would never use it on her—or anyone else, for that matter. She doubted he knew how to load it, let alone shoot it. Regardless, her expression must have registered some apprehension, because Robert reseated himself with a self-satisfied smirk on his face.

"We've an appointment at St. Trinity tomorrow morning," he explained. "I have two witnesses meeting us here. We'll tie you up and cover you with my cloak. The proprietor here already believes you're ill; he'll think naught when we carry you out and over toward the church."

St. Trinity was in the Minories. If he planned on carrying her there, they must still be in the City, or at least somewhere in greater London. That was welcome news.

Robert would have to leave sometime, at least to

order some food, and perhaps she could untie herself, knock him senseless upon his return, steal the key and escape, losing herself in the rabbit warren of streets that made up London. She'd take his cloak to cover her nightgown . . .

". . . gown and slippers will be delivered for you within the hour," Robert was saying. So she'd have something to wear. Things were looking up. "I've arranged for food to be delivered." *Damn.* There went his reason for leaving. "Are you hungry?"

"It doesn't signify. I'd not sit at table with you in either case."

"You're right. You're staying in that bed."

They glared at each other. Robert looked away first.

Amy kept her gaze on him. "No banns have been posted."

"No matter. 'Tis a privileged church. You've heard of them, I presume?"

She nodded curtly. "I'll not say 'I will.' "

"Oh, you'll say it." He picked up the gun, hefted it as emphasis to his words. "I doubt the curate cares what you say, anyway. So long as he gets his blunt."

He had an answer for every protest. Nonetheless, from somewhere deep inside, Amy was confident she'd find a way out.

The alternative was too ghastly to consider.

"I know not where he is, my lord. I'm sorry."

"Think, Mr. Stanley. *Please,*" Colin begged. "I must find her. I—I love her." There. He'd said it. Out loud, to another human being.

All the same, his confession, however difficult, did not seem to make any profound impression on Robert's father. "I'm sure Robert loves her too, my lord," James Stanley said warily. He was an older, much fatter version of Robert, exhibiting the likely result of an inactive life seated at a jeweler's bench. He looked affable enough, in much the same way Robert did. Still, the sheer resemblance of the two men led to Colin's instant resentment.

Was this jealousy? If so, 'twas a deucedly intolerable emotion.

"She's been promised to him since they were children," Mr. Stanley continued in a reasonable tone of voice. "They come from similar backgrounds. They can build a life together. What can you offer her?"

"That is none of your damn business."

James Stanley's face shut down, the straight line of his mouth indicating his unwillingness to cooperate.

Colin sighed, dropping his head. He stared down through the glass of the empty jewelry case. The little shop was closed, it being Sunday, but Colin had pounded on the door until Mr. Stanley came downstairs.

Confident until now, Colin had been on his quest for half a day already. Cheapside was still in ashes; no one near the ruins of Goldsmith & Sons had known of Robert Stanley. But on the Strand, home to more than fifty jewelers for the past two centuries, he'd hit gold: the elder Stanley's name and location. Weaving Ebony across town through London's afternoon traffic, Colin's spirits had remained high. He was counting on a potent combination of ingenuity and sheer determination to help him locate Amy in this city of over a quarter million inhabitants, and he'd convinced himself James Stanley would know his son's plans.

Apparently, Mr. Stanley either didn't know or wouldn't tell. And now Colin had alienated him with that thoughtless, hotheaded remark. He swore silently at himself; he hardly recognized the man he'd become since he found Amethyst Goldsmith outside her blazing shop. He stared down at his reflection in the case's glass, and narrowed green eyes stared back up at him. His jaw was tense, his mouth twisted into a threat. He blinked, shocked at his forbidding countenance. He'd not send such a man after his son, either, he supposed.

Determined to regain his self-control, he forced his lips to part in a stiff, toothy smile and looked back up at James Stanley. "I just want to make sure this is what

Amy wants. I would never harm her, physically or otherwise."

"Robert would never harm her, either," the older man snapped.

Colin lifted his chin, meeting Stanley's icy blue gaze—so like Robert's—straight on. "There was blood on the sheets, Mr. Stanley." The words were calm, unemotional. Inside, Colin was seething, but this man was his best hope for information, so he couldn't afford to let him see it.

James Stanley blinked, and his sharp indrawn breath revealed his shock. "I honestly know not where he is," he said after a few moments. "He doesn't confide in me. But he spends his free hours at the King's Arms, on Holborn."

Robert pushed the spoon between her lips, but it met clenched teeth. "Damn it, Amy, you have to eat. I'll not have you fainting in church tomorrow."

"Untie me, and I'll feed myself. Otherwise . . ." She shrugged.

Robert dropped the spoon in the bowl; ragout of mushrooms, sweetbreads and oysters splashed up; brown bits landed on the coverlet. "Have it your way. You'll let me feed you when you get hungry enough."

Never, Amy thought. She'd never grant him the satisfaction.

He rose from the bed and wandered to the window, rubbed a fist on the grimy pane in an effort to see out. Then, giving up, he threw himself onto one of the wooden chairs, his legs sprawled out in front of him in an awkward attempt to recline.

Amy's carefully veiled eyes followed his every move. He was growing bored, tired of waiting. Good. Perhaps he would become restless enough to consider leaving for a while.

He yawned, loudly, not bothering to cover his mouth. She grimaced at the sight of his overlapping teeth, wondering how she'd ever had the stomach to let him kiss her.

He yawned again. This was encouraging. If he fell asleep, she'd have a chance to untie herself. She ground her teeth lightly, anticipating using them to loosen her bonds.

A knock at the door jerked Robert back to life.

"About time," he growled, rising to answer it.

A man pushed a large box into Robert's arms. Reaching into his pocket, Robert fished out a coin and slapped it into the man's palm, then turned and kicked the door shut behind him. He set the box on the table. "Want to see it?"

Without waiting for an answer, he threw aside the box's lid and pulled out an ice-blue gown. Shaking it out, he held it up. "See? It matches my suit," he pointed out, grinning. He was obviously pleased with himself, his good humor restored. And why not? Amy reflected. He had planned everything down to the last detail, and 'twas all proceeding perfectly.

"We'll appear the proper bride and groom," Robert boasted.

Amy snorted. Matching his outfit was the last item on her list of priorities. She had to admit, though, he had good taste. However had he managed to procure such a lovely gown on a few hours' notice on a Sunday? The satin was embroidered with silver flowers and leaves, and scattered clusters of pearls suggested bunches of grapes. He spread it across the foot of the bed and laid coordinating blue slippers on top; they looked as though they might fit.

Amy was heartened. In such a gown she could flag down a hackney without the driver suspecting she had no means to pay. Another problem was solved.

She allowed herself a smile—but just a tiny one, so he'd not suspect.

The sign on the middle-class tavern swung gently in the light wind, the words "Kings Arms" spelled out in bright new paint. Colin stepped inside.

The clientele were seated in convivial bunches at long, clean-scrubbed wooden tables with matching benches. They were by and large a well-off group, although not of the aristocracy—merchants and solicitors, architects and publishers, gathered to share the news and some companionship at the end of a busy day. Many drank coffee, well known as a means of overcoming drowsiness and stimulating the wits, and the cheerful room was filled with the buzz of animated conversation and the faint scent of tobacco smoke. Colin could well imagine that a titled peer or two stopped by this warm, friendly establishment when they felt like slumming with the common people.

From behind a serving counter, the proprietor looked up. He bustled over, noting Colin's sword and spurs, and the fine fabric and cut of his surcoat, immediately taking him for exactly what he was. "May I be of service, my lord . . . ?"

"Greystone. I'm looking for a man said to frequent this establishment, a Robert Stanley."

The proprietor's dark, intelligent eyes scanned the room. "Your information is correct. He is not here now, however."

"Perhaps someone here may know of his whereabouts?"

"That is a possibility. He usually sits over there—men are creatures of habit, you know." He indicated a table in the center of the room, crowded with jovial young men with tankards of ale before them.

Their conversation ceased as Colin approached and they all turned to view this imposing stranger. Colin did his best to put a smile in his voice as well as on his face.

"I'm looking for Robert Stanley."

Silence reigned for a moment, the faces around the table cautious and suspicious. "Is he in some sort of trouble?" one man asked slowly. "Lately, he's been—" His words were cut off when the man beside him dealt him a sharp elbow in the ribs.

The smile left Colin's face. He surveyed the table, focusing on each of Robert's friends in turn. "This is a matter of some urgency. It seems Mr. Stanley has abducted a lady of our mutual acquaintance. I'll pay for information."

Friendship apparently went only so far. Whether 'twas the severity of the charge or the offer of money, Colin knew not, but the men suddenly came alive.

"He's been searching for his betrothed for weeks. Is it her? She may have gone willingly."

"He paid someone to show him the Marquess of Cainewood's house."

"Yesterday, he asked where to find a privileged church. I told him St. Trinity, in the Minories."

"I told him m'sister was wed at St. James."

Privileged churches. A forced marriage. Colin wanted to kick himself for not thinking of the possibility. He could have saved hours by simply enquiring as to where such churches were located and riding straight there.

Well, Ford's hunch, though slightly miscalculated, had led him to the truth. Colin drew a deep breath; he was on the right track. "Might anyone know where he is now?"

The men shook their heads. "He's not been here since yesterday," one of them volunteered.

"Where is St. James?"

"In Duke's Place."

"Thank you, gentlemen." Colin dug in his pouch and threw a handful of silver coins on the table. He left without another word, at a run. The two churches in question were just outside the City walls, and Amy had been taken last night. If Robert Stanley had timed it early enough, she might be a wife already.

"So . . . are you ready to talk?" Robert leaned back, balancing precariously on the hind legs of the rickety wooden chair, picking at his teeth with a fingernail.

Watching him, Amy shuddered. She hoped he'd fall over and crack his head open. "You mean, discuss something? As if you still lived in my father's house and we cared about each other?"

"I care about you, Amy."

"You actually sound sincere." She lifted her tied wrists, the skin red and raw. "You have an unusual way of showing it."

He leaned forward, and the front chair legs met the floor with a loud *bang*. "That is for your own good. We were meant to be together, and you refused to cooperate. After we're wed—after you have my babe—you'll agree."

She'd never have his babe, Amy promised herself—*never*. She'd drink a thousand purges first. She'd throw herself down a staircase. Whatever it took.

"Where's the jewelry?" he asked suddenly.

She stared at him, unblinking. "I don't have it."

"That is quite obvious. 'Tis unfortunate; I'm sure you'd like to choose a few pieces to complement your wedding gown tomorrow." He flashed a facetious grin, but it faded swiftly. "No matter. It will all turn up once the deed is done, will it not?" He rose from the chair, walked over to the bed and leaned over her. *"Will it not?"*

She spat in his face.

He hovered above her for a moment, disbelief marking his features, then his hand shot out and slapped her across the face, snapping her head to one side.

Tears sprang to her eyes, but she'd not cry. She'd not allow him the gratification of seeing her reduced to a quivering bundle of emotion.

"*That* was a mistake," Robert ground out from between clenched teeth. "Care to try it again?"

She shook her head infinitesimally.

"Very well, then." He turned and slunk back to the chair, stretched out his legs and crossed them at the ankles. "Now, you said earlier you were sorry we quarreled, and you were willing to work something out. Were you lying?"

She didn't answer.

"Were you lying?"

She turned her head. "I'll not marry you," she whispered.

"What? What did you say?"

"I'll not marry you, Robert Stanley!" she fairly yelled. "Not now, not tomorrow, *not ever*!" She knew 'twas the wrong thing to do; she should act as though she were willing and wait for her chance to escape. But the rebel in her took over, and she couldn't help herself.

He leapt up to stand over her again. "Oh, yes, you will. I'm a second son. There are no jeweler's heiresses lining up to wed me. If I haven't you, I have nothing. That pistol"—he gestured toward the table—"will guarantee you'll marry me." At that moment, he looked angry enough to use it.

"You'd never—" she started.

"And as insurance," he continued, his pale eyes flashing and wild, "I've a mind to take your maidenhead tonight." He paused, licking his rubbery lips as he considered the idea. "Yes, a consummated betrothal is as good as a marriage, is it not?"

Amy struggled up on her elbows. "Our betrothal papers burned in the fire. 'Twould be your word against mine. My Aunt Elizabeth would swear her brother never betrothed me to the likes of you."

His face went slack, but only for an instant. "I can still ruin you for anyone else, can I not? You'd have no choice but to marry me then."

"You're too late, Robert Stanley," Amy shot back without thinking. "Someone else has already claimed the honor." She glared at him, unflinching, even knowing how angry the admission was likely to make him.

He pounced on the bed, crouching over her with his hands on either side of her head. "Who was it?" He pushed his hands down at each word, for emphasis. *"Who was it?"*

She dared not tell him.

"Whoever it was, I'll kill him, I swear it. You're mine." The mattress continued to bounce, punctuating his words, swiftly escalating her diminished headache into a virulent pain.

Suddenly, he growled deep in his throat. " 'Twas Greystone, wasn't it? *That bastard.*" The fear in her eyes was all the confirmation he needed. He raised a fist and slammed it toward her, but she was ready and jerked her head to the side in time.

"Robert!" she screamed. "What have you turned into? Look at yourself!"

And miraculously, he did. He picked up his fist from where it was buried in the mattress and stared at it as though it were a foreign body. Then he slowly climbed off the bed and wandered over to the table. He sat down, dropped his head to the surface with an audible bump, and stayed there, perfectly still.

Amy released her breath. She was shaking from head to toe.

She had to get out of here before he raped her. She choked back a sob at the mere thought, the possibility of him violating her body, pushing himself into her. It seemed a completely different act than what she had done with Colin, and she didn't think she could bear the disgust and humiliation.

Robert lifted his head from the table. His breath came in loud, ragged gasps. "You enjoyed it, didn't you?" he asked in an ominous, deep whisper. "Cold, proper Amethyst Goldsmith." He swung around to gaze at her, but she didn't answer, just watched his steely blue eyes, preparing herself to react should he attack her another time. She flinched when he whispered again. "You'd better pray you're not carrying his child, because if you are, I swear I'll kill it."

His expression grew hard and resentful. When he spoke again, his voice was absolutely emotionless. It sent a chill slithering down her spine.

"Robert Stanley," he stated, "will not raise another man's child."

Chapter Nineteen

Colin reached St. James, the first church outside Aldgate, just as the evening service was concluding. The congregation was sparse; religion had lost favor when Charles and his loose-moraled court took over London, and no one save a few tradesmen and peasants bothered attending church for anything but the obligatory baptisms, weddings, and funerals. No exception to the norm, Colin shifted impatiently, twisting his ring back and forth as the curate completed his long-winded, boring sermon.

The minute the parishioners began shuffling out, Colin strode toward the pulpit, jostling shoulders in his haste. "Excuse me, Father," he called when he was but halfway down the aisle. "Did you marry a couple yesterday—he red-haired, and she small with black hair and—"

"Would you care to examine the marriage register, my son?" Colin winced at the humor in the curate's voice; 'twas obvious the man was no stranger to lovesick swains having their intended brides stolen out from under them.

The register was duly produced, and there were nine recorded weddings dated the previous day—none of them Robert's or Amy's. "Did you see them?" Colin persisted. "Perhaps you know where—"

"No one came to be wed yesterday who was not accommodated. Perhaps they went to St. Trinity?"

Colin was already out the door.

The marriage register at St. Trinity had logged eleven ceremonies, and Colin's heart seemed to grow larger and larger in his chest as he scrutinized the long list. When he reached the end without seeing either name, he stumbled to a front-row pew and plopped down.

"Is there a problem, my son?" the plump curate asked kindly.

"No. 'Tis good, in fact." Amy was yet unmarried. Colin slumped on the bench, his pulse returning to normal. Until another thought occurred to him.

He jumped up. "Is there another place in London where one can be wed—ah—in a hurry, without a license?" Robert's friends had recommended only the two, but—

"Nay." The curate grinned, clearly pleased that he shared his lucrative business with only one other clergyman. "Not in London. In the countryside, near Oxford . . ."

Colin exhaled a long sigh of relief. "Too far to signify. They got a late start last night."

The curate ran his tongue over his uneven teeth, thinking. "This couple, from late last night. He'd not have had red hair, would he?"

Colin's heart skipped. "Yes! And she's small, dark-haired—"

"I never saw her. He said she was waiting outside, and she was likely to be . . . reluctant, I believe he termed it."

Thank God. Having abandoned Amy at the town house without so much as saying good-bye, a tiny, insecure part of Colin had been wondering if the blood could have been an honest accident, if Amy might marry Robert willingly, given the circumstances.

"I expect them back here in the morning."

"No, I must find them tonight. She could be injured . . ."

The clergyman frowned. "They're likely close at hand since he's planning an early return. Perhaps at a nearby inn. You might try Fenchurch Street."

"Thank you, Father." Colin was so relieved, he felt like kissing the fat, bald man, but he thought that would be improper with a man of God. Instead, he dropped a coin into the collection box on his way out.

The curate hurried to retrieve it when the door shut. Silver. His big teeth gleamed in the candlelight as he pocketed the coin.

He may have lost himself a wedding fee, but it mattered not much. Over fifteen hundred anxious couples a year found their way to his altar.

No ransom note arrived.

A crackling fire warmed the drawing room, but the cold knot inside Kendra refused to thaw. Ford sat next to her and held her hand, which may have provided a small comfort if Jason's constant pacing weren't driving her to distraction.

She bit the inside of her cheek, worrying the soft flesh with her teeth. She couldn't shake the feeling that she was partially at fault. She should have checked on Amy much earlier. She should have taken Robert's threat more seriously. Over and over, she replayed yesterday's scene in her mind, looking for a clue to his plans.

Suddenly, the blood drained from her face, and she sat up straighter. "I just remembered something," she breathed.

Jason stopped in mid-track. "What?"

"He said he spent his time drinking at the King's Arms. Maybe someone there—"

"Oh, *that* is bloody useful information," Ford scoffed. "The King's Arms." He rolled his eyes. "There must be two dozen of them in town, at least. Not to mention the King's Head and other assorted Royal body parts—why, half the taverns and inns have been renamed since the Restoration."

Kendra stood. Planting her feet in a wide stance, she placed her hands on her hips and drew a deep breath. "I cannot just sit here, waiting, any longer," she declared.

Ford's gaze swung to Jason's, inquiring, and Jason's arched eyebrows rose as he shrugged in return. "I suppose 'twould not hurt to ask around," he sighed. And

Kendra was out the door, leaving her brothers to follow in her wake.

As the sun disappeared, the grimy window darkened to black. Amy struggled to stay awake. Her life depended on it. If she nodded off and slept until morning, her chance for freedom would be lost.

And life as the forced bride of Robert Stanley was not worth living.

Her only hope lay in his falling asleep, deeply enough for her to escape her bonds and retrieve the key from his pocket. He had dozed a couple of times, but his body would jerk awake, his cold, suspicious eyes searching her out.

He'd said not a word since he threatened to kill her child.

While she waited long hours for him to nod off, her emotions swung wildly. Deep inside, she seethed with mounting rage at his ability to control her just because he was bigger and stronger. Other young men took fencing lessons, trained with knives and pistols, spent hours in boxing parlors perfecting their skills. Not Robert. He spent his off-hours drinking, gambling, and wenching, and had the soft physique to prove it. Yet that unhardened body was twice her weight, coupled with a deranged force that rendered her well-nigh helpless.

She lay still, as unobtrusive as humanly possible in an effort to avoid his wrath, feeling alternately angry, defiant, despairing, determined, and frustrated. In between, she made paltry attempts to calm her irregular pulse, telling herself to think of better times in the past and those to come, when she somehow extricated herself from this impossible situation.

Mostly, she thought about Colin.

She placed her bound hands over her stomach protectively. Was it possible? She'd never considered the hypothetical consequences when she'd lain in Colin's arms. Had he? She'd heard there were things women could do to prevent pregnancy, but the details were hazy. Were there things men could do as well? Had Colin done any of them? Though embarrassed at her lack of knowledge, she thought not. He'd seemed too emotionally involved to have concerned himself with any precautions.

She counted back carefully. 'Twas sixteen days since she'd first lain with Colin. Her monthly flow had been due last Friday, but she'd thought nothing of it when it hadn't arrived; her body was notoriously irregular.

'Twas way too early to jump to any conclusions, but still . . . her heart beat an erratic tattoo at the thought. Even now, Colin's son might be cradled within her. She never even considered it might be his daughter. In her mind's eye, her body harbored a tiny little replica of Colin Chase.

Now she had still another reason to make sure she escaped. If she should be so fortunate as to have conceived Colin's child, she would cherish him her whole life. She would set herself up as a jeweler's widow and raise their son in Paris. She would have a piece of Colin forever.

She smiled a slow, secret smile at the thought, before she remembered her predicament and her gaze swung across the chamber to Robert. He was sleeping, his head lolling to one side, his mouth open and slack. His breathing was deep and measured.

Thank God.

Her heart galloped with excitement. She brought her wrists to her mouth and tested the knot. Her teeth slipped off the hard knob and clicked together with a sound that seemed loud in the still room, but Robert didn't stir, and she continued working at the knot, loosening it bit by bit. Half an hour later her arms ached from holding them up, and her lips were chapped and sore from rubbing against saliva-drenched fabric, but her hands were free.

She made short work of the bonds on her ankles and stood on shaky legs. After twenty-odd hours flat on her back, her knees threatened to buckle under her, but she refused to give in to her weakness. Sternly forcing her body to comply, she drew the ice-blue dress off the foot of the bed and dropped it over her head, holding her breath when the satin rustled as it settled into place. She shoved the nightgown's sleeves up under those of the gown, jerked the lacings closed over her breasts, and attached the stomacher haphazardly. She could finish dressing properly when she was safely outside.

Slipping her feet into the matching slippers, which were a little large but would have to do, she tiptoed over to Robert. Her heart was pounding so loudly she was half-convinced it would wake him.

Silently blessing the powers that be for decreeing loose breeches with deep pockets were fashionable, she crouched behind him and eased her hand into one pocket. Her first try found a small gunpowder flask and a few balls and cloth patches, but no key.

She paused, taken aback by the evidence that he was prepared to fire the pistol. As she pulled out her hand, Robert took a deep, ragged breath, inhaling with a resounding snore, and Amy froze for a good two minutes before daring to try the other pocket.

When her fingers closed around the cold, heavy key, she could barely contain her glee. She was mere steps from freedom.

She stood, reminding herself to be light-footed regardless of her haste, and her gaze lit on the gun on the table. It gleamed in the weak firelight, the stock profusely inlaid with silver wire in a display of workmanship akin to the finest jeweler's. She briefly considered taking it, but the gown had no pockets, and she'd not the faintest idea how to shoot it, in any case. Forcing her eyes away, she tiptoed to the door.

The key in the lock made a hideous grating noise, but she didn't look back. She bolted into a dim, dusty corridor.

She tripped and stumbled as one of the too-loose slippers threatened to come off. Suddenly she heard scuffling behind her, then a horrible ripping sound as, for the second time in as many days, she found herself tugged to her knees. Robert's considerable weight landed on her back, and she plunged forward.

"Holy Jesus," he hissed into her ear. "I'd have thought you'd've learned your lesson by now." He jerked her up, one hand coming around to cover her mouth and muffle her impending scream. She glanced frantically around the dingy corridor, but there was no one to help her.

The cold steel of the pistol's barrel pressed into the side of her neck. She should have taken it.

Colin had checked the eight inns closest to St. Trinity, but there was no sign of Amy. His disappointment was a physical pain, a heaviness in his chest that was weighted with a creeping sense of foreboding.

To have come all this way, crisscrossing the City, from one clue to another, and then . . . nothing. And somewhere out there, Amy was . . . what? Sleeping, suffering, frightened, abused? Well, 'twas still Sunday, so even if they'd left London, he was fairly certain she wasn't married.

Yet.

Perhaps he was on the wrong track. Perhaps he should go back to Robert's father or the King's Arms, and see if anyone had heard from Robert in the past few hours. Intending to make the depressing rounds again, he'd no sooner untied Ebony when a yellow glow caught his eye, penetrating the fog from up the street. At this hour, in this neighborhood, where citizens couldn't afford the luxury of candles at midnight, where decent folk went to bed with the dusk and rose with the dawn, that light could mean only one thing: a tavern.

He leaped onto Ebony and clip-clopped down the dark, empty street toward the glow. Bereft and desolate, Colin could only muster a faint hope that he might have reached the end of his search. As he drew nearer, the light from the grimy window illuminated a cracked wooden sign proclaiming it the Cat and Canary, and a swift glance up at the overhanging story assured him that it did, indeed, boast a few rooms for rent.

Colin tied up Ebony in a rough shed across the street, then took the time to thank him for his service and companionship with a bucketful of brackish water and a forkful of hay. After all, of all the multitudes of places in London, he had no real reason to think Amy was here.

The tavern's door swung open with a prolonged creak, revealing a plain wooden interior encrusted with years of accumulated dirt. A nauseating reek of rancid food choked the air. He glanced around, grimacing, thinking 'twas a shame the fire had missed this street; this was the kind of firetrap London needed to rid itself of.

A few unkempt customers sat conversing morosely at one table; no proprietor was in sight. All was quiet. Colin couldn't imagine Amy in a place like this, even as Robert's hostage.

He turned to leave, but caught himself glancing uneasily over his shoulder. After a pause, he addressed the motley group at the table. "Pardon me, but is anyone staying above?"

The answer was a mixture of shrugs and grunts that he took to be a negative. One man looked up at him, his bloated face showing surprise at finding someone of Colin's class in this tavern. Colin focused on him. "I'm looking for someone . . ."

"Anyone you'd be lookin' fer'd be on Leadenhall Street," the man offered, inclining his head toward a street across the way, behind the shed where Colin had stashed Ebony. "Try the Rose 'n' Crown."

"Thank you kindly," Colin replied, moving to the entry. He couldn't wait to get out of this depressing establishment.

Halfway through the door, he heard a thud from above. His blood chilled. He swung back around. "Are you certain no one is up there?"

He would swear he heard a muffled yell. The men didn't react. One of them stood slowly, the legs of his chair scraping back on the wooden floor. "No one is up there," he stated, running a dirty hand through shaggy, greasy hair.

A scream. Hysterical. Unrelenting. Anxiety sent Colin's pulse racing, and he felt as though his chest might burst. He pulled a gold guinea from his pouch and flung it on the table, his eyes boring into the other man's. "Room four," the man muttered, scooping up the coin and testing it between his teeth. Colin bolted up the rough staircase.

The numbers on the doors were too faded to read in the dim light emanating from downstairs, but it mattered not. There was only one room he could possibly be interested in, and Amy's unmistakable sobs led him straight to it.

Robert had shoved Amy back into the room and thrown her on the bed. He pointed the pistol in her direction with one shaking hand while he attempted to lock the door with the other.

"Please, Robert—"

"*Shut up*. I'll hear not one word from you." He frantically worked the lock, his hand fumbling. "God damn it to bloody hell. You'll pay for this, Amy. Mark my words." The lock clicked into place, and he whirled around, wild-eyed, searching the room. With a sinister laugh and a flick of his wrist, the key landed in the flames of the fireplace.

"There," he growled. "I'll take it back in the morning, when the ashes grow cold. Until then, we'll not be needing it, will we?"

Cringing, Amy scooted back until her spine pressed against the dirty headboard, then pulled up her knees and wrapped her arms around them, clasping tight.

Robert raised his arm and aimed the pistol at her again. "Lie down!" he barked, waving the gun wildly. She dropped to the mattress, curled into a fetal position, and let out a whimper as panic like she'd never known before welled up in her throat. She whimpered again as she watched Robert switch the pistol to his left hand so he could work the buckle on his belt with his right.

She shut her eyes tight, as if by doing so she could banish Robert and his pistol and his belt from the earth. Any second now, she expected to feel the belt on her, the leather ripping shreds of her tender flesh in Robert's fury.

Instead, she felt Robert throw himself on top of her, flattening her to the mattress. The gun fell to the wooden floor with a meaty thud, and she twisted under him, intending to lunge for it. But Robert pressed her shoulders against the bed with his two fleshy hands, and his head descended on hers, blocking her vision and her access to the weapon.

He ground his lips against hers in a cruel ravishment of her mouth, until she tasted coppery-tinged blood. Her hands came up and pushed at his head, but to no avail; he was quite simply stronger and heavier than she. He forced her teeth apart with his, plunging his slippery wet tongue into the deep recesses of her mouth. She bit down on it, hard, but he seemed not to notice, even when his hot, salty blood flowed into her mouth.

She gagged. And she wished he had beaten her instead.

A lifetime later, after pinning Amy beneath the weight of his body, Robert came up on his elbows. Her mouth finally free, she screamed.

Robert laughed wildly. "No one will come," he taunted. "They all think you're delirious. And they've been well paid. You'll be *mine* after tonight," he growled. "No man will ever want to touch you again."

Amy heard him, but his words did not register. The blood was pounding in her ears, and all her senses were turned inward, as if she had encased herself in a cocoon in a desperate attempt to escape reality.

Lifting himself further, he ripped off one side of the stomacher and clawed at her laces. He parted the front of her bodice and freed her breasts with one long tear of the nightgown's fragile fabric, then grabbed them in both hands and pushed their lushness together. His pale eyes gleamed recklessly, and he smacked his lips.

He fell to, sucking and biting her sensitive flesh, heedless of Amy's fingers tugging on his neckcloth and pulling on his hair. His breath was heavy and labored; the stench of stale ale and old vomit suffused the air around them. He wedged a hand between their bodies, working frantically to unlace his breeches.

She clawed long, bloody scratches along his cheeks. But instead of relenting, he growled low in his throat and tugged at the voluminous skirts of the wedding gown, bunching it and the nightgown around her waist.

Though she'd thought she could feel no more panicked, the cool air on her extremities fueled her useless howling to new heights. Robert shoved his knees between hers to force her legs apart, and her anguish was so acute that it overwhelmed any physical pain.

"Stanley!" Colin pounded with both fists on the rotting wood that separated him from the woman he loved and her abductor. "Open up! *Now!*"

He ripped off his surcoat and threw it to the floor. Backing up a few feet, he made a run at the door and rammed it with one brawny shoulder—the old lock gave with a satisfying snap, and the door flung into the room and slammed against the wall, barely staying on its hinges.

Startled into action, Robert rolled off Amy and slid over the edge of the bed, scrabbling to find the pistol on the floor.

The chamber was lit by only a dying fire and a few candles, but Amy knew 'twas Colin from his tall, familiar outline framed in the open doorway. She knew it, but she could not believe it. She had prayed her screaming would result in help, but she had never imagined the help would be Colin Chase.

She pushed herself up to a sitting position, blinking and whimpering in her confusion. The confrontation seemed like an eternity in slow motion, but took only a few seconds.

Robert stood up, one hand clutching the waistband of his breeches, the other clenching the pistol. A feral look hardened his bloodied features, a primitive reaction to the invasion of his territory. Colin took a step forward.

"Stay back, Greystone, you bastard." The pistol wavered as Robert growled. "She's *mine*." The flintlock had been half-cocked, primed and ready, and now Robert pulled back the lock. The room reverberated with an ominous click.

Colin advanced, his expression thunderous. Robert's face registered sheer, unreasoning panic; his arm swung wildly as he squeezed the unfamiliar trigger, and he brought his other hand up to steady it, but in the scant second or so of time, he only managed to throw off his aim even more. The pistol went off with a loud report that left Amy's heart in her mouth, and her eyes went wide as she watched a horrible red stain blossom on Colin's shirt, under his left arm.

She let out a shriek of terror, but Colin didn't flinch; his advance continued unchecked. The bullet was lodged in the wall of the corridor. Robert was left with a smoking gun in his shaking hands, the pungent scent of exploded gunpowder swirling around him.

There was insufficient time for an expert to reload, and Robert was no expert. He flung the heavy pistol at Colin's head.

Colin ducked, and as his head came back up, he pulled his rapier out of his belt with smooth, practiced ease.

Without the false sense of security the pistol had provided, Robert seemed to shrink into himself. Amy saw the truth in his eyes: Robert knew he was no match for the Earl of Greystone—had known it from the moment Colin came into the shop, three long months ago. Robert backed up against the wall, his pale eyes glassy with terror, fastened on the gleaming silver length of Colin's blade.

Flinging the sword away, Colin rounded on Robert

with his fists clenched. He grabbed the shorter man's shoulders and pulled him away from the wall, then rammed him back into it with a raging force. There was an audible *crack*! as Robert's head met the rigid wood, and when Colin let go, Robert slid to the floor in an ungraceful heap.

The fight was over before it began.

Amy watched, silent, as Colin bent down to reclaim his sword. "Do you want me to kill him?" he grated out, his breath coming in large gulps as he fought to control his fury.

She shook her head violently, still mute. Colin stood motionless for a moment, registering the shock in her disbelieving eyes. Then he slid the sword into his belt and moved to the bed, reaching down toward her.

"You're . . . you've been *shot,*" she whispered, beginning to shake.

He straightened and looked down to where her gaze was riveted, surprised. His shirt was plastered to his ribs by a dark, sticky patch of blood, but 'twas not spreading. " 'Tis but a scratch," he said. He still couldn't feel it—the white-hot maelstrom of his emotions overrode any pain.

Still, he had enough presence of mind to retrieve his surcoat from the corridor and shrug back into it, wrapping it tightly around himself to cover the blood before he scooped her up in his arms.

She trembled in his embrace. With a lingering, murderous look at Robert's still form, he carried her down the stairs and out into the street.

Chapter Twenty

Only a street from the ramshackle Cat and Canary, the aristocratic Rose and Crown seemed a world away. Amy seemed a world away, too.

"I'm cold, Colin," she whispered as he gently laid her on the bed.

After starting a roaring blaze in the fireplace, he went downstairs to ask for a bath to be prepared. He returned to find Amy huddled in a chair, staring into the flames. Concerned, he glanced back at the bed.

"I've been tied to a bed . . ." she murmured in answer to his unasked question. He unbuckled his sword and set it on a low table, then lifted her up, took her place in the chair and settled her onto his lap. Silent, they watched the fire together, Colin holding her close, her head against his chest.

He buried his lips in her tangled curls, and they stayed that way for a very long time, motionless except when Colin's mouth moved against her hair. His kisses were gentle, slow and warm. Possessive, healing. Not sensuous, but cherishing. His heart seemed to burst with tenderness at the miracle of her back in his arms.

Servants dragged a tub into the chamber and filled it with bucket after bucket of steaming water, scented with oil of roses. Hard-milled perfumed soap was left, along with a comb and a brush and large linen towels.

Alone again, Colin rose and stood Amy on her feet. He pushed the blue dress off her shoulders and down her unresisting body. It whispered to pool on the floor, a pale shimmer in the firelight. He drew the ripped nightgown over her head.

"I should have killed him," he whispered, looking at her. Her knees and elbows were scraped and scabby, her wrists and ankles raw and abraded. Purple marks marred one side of her face, dried blood crusted her forehead. Her lips were bruised and swollen, her hair a tangled mess tumbling down her back . . .

He had thought he would never see her again. She looked beautiful.

He took her hand and led her to the tub, helped her lower herself into the soothing, fragrant water. She melted into the warmth, leaned her head back on the rim. Through half-closed eyes, she watched him shrug out of his surcoat, cringing when his bloodstained shirt was revealed.

" 'Tis naught but a scratch," he reminded her, his voice low and steady. He turned away so she'd not see him wince when he pulled the fabric from the wound and slipped the shirt off over his head. But it *was* just a scratch, the barest graze, and 'twould not even require stitches. It stung, but not so much that he couldn't ignore it. *A quarter of an inch to the right*—Colin drew a deep breath. A broken rib, perhaps bone fragments puncturing his lung. It would have wreaked havoc, would certainly have impaired his swift action, if not killed him outright. Well, it had not happened. He'd been lucky—very, very lucky—and he would never reveal to her just how narrow their escape had been.

He knelt by the tub, dipped a towel into the water and dabbed at the blood until the shallow laceration was clean.

"Look, Amy." He turned toward the light. " 'Tis nothing." She reached out tentative fingers, touching him lightly, and when he didn't flinch, she settled back, satisfied.

Taking up a soft cloth, he cleaned her slowly and gently. He washed away the blood, the dirt, and—he hoped—the memories.

She said not a word and neither did he. 'Twas the most impersonal bath he had ever given a lady, and the most personal at the same time. His cloth ran over her tender breasts, her white belly, between her thighs. When her ivory skin gleamed clean in the firelight, he lathered her hair with the scented soap and poured buckets of water down her back. His arousal, long denied, grew until he hurt, but he trained his face to remain impassive, his touch to be no more than methodical.

'Twas the hardest thing he'd ever done.

With a hand in hers, he helped her stand. The water sluiced down, leaving droplets that shimmered on her graceful form. Colin's jaw tightened, and his eyes fluttered closed momentarily. Her wounds were merely surface deep, nothing that wouldn't heal in a few days at most. But he was furious nonetheless, feeling somehow responsible for her suffering, for the damage to her perfect young body. He should never have left her.

He would never leave her again, he promised himself as she stepped from the tub and he patted her dry. The nightgown was ruined and the blue dress ripped in the back, so he wrapped her in a dry towel, swallowing hard as he tucked the end between her breasts.

He dragged the chair closer to the fire and drew her long hair out as she sat down, draping it over the seat back. Then he sat behind her to brush it dry. He hummed as he worked, a soft lullaby his mother used to sing to him, bcfore the War.

The firelight played off the shiny black silk, and he wished he could sink his fingers into it, wrap it around his hands and pull her head back, devour her mouth with passionate kisses. But he willed his hands to continue the systematic strokes, his traitorous body to ignore the sensual stimulation the simple act elicited.

" 'Tis so beautiful . . ." he whispered once despite himself, pausing to rub the glistening mass between his palms. She froze as though she were surprised, and he would swear she even stopped breathing for a few seconds, but she said not a word, and he went on with his task.

He toyed with the idea of setting her up as his mistress, installing her in his beloved castle and building Priscilla the modern manor house she coveted. But deep inside, he knew 'twould never work. And he daydreamed of taking Amy to wife, living with her openly, without pretense.

Still, old convictions were difficult to overcome.

Her hair was dry and gleaming now. She rose when he did and turned to him with a gentle smile. "Thank you," she whispered. "I feel much better now."

"I'm glad." She stood so close he could feel the heat from her body. He swallowed hard. "Can you face the bed now?"

She nodded, her smile wobbly but determined. " 'Tis a different bed."

"Yes, it is." He led her to it and lifted a corner of the covers; she unwrapped her towel and slipped between the sheets.

Her gaze followed him as he poured water from the ewer to rinse the bloodstain from his shirt, then moved to the hearth to lay it out to dry. His heart warmed at her peaceful, sleepy expression. When his boots hit the floor with two dull thuds, she closed her eyes. He undressed and blew out the candles, then slid into bed beside her.

"Amy?"

"Mmmm?"

He had to know. "Did he? . . . I mean . . ."

She rolled to face him, opened her eyes to search his. "No. He didn't," she whispered. "You arrived in time. Like magic."

His body sagged into the bed with the release of tension he'd not known he'd been holding. Amy touched his face with feather-light fingertips. "It has only ever been you, Colin. Only you."

If he'd not known it before, in that moment he knew for certain she was destined to be his. It seemed the harder he tried to ignore the truth, the more it persisted. He swallowed past the lump in his throat, unable to respond to her artless admission.

"I still cannot believe you're here." Her eyes turned luminous as her fingertips stroked his jaw. "Am I dreaming?"

His hand came up, and his fingers laced with hers. "No," he managed to say. "You're not dreaming."

"You were far away—at Greystone—then suddenly you were here. Exactly when I needed you. Just like during the fire." The wonder in her voice, the total trust her words implied, made Colin's heart skip a beat.

"I'll always be here when you need me," he said simply. "Always."

He squeezed her hand, tight, then drew her head down to rest on his shoulder. She closed her eyes and settled her small, soft body against his. He stroked her satiny skin, feeling her respiration settle into an even pattern, her body relax in the solace of long-denied sleep.

The weight of her head on his shoulder, the warmth of her breath on his neck, the silky pillows of her breasts nestled against his side—all were heaven. Yet he felt as if he were in hell.

Though his heart told him 'twas so, it seemed impossible to admit that the pure essence of Amy—her inherent goodness, her intelligent strength, her passion for life—overcompensated for any drawbacks in her background. She would make a wonderful mother someday; her warmth and compassion would create a haven of security no pedigree could provide; he saw that now. The bond he felt between them—as though she existed for him alone—would extend to children of their bodies as naturally as passion darkened her amethyst eyes.

And yet, he remembered another strong bond: that of a little boy for his parents. And he remembered the heartrending pain of abandonment.

How had this happened to him? He was rational, determined. He'd had a plan.

He'd wanted not to love anyone.

* * *

There was a King's Arms not three blocks from the Chases' town house. The few patrons still there had never heard of Robert Stanley, but the innkeeper directed them to another King's Arms, which directed them to a third.

The place was deserted, but a weary serving maid was still in the back, sweeping up, and she was able to confirm that they had indeed found Robert Stanley's haunt. Perking up at the sound of his name, she informed them that rumor had it he'd taken off with his love, bound for either St. James or St. Trinity.

"There would be no marriages on Sunday." Kendra's eyes sparkled with excitement. "Perhaps we're not too late. We'll go and warn—"

"Oh, no, we will not," Jason interrupted in a tense, clipped voice that forbade any argument. "There is no sense in chasing out there tonight. The morning will do fine."

"But—"

"Listen, Kendra," he said more gently. "We're as concerned about Amy as you are. But I know that neighborhood—'tis no place to visit late on a foggy night. The clergy will have been long since abed, anyway. We'll go first thing in the morning."

Crestfallen, Kendra's enthusiasm evaporated. It had felt so good to be in active pursuit. Still, she knew there was nothing to discuss—Jason made perfect sense. "I want to get there early," she proclaimed. "Before anyone can possibly be married."

"We will. We'll be there when the sun rises."

"Promise?"

"Promise."

Ford put a sympathetic arm around Kendra's shoulders and drew her out of the tavern, and she resigned herself to a sleepless night of waiting.

Colin was awakened by a warm, delicate kiss brushed across his mouth. He opened his eyes lazily, looking up through half-closed lids. In the hazy light of dawn, he gazed upon Amy's face just inches from his, her sweet breath lightly caressing him from between her parted lips.

"Colin, make me forget the feel of his touch," she whispered before lowering her mouth once again to meet his.

He returned her kiss gently, mindful of her bruises. How could he resist such a heavenly invitation? His resolve melted away. Concerns for her battered anatomy and fragile state of mind were pushed aside as his body responded to hers with a will of its own.

Rolling her over slowly, he brushed the hair off her forehead and framed her face in his hands. His eyes searched hers for permission and approval, but what shone from their amethyst depths was such a deep, abiding love that he was momentarily taken aback. His breath caught in his chest, and he blinked, but when he opened his eyes the look was still there. Unconditional and unfaltering.

Her arms came around his back, and she opened her mouth in encouragement. With a soft groan, Colin's lips moved to hers; his tongue plundered her warm mouth with reckless abandon until they were both breathless.

When he lifted his head, breaking contact, in the still room he could feel her heart beating against his. He bent to place a kiss in the hollow of her throat and inched one hand down to caress her breast, but she shook her head.

"Now," she said, her voice shaky and tremulous. "Come inside me *now*. Please."

Her sensuous plea sent the blood racing through Colin's veins. A man given to leisurely, playful lovemaking, in this case he was only too eager to comply.

He came over her, slid inside her welcoming body with one swift thrust. Her answering moan of pleasure drove the last lingering thoughts of restraint from his mind, and his body took over, innately establishing the glorious tempo that bound them together, body and soul.

She cried out, clutching him, and his heart leapt. In that moment, he knew with a stunning clarity they would marry—he would never give her up again. He had tried to protect his heart—tried and failed. Now 'twas bursting with love, and he could deny it not a moment longer.

He pushed into her again, and the sweet sensation of her convulsing around him sent hot fingers of fire sprinting along his nerves, enveloping his entire body in explosions of pleasure.

He slowly spun down to earth and came up on his elbows, brushing the tangled curls off her face with shaking hands. His lips grazed her eyelids, the warm swath of her forehead, and one shell-pink ear. "I love you," he whispered there.

Amy's breath came in uneven gasps. "Wh-what?"

He kissed one downy cheek, the tip of her nose and the other cheek, before his tongue flicked inside her other ear. "I love you," he murmured, his voice husky and unsteady.

"No. You cannot. We cannot."

His head snapped up. "But I saw it in your eyes. I thought you—"

Amy's arms tightened around him, crushing him to her. "I love you, too," she whispered fiercely. "I do. 'Tis just—"

Colin touched his fingers to her lips. "I've never told anyone that, you know," he admitted with rueful candor. "You've disrupted my entire life, Amethyst Goldsmith." In contrast to his words, he felt immensely pleased with himself and his world. He kissed her with all the exquisite tenderness he felt in his heart, completely at peace for the first time in months.

"Tell me again," she begged, a smile in her voice.

"I love you," he said simply, and 'twas easier than he had ever thought possible.

He lifted himself off her, sliding from her body, and a small sound of loss escaped her lips. "Oh . . ."

Chuckling, he settled himself beside her and propped

his head up on one hand. "I'll be back," he promised, shooting her his best irresistibly devastating grin.

"Mmm . . ." Her response was a gentle smile, intimate as a kiss. It sent currents of desire racing through Colin's body, and he snuggled against her suggestively. "Be not too long . . ." Amy said in a seductive whisper, and she blushed, obviously pleased at her own boldness.

To his amazement, Colin's body responded immediately, his arousal rising against her thigh. When he opened his mouth to speak, the words were rough with renewed passion.

"Has it been long enough yet?"

Chapter Twenty-one

'Twas still dark and foggy when Kendra and Ford dropped off Jason and a footman at the deserted St. James. A bleary-eyed Kendra was relieved to confirm they were not too late—at least not at this church.

The twins traveled on to St. Trinity and were elated to find it empty as well. They slipped into a back pew to wait, resting their exhausted bodies and chatting quietly. A couple arrived with two witnesses in tow, and then another couple, the woman visibly pregnant. The two groups stood in separate clusters in the back of the sanctuary, shifting nervously on their feet as they waited for their respective ceremonies to commence.

The light grew steadily brighter, passing through the ancient leaded windows and projecting brilliant colored patches on the walls and floor of the church. At last, a door opened at the other end, and the plump curate entered. He bustled about, lighting a few tapers before turning to address the small crowd.

"Now, who was here first?" A satisfied smile spread on his face as he viewed the assemblage.

"We were, Father." Kendra stood, tugging on Ford's hand to pull him up after her and down the narrow aisle.

"Where are your witnesses?" the curate asked as the twins came up before him.

"But—but," Ford sputtered, "she's my sister!"

The man's crooked teeth disappeared as his smile reversed to a stern frown. "Young man, I realize we're known for being, ah, *tolerant* here at St. Trinity, but the church expressly forbids—"

Kendra's laughter rang through the sanctuary. "We're not here to be wed, Father! We're here to find out if someone else was wed on Saturday, and prevent the marriage if it's not already taken place."

"Well, why did you not just say so?" the clergyman asked peevishly. "Whom are you inquiring about?"

"Amy—Amethyst—Goldsmith and Robert Stanley."

The curate's eyes opened wider. "I declare, I cannot recall the last time there was so much interest in one wedding. Why—"

"Then they're already married?" Kendra interrupted, her voice shrill.

"No. Not to my knowledge." When Kendra sagged in relief, the clergyman smiled. "I believe they were here Saturday evening, however, and yesterday a tall gentleman with dark hair—"

"Our brother," the twins said in unison.

The stout man looked them both over thoughtfully. "Yes, he could have been. In any case, the groom in question planned to return this morning, and your brother went off to search the inns on Fenchurch Street last night."

"Thank you *so* much." Kendra's smile was contagious. She handed the man a coin.

The curate's uneven teeth reappeared, although his gaze was already shifting to the other couples. "Now, who was next?"

Kendra and Ford retreated to the front steps of the church, where they quickly decided Ford would wait inside in case Robert and Amy appeared, while Kendra fetched Jason.

She arrived at St. James to find Jason pacing by the doors. He strode to the carriage. "What's news?"

"They're not wed." Kendra grinned. "But he plans to wed her today, at St. Trinity. Jason . . ."

"What?" He climbed inside and pulled the door shut.

"I'm hoping you'll not mind, but I asked Carrington to head for Fenchurch Street. The curate said Colin was searching the inns there last night. I'm thinking perhaps he grew tired and slept there overnight." Jason started to protest, but Kendra held up a hand, rushing to finish. "Check a few of the inns, *please*? I cannot just sit and wait."

"But you said Robert and Amy are due back at the church."

" 'Tis still early. Besides, Ford will take care of matters should they show up."

"There's no arguing with you once your mind is set, is there?" Jason muttered. For the next half-hour, he obligingly walked along Fenchurch, checking a few likely places while the coach followed at a crawl.

Kendra regretted the detour almost immediately. Waiting in the carriage, she grew more and more impatient as she watched Jason go in and out. She noticed a sign in the window of Mr. Farr's Tobacco Shop, proclaiming it had "The Best Tobacco by Farr." A few shops down, there was another sign, that of his rival, "Far Better Tobacco than the Best Tobacco by Farr." She smiled, but mostly she was bored and restless, wondering what was happening back at the church.

Coming out of the fifth inn, Jason stalked to the carriage, his face set in purposeful lines. The door was flung open just as he arrived.

"Kendra, this is—"

"—a waste of time. They may have turned up at St. Trinity by now. And much as I trust Ford to intervene, I'd hate to miss the resulting scene. It ought to be better than Shakespeare."

Worn out as he was, Jason couldn't help but smile. "You're something else, you know that?"

"I'm *your* sister." Kendra's return grin lit up her face. "Come along."

Before climbing inside, Jason instructed his coachman to turn around at Mark Lane and head back to St. Trinity. But they'd driven less than half a block when Kendra started banging on the roof of the carriage. "*Stop! Stop!*"

Nonplussed, Jason groaned. "What the devil—"

"That's Ebony! There, in that shed. Colin is here!"

She was down from the coach before the wheels stopped turning. Jason reluctantly followed her out. "Now, Kendra, not every horse with a white star on his forehead is Ebony."

But it was. Whickering softly as they approached, Ebony bent his big head to search Jason's pockets for a treat.

"Colin must be in there." Kendra indicated a dubious establishment called the Cat and Canary.

"I think not." Jason shook his head. "Colin wouldn't stay in a place like that, no matter how tired he was."

"Then where?"

He pointed to the back wall of the shed. "Behind there is Leadenhall Street. And a very nice inn, if I'm not mistaken."

Minutes later, they were knocking on the door to Number Three at the Rose and Crown. A sleepy Colin came to answer, his breeches unlaced, his hair in disarray, and a dopey, satisfied smile plastered on his bristled face.

Kendra pushed past him, needing no other evidence to guess she'd find Amy in his bed. "She's in here, Jason," she shouted, wondering whether to be thrilled she'd found Amy, or angry to find her sitting in bed, a quilt clutched to her bare chest and a smile matching Colin's on her face.

Jason shoved Colin back and followed him into the room, shutting the door with a little more force than was necessary. "Now you've done it."

Colin's smile was infectious. "I know. I found her. I can scarcely believe it myself." He ambled over to retrieve his shirt and slipped it over his head. "A fine bit of sleuthing, was it not? Hey—how did you find us, anyway?"

"That's not what I meant," Jason growled. "Once again, you've—"

Shouldering Jason out of the way, Kendra took his

place before her obstinate brother. "What he meant is, you'll have to marry her now, you—"

"I fully intend to," Colin said toward the floor as he tucked in his shirt and laced up his breeches. His words were quiet and matter-of-fact—so much so that Kendra failed to register them.

But Amy did. She let out a small gasp of surprise. *Marriage!* Colin had said he loved her, but never mentioned . . .

No, 'twould never work. Her stomach felt leaden and her eyes grew misty, but the siblings were too busy with each other to notice.

"Why are you grinning, you idiot?" Kendra railed. "You could not just bring her to the town house, could you? Once again, you've—"

Jason shoved Kendra over with his hip and stood next to her, the two of them effectively making a solid wall that obscured Colin from Amy's view. "You've really made a mess of things now, Colin Chase." Usually the calm one, Jason's voice seethed with uncharacteristic rage. "You couldn't leave well enough—"

"Jason. Kendra. I said I'm going to marry her." Though Amy couldn't see Colin, she could hear the smile in his voice. He was enjoying this little scene. And she'd not heard wrong the first time—he really did intend to make her his wife.

God in heaven, she couldn't marry him. Her father would never forgive her.

A prolonged silence settled as Kendra and Jason were shocked speechless. Then Kendra whirled to face Amy. "Is this true?"

Amy clutched the blanket closer to her body. "I—no. No." She shook her head, slowly and then faster, trying to convince herself as tears sprang to her eyes. "No."

"What?" Colin strode to the bed and stood staring down at her. "I told you last night—"

"—that you loved me." It hurt to look at him; she dropped her gaze, picking at the edge of the quilt. "I love you too, but I cannot marry you, Colin. I cannot. I have to reestablish the business—I told you that. I vowed I would see it carried on. And you said a nobleman's wife cannot run a shop. When we were at Greystone, you said if I married a nobleman, I'd never be able to reopen Goldsmith & Sons." She swallowed hard and looked up. "You said it, Colin—I heard you."

"Of course I said it!" He opened his mouth as though to say more, but just stood there, red faced and tongue tied.

"You would choose a business over my brother?" Kendra shifted on her feet. "Over becoming a countess?"

" 'Tis not a matter of choice!" Amy brushed angrily at her tears; why could these people not understand? "I was born to a craft. And I hold in trust a fortune—I cannot just turn the Goldsmith inheritance over to a husband . . . it belongs to future business generations."

"I'd not take it, Amy. You have my word on that."

"What?" 'Twas Jason's turn to look astonished. His lips thinned beneath his narrow black mustache. "You were right when you said they belong together, Kendra. They're both totally, completely insane."

Colin took a deep breath, the red fading from his features. "You have to marry me," he said calmly.

"Is something wrong with your hearing?" How many times could she refuse him without giving in? Every denial cost her a piece of her heart. "I said I cannot marry you. I cannot."

"You must."

"I said—"

"Robert is still out there. Bloody hell, I knew I should have killed him." He looked thoroughly disgusted with himself. "He'll find you, Amy. Even in Paris. He'll find you and he'll try again to force you to the altar. Maybe he'll succeed next time, or maybe he'll just murder you instead. Then he can petition for your wealth on the basis of the betrothal . . ."

Amy felt the blood drain out of her face. She put her hands to her cheeks. Dear God, Colin was right.

". . . If you marry me, 'twould do him no good to come after you—"

"Because my fortune would belong to you, then."

"Only legally." His emerald eyes burned into hers.

" 'Tis meant for the business," she whispered.

" 'Tis meant for your descendants. As security, no?"

She nodded.

"They'll have it."

"Colin—" Jason interrupted.

"Just shut up." Colin waved him off. "They'll have it," he repeated. He knelt by the bed and took her hands in his. "Now . . . will you marry me?"

She stared at him, his beloved features wavering through her tears. To wed Colin Chase—her heart's most selfish desire—so selfish she'd not even dared to let herself consider it. But he was right—she had no choice. 'Twas either wed him or Robert, or forfeit her life.

Forgive me, Papa, she intoned in her head, then nodded at Colin. His hands tightened around hers, almost painfully, and he raised himself to brush a kiss across her lips. An unfamiliar and unexpected warmth surged through her—a feeling of belonging to someone that she'd not experienced in a long time.

Her senses were already spinning when Kendra let out a whoop of joy and threw herself on the bed, almost dislodging Amy's quilt. She pulled Amy to her in a tight embrace that reminded Amy just how bruised and battered she was, but Amy cared not. It felt so good to know she was about to be part of a family again. And when Kendra gushed, "Oh, Amy, you'll really, truly be my sister now," Amy was so happy she thought her heart would burst.

"Good job, Colin." Jason slapped his brother on the back, beaming. "You finally came to your senses."

Kendra disentangled herself from Amy and put in, "You were such a bloody blockhead, I was ready to strangle you."

Colin just stood there grinning like an imbecile. Jason

walked to the bed and leaned to kiss Amy on both cheeks. "Welcome to the family," he said warmly, and Amy would have thrown her arms around him if she'd not been in such an embarrassing state of undress. As it was, tears welled once more in her eyes. She blinked them back, and Jason straightened and cleared his throat. "We'll have it at Cainewood," he said to Colin.

Colin had just sat down to put on his stockings and boots. "Have what?" he asked blankly.

Kendra made a rude noise. "The wedding, of course." She turned to Jason. "He's still not himself, is he? A spring wedding . . . We'll have to start planning immediately."

"Oh, no." The words were uttered in a voice that brooked no nonsense, and three pairs of eyes swung to Colin. "No spring wedding. We'll be married *today*."

"You cannot," Kendra protested. "You have no license. No banns have been posted."

"Amy was to have been wed at St. Trinity this morning, and wed there she will be. There's a madman loose. And even were that not so, I would wait not a minute longer than necessary to make her my wife." Colin's gaze locked on Amy's, and any objections she may have had to being married in a place of Robert Stanley's choosing were swept away in an instant. Colin wanted her, and that was all that mattered.

"But . . ." Not one to be dissuaded easily, Kendra turned on Amy. "You want a real wedding, do you not? With guests and a wedding gown and dancing for hours afterward?"

Amy slowly shook her head. She had planned a big wedding once, with a plethora of guests and a dress covered in love-knots, and she'd been altogether miserable. Suddenly a simple wedding today, even at St. Trinity, seemed perfect.

And she'd be Colin's wife by tonight . . . It still did not seem real. 'Twas too good to be true. *You cannot have everything,* she could hear her father saying—and he'd been right. But she had no choice. Joy bubbled up inside her, and she hugged herself in blissful disbelief.

Now that was settled, Colin became all business. He strode to the hearth and picked up the ice-blue gown from where they'd left it in a crumpled heap on the floor. It rustled as he shook it out, saying, " 'Tis ripped in the back. Damn."

Amy froze.

"Let me see." Kendra reached for the gown. No one noticed the color draining from Amy's face. " 'Tis just a seam. I'm sure someone belowstairs can stitch it up in no time."

"No." The word was almost a whimper, and three sets of concerned green eyes fastened on Amy huddled on the bed. "I was supposed to marry *him* in that gown. I'll not wear it."

Colin spread his hands and glanced around the room as though he expected a wedding gown to materialize out of thin air.

"I will not wear it," Amy repeated through clenched teeth.

Colin's hands dropped; his fingers drummed against one thigh as he stared at the gown in Kendra's arms, its icy blue contrasting with her own bright green dress. His fingers stilled, and he brightened. "Kendra, why do you not simply—"

Before the words were out of his mouth, Kendra wadded up the offending garment and thrust it into the fireplace.

It ignited with a great *whoosh,* sending sparks flying into the room, and Colin blinked, dumbfounded. "What did you do that for? I was going to suggest—"

"A typical logical male solution—my swapping gowns with Amy. You poor fool. I can assure you she doesn't want that dress in the same city, let alone standing next to her as witness to her marriage." Shaking her head in mock exasperation, Kendra turned to Amy. "Men can be so stupid sometimes. Are you sure you want to marry this one?"

Amy's answering giggle brought a grin to Colin's face. He bowed in Kendra's direction. "Your servant, my lady. Since you're so intelligent, I'm awaiting your instructions on how to deal with this problem." He bent down and picked up the filthy shredded nightgown, dangling it at arm's length from two fingers. "Shall she wear this, do you suppose?"

Another giggle from Amy was drowned by a loud guffaw from Jason. Kendra rolled her eyes. "No, I don't suppose. But I do have a plan."

"By all means, inform us. We're all dying of curiosity."

Kendra took a deep breath. "You, Colin Chase, are going to have to wait a few hours for your wedding. Do you think you can handle that?"

He raised one eyebrow, apparently reserving judgment. Kendra continued in authoritative tones. "Being Monday, Amy's gowns are now ready at Madame Beaumont's. I shall fetch one and bring it here. *You* will go home, clean up, and return in appropriate wedding attire. Look at you—your shirt is ripped."

"A bullet will do that," Colin said wryly.

"A *bullet*?"

He waved off her concern. "'Tis nothing, just a scratch."

"Colin—" Jason started.

"'Tis *nothing*. Amy?"

"'Tis nothing," Amy said with a small smile. She loved this bickering family.

Colin turned back to Kendra. "Continue."

"Well, then, you've not shaved in two days!"

"I apologize for offending you," Colin drawled, rubbing his whiskered chin. "I've been a mite busy."

"Well, I'll admit we do have evidence you were occupied," Kendra returned, looking pointedly at Amy.

Amy had been so busy enjoying their argument and basking in the warmth of their acceptance, she'd almost forgotten her unseemly predicament. Now the center of their attention, she blushed from her hairline to her toes.

Colin grinned with masculine pride, but Jason took pity on her. "Now that you've thoroughly embarrassed Colin's bride," he said to Kendra, "are you quite finished?"

"Yes," Kendra muttered. "Sorry, Amy."

"Colin, you seem to have forgotten one large obstacle to this hasty wedding." The good-natured bantering tone had disappeared from Jason's voice, and he looked toward Colin with all seriousness.

"What could that be?" Colin held up a hand and ticked off imaginary impediments on his fingers. "Apparently there's a gown waiting for Amy, and we've established my need to shave and change my shirt . . . What? What is it?"

"The simple matter that you're betrothed to someone else?"

"Oh. There is that."

Amy's heart skipped in her chest.

Jason kept his eyes trained on Colin. "Yes, there is."

"You don't suppose I could just write her a letter afterward?"

"No, I don't think that would quite satisfy my sense of propriety."

"I didn't think so." Colin paused, staring at his boots for a moment, and Amy held her breath. "Well, there's nothing for it," he said at last. "I shall ride to Priscilla's house straightaway and explain myself. I don't expect they can force me to the altar."

"Let us hope Lord Hobbs agrees. There's the matter of the dowr—"

"Shh." With a furtive glance at Amy, Colin held up a hand. "He has no choice. He's a cold, calculating buzzard, but he'll not get the best of me." Colin suddenly smiled, and Amy started breathing again. "Can you imagine anyone voluntarily becoming his son-in-law?" he asked playfully. "Or, even more unbelievable, taking his daughter to wife, when she's such a—"

"Snob?" Kendra supplied helpfully.

"Exactly."

Jason clapped Colin on the shoulder. "Are you still determined to accomplish all this today?"

Colin ignored his brother, smiling at Amy instead. "Absolutely." He locked his eyes on hers, and she melted a little inside.

"Shall I come along with you?" Jason offered.

"No. I do believe I'm actually looking forward to clipping this buzzard's wings." His smile widened, his eyes crinkled at the corners, and she melted a little bit more.

"Very well, then. Kendra and I will fetch Amy's clothes and meet you at the town house. We'll all return together."

Frowning, Colin tore his gaze from Amy's. "Wait a minute—we cannot leave Amy alone. That scoundrel Stanley is still walking the earth—an error I am regretting more with each passing minute."

"I'll send up one of the footmen to guard the door."

"Make that two," Colin said. "And Amy will need breakfast sent up as well."

Jason nodded. "Done." Smiling, he swiped Colin's swordbelt off the table and tossed it to him. "I'll have to cancel some appointments, but I suppose this takes precedence."

Colin caught the sword and buckled it on, grinning mischievously. "Are you sure, now? I'd not want to be responsible for upsetting your schedule."

"I'm sure." The brothers' eyes met, sparkling leaf-green to glittering emerald. Jason moved to enclose Colin in a bear hug. "God, I thought this day would never come. A Chase, married."

" 'Twas bound to happen sooner or later," Colin said, his voice a bit choked. "Shall we?" He accepted the surcoat that Kendra held out, flinging it over one shoulder, then went to Amy and leaned to brush a kiss across her forehead. Her heart pounded at his nearness and the realization that he would be hers—all hers—from now on, and she risked releasing her blanket to reach up her arms and wind them around his neck, pulling his mouth down to hers. Their lips met and clung for a long, sweet minute, until Jason cleared his throat.

"Get some rest, love." Colin's tone was more suggestive than his words. "I don't plan on letting you sleep tonight."

His sister gasped. "Col-in!"

"Hang it, Kendra, this was your idea in the first place."

Amy snuggled down in the bed, listening to Kendra's exaggerated sniff, Jason's infectious laugh, and Colin's hurried footsteps as they left to prepare for the wedding. Her family—almost.

The door closed behind them, but she could hear Kendra's exclamation through the walls. "Oh, my God—we forgot Ford!"

Colin leaned against the mantel in the Hobbs's massive drawing room, twisting his ring and steeling himself to face Priscilla. Breaking the betrothal had seemed such a simple matter at the Rose and Crown; now that he was here, he suspected 'twould be harder than he'd thought. Priscilla would be unhappy, mostly out of humiliation, if he didn't miss his guess—he was well aware she harbored little genuine affection for him. He wondered if she were even capable of deep feeling.

Her father would be furious. Lord Hobbs had searched high and low for a son-in-law with Colin's connections, thrusting his daughter at every likely candidate. He'd not take lightly to having his careful plans thwarted.

Hearing heavy footsteps on the parquet floor outside the room, Colin stood up straight and tugged his surcoat tighter around his middle, hoping to conceal the rip in his shirt. His jaw tightened when Lord Hobbs entered, alone. A tall, pale man, he was most definitely his daughter's father, though he did have a more animated personality—one that had always rubbed Colin the wrong way.

"Lord Hobbs. I had asked to speak with Priscilla."

"My daughter is not home at the moment. I was thinking we might share a drink while you waited. King Charles—" Hobbs broke off and looked critically at Colin, his gray gaze sizing up the younger man's rumpled form. "My God, Greystone, you look positively disreputable. Have you fought a duel, or what?"

"Something like that," Colin muttered, rubbing his stubbled jaw. "When will Priscilla be returning?"

"Lord knows. She's off shopping with a few friends—spending my money like there's no tomorrow, no doubt." He poured Madeira into two goblets and handed one to Colin with a jovial slap on the back. "Glad that will be *your* problem soon."

Colin couldn't dally until Priscilla returned; Amy was waiting. "That is what I wanted to talk about, sir. I'm sorry Priscilla is not here, but perhaps 'tis best I talk to you, in any case."

"About Priscilla's spending habits? I suppose you can put her on an allowance, but she'll not take kindly—"

"No, sir. About our marriage." Colin took a mouthful of wine and swallowed it deliberately. "I want to call off our betrothal."

"You *what*?"

Colin hadn't eaten in two days. The Madeira burned a path down his throat and into his stomach, and courage flowed in after it. "I want to call off our betrothal," he repeated firmly. "Your daughter and I—we aren't suited. 'Tis not a good match."

"Not a good match? You need her fortune, and I need the King's ear in order to obtain a license to develop my land outside London. 'Tis a perfect match."

"I don't love your daughter, sir."

"Pshaw! What does that matter? Take a mistress—my daughter is not the warmest of women—you think I've not noticed? I'll not think the less of you for it." Hobbs put an arm around Colin and tugged him close to his side. "A warm, willing wench in the City and a beautiful heiress in the country—what more could a man want, eh?"

Hobbs's hot, alcoholic breath washed over Colin's

face, and Colin pulled away before he retched in response. The man was making him physically sick. Colin felt sorry for Priscilla—'twas not her fault he couldn't love her—and angry with Hobbs for treating his own daughter so callously. The despicable buzzard. He took a deep breath and moved farther away from the man.

"I'm marrying someone else this afternoon," he said quietly.

Hobbs's jaw set, and his breath became labored. "You would leave Priscilla for another woman? *My* Priscilla? After a formal betrothal? After you—you *ruined* her?"

Despite the gravity of the situation, Colin felt an absurd urge to laugh. "Ruined her?" he said, incredulous. "That's a joke."

Hobbs's gray eyes darkened in anger. "Not everyone shares our good King's lack of morals, young man. Priscilla was raised properly, and—"

"Do you honestly believe she was a virgin when I took her to my bed?" The outraged father role did not fit Hobbs well; Colin could see the truth in his eyes, and he'd had it with the man's pomposity. "After you tried to pawn her off on half the Royalists in England?"

"You . . . you . . ."

"There is not a name you could call me that would change my mind." With an outward calm that he didn't feel, Colin set his goblet on the table, spread his feet and crossed his arms. "What will it take to satisfy you, Lord Hobbs?" His hand moved to his sword. "You may draw my blood if it will appease your sense of honor, but I warn you: I do not intend to lay down my life in order to be released from this betrothal."

The older man's eyes flickered toward Colin's sword and back up, then narrowed connivingly. "I'm certain we can find a civilized way to settle this, Greystone."

"What do you want?"

"A private audience with His Majesty."

'Twas naught but an audience—'twould cost Charles nothing but a few minutes of his time. He'd do it if Colin asked. But it made Colin furious that he would have to ask. "I'll get you your audience. I'll get you ten audiences. You can have a standing appointment—"

"Just one audience. As long as you can guarantee my license will be forthcoming."

Colin paused. 'Twas a tall order. Though Hobbs had professed neutrality throughout the War, he was rumored to be a closet Parliamentarian. The King did not look kindly on those responsible for beheading his father; Charles didn't merely disregard Hobbs, he actively disliked the man. More than a simple request, this would mean asking a special favor of Charles. But Charles owed the Chases favors. And a license wouldn't cost Charles, either—to the contrary, he would probably milk Hobbs for an exorbitant fee. It grated on Colin, a scheming buzzard like Lord Hobbs getting his way, but 'twould not be a problem.

He nodded once. "Consider it done."

Hobbs didn't smile. He seated himself at the drawing room's marquetry writing table and waved Colin into a chair. "I'll expect my funds returned within the week, of course."

Colin's stomach knotted; this was the part he'd been dreading. "No, sir. I . . . haven't the funds. They were used for renovations to—"

"Then the deal is off. You were legally betrothed, and you accepted part of the dowry. Surely you do not expect—"

"I'll pay it back. Just"—Colin sucked in a breath—"give me some time."

Hobbs fixed him with an icy stare. "You will sign a note. Eight percent interest, with the balance due before we see 1668."

A year. One year. If the renovations were halted, the fields produced a bumper crop, the quarry was extra-productive, the sheep thrived . . . 'twas a terrible gamble. Colin pictured Amy waiting for him at the inn, and his vision blurred.

He would have Amy's inheritance. But he'd promised her he wouldn't take it.

"I'm waiting for your answer," Hobbs pressed. "Unless you'd prefer to pretend you never walked in here today."

Colin blinked. "I'll sign it."

Hobbs wasted no time producing paper, quill, and ink. He scribbled a hasty contract, which Colin signed, a weight in his gut, the scratch of the quill sounding like nothing so much as a death knell. Hobbs dripped wax by the signature, and Colin used his ring to set his seal, remembering the day he ordered it from Amy. How he had walked away that day, expecting never to see her again.

Hobbs sprinkled sand on the ink, then dusted off and rolled up the contract. "If you fail to pay up, as God is my witness I'll have you slapped into Newgate Prison so fast your head will spin. You'll see the devil in heaven the day I show you mercy."

Although 'twould never come to that—Hobbs would end up with Greystone instead—the thought of squalid, vermin-infested Newgate made the bile rise in Colin's throat. He pushed away the image. He'd find some way to pay back the money. Whatever sacrifices were necessary would be worth it in the end.

Hobbs tucked the scroll in a drawer, poured himself another goblet of wine, and downed it in one gulp. "I won, you know." He swiped a hand across his mouth. "I'll have my license, and I still have my daughter."

"To sell to the highest bidder? The man with the next item on your agenda?"

"That is what daughters are for. You'll learn it when you have your own."

Colin ignored that, setting aside his own goblet of Madeira in disgust.

"Who is she?" Hobbs asked suddenly.

"It doesn't signify. She has nothing to do with my lack of love for your daughter."

"Love, hah! You're a weak man, Greystone—my daughter is well rid of you."

Hobbs's stare dared Colin to respond to the insult,

but Colin forced himself to ignore him once again. "Please give Priscilla my regards, and my sincere apologies."

"She'll be fine. She'll suffer some loss of face, but she'll survive. I'll remind her how little she liked you—and your 'countrified' family, as I believe she called them."

That should have hurt Colin, but it didn't. He felt nothing but relief and an overwhelming compulsion to escape.

He stood. "I'll take my leave, then."

To Colin's vast surprise, Hobbs held out a hand. "A pleasure doing business with you, Greystone."

Colin blinked. "There are no hard feelings, then?"

Hobbs shrugged. " 'Twas all for the better."

"That it was," Colin muttered, proffering a half-hearted handshake. He shuddered to think how narrowly he'd escaped becoming this man's son-in-law. Claiming one favor from Charles and acquiring a monstrous debt were small penalties indeed for avoiding the biggest mistake of his life.

Still and all, if he never saw that buzzard's face again, it would suit him just fine.

Chapter Twenty-two

With Kendra in tow, Madame Beaumont bustled into the room and made her way to the window, throwing open the shutters. "Get up, mademoiselle. We must make you ready for the *mariage*!"

Amy sat up, blinking the sleep from her eyes. She winced as Madame clutched her chin, turning her poor bruised face this way and that to examine it in the early afternoon light.

"Mon Dieu!" Madame exclaimed, shaking her head, "we have a lot of work to do!" She gestured at the door. "Come in, come in." Two footmen entered, toting a large wooden box. Madame indicated a spot on the floor where she expected the box placed, then shooshed them out with an impatient wave of her hand.

Kendra giggled, hiding her face as she rummaged in the big box. She pulled out a dressing gown fashioned in peach-colored fabric with a lavish lace edging. An amused smile played around her lips as she helped Amy out of bed and into the garment, tying it at her waist as one would for a small child.

While Kendra sat Amy at the dressing table, Madame took a small wooden case from the box. Carrying it by its ornate brass handle, she brought it over and opened its hinged lid with a flourish. The contents were a jumble of brushes and pencils, jars, bottles, pots and boxes filled with mysterious colored powders and pomades, all of which Madame set about the tabletop.

"Now . . ." she said, lifting a sinister metal tool. In her jewelry shop, Amy had used something similar to pick up loose gemstones. She flinched as Madame tilted her chin up and leaned over her, the device hovering in the region of her forehead. "Oooh, *charmant,*" Madame gushed suddenly. "Perfectly arched. Just look." As though Amy were nothing more than a doll, Madame swung her head around toward Kendra, then dropped the implement on the table. "No plucking," Madame declared, and Amy's eyes widened as she glared at Kendra. Plucking, indeed!

Madame set to work, conferring with Kendra from time to time, and Amy relaxed, as no other instruments of torture seemed to be forthcoming. They chatted excitedly about the upcoming wedding and Colin waiting below in the taproom, "probably drinking himself into a stupor," according to Kendra.

Amy bit her lip. "I've never worn cosmetics."

"No?" Using a hare's foot, Madame powdered Amy's face.

"No. My father . . . I mean, the merchant class . . . 'tis not considered acceptable . . ." At their vague smiles, her voice trailed off. Could she ever fit in their world?

She sneaked a wary glance in the mirror, then gasped. "Marry come up! The bruises are gone!" She touched her fingers to her face in wonder. "And the dark circles under my eyes."

" 'Tis the Princesses Powder." Madame brushed away her fingers and applied more to repair the damage.

"Princesses Powder?" Amy clenched her hands in her lap to keep them from shaking. Merchants' daughters didn't wear powder made for princesses. And they didn't wed earls, either . . .

" 'Tis so called because four princesses, whose great *beauté* is known throughout Europe, have used it with such success they've preserved an air of youth 'til seventy years of *âge*."

"Seventy years?" Kendra touched non-existent crow's feet at the corners of her eyes. "I *must* have some."

Madame turned away to swipe powder on Kendra's cheeks. "You can procure a supply from Madame Elizabeth Jackson, near Maypole in the Strand, for a price of sixpence per authentic packet."

Amy stared at her reflection. Would her father be disappointed if he were here? She was breaking her promises, but he'd loved her . . . would he really deny her love for Colin?

"A bargain at twice the price." Kendra's face appeared behind Amy's in the mirror. She frowned at her newly-powdered complexion, then smiled. "I shall visit Elizabeth Jackson tomorrow. Will you come, Amy?"

Amy shook her head slowly, pressing her lips together to hide the telltale quiver.

"Of course not; how silly of me." Kendra's grin grew wider. "You'll want to be with Colin, will you not?" She handed Madame a kohl pencil.

With Colin. What a wonderful, magical thought. "Yes, I will," Amy said, surprised at how clear and sure her voice rang through the room.

Turning Amy from the mirror, Madame rimmed her eyes with the kohl and darkened her lashes and brows with the end of a burnt cork. "Oh, did I get some in your eyes?" Concerned, she leaned closer, peering at Amy. "*Je regrette.* I'm so sorry."

" 'Tis all right." Amy blinked back the tears, chagrined that she couldn't seem to control herself. She stole another glance in the looking glass. "My eyes look huge," she worried. "Maybe Colin won't like me with a painted face."

"Don't be a goose." Kendra giggled. "I expect I'll have to wipe the drool off his chin."

Madame tore a sheet of red Spanish paper out of a tiny booklet and rubbed it lightly on Amy's cheeks.

"Did Colin talk to Priscilla?" Amy hesitantly asked Kendra.

"No, her father."

"And?" Amy watched as Madame took up a small pot. "What happened?"

"Shh," Madame interjected, applying pomade to Amy's lips.

Kendra shrugged. "I know not exactly, but everything is taken care of. Talk not to him of it. He's rather furious. Still muttering about the buzzard or some such."

Amy was about to ask another question, when Madame took her by the shoulders and swung her around to fully face the mirror.

She stared, her eyes sparkling. "I-I'm beautiful," she breathed, watching in wonder as the words came from between her glossy parted lips.

"No," Kendra corrected. "You're magnificent. You've always been beautiful." She bent to wrap Amy in a hug. "My beautiful sister—can you credit it?" Sniffing, she wiped her eyes, and Amy wiped her own, too. "Oh, we're both going to ruin our faces! Let us get you dressed."

As Madame fetched her clothing from the box, Amy stood in a daze, trembling from head to toe, plagued by second thoughts, yet excited at the unbelievable miracle of wedding Colin. Madame and Kendra seemed not to notice as they slid off her dressing gown and pulled a new chemise over her head, taking care not to disturb her carefully applied face. Next came the sapphire and cream gown Amy had despaired of ever having the occasion to wear.

The minute they smoothed the satin skirts over her hips, her doubts scattered. 'Twas going to happen. God in heaven, she would be a countess before the day was out.

"Mine, I hope they fit." Interrupting her thoughts, Kendra held out stockings and a pair of fashionable Louis-heeled shoes.

With a distracted smile, Amy drew on the stockings and stepped into the shoes, teetering on the high heels while Madame twisted a sleeve here and tweaked the waistline there until she was satisfied. She led Amy back to the dressing table and tucked a kerchief into her low decolletage, to protect the exquisite pearl-studded lace while she powdered Amy's neck and cleavage to match her face.

A curling iron was set to heat at the edge of the fire, and Madame set to work on Amy's hair. "You really should cut this if you wish to be *à la mode.*" With the edge of her hand against Amy's neck, the seamstress indicated the preferred length, just below ear-level. Remembering the feel of Colin's hands caressing her hair, Amy blanched and gathered her long tresses into both fists. Madame chuckled. "Perhaps not today."

"Colin wouldn't like it," Amy stated flatly, and that was that. Madame's deft hands twisted, braided, and curled, and before long Amy's hair was arranged in a semblance of fashionable style—long ringlets at the sides and a bun plaited together with sapphire ribbons in the back.

"No wires." Madame patted Amy's thick mass of curls.

"No fair," Kendra pouted. "I need wires and false ringlets besides."

"Now *you're* being the goose," Amy said. "What I'd not give for that rich red color. And have you any idea how long it takes to dry this?"

"*Mon Dieu,* mesdemoiselles," Madame clucked. "We all have to work with what God gives us, and you're both lovely." She rummaged with a fingertip through a tiny box of black beauty patches. "Hearts, stars, flowers . . . which do you think?"

"Hearts," Kendra decided. " 'Tis for a wedding, after all."

"No patches. I'm painted enough as it is. Colin will scarcely recognize me."

Kendra snorted. " 'Tis not as if you're painted like an actress. One patch?"

"This is not a negotiation." Amy laughed. "No patches."

"Madame?"

Madame took Amy by one elbow, stood her up, and guided her to the center of the chamber. Amy stood stiff as a poker while Madame walked all the way around her, looking her up and down. The seamstress backed across the room, her eyes narrowing as she contemplated her creation.

"Her complexion is flawless," she said to Kendra.

"What difference does that make?" Kendra wondered. "Patches are all the rage; they're not just to hide pimples and smallpox scars anymore."

"She's a perfect bride, *n'est-ce pas*?" Madame led Amy to the pier glass. "Look."

Amy gazed in the mirror, mesmerized. All evidence of her mistreatment was hidden. Veiled by the cosmetics, her face, neck and shoulders appeared creamy and unblemished. Vanilla lace spilled from her sleeves and over her wrists, concealing the unsightly abrasions. The glossy sapphire satin shimmered; the pearls on her collar and underskirt gleamed. Fat, springy corkscrew curls spilled artistically over her shoulders, and suddenly, the ebony color seemed to suit her perfectly. To her vast relief, she did not look overpainted—to the contrary, owing to Madame's skill, she looked very much like herself, only enhanced. Her eyes met Kendra's in the glass, and they shared a smile. Amy had never felt so beautiful.

She would have stared at herself forever, but Madame gave them both a little push. "The groom is waiting. *Allez-y!*" With a graceful wave of her hand, she dismissed them.

The brothers' conversation had long since turned to discussing the interminable length of time women always took to get ready. Colin popped the cork on yet another bottle of sack, saying, "I vow, they must have food in there."

"Food?"

"Food. They never eat much in front of us, yet they always complain about how full they are after a few bites. My theory is they sneak food into their dressing chambers. They likely take no longer than we do to dress." Colin paused for a swallow of wine from the green bottle. "While we're out here, waiting and starving, they're dining and laughing at us."

Ford chuckled. "Just how long do you hypothesize this has been going on?"

"Since the dawn of time, at the very least."

Jason stroked his mustache. "And they've kept this a secret over the centuries?"

" 'Tis a vast conspiracy—every female is sworn to secrecy from birth." Colin spoke solemnly, but the glitter in his eyes betrayed his amusement. He lowered his voice and leaned into the center of the table. "We've always teased Kendra because she eats her dessert first. Well, that is because she already—"

An apparition coming down the stairs claimed Colin's attention, effectively cutting off his words. A vision in sapphire and cream, Amy glided toward him. His breath caught as he wondered how he'd ever considered letting her go.

The gown's bodice fit like a second skin, emphasizing her slim waist. The skirts flared over her hips, reminding him of the lush curves underneath. Satin and lace, ribbons and pearls; she lacked only some of her exquisite jewelry to look every inch the countess she was about to become. But it mattered not—she could be wearing a burlap sack and he would marry her.

When Jason jiggled his elbow, Colin slowly stood up.

"Dear God in heaven," Amy whispered. He was quite simply the most magnificent male she had ever seen. Once, months ago in her shop, she'd been overwhelmed by his almost-beautiful countenance, but her initial impression had long since been replaced by a sense of the complex mix of body, heart, and intellect that, to her, was Colin. Now, seeing him dressed for his wedding—*their* wedding—the awe came rushing back.

The handsome planes of his face were clean shaven, and his freshly washed hair hung in dark waves to his shoulders. But 'twas his formal clothing that transformed him in Amy's eyes—a black velvet suit that reminded her of the one she'd seen in his bedchamber's chest.

Given Colin's tastes, the suit was a passable nod to fashion, the breeches fuller than he preferred, though not the petticoat breeches—actually divided skirts—that were in vogue. Where a dandy's apparel would be dripping in looped ribbons—cuffs, waist, and epaulettes—Colin's was finished with gold braid. His full, snow-white shirt was trimmed with lace at the gathered cuffs. Matching lace decorated the cravat that flowed over the collar of his short doublet, Amy's gold-edged cameo pinning it in place. The signet ring she'd made for him was his only other jewelry.

Though Jason and Ford were decked out in similar finery, she had eyes only for Colin. When he started toward her, she saw he was wearing shoes—*shoes*, not boots!—heeled, with high tongues and stiff narrow ribbon bows. Amy could scarcely believe this model of masculine perfection was about to be hers. She felt breathless, lightheaded. She almost tripped at the bottom of the stairs, but Colin was there and caught her in his arms.

"No fainting, now," he quipped. "I may look like a peacock, but I assure you I'm the same man you consented to marry."

Clad head to toe in black and white, he hardly looked like a peacock. "No . . . you look . . ."

"Like a featherbrained fop, no doubt." Setting Amy down, Colin threw a peevish glance in Kendra's direction. "These are my Court clothes. She *made* me wear them."

Kendra's laughter floated down the stairs. "No one makes you do anything, Colin Chase. Though, God knows we've tried."

"Besides," Amy declared, "I was about to say you look incredibly handsome."

Colin's face flushed pink under his fading tan, revealing his embarrassment at the public compliment. He clutched the sides of his full breeches in a show of annoyance. "Just don't expect me to dress like this often. A man cannot move properly with all this extra fabric hung about his person."

"To the contrary," Ford put in, "I'm certain Amy

would prefer you with no fabric hung about your person at all." General laughter greeted his comment, and Amy's face flamed—though she'd been thinking the very same thing.

Moving closer, Colin linked his arms loosely around her waist and captured her eyes with his. "My sentiments exactly," he murmured, his husky voice low so only she could hear. "Though you look unbelievably splendid in that gown, I can hardly wait to remove it." Amy's cheeks burned even hotter.

Someone cleared his throat, and she broke out of Colin's embrace. Jason nodded toward her. "In the absence of your father, Amy, may I have the honor of giving you to my brother?"

For the countless time since this incredible day had started, Amy's throat closed with emotion, and her eyes filled with tears. She was saddened by the absence of her parents, and oh so gladdened by her acceptance into this marvelous family.

She nodded mutely.

"Well, then, what are we waiting for?" Jason's smile was warm and understanding as he offered Amy his arm. With a return smile and a swish of her satin skirts, she sailed past Colin and linked arms with her almost brother-in-law.

Amy couldn't really remember her wedding. From the moment they entered St. Trinity—the curate lifted a heavy eyebrow at Colin and uttered, "*This* was worth chasing after"—until the plump clergyman handed her a rolled parchment declaring her officially Amethyst Chase, Countess of Greystone, the time swept by in one incoherent blur of unreality.

Oh, she remembered saying "I will" and hearing Colin's "I will" boom confidently through the sanctuary. She remembered him slipping a cool circlet of metal onto her ring finger, and she remembered his long kiss, sealing her to him forever, his sweet taste tinged with the sack he'd sipped while waiting. Jason had finally tapped Colin on the shoulder, and he'd reluctantly released her, and she remembered that, too. But the curate's words—the incessant drone that tied these events together—were filtered through a distracted fog.

The ceremony was followed by a hastily prepared wedding feast at the Chases' town house. Their formal dining room was filled with laughter from the intricate inlaid wooden floor to the ornate painted ceiling.

Portraits of ancestors watched the proceedings from the walls overlooking the laden table. Silver platters bearing suckling pig, a roast round of beef, and duck stuffed with oysters and onions were brought steaming to the table, surrounded by bowls of peas, cauliflower, lettuce, corn, turnips, and rice spiced with saffron and chopped nuts.

The scent of fresh, hot bread and sweet butter tickled Amy's nose. Her cup was refilled with claret wine punch spiked with brandy, nutmeg, sugar and the juice of a lemon. As she drained it for toast after toast, she grew giddy with laughter and companionship, not to mention the unprecedented amount of liquor she consumed.

In the center of the table sat a white-iced wedding cake decorated with candied violets and roses—in the middle of winter!—which Kendra insisted they cut and serve immediately in celebration of their marriage. Amy and Kendra ate their portions, but the men pushed theirs aside to have later. Colin raised one eyebrow, his gaze searching out each of his brothers in turn. "See?" he asked them, his tone deep with hidden meaning. " 'Tis just as I said . . ."

Ford and Jason laughed, while Kendra and Amy looked at each other, confusion written plainly on their faces. But then dishes were passed back and forth across the table, plates were filled, more toasts were drunk, and the odd comment was forgotten.

Amy could eat no more than a few bites of the impressive feast. Her stomach churned with a combination of excitement, exhaustion, and a tinge of inebriation. Besides, the slow pressure of Colin's thigh against hers, under the cover of the table, kept her thoughts elsewhere.

Conversation whirled about her. She paid scant attention to most of it, but she did take notice of Kendra's reaction when Colin announced they were leaving. Kendra was not at all pleased to be having her brand-new sister snatched away so soon.

"You cannot!"

"The devil we cannot. If you think I'm spending my wedding night with my little sister hanging outside the door—"

"But you have only Ebony. Surely—"

"You can borrow my coach," Jason offered pleasantly.

"Thank you, but there is no need. I sent for my own coach this morning."

"But—but—" Colin smiled when his sister sputtered. "Amy has no clothes!"

"She has a trunk full of clothes that you picked up from Madame Beaumont only this morning."

"She has no shoes, no stockings, and no nightclothes," Kendra returned smugly.

"Surely you can lend her a pair of shoes and some stockings." Colin shot his sister a wicked grin. "She *certainly* has no need of nightclothes."

His prediction proved true. Amy hazily remembered being bundled into Colin's coach and settling her head against his shoulder. The next thing she knew, she was back at Greystone, in his—*their!*—bed, wearing not a stitch of clothing. But she wasn't cold. There was a roaring blaze in the fireplace, and Colin's breath was hot on her neck where he'd nuzzled her awake. "Have you slept long enough yet?" he'd whispered, and then, with calculated, skillful maneuvers, proceeded to keep her awake until dawn illuminated the sky.

Not that she was complaining.

Judging by the bright sun through the window, 'twas afternoon now. Amy stretched under the sheets, content. She ran her hand over the shallow hollow where Colin had lain, imagining she could still feel his warmth and sniffing deeply of the distinctive scent he'd left behind. She had no cause to be concerned about his disappearance—he was her husband now.

The thought brought a smile and a vision of herself standing beside him in the ancient church. Sapphire and cream, black and white. They'd not matched. It had been perfect.

No . . . no, it had *not* been perfect. A disturbing emptiness seemed to open in Amy's middle. What had she done? She'd taken one vow and broken another—she'd never be able to reestablish Goldsmith & Sons, now. Dear God in heaven, would her father ever forgive her? Would she ever forgive herself? Generations of craftsmanship, all ending with her, ending with her selfishness.

She should have married Robert in the first place, and none of this would have happened. No matter that the mere idea twisted her insides; she would have had the solace of Goldsmith & Sons, of her craft, of knowing she'd done the right thing. She'd done Colin no favor, either. What had he said? *Bloody hell, I knew I should have killed him.* Instead, he'd married her to save her from Robert. And now he was stuck with a commoner for a wife, when she knew he'd wanted a titled lady.

Did he really even love her? She curled into a ball and squeezed her eyes shut tight. Strange patterns danced behind her lids, making her dizzy. The claret punch from last night was not sitting well in her stomach.

What was done, was done. She forced herself to breathe slow and steady, her heart to gradually calm. She would have to bury the guilty feelings deep. Her love was so overwhelming, surely everything would work out. She'd had no choice.

No other choice she could have lived with.

Opening her eyes, she uncurled her body and gazed up at the cream-colored canopy. A warm fire crackled on the gray stone hearth. Yellow sunshine streamed through the window. A brilliant flash of purple arced from where her hand lay on the blanket.

She sat up, drawing a quick breath. In all the excitement, she'd not found time to inspect it last night, but the ring was magnificent: a large heart-shaped amethyst surrounded by tiny seed pearls and table-cut diamonds, set in a framework of delicate filigree reminiscent of the finest sixteenth-century artistry.

Where had Colin come by such a masterpiece on such short notice? She waved her fingers, watching the play of light on the deep purple amethyst and old diamonds. 'Twas eighteen karat, the shank worn thin with age and use, but still a rich yellow. Lovely, yet strange somehow . . . foreign . . . she'd never worn jewelry not made by a member of her family.

She pulled off the ring.

At her burst of laughter, Colin appeared in the doorway, his face split into a wide grin.

"Good afternoon, sleepyhead. What is so funny?"

Sunlight flashed off the amethyst in the palm of her hand. "This," she choked out between giggles. "This ring."

His smile disappeared, replaced by a frown of hurt chagrin. " 'Twas my grandmother's," he mumbled grimly. "I thought . . ."

Her laughter died as she realized he thought she was disparaging the beautiful piece of jewelry. Clutching the quilt around herself, she jumped off the bed and rushed to his side. "No, 'tis lovely," she cried. "But look—just look inside."

Colin took the proffered ring. "Inside?" he asked blankly.

"Yes! Look there—do you not see it?"

He frowned, squinting at the tiny marks. "An eagle?"

"A falcon! And the letters GSJ."

"So . . ."

"Goldsmith & Sons, Jewellers. Colin, someone in my family made this ring."

He glanced up quickly, then back down, staring at the ring in disbelief. "Are you sure? There's also an animal head of some sort stamped in here."

"A leopard's head. That means the gold was assayed

at Goldsmith's Hall in London. 'Tis why we call it hall-marking. And the leopard's head is in a circle—an old style mark used only before 1519. Colin, this ring must be over a hundred and fifty years old."

"I knew 'twas old, but . . ."

" 'Tis *very* old. And very wonderful. Look at the filigree." Before Colin could look at the filigree or anything else, she snatched it back and slipped it onto her finger. Extending her arm, she gazed at the ring possessively. "However did it survive this long? Most of our business was designing new mountings for old stones; fashionable people have their jewels reset every two or three years."

"Grandmother was never fashionable. She gave the ring to Jason—otherwise it would have been sold to help fight Cromwell years ago. Is it valuable?"

"Very. Large amethysts are rare—they call amethyst the Jewel of Royalty. But 'tis the workmanship I treasure . . . I wonder who made it? My great-great-grandfather?" Happiness spurted through her as she looked from the ring to her husband. "Oh, Colin, this is the best wedding ring ever!"

Colin's eyes glittered emerald in response. He moved to her, slipping his arms beneath the blanket to encircle her waist. "I'm glad you like it, love," he murmured huskily before his mouth descended on hers. "And I second your opinion concerning the rarity and value of Amethyst . . ." His large hands were warm on her bare back, and he kissed her long and deep, breaking off only when the quilt slid from her shoulders and she pulled away and stooped hurriedly to retrieve it.

Colin wrapped the blanket back around her. "Benchley has our dinner waiting. How quickly can you dress? Unless you'd rather have, uh, dessert first?"

"Kendra has dessert first."

Colin chuckled deep in his throat. "That was not what I meant." He leaned down to her, and his tongue traced her lips, sending a tremor through her body. When he pulled back, his eyes bore into hers suggestively.

Two hot spots burned on Amy's cheeks, but nonetheless she murmured, "Oh. Dessert would be nice." This time, when the blanket fell, she didn't reach for it.

And as he carried her to the bed, she told herself 'twas impossible for something this perfect to be wrong.

She would not let it be.

Chapter Twenty-three

"Will you come upstairs with me, love?"

Amy's reflection looked puzzled in her dressing-table mirror. "Upstairs?" She folded the letter she'd been writing to Aunt Elizabeth with the news of their wedding, then glanced back at Colin. "For three weeks you've been telling me 'tis dangerous up there. Besides, do we not need to leave for Cainewood?"

"Christmas Eve can wait a few minutes yet." Hard put to keep a smile off his lips, he took her by the hand and led her down the corridor toward the staircase.

"When will the upper level be renovated?"

Halfway up the stairs, his step faltered. "I'm not sure. I've put all the renovations on hold. The farmstead is almost self-supporting, and then . . ."

He turned when he felt her stop. Her words came forced and quiet. "Colin, I have a trunk full of gold."

"So you do." He backed down a step, twisting his ring. "I promised you I wouldn't touch it."

"But—'tis yours. Legally, 'tis yours." Her fingers trailed back and forth along the oak rail. "You . . . you'd have taken Priscilla's dowry, would you not?"

Colin noticed the catch in her voice. 'Twould kill her if he spent her gold—kill their marriage. Kill her love for him.

"Priscilla was different," he said carefully. "That was a business arrangement." He moved down another step to encircle her in his arms. "I love you," he said low. "We'll wait, see what happens. If you don't mind living like this for now—"

"I could live like this forever," she said quickly.

Very quickly, Colin thought. Very, very quickly. As he took her lips in a gentle kiss, a disturbing image of Lord Hobbs flashed in his head.

He didn't have forever.

"So what is up here?" Amy asked, pulling back. What she saw in his eyes troubled her. He seemed so very serious, unhappy even. But his step lightened as, without answering her, he led her the rest of the way up the stairs and down the corridor. Despite his earlier warnings, she saw no rotting wood, no holes in the floor. He stopped in front of a stout, arched oak door and slipped a key into the lock.

It clicked open with a rusty screech, and he took her hand and placed the key in her palm. 'Twas warm, retaining his body heat. She closed her fingers around it and looked up at him.

"Go ahead. 'Tis yours," he urged, indicating the door and whatever lay beyond.

The door squeaked a protest of disuse as she pushed it open. The smallish chamber had a carved marble fireplace set into one wall. A long upholstered couch sat in the center, flanking a heavy, dark wooden desk that belonged to the previous century. But best of all were the books, multitudes of them, lining the walls from floor to ceiling.

"A library . . ." Her mood suddenly lifted, her uneasiness flitting away as it tended to do in the bliss of being wed to Colin. If they really loved one another, it should be enough.

It *would* be enough.

" 'Tis yours," Colin repeated. "Your own place, like the study is mine. Though I'm hoping you'll let me in now and then. To borrow a book, you know."

He winked at Amy, but she only smiled faintly at his humor. She moved to the windows and gazed down into Hidden Court. The plants were mostly dead from the cold and last month's brief snow, but 'twould be lovely come spring. And the little library was perfect; she could already imagine herself curled up before the fire with a stack of books by her side.

"Do you like it?" From behind her, Colin's voice sounded warm and pleased, as if he knew her answer. It flowed around and over her, making her tingle with contentment and the physical need for him that always lingered just below the surface.

She turned to face him. " 'Tis wonderful. Thank you."

"We'll furnish it however you like. Benchley cleaned it for me. I know not about the books—they've probably not been disturbed in decades."

She wandered to the bookcases and ran a finger down the dark green leather spine of one volume. Her finger came away smudged, leaving the green stripe noticeably brighter than the rest of the cover. But it mattered not; cleaning and organizing the books would be a joyful endeavor—she'd felt rather useless as a countess these past three weeks.

She looked back to Colin. Winter sun streamed through the windows and seemed to create a halo around him, swimming with brilliant dust motes from the recently swept room. At the sight, she melted inside a little bit more.

His lips curved in a wry smile, and he gave an elegant shrug. "I had nothing else to give you for Christmas."

Amy's heart plunged. "Oh, Colin, I have nothing for *you*. And this—this"—she gestured helplessly—" 'tis so *much*."

Colin chuckled at her obvious distress, moving to enclose her in his warm, strong arms. His face mere inches away, he locked his eyes on hers, and she lost herself in their emerald depths. "I need no gift from you, love," he said, his voice low and slightly rough. "You're my Christmas present. You're all I want and more than I deserve. Besides, how could you get me anything? I've not left you alone for a heartbeat."

He grinned, and it had a devastating effect on Amy's insides. Suddenly, she realized she did have a gift for him. She smiled to herself. An idea flickered in her brain . . . a mischievous Christmas prank . . . she'd need Kendra's help . . .

He kissed her then, his mouth hot and demanding on hers, and her fledgling plans drifted away, replaced, as always, by the overwhelming feelings Colin engendered with his slightest touch.

His touch now was by no means slight. They made love on the couch—"christening" her room, as Colin put it devilishly, and disturbing years of accumulated dust in the process. Afterward, Colin ran a fingertip down the bridge of her nose, as she'd done to the book.

Laughing, he called for a bath, and they moved downstairs to wash each other in their enormous tub. Benchley had the horses hitched and had been waiting a good half hour by the time the pair emerged and climbed into the coach to make their way to Cainewood.

The road was hard and dry today, and their carriage barreled toward Cainewood in record time. Besides clothing for a short stay, their trunks had small packages tucked inside—Christmas gifts of jewelry they'd chosen the night before. Amy's cheeks flushed with excitement at the thought of everyone's pleasure in their gifts, especially the surprise she was planning for Colin.

Before she knew it they were in the village, knocking on the door to Clarice Bradford's whitewashed cottage. Little Mary came to answer, Clarice at her heels. The child looked well fed and pink cheeked, and with a whoop of joy she threw herself into Amy's arms.

"Oh, my lady—I mean, Amy! I knew not if ever I'd see you again!"

Amy knelt to return the embrace, then pulled back. The girl's big blue eyes sparkled with happiness, and not just at seeing her old friend. She was happy as Clarice's daughter—the two had needed one another. Just as she and Colin were meant for each other.

"I *am* a lady now, Mary. Can you believe it? I've married Lord Cainewood's brother. Do you remember him?" She rose and put her arm around Colin.

" 'Course I 'member him." Mary tilted her head back

to look up at him. "You saved me so I could be Mama's little girl." Amy had to jump to the side when the girl launched herself at him, wrapping her arms around his neck and her legs around his waist. "Oh, my lord, thank you!"

"I cannot find the words to tell you how grateful I am." Clarice bowed her head and bobbed a curtsy. She reached for her daughter, but Colin shifted Mary to his hip, supporting her with one arm while he gave Clarice's hand a quick squeeze.

" 'Twas my pleasure." He smiled at Mary, brushed blond ringlets from her face, touched her little nose with one long finger. "I am delighted to see Mary so happy."

"No more delighted than I am to have her." Clarice reached again, and this time Colin handed Mary over. "Thank you, my lord." She cradled her daughter tight, tears brightening her gray eyes.

"I brought you something, Mary." Amy held out a tiny package wrapped in bright cloth and tied with a pink ribbon. "For Christmas."

"For me?" Mary's mouth dropped open in a little O. "What is it?"

"Open it and see."

Clarice set her down, and she fumbled with the ribbon until Colin took it and untied it for her. The cloth fell open in his hand, and Mary gasped. "Is it really for me?"

Without waiting for an answer, she reached for the tiny gold ring, slipped it on one finger and then another until she found a fit. She fisted her hand and brought it to her lips. "Oh, my lady, thank you!"

Clarice eased Mary's hand from her mouth and bent to inspect the ring. "A heart." She smiled at Amy. "Mary loves hearts. 'Tis lovely, my lady."

"I made it a long time ago." Amy took the pink ribbon from Colin and tied it in Mary's curls. "When I was yet a girl in London."

"I have something to give you, too." Mary dashed into the cottage.

Clarice spread her hands in question, but Mary was

back in a moment, holding forth a scrap of paper. "For you," she said, handing it to Amy.

Tears pricked the back of Amy's lids as she stared at the picture Mary had drawn. The cottage. A smiling sun. And two stick figures with a crooked heart between them. "Surely your mama would like to keep this."

"Keep it," Clarice said simply.

Amy bent to gave Mary a heartfelt hug. "I will treasure it always."

Thank you, Clarice mouthed with a gentle smile. "Will you come in and share some Christmas cake?"

"I could use some sustenance," Colin declared, and they all laughed.

Back in their carriage on the way to the castle, Amy leaned across to take Colin's hands. "Was that not wonderful?"

"Yes, it was delicious. I was starving."

"You and your stomach." Giggling, she tried to pull her hands back, but he held them tight. "I meant Mary, and how happy she is."

"Oh," he said with an innocent grin. He squeezed her fingers, arched one dark brow. "I'm hoping you'll give me a little girl just like Mary."

She looked pointedly as his dark head, then freed her hands to sit back and lift a hank of her own ebony hair. "I think not, no matter how hard I tried."

Colin laughed. "I meant not golden haired, but sweet. Surely you can give me a sweet daughter? We will have to work on it more often."

"Have we not been?" Amy mused with a secretive smile.

As they pulled through the gatehouse and onto Cainewood's private road, he grumbled under his breath, "So much for working on it."

"Pardon me?"

He reached to take Amy's hand and pull her onto his lap. "Our days of solitude are over—not to mention our nights."

Amy laughed. " 'Tis not so bad as all that! Surely we'll

have time alone together. And the family . . ." Amy was very much looking forward to spending time with her new family.

"The family. The loud, boisterous, meddlesome, teasing . . ." He swept the hair off the nape of her neck and bent his head to kiss her there with each word. "Argumentative, childish, outspoken, pigheaded—"

Amy turned on his lap. She touched her mouth to his, just barely, so he could feel her lips move. "Affectionate, generous, enthusiastic." She kissed him lightly. "Playful, thoughtful, *alive*." Another kiss, more forceful. "Intelligent, lovable—"

Colin pulled back in mock surprise. "Good heavens, are we as wonderful as all that?"

"Well, *they* are. I'm not so sure about you." The carriage wheels clattered over the drawbridge, and Amy leaned back to part the curtains as they came through the barbican and into the quadrangle. "Oh, Colin, *look*."

All around the quadrangle, garlands of ivy graced the ancient walls. A large red bow hung over each door and window, the swagged ends wound with holly and laurel. " 'Tis beautiful!"

"Wait 'til you see inside," Colin promised drolly. "Kendra quite outdoes herself this time of year." But he was smiling, clearly caught up in the Christmas spirit despite himself.

Inside, the monotone, cream-hued Stone Hall was a-splash with red and green. Winter foliage and red ribbon twisted around the gray handrail, marching up the stairs and across the balcony at the top. Hundreds of beeswax candles sat at intervals, waiting to be lit when darkness fell. Cloth of gold swagged lavishly between the columns, held in place with huge red bows.

Amy paused on the threshold, aghast at the splendor, and Colin seized the opportunity to kiss her, reaching overhead to pull a berry off the mistletoe afterward.

"Ah, the newlyweds," Kendra called, coming down the stairs. "Thank God you've arrived. Our mistletoe's been sadly neglected this season."

"We can remedy that situation." Colin laughed, giving Amy another light kiss and removing another berry.

Moments later, the brothers appeared. They both had resounding kisses for Amy, and the mistletoe was relieved of two more berries. Then Kendra claimed a kiss from Colin, albeit a mite more brotherly, and another berry was plucked. Kendra giggled, looking up. "At this rate, 'twill be bare before evening!"

"Hey, down here!"

Amy looked down from the wall walk to see Kendra waving frantically and Jason and Ford toting a large saw between them. Colin laughed at the question in her eyes. "Come, love, we're going to cut the Yule Log," he said as he beckoned her to follow him down.

Spirits high, the five of them trudged outside the castle walls and into the bordering forest. Much good-natured arguing followed, as each claimed to have discovered the largest tree trunk. Teasing laughter pealed through the fragrant woods until Jason, as usual the peacemaker, swept off his cloak and shivered stoically while they used it as a crude measuring device.

Amy's tree was the winner. Her cheeks bright with the flush of victory, she watched the Chase men struggle manfully to cut it down. At last it fell, with a resounding crash and a great cheer from all. They cut a long chunk from the thickest part, which Amy eyed incredulously, considering they had brought no cart or horse.

"How will we get it back to Cainewood?" she asked Jason.

"We'll manage." Under their cloaks, Jason and Ford both had lengths of rope coiled about their waists, which they unwound and tied around the colossal log, creating six long looped handles to pull it by. "Can you and Kendra handle the saw?"

"Of course, but must the log be so big?"

"Tradition says it will be a good year if we can keep it smoldering through Twelfth Night." Ford made a small grunt as he tugged a knot tight. "The bigger, the better."

"But that couldn't possibly fit in the fireplace."

Colin's laughter rang through the trees. "Don't be such a worrywart, love, we've done this a time or two."

"Hmmph. You're the one who has to carry it, not me." Tilting her nose in the air, she moved to help Kendra with the heavy saw.

Despite the frosty air, the men were covered with a thin sheen of sweat by the time they managed to haul the log to the front door. They needed the help of three additional men to lift it over the threshold and carry it into the Great Hall.

"Careful, the floor!" Kendra warned. " 'Tis just been polished."

In fact, the servants were not quite finished; at the far end they were still spreading the milk that would dry to a high sheen. Amy gawked at the buzz of activity. From the planked floor to the intricate oak hammerbeam ceiling, the immense Great Hall swarmed with workers. Paintings were dusted, tapestries cleaned and rehung on the stone walls. Servants chatted excitedly as they brought in heavy, ancient trestle tables and set them with row after row of trenchers and cutlery.

"What is happening?" Amy asked, one eye on the men struggling to set the log into the enormous fireplace.

Kendra crossed her arms and tapped a foot disapprovingly. "Did Colin not tell you about Christmas at Cainewood?"

"For God's sake, Kendra," Colin called across the chamber. "We've been wed but three weeks. Did you think we'd be spending our time talking about family traditions?"

Amy felt red heat flush her face, but the others laughed until she was prompted to a smile. "Is there to be an entertainment tonight?"

"Tomorrow. All the castle retainers, tenants, and villagers will come for Christmas dinner, complete with gifts for everyone." Kendra waved a hand expansively. "Is it not glorious? I love Christmas!"

Amy laughed. "I love Christmas, too. I missed it during the Commonwealth."

"May Cromwell roast in hell." Kendra wiped her tongue and spit. "That I should even say such an evil name. Eleven years with no Christmas . . . Look, Amy, it fit!" She clapped her hands.

The log snugged in the fireplace with room to spare. The brothers were remarkably well behaved, throwing nothing more than a few gloating glances Amy's way.

"You told me so!" she said for them with a giggle, and their answering laughter echoed in the cavernous Hall.

"Food." Colin wiped his palms on his breeches. "After all that work, a man needs food."

"Christmas Eve supper awaits," Kendra announced.

In contrast to the Great Hall, the private family dining room seemed small and intimate, the air suffused with savory scents that made Amy's mouth water. Colin loaded her plate with clove-studded goose, Yorkshire Christmas pie, artichoke bottoms in pastry, a spinach tart, and one of the new French rolls. Kendra started with a slice of almond cheesecake, a wedge of cherry pie, and an apple taffety tart.

"Kendra, Kendra." Jason heaved a good-natured sigh. "Cherry pie when there's Yorkshire pie on the table?" He spooned up a bite, the hearty crust filled with a mixture of turkey, goose, partridge, pigeon, hare and woodcock, all swimming in butter. "When will you grow up?"

"Buttered ale?" Kendra said sweetly, ignoring him as she poured a dipperful from the huge wassail bowl that dominated the table, garlanded with ivy. She floated a square of brown toast on top and handed the cup to Amy.

"Thank you." Amy sniffed deep of the hot ale, mulled with beaten eggs, sugar, spices and the pulp of roasted apples. When she took a sip, it warmed her to her very bones. " 'Tis so lovely here," she sighed, thinking of Christmases past in the single room her family had used for cooking, eating, and socializing. "A different world. Look at the firelight dancing on the beveled windows."

"It holds not a candle to the sparkling of your amethyst eyes." Colin reached for another roll. "Or the blush on your cheeks," he added with a laugh.

When everyone had crammed in the last possible bite, they all walked slowly to the Great Hall, with many competing groans of regretted gluttony. There they lit the Yule Log and sang the traditional Christmas carols while Kendra accompanied on the harpsichord, moved into the Hall for the occasion. They were dwarfed by the huge Hall, but warm and merry, clustered at one end with the fire burning cheerfully. When they ran out of songs, they opened their gifts.

Jason's serious face split into a smile when he saw his pearl cravat pin, and he put it on immediately. Kendra slipped the emerald ring on her finger and declared it her favorite piece of jewelry. Ford disappeared upstairs after opening his gift, returning with his new jeweled hatband adorning a fashionable wide-brimmed hat, which he wore the rest of the evening. Amy could not have been more pleased.

Kendra's gift to Amy was a large assortment of shoes, stockings, ribbons, and nightgowns—the latter so sheer that Amy blushed when she unwrapped them. Colin made her stand up and display each one, finally declaring that he supposed she would be allowed to wear nightclothes after all, so long as she kept her selection limited to *these*. His disarming smile and appraising gaze told her they'd not stay on for long.

Jason had wrapped up the history books Amy had left piled on the mosaic table in his library, and she clutched them to her chest in delight. Ford presented her with a selection of hard-milled scented soaps, floral bath oils, and French perfumes that had Colin wondering aloud at why such a gift would come from his *brother*—until Amy punched him playfully in the stomach. He doubled over, in laughter, not pain, and Amy couldn't remember when she'd had as much fun.

After everyone's gifts were opened—a long proceeding, as each individual present was passed around and properly admired—Jason called for the plum porridge.

Amy groaned. "I cannot eat another bite."

"Oh, but you must have a serving." Kendra scooped a healthy dollop and plopped it in Amy's bowl. "Hidden within it are tokens that foretell of the year to come."

Colin's bowl held the first prize, a silver penny, predicting a fortune in the offing. "I've fortune enough for a lifetime already," he declared in a chivalrous tone, his gaze fastened on Amy.

The others laughed as Amy slowly turned red.

"Oh, no." Jason pulled a ring from his mouth, rolling his eyes as he licked it clean. "This should be Kendra's, surely."

They all laughed again. "What does it mean?" Amy asked.

" 'Tis a sign of marriage," Kendra explained. "Ah, the thimble!" She placed it on a fingertip, flashing an angelic smile. "A life of blessedness."

"When are you joining the convent?" Ford chortled.

She threw the thimble at his head, and obligingly he doubled over, moaning loud and long as he clutched his head in a show of great pain.

"Well, so much for the tokens," Colin announced when Ford's act was over.

"Thank God." Amy set down her bowl.

"Are you not going to finish it?"

She shook her head. "I've had enough," she said quietly. "I'm really not feeling too well." Kendra glanced up, and Amy threw her a surreptitious wink. "I think I should go to bed," she said to Colin.

He shot up at once and placed a hand on her forehead. "You're not feverish," he reported, visibly relieved. "But if you feel ill, then of course we must go to bed." Grasping her by one hand, he pulled her up and put a protective arm around her.

"But the games . . ." Ford protested.

"What games?" Amy asked innocently, finishing with a weak cough for effect.

"We always play games on Christmas Eve, charades and the like, until the wee hours." Colin pulled her toward the door. "But that was before one of us was married. Besides, your health is more important."

"You must stay and play, Colin. 'Tis only fatigue, I'm certain, and overeating and a bit too much buttered ale—though 'twas all delicious." Amy sighed prettily and placed a delicate hand over her abdomen.

Unfortunately, Colin proved to be overly solicitous, and the best they could do was convince him to see her to bed and then return for the games. He undressed her himself, pulled one of her new nightgowns over her head, then stood back to judge the effect.

He gave a low whistle, and one eyebrow rose provocatively. "Are you certain you're ill, love?"

"Quite certain." She forced another cough and clutched at her stomach. "Leave now, please, before I embarrass myself in front of you." She climbed into the bed, moaning softly to demonstrate her illness. "Bring the chamber pot here before you go."

"Sickness is nothing to be embarrassed about," he assured her. With a small thud, he deposited the chamber pot on the bedside table. "Are you sure you don't want me to stay?"

"Positive. Go enjoy the games." He stood still as though not quite convinced, and she added, "If you'll but let me rest, Colin, *alone,* when you return in a few hours I'm certain to be feeling better."

"Well . . ."

"*Much* better," she repeated meaningfully. She watched his eyes light up as he grasped her implication, then she rolled away with an audible groan and pulled the covers over her head.

He left a few seconds later. No sooner had she heard the soft click of the closing door than she jumped up and started redressing, donning a carefully chosen gown, one of Madame Beaumont's new creations. On Kendra's instructions, a maid came in to help Amy and direct her downstairs, where several burly servants stood by in one of the many chambers that were usually closed up.

Half an hour later the charades game was interrupted by the head butler as, with an admirably straight face, he announced the unexpected delivery of a crate. They all hurried to the Stone Hall to see what it might be.

'Twas enormous, standing taller than Colin himself, and his name was scrawled across the front. There was no indication of where or whom it had come from.

"Do you suppose it is a wedding gift?" he asked, coming up to stand beside it.

"Open it and see," Jason suggested. The buoyancy in his voice had Colin turning to him sharply.

" 'Tis from you, then?"

"I didn't say that. Just open it."

"It must be furniture. A nice thought, Jason, but much too generous—and besides, I have no place to put anything yet."

Jason laughed. "Look, 'tis not from me. Just open it."

Colin considered. "Very well, but Amy should be here. Perhaps she's feeling better now. I'll just go and check."

"Let her sleep. She felt beastly," Kendra insisted. "You mustn't take the chance of waking her."

"Well, then, this will wait 'til morning," Colin said slowly, twisting his signet ring all the while.

Kendra jumped on his indecision. " 'Tis addressed to you, not Amy. She can see it in the morning. Open it, please—or I'll do it for you."

"Well . . ."

"I'll fetch some tools," Ford offered after a meaningful glance from his twin. Before Colin could change his mind, Ford was back, and together they pried off the front of the wooden box—only to find another box enclosed inside.

They pulled the other three sides of the box apart, but there was still no clue to the contents. The new box was unmarked.

"It must be fragile," Colin remarked uncertainly. "Let us be more careful opening this one."

The second box revealed nothing more than a slightly smaller version of itself hidden inside.

He threw his siblings a sidelong glance and silently set to opening it. When a fourth featureless box was revealed, he grinned at the profusion of lumber littering the Hall. "What the hell is going on here?"

"I'm sure we know not," Kendra protested.

"We were just minding our own business, playing charades," Ford offered.

"Just open it," Jason said.

Colin looked at them all and shrugged, trying to hide a smile. He loved a joke played on himself almost as much as being the perpetrator of one. "I think I'll wait until morning, after all," he said blandly, turning to leave.

Kendra lunged at him, tugging on his shirt. "Colin Chase, you open that box right now. I'm—I'm *dying* of curiosity."

He turned back and fixed her with an innocent look. "Well, then, I suppose I must. I'd not want you to *die* on account of me."

They laughed as he pulled the box apart, and he was not at all surprised to find a fifth box inside. This one had a sign on it, though, spelling out the words CONTAINS THE EARL OF GREYSTONE in neat block letters.

"It should say '*Contents for* the Earl of Greystone,'" he pointed out. "Somebody knows not how to spell."

His siblings shrugged.

"It cannot contain the Earl of Greystone," he insisted, staring at their blank faces. "*I'm* the Earl of Greystone, and I'm quite obviously not in that box. I'm not certain I would even fit," he added as an afterthought.

A discrete cough came from within the box. Colin swung around. "What the devil . . ."

The top was hinged. He threw it open. Amy slowly rose, completely captivating in a soft peach gown, a dazzling smile on her lips and in her eyes.

"*You!* Uh—are you not sick?" Colin sputtered.

"Do I look sick?"

"No. And you look not like the Earl of Greystone, either."

Laughter came from behind him, and he turned, confused. "Do you not like your Christmas present, Colin?" Kendra prompted.

A grin of amusement twitching on his lips, he turned back to Amy "You're lovely, but you're not a present, love. I have you already." He grasped her under her arms, effortlessly lifting her out of the box. " 'Twas a good trick, though," he conceded as he set her on her feet. "Even if the sign was spelled wrong."

"No, 'twas spelled correctly," Amy said.

He remained silent, his brows drawn together in puzzlement.

"The box contains the *next* Earl of Greystone."

Colin could sense all their eyes on him, but his brain refused to work. His head felt completely blank. He leaned over a little, gazing into the empty box.

"It *contained* the next Earl of Greystone, I mean," Amy continued. "He's not inside the box anymore."

Colin blinked stupidly.

"You'll have to wait to see him, though—about seven months, I suspect."

His heart faltered in his chest.

"He's inside *me,* Colin," Amy finished softly.

His mouth opened, closed, then he let forth a whoop of joy, picked Amy up and swung her around and around in a wide circle. Self-conscious grins split Jason's and Ford's faces, and tears brightened Kendra's pale green eyes.

Suddenly, Colin stopped and set Amy down with exquisite care. She laughed as he asked earnestly, "Have I hurt you? Either of you?"

"No, we're not that fragile. Though 'tis a good thing I seem not prone to morning sickness."

"You'd have gotten it straight in your face, I expect," Ford chortled.

"Ford!" Jason and Kendra shouted together. "Forgive him," Jason continued to Amy. "He's hopelessly uncivilized."

"*I* think he's funny," Amy declared between giggles. "And quite handsome, besides." Ford's blue eyes deepened with pleasure, and he and Amy shared a smile as a faint blush spread up from his neck.

"Well, Colin, I reckon the honeymoon is over," Jason proclaimed, his smile belying the seriousness of his tone.

"Come again?"

"She played a joke on you. She's challenging your virtuosity as a prankster already."

Colin looked at his bride, his heart swelling with emotion. *"Au contraire,"* he said slowly. "The honeymoon is only beginning." He swept her up, bearing her slight weight as one would a sleeping child, his arms beneath her shoulders and knees. Cradling her against his upper body, he strode toward the stairs.

"Wait . . . the games!" Kendra shouted.

"Go ahead, children," Colin called over his shoulder. "We have our own games to play."

Chapter Twenty-four

Colin kicked the door closed behind them and gently deposited Amy on the bed. The apprehension in her eyes made his gut clench. "Are you truly pleased?" she asked in a small voice. "I mean, 'tis so soon . . . and I should have told you first, privately . . ." She looked away, staring up at the underside of the canopy.

"Oh, love, how could you doubt it?" He lowered himself to the bed and turned her face toward him with a fingertip. "A family . . . a babe . . ."

Amy's breath rushed out, and she offered him a shaky smile. "A son," she said. "I know not why, but I'm sure of it, Colin."

He cared not whether she carried a son or a daughter; either way, his throat tightened as he thought of their child growing within her. But he knew better than to argue with a pregnant woman. "A son," he echoed, suppressing a chuckle. "How long have you known?"

Her fingers toyed with a lock of her hair. "I think it must have happened the very first time, at Greystone. I first thought of the possibility when I was . . . attacked by Robert." At Colin's wince, she rushed to add, " 'Twas that thought that kept me going, made me fight."

"But you said nothing."

" 'Twas too soon to tell, barely more than a fortnight," she defended herself. "Besides, I would never have trapped you into marriage that way."

No, she'd not do that, Colin agreed silently. She was much too honorable to pull such a stunt. He wished he could say the same for himself. She'd known they were not meant to wed, but he'd manipulated her by bringing Robert's threat into the equation. And look where it had gotten him: He was happy beyond belief, but those days were numbered. A year—one precious year—until that buzzard's debt was due.

He laced his fingers with hers. He'd been right all along; marrying for love was illogical. A mistake. But one he couldn't bring himself to be sorry for—yet.

"Go on," he said, squeezing her hand.

She took a deep breath. "When I became convinced—and ask me not how, I just *know*—I knew not how to tell you. Whether you would be happy or not. After all, 'tis so soon, and . . . the baby will come early, before we've been married nine months, even," she blurted out in a rush, then bit her lip. "But I wanted to give you a Christmas present. 'Twas all I had." Her mouth curved in a tiny smile. "Since you'll not take my diamonds and gold."

"My Amethyst is the most precious gem of all," Colin teased. "Why would I want any others when they all pale in comparison?" He brushed a gentle kiss across her lips.

"Then you're really, truly pleased about the babe? You're not vexed that he will come early?" Amy wiggled closer, pressing the length of her body against his. "Because, God forgive me, I just cannot be sorry about it. I want your son more than anything in the world," she finished on a sigh.

What had he done to deserve her? And how—bloody hell, *how* could he manage to keep his promise and save Greystone, too?

Her amethyst eyes still radiated worry. "I'm more than pleased," he assured her. "I'm overjoyed . . . delighted . . . enchanted . . . elated . . ." A kiss punctuated each word, and his voice grew unmistakably husky. "Ecstatic . . . intoxicated . . ."

"That's the buttered ale, I think." She giggled.

"No, 'tis you," he protested.

She blushed and cleared her throat. "Well, now that

you've relieved my fears, we may as well go join in the games." Belying her own words, she arched herself nearer, her fingers exploring seductively on his skin.

Colin laughed, the sound bubbling up from deep in his chest. "I think not," he said flatly, one arm coming around to hold her hostage, in the unlikely event she would actually try to escape.

"But I've never before had a large family to play games with." He nuzzled her neck, smiling when he felt her pulse speed up. "I-I was so looking forward to it," she stammered out, her eyes closed.

His tongue traced a shivery trail to her ear. "I have much more interesting games to teach you," he whispered there. "But first, I would meet my child."

"Your son." Amy stilled; her hands froze on his body. "But he'll not be arriving for many months."

"It doesn't signify." Coming up on his elbows, he set about removing the embroidered stomacher from the front of her gown. "I shall meet him anyway." The stomacher dropped to the floor, and he unlaced her bodice, placing small, damp kisses on each bit of skin as it was exposed.

Her body seemed to melt bonelessly under him. "Dear God," she breathed. " 'Tis like your mouth sends messages to . . ."

"To where, love?" He smiled against her cleavage.

"Mmmm." Her breath came quicker. "Mmmm . . . never mind."

Chuckling, he spread her bodice wide. Her breasts had always been pleasingly full, but did they not seem especially lush, the tips darkened and inviting even through the diaphanous fabric of her chemise? He couldn't be sure. Lifting her a bit, he drew the gown over her shoulders and down past her waist. Her stomach was as flat as ever, he marveled, skimming one hand over the thin material.

All at once, his heart soared. Though he hoped to God he would never be forced to spend her inheritance, now, thanks to this miracle, he'd have something to bind her to his side. Their baby . . . surely she'd stay with him always for the sake of their child, even if he lost Greystone or depleted her gold in saving it.

Sweet Mary, he was so damned lucky to have her. Suddenly he was overcome with a desire to see her unclothed, to touch the body that harbored his child, to feel her smooth skin against his. With impatient hands, he tugged off her gown and chemise, removed her shoes and stockings.

After making short work of divesting his own clothing, he took a deep breath and leaned over her, running his fingers through her dark tresses and arranging them artistically on the pillows, before his mouth met hers in an ardent kiss.

"Ahhh," he said with a long, drawn-out sigh. "I've not been able to touch you properly since morning."

"Improperly, you mean." Amy giggled, feeling lighthearted for the first time since she'd decided she was pregnant.

He smiled, that devilish grin that made her heart flip-flop. " 'Tis deucedly inconvenient having the family around." His stern voice didn't fool her. "I warned you."

She lifted her head for another kiss. He tasted sweet and spicy, buttered ale and plum porridge and Colin, all mixed together. "It has its compensations," she said, watching the firelight play over his perfect features. His body against hers felt impossibly warm and masculine, she thought blissfully.

"Such as?"

"Such as . . ." Colin's fingers played over her sensitive breasts, making concentration difficult. "They're quite helpful with practical joke arrangements."

"I see." He cupped one breast in his large hand, squeezing experimentally, as though gauging its expanded weight.

"They . . . make interesting supper conversation," she managed to say.

"Is that so?"

"Mmm-hmm." His thumb rubbed the peaked nipple

in a circular motion that sent Amy's senses spinning to match. Then his dark head bent and his warm mouth closed over where his thumb had been, and their inane discussion came to an abrupt end as her body responded with newly heightened awareness.

Amy's hands stole down to the ribbon securing his hair, and she untied it and tossed it aside. Colin's wet tongue trailed to her other breast, and the rosy bud hardened instantly. She held his head captive, her fingers tangling in his midnight locks as he suckled and licked. More gentle than usual, his teeth grazed her ever so lightly, but her baby-swollen breasts surged in response, sending fiery sensations to the core of her being.

When his lips reclaimed hers, her heart swelled with emotion. She touched him wherever she could reach: his muscled chest, his sleek side, the hard, smooth planes of his back. He felt divine against her palms: warm, large and solid, firm, yet silky soft.

His fingers brushed the soft curls that shielded the center of her pleasure, then delved deeper, caressing until the petals guarding her entrance became dewy with moisture. He slipped one finger inside, probing with a heavenly skill that made her squirm with excitement and tore a ragged sob from her throat.

"Now," she begged, her voice low and raspy, foreign to her own ears. Her hand moved down to encircle the warm velvet of his erection. "Now, *please*."

She parted her thighs further, anxious to receive him. But though he moved over her, he glided down, until the roughness on his chin and cheek grazed against the softness of her belly.

"Are you in there, little one?" His voice vibrated into her body, low and disturbing. " 'Tis your father." His lips moved against her stomach, his breath moist and warm. She groaned, half with the frustration of delayed gratification, half with delight in his tenderness for their child. Her hands reached down to tug impatiently at his shoulders.

"Your mother wants me now," Colin gloated to his

son with a low chuckle of satisfaction. "But first I want to say . . . we love you."

"Colin . . ." His mouth was hot and wet on her skin. She yearned for it on her mouth, ached for his weight on her body, burned for him to bury himself inside her.

"Good-bye for now," Colin murmured just as she decided she couldn't bear this father-son meeting a moment longer. "We'll talk again soon." He lifted his head, and his warm breath wafted over the wet patch he'd left on her belly. She opened her eyes and gazed down at him, questioning his hesitation.

The eyes that blazed into hers were a deep, fathomless green, overflowing with a surfeit of emotion that words could never convey. His breath came in a deep, ragged rhythm as he hovered there, and she could feel his life force sluicing through his veins, to match the insistent throbbing between her legs.

Then he moved down instead of up.

His lips traversed her sensitive inner thighs, one and then the other, leaving a moist, fiery trail of kisses in their wake. Warm and damp, his breath washed over her most secret places. She froze, sure he could hear her heart pounding.

Then, with the tip of his tongue he touched her, lightly at first, then more emphatically. Unbelievably soft and intimate, gentle and rhythmic, his caress was almost unbearable. Her knees felt weak, her hands and feet tingled. She'd not known such things happened between a man and a woman, not conceived of it in her wildest dreams, but she'd not have stopped him for the world.

His tongue was hot and slick and just the tiniest bit rough, enough so she felt every movement with exquisite sensitivity. Her breath caught as he licked maddeningly slow along the length of her pulsing cleft.

Twisting beneath him, she cried out his name in a manner so wanton that somewhere deep inside she was shocked at her unabashed reaction. And what he was doing to her, for God's sake, this . . . this unthinkable thing. It must be wicked. But everything between Colin and herself seemed incredibly perfect, as though they belonged together, each and every minute particle of their bodies and souls. Her heart knew they were meant to be, even if her head told her otherwise.

She trembled uncontrollably, lifting her hips to get closer still, until suddenly she was overcome by an awesome burst of joy, an irrepressible, shuddering release of passion. He met her high piercing cry with a low moan of pleasure, and he lifted his head, pausing for a long, torturous moment before he slid slowly up her body and settled his hips into the cradle of her thighs.

Eased by the nectar of their lovemaking, Colin plunged inside her, and Amy let out a long, soft moan. It felt so right, like paradise, to have him filling her body, that tears of wonderment came to her eyes.

He kissed her then, his mouth urgent and hungry, and she tasted herself on his lips. He rocked against her, his hips maneuvering in a rhythm as ancient as time, and she matched his every move. She could feel him holding back, feel the uneven tempo of his breath as he struggled for control, feel the staccato beat of his heart against hers. And then, with a groan of capitulation, he let go, and she felt him pulsing inside her, his hot seed pouring over her womb where their baby lay safe inside. Arching herself closer, she cupped his buttocks and pulled him deeper as her own contractions burst forth, matching and melding with his until she could tell not where one of them stopped and the other started.

Long minutes later, when their breathing had calmed and their hearts slowed, Amy sighed luxuriously. "I like that new game."

"Then we'll have to practice it some more, love, until we get it perfect."

"Mmmm." She moved under him, feeling languid and seductive. "Colin?"

"Hmmm?"

"Can I do that to *you*?"

'Twas a straightforward query, but Colin groaned, and she felt his body tense in response. "You're going to kill me, Lady Greystone," he murmured into the curve of her neck. "You're going to kill me." He paused so long she nearly voiced her confusion.

"But I'll die a happy man."

Chapter Twenty-five

Six months later

Colin slid his knife under the red seal and scanned the brief missive. Bloody hell, just what he needed. Rubbing his temples, he dropped the vellum letter atop the ledgers and journals that covered the scarred wooden surface of his desk—ledgers and journals he would be forced to abandon for the next few days. Beyond the castle walls, he imagined the rolling land, freshly green with the first new shoots from spring planting. Although 'twas all too far away to hear, he swore he could make out the bleat of distant sheep, the dull thud of a log being felled, the vague bangs and scrapes of quarrying—all work he was loathe to let continue without his supervision. The estate needed his attention too, damn it.

The year was halfway over, and he had saved nowhere near half of his debt to Hobbs.

The door cracked open. "Are you napping, my lady?"

"Hah." Amy looked up from her book as her buxom blond maid stepped inside. "My belly is so big and itchy, I cannot find a good position no matter how many I try." As though he'd heard her complaint, her son swished in her womb, poking out fists, knees, elbows and feet all at once, it seemed.

"Lud, that looks uncomfortable." Lydia's kittenish blue eyes narrowed as she contemplated the rolling lumps on her mistress's stomach.

Amy laughed and set the book aside. "Sometimes I'm convinced I'm carrying a human octopus, or at the very least an accomplished acrobat." She pushed herself to stand. "Did you need me for something?"

"The lord said he has a matter to discuss. He waits in the study." Frowning, Lydia flipped through the gowns in Amy's wardrobe. "Cuds bobs, milady, you've got nothing decent to wear that will fit your ballooning midsection."

"Marry come up, Lydia! I needn't dress up to visit with my husband!" Giggling, Amy went next door to see him in the study.

She quieted when she came upon the slightly open door and heard Benchley's voice. "Fernew was asking when the new thresher will arrive."

"I canceled delivery." At Colin's grim words, Amy froze, her hand on the latch.

"You—"

"Canceled it. Fernew will have to get along without it. Tell him 'tis only 'til next year." The defeat in his voice gnawed at Amy's insides.

"And the mill?"

She grimaced at Colin's heavy sigh. "That will have to be repaired; there is no way around it. Have Jenner order the parts; I should be back to help well before their delivery. No sense paying for more labor when 'tis not necessary. Anything else, Benchley?"

"No. No, my lord." Amy jumped back when Benchley opened the door. She stepped into the room as his footsteps receded down the corridor.

Colin was bent over a sheet of vellum, shaking his head. She bit her lip. Another financial problem he couldn't solve, thanks to wedding her?

"Ah, Amy." He glanced up with a distracted smile. "Come here, love."

She went to him, smiling in return when he ran a hand over the swell of their child, learning her ripening form and feeling for signs of movement.

"Charles wants to see us. Tomorrow night," he said, looking up from her belly with thinly veiled disgust.

"Charles?" Amy eyed the paper in his other hand. A large red seal was attached, broken but impressive nonetheless. "Charles who?"

"Charles. The King."

Her heart pounded in her chest. In an intellectual sense, she had known that Colin was intimate with the King, that she was a countess and expected to move in Court circles. But here at Greystone, in their own little crumbling castle, she'd felt very removed from the possibility. "But . . . why?"

"Who knows? Perhaps he's miffed that I didn't ask his permission to marry you."

She leaned weakly against the desk. "His permission?"

Colin sighed, tossing the summons onto the desk with a flick of his supple wrist. "As a peer of the realm, ancient law says I'm obligated to obtain the King's approval. Of course, no one actually asks—not even his own brother James before his secret marriage to Anne Hyde." With the heels of both hands, he rubbed his forehead, as though a massive headache had just arisen. " 'Tis archaic; I'm certain no one has asked for centuries. Still, Charles and I were close once." He squinted, and his eyes turned a glazy dull color as he tried and failed to ascertain a reason for the summons. "I don't know."

"Can you not just send him a note? Tell him you're busy and I'm with child?"

Colin's laughter was immediate; his eyes cleared and turned to her, a glittering emerald green. He caught her hand and pulled her onto his lap. "No, we cannot just send a note, love. When the King calls, one answers. 'Tis off to Whitehall for us, I'm afraid." He was silent a minute, his fingers absently twirling one of her long ebony ringlets. "We'll leave first thing in the morning, to arrive at the town house by noon. You can nap before the evening festivities."

"I'm sure I'll not sleep a wink tonight." She groaned

softly and moved her hand to cover where their child registered his own protest, in the form of a particularly violent kick.

Warm as always, Colin's large hand enveloped hers. " 'Tis nothing to be worried about. Charles is an affable sort."

"But there will be all those people . . ." She imagined hordes of svelte ladies, all dressed in the latest fashions. And haughty lords, beribboned and bejeweled, looking down their aristocratic noses at her bloated form.

"You already know most of them," he reminded her patiently, "from your shop."

"As *customers*. Oh, Colin, look at me! You're going to be sorry you ever married me, I just know it."

His fingers stilled in her hair, and he said very quietly, "I will never, ever be sorry I married you, Amethyst Chase. You're the best thing that ever happened to me." His hand moved to cup the back of her neck, and he pulled her toward him and kissed her lightly, and she almost believed him. "And you're beautiful, as beautiful as ever. I swear it." He kissed her again, this time long and deep, his mouth warm and possessive, and she did believe him. For two seconds, at least.

"And when Harry kisses me . . ." Lydia shuddered expressively. "Oh, I cannot think how to put it."

"Ooh, la, la?" Madame Beaumont suggested, putting the finishing touches on Amy's face.

Lydia laughed. "Ooh, la, la, exactly!"

"Ooh, la, la?" Amy echoed distractedly.

Madame Beaumont helped her to stand. "You're a million miles away, my lady."

"What? Oh . . . yes, I'm afraid you're right." Sighing, Amy set down the amethyst necklace she'd brought from Greystone. The deep-violet pear-shape gems glistened on the dark wood of the dressing table, beckoning her to hold them again. She flexed her hands and forced a smile. "I was daydreaming about wax and knives."

"*Pourquoi?*"

"Lady Greystone used to be a jeweler," Lydia explained, hiding a smile of her own.

"Oh, I see."

Madame looked as though she saw not at all, but she didn't seem shocked or disapproving, either. Amy gave the older woman's hand a quick squeeze. "I cannot thank you enough for coming." Having received her frantic messengered note yesterday, Madame had been waiting at the London town house this morning, gown in hand. "You saved my life."

"Surely you exaggerate." Amusement twitched on the seamstress's lips as she drew off Amy's dressing gown and laid a gentle palm on her abdomen. Amy jumped a bit, then relaxed. Of late, she'd noticed everyone thought they had a right to touch her since she'd swelled with the child, as though her body were public property.

Madame slipped a lacy new chemise over Amy's head, and Lydia held out the gown. "*I* never exaggerate," the blond maid giggled. "Lud, my Harry is so virile."

"Pray tell, Lydia, where did you find this *amour*?" Madame set the curling iron to heat in the glowing embers of the fire. "This paragon of masculinity?"

Amy grinned. "In our stables. Colin recently hired him to relieve Benchley of some duties. Your dream man, is he, Lydia?"

"Hmmm," Lydia murmured noncommittally. Hiding her face, she made herself busy adjusting the gown over the bulge of Amy's stomach. "In bed, yes, but . . . all is not perfect with Harry."

"Do you not discuss your problems?" The seamstress pushed Amy into a chair and set to work on her hair.

Lydia puttered around the room, folding Amy's dressing gown. She sighed. "I've tried. I suppose I should try again."

"I wish you luck." Amy frowned into the dressing table mirror. "Men do not care to discuss our problems. They always think they know what is best."

Madame's eyes met her reflection; her hands braided faster.

" 'Tis true," Amy muttered defensively. "When I talked to Papa about my marriage, he disregarded my feelings entirely."

"Not all men are like that." Madame's fingers caught and pulled at her hair. "Not my François."

"Surely not the earl?" Lydia's face appeared beside Madame's in the mirror, puzzled. "You confide in him, do you not? He loves you so."

Did he really? Amy bit her lip. 'Twas pointless to confide in Colin, anyway; he'd made it clear before they wed that a nobleman's wife would never run a business. And he'd become more and more closed and distracted over the months.

The other women were still staring at her. "Oh, I suppose you're right," she said. " 'Tis just one of my silly notions."

"She's breeding," Madame said knowingly.

"That doesn't make me a nimwit," Amy huffed.

Lydia nodded, ignoring her outburst. "I've seen five different ladies through five different pregnancies. They're all this way."

"Hmmph." Looking down to her crossed arms, Amy glimpsed her cleavage exposed in the purple dress's plunging neckline. "God in heaven," she whispered, her hands fluttering up to cover her bare chest.

Madame's laugh tinkled through the room. "You'll be the most modest lady at Court, just you wait and see."

Hopefully the brazen display would draw attention away from her unfashionable high waistline, but Amy felt daring and embarrassed at the same time. She hoped Madame was right.

"Voilà." Madame tied the last ribbon in Amy's hair, and Lydia clasped the amethyst necklace around Amy's throat. Aching to make something like it again, Amy's fingers moved to touch the twenty carat gem that dangled between her breasts. She stared at its flashing brilliance in the mirror.

"Milady?" Lydia held out the matching earrings. "Shall I put these on for you?"

"Heavens, no." Amy took a deep breath and blew it out. She fastened the earrings on her lobes and smiled, shaking her head to set them swinging from their clustered diamond tops.

"That's more like it." Lydia slipped a simple amethyst and diamond bracelet onto Amy's left wrist, where 'twould complement her heart-shaped amethyst wedding ring. The maid stood back and grinned. "Cuds bobs, if you don't look the perfect lady. I'll just go tell the lord you're ready to leave."

"Come, see if your Lydia wasn't telling the bare truth." Taking her hand, Madame helped Amy rise from the chair and led her to the pier glass.

The rich purple silk gown shimmered as Amy approached the mirror, beaming at her reflection. The seamstress had worked her magic yet again. A gold tissue overskirt looped up, held on each side with golden bows; matching gold bows marched down her full sleeves. The purple underskirt sparkled with hundreds of golden stars.

A low whistle of appreciation came from behind her. She turned to see Colin leaning against the doorjamb, his gaze fastened to her deep, scooped neckline. She melted a little at the sight of him, even after six months of marriage. He was devastatingly male. Would she ever get used to it? She thought not. Not in six months, or six years, or sixty years, even.

"You'll be the most beautiful woman at Whitehall," he said softly.

"And you, the most beautiful man."

Colin laughed. He was dressed, predictably, in the same black velvet suit he had worn for their wedding, identical down to her cameo pinned in the lavish lace of his cravat. His crisp, dark hair was loose and fell in waves to his shoulders.

Amy felt a lump of emotion swell in her throat. She was so lucky to have him; their marriage was beyond wonderful, and she had no cause to dwell on melancholy thoughts, especially on a day like today. She moved toward him and looped her arms around his neck, threading her fingers in the hair at his nape. She heard Madame bustling about, putting away cosmetics, but the sounds seemed to fade as Colin brought his lips to hers.

He kissed her gently, and she tried to pull him closer, but he tugged away and grinned.

"Later, love. We'd not want to spoil Madame Beaumont's accomplished artwork."

Amy's face flamed, and she stole a glance at Madame. But the seamstress was studiously looking elsewhere.

"Shall we?" Colin curled an arm around her waist and drew her from the room.

Was she really on her way to Whitehall Palace, to be presented to England's King and Queen? She, Amy Goldsmith, merchant's daughter? It didn't seem possible.

Colin interrupted her thoughts. "Why so quiet, love? You're not worried about tonight, are you?"

"A little, maybe. 'Tis . . ." Her chest ached with the need to tell someone, and she shot him an appraising glance. But then she heard the old words again, *You cannot have everything*, and God help her, she could tell not if it were her father's voice or Colin's. " 'Tis nothing."

"Then . . ." The fingers of one hand drummed against his thigh.

"Heavens, Colin." Forcing a smile, she pulled him toward the front door before he could question her further. "You know how moody pregnant women are!"

Chapter Twenty-six

Amy shivered as she stood in line outside the Presence Chamber, a mixture of anticipation and sheer terror shuddering through her. Colin clasped her hand tighter and looked down at her sympathetically. "They're only people, love," he whispered.

Oh, but what magnificent people they were! In front of her stood a lady in a satin gown of deep magenta studded with pearls, and Amy was forced to stand ten feet behind her long, ermine-trimmed train. Amy peeked behind at a lady wearing a splendid gown of rich turquoise with a silver lace overlay, then spun back and clapped a hand to her open mouth. Why, the woman's bosom was all but falling out of her low neckline, and the top halves of her nipples were showing!

Beside her, Colin chuckled. He raised her hand and pressed his warm lips to the back in a soft kiss. Amy looked up at him, offering a shaky smile. She was surrounded by men in long, elaborate crimped periwigs. Their satin and velvet clothing dripped with ribbons and lace in such profusion as to rival the ladies. Their fingers were bedecked with garish gemstones, their necks adorned with ropes of huge, costly pearls. Still, she was certain that Colin was the most stunning male specimen within twenty miles of Whitehall.

They advanced slowly, until suddenly it was their turn to be announced. The usher puffed out his chest and took a deep breath. "The Earl of Greystone. The Countess of Greystone."

As they entered the Presence Chamber, the throng of

spectators in the gallery above leaned forward en masse. Heads turned to ogle the new arrivals. Amy heard a distinct murmur from the lords and ladies lining the walkway.

Gliding down the endless aisle on Colin's arm, she stared straight ahead. "What are they all saying?" she asked low, trying to keep her lips from moving.

With an easy smile, Colin inclined his head toward hers. "They're saying, 'Ahhh . . . the rumors are true. Lord Greystone jilted Lady Priscilla for an uncommon beauty.' "

"Shh!" Amy blushed and giggled. "They're all looking at us."

"Of course they are. See those ladies talking behind their fans? They're saying, 'Such a shame the earl is no longer available. But at least his gorgeous lady is taken and therefore out of the competition.' "

Amy almost tripped. "I was never in the competition," she chided. "I was only a merchant's daughter."

"Tsk. They're deluding themselves, anyway. You may be out of the competition for marriage, but at Charles's Court, 'tis assumed one is always available for an *affaire d'amour*. It is taken for granted that wives are as unfaithful as husbands; the men here demand fidelity only from their mistresses."

"Not all the men, I'm hoping." She looked up at Colin with a sparkle in her eye.

He raised one eyebrow devilishly. "Oh, there might be one or two holdouts."

In spite of her anxiety, Amy grinned, but the smile faded from her lips as her attention was drawn ahead, to where Their Majesties sat awaiting her.

Their thrones were set on a raised platform, framed with a swagged canopy of crimson velvet decorated in silver and gold. But 'twas not the magnificence of the setting that held Amy's attention. 'Twas the King himself.

The most compelling figure she had ever seen, His Majesty sat tall on his throne, dwarfing his queen next to him, his long legs sprawled carelessly before him. Though he'd already reached the advanced age of thirty-seven, his volumes of shining black hair held nary a hint of gray. His face was lean, with a thin, curly black mustache over a generous, sensual mouth.

The prospect of actually meeting him was terrifying.

The magenta-garbed lady rose and moved out of the way, swishing her fur-edged train behind her. Charles looked up; his quick, heavy-lidded black eyes settled on Amy. A small smile twitched at his full lips, and Amy's heart clenched in her chest.

Colin drew her forward. He walked with the sure steps of a man greeting an old friend, while Amy's feet hesitated along the carpeted approach. When they reached the dias and Colin knelt down, Amy tore her gaze from King Charles and dipped into a deep curtsy. She looked back up into the large, liquid brown eyes of Queen Catharine of Braganza.

Queen Catharine's olive-tinted features were pleasant rather than pretty. Tiny and dark, with a long nose and high forehead, she looked very, very foreign. She smiled at Amy, revealing small teeth that protruded slightly.

"Lady Greystone," she said, her Portuguese-accented voice beautiful and melodious. Her eyes were compassionate, as though she understood Amy's nervousness. They flickered toward the King and back; though theirs was an arranged marriage, Amy thought she looked very much in love with her husband.

Catharine was dressed in soft yellow, an unfortunate choice of color that did nothing for her naturally sallow complexion. She proffered a slim hand for Amy's kiss, smiling graciously at Amy, and down to Amy's rounded belly. Was that a trace of jealousy that fluttered in Catharine's welcoming expression? Sadly, in five years of marriage, the Queen had not proven able to present Charles with any Royal children. There was constant talk of Charles setting her aside to replace her with a queen who was not barren.

She was brave and kind, and Amy decided she liked her very much.

"Ah, Lady Amethyst Chase, Countess of Greystone," she heard King Charles say. " 'Tis a pleasure to finally meet you, my dear." He held out a shapely hand, and Amy moved closer to kiss it. "A pleasure," he repeated, holding onto her hand a bit longer than was necessary.

"It . . . is *my* pleasure, Your Majesty," Amy replied after she found her voice. Charles's eyes locked with hers, signaling a warm welcome, and she decided he was not frightening after all.

"You've done well for yourself, Greystone," Charles drawled, with a wink in Colin's direction.

"Then you're not . . . displeased?"

"Displeased, Colin?"

"I assumed, when I received the summons . . ."

"Od's fish! What an idea. No, I asked you here for quite another reason altogether. Later, when all this"—he gestured impatiently—"rigamarole is dispensed with, we'll discuss it."

Amy smiled to herself. Colin had told her that Charles was notoriously intolerant of Court ceremony, considering it a waste of time. He much preferred to be out among his people, and made it a point to be available to them casually, in public places such as parks, as often as possible.

Their exchange left Amy curious, but at least reassured as to Colin's relationship with the King. It sounded as though Charles were not perturbed with him in any way. With another curtsy and a quick bow, Amy and Colin relinquished their positions to the next in line.

Colin drew her into the crowd. " 'Twas not so hard, was it now?"

"I expect I survived." Amy turned in a slow circle, taking in the splendor of her surroundings. The Presence Chamber was lit by hundreds of candles in wall sconces and liveried yeomen holding flaming torches. Dressed in every color of the rainbow, lords and ladies shimmered in the blazing light. "Look at everyone, Colin. Sequins, fur, pearls, gems, ribbon, braid, embroidery . . . on men and women alike."

"You can tell which are the ladies, though; they're the ones fanning themselves with those absurd painted creations."

Amy laughed. "You surely cannot judge gender by who is wearing the jewels." Ornaments of every description glittered from necks, wrists, waists, fingers, and ears. Seeing it all, Amy's fists tightened against the urge to make jewelry.

One tall, pale lady separated herself from the throng and came up to tap Colin on the arm with her folded fan. He started and turned to her, wondering briefly why he was surprised to see her there. Thankful that Amy was engrossed in watching the extravaganza, he pulled the woman a few feet away.

"Priscilla."

"Greystone," she said coolly. "To what do we owe the honor of your presence at Court? I was under the impression you abhorred this type of gathering."

"I was summoned by Charles," he said smoothly, refusing to rise to her bait. "Did you receive my letter of apology? I regret—"

"Well, *I* do not," she interrupted. "Buckhurst is courting me now—though I've yet to decide whether I want him."

As if she were the one who did the deciding, Colin thought. Her father would never accept Lord Buckhurst. A handsome devil, and popular—Priscilla undoubtedly basked in reflected celebrity—Buckhurst was one of the "Wits," or "Merry Gang," as they were called. These high-spirited gentlemen enlivened society with their sardonic and often vulgar poetry, plays and literature. They were tolerated at Court because Charles found them amusing, but they wielded no power. Buckhurst was most certainly *not* what Lord Hobbs was looking for in a son-in-law.

"I wish you every happiness with him," he told her.

She smiled smugly.

Amy glanced around, having finally noticed that Colin was no longer by her side. She recognized Priscilla with a jolt of surprise, and was even more surprised to find herself not worried or jealous in the least. Seeing them together, she was suddenly sure Colin didn't love Priscilla and never had. She glided up to where they faced each other, and with a warm smile, Colin moved aside to include her.

"Lady Priscilla, may I present my wife, Amethyst—"

"Amethyst," Priscilla repeated under her breath, her eyes narrowing as she struggled to remember something. "Amethyst." Suddenly, the gray eyes snapped open wide. "You!" she exclaimed.

" 'Tis nice to see you again, Lady Priscilla."

Colin's brow furrowed in a frown of puzzlement. "You . . . know one another?"

Priscilla didn't answer. Her beautiful mouth was slack with disbelief.

"We met once, at Madame Beaumont's," Amy explained, clutching Colin's arm in a subconscious message of possession. "Before . . . before we were wed."

Priscilla finally found her voice. "I do not believe this," she spat.

Colin laid a hand over Amy's where it rested on his arm. "You do not believe what, Priscilla?"

"I do not believe you broke *our* betrothal to wed *her*," she burst out, as though Amy weren't there. She had a nasty habit of doing that, Amy thought. "Why, she's not—she's only—" Priscilla sputtered, "she's—"

"My wife," Colin supplied. "And a countess. The Countess of Greystone. A smallish estate, with a charming medieval castle. You'll remember it, I'm sure?"

Priscilla stared at him for a moment, her eyes so cold that Amy half-expected Colin's arm to turn to ice under her fingers. Then Priscilla lifted her perfect chin, turned and walked away. She'd not taken more than three ladylike steps when Amy and Colin convulsed in laughter; Amy was sure Priscilla could hear them, but she cared not.

"I do believe she'll be asking Buckhurst to send for the coach forthwith," Colin said with more than a little satisfaction. "She's certain to have a headache this evening."

"Is she, now?"

"Based on my experience, I'd wager on it. And this time, I find myself perversely pleased to be the cause of it." He took her hand. "Come, the dancing is about to begin."

The musicians were tuning up at one end of the chamber, and the presentations were complete. King Charles stepped down from the dias and gave the signal for the music to start.

He danced the first dance with Catharine, as was only proper. 'Twas a courante, slow and grave, a pantomimic dance suggesting courtship. Amy watched in awe, unable to believe she was in this place, at this time, watching the King of England dance with the Queen. He moved with a rare grace for so large a man and cut a dashing figure indeed. In fact, he was put together in quite a pleasing fashion and, being a man who enjoyed and excelled at all types of sports, had not an ounce of spare fat on his well-formed frame.

The next tune was an English country dance, a few simple steps executed by many couples in a double line. Colin pulled her into the queue, and there she was—dancing at Whitehall Palace. Amethyst Goldsmith, merchant's daughter. Incredible. When the ladies' line passed the men's, she could feel Charles's gaze on her.

Following the country dance was a branle, a group dance featuring pendulum-like movements combined with much running, gliding and skipping.'Twas a bit too energetic for Amy in her present condition, so Colin led her off to the side.

"Greystone!" The voice was light and self-assured, and Amy turned to see its lush, sensual owner. The lady's deep blue eyes were set in a classical face framed by auburn curls.

"My Lady Castlemaine." Pleasure at meeting her was

evident on Colin's expressive features. "Amy, this is Barbara, the Countess of Castlemaine. Barbara, my wife, Amethyst."

So this was the King's longtime mistress. "I'm glad of your acquaintance," Amy said with a little bow, perfectly mimicking the behavior of the lords and ladies around her.

Barbara looked Amy up and down, nodded her approval, then leaned forward for the obligatory casual kiss. "I'm glad of your acquaintance, also," she returned with, to her credit, as much warmth as she allotted to any woman. Colin smiled to himself. A natural predator, Barbara's charms were mainly reserved for men.

"Where is your rival tonight, Barbara?" He took advantage of his excessive height to give the chamber a sweeping glance.

"My *rival*?" Barbara's tone bordered on offended, as if she thought it absurd that anyone could rival the celebrated Countess of Castlemaine. But she wore a broad smile on her face, attesting to her good humor.

"Frances. *La Belle* Stewart."

"Frances? Have you not heard? My God, Greystone, whyever do you hide yourself away in the country like that? You miss all the fun."

"Heard what? Is she ill?"

"Only in the head. The ninny up and married Richmond in April—eloped, they did. Charles is livid. He'll not stand to see her, at Court or anywhere else."

"But why?" Colin asked dryly. "Certainly so inconsequential a matter as marriage wouldn't affect his pursuit of her." At the same time, he put an arm around Amy's shoulders to draw her near.

"If it were anyone else, you'd be right." Barbara looked from Colin to Amy and back. "*Almost* anyone else," she amended pointedly.

Colin's lips quirked in a half smile. "But not Frances?"

"Not Frances. She's behaved with nauseating correctness—to the extent of returning all the jewels that Charles had given her. Can you *imagine*?"

Of all people, Colin reflected, Barbara would have a hard time imagining *that*. "Perhaps she simply values a wedding ring over the benefits of being a Royal mistress," he suggested.

"Hummph!" Only Barbara could snort so regally. "As if she couldn't have both!" Barbara's voice dropped suddenly. "Do you want to know the real reason Frances has never graced the King's bed?" She motioned them closer, and the three huddled together as she revealed conspiratorially, "She doesn't like it. She was terrified before she was married, and now that she is, she finds it disgusting. So much for the Duke of Richmond's prowess!"

Amy's eyes widened in disbelief as this tidbit was revealed, and Barbara burst into laughter. "From the look on your bride's face, Greystone, I would wager you share none of Richmond's shortcomings!" she crowed.

Try as he might, Colin couldn't help but laugh at Barbara's observation, and after taking a moment to digest Barbara's meaning, a red-cheeked Amy joined in.

"Ahh, Colin." Barbara's blue eyes danced with mischief. "I see you finally found someone with a sense of humor."

Amy cocked her head; a slightly bewildered look overcame her features. " 'Tis old history, my dear," Barbara explained with a wave of her elegant hand. "But let me be the first to welcome you to Court. So refreshing to have a new face in the crowd. We're all so bloody bored of one another!"

Colin was inordinately pleased. 'Twas the most ringing endorsement he had ever heard Barbara give another woman, and it boded well indeed for Amy's acceptance into society.

Just then a courtier came up to curry favor with Barbara, and with a roll of her eyes, she departed.

Amy turned to Colin. "I knew not that you were friends with Lady Castlemaine."

"As Barbara said, love, 'tis a small circle. Everyone knows everyone else."

"But you seem to know her *especially* well," Amy pointed out, her voice tinged with an unmistakable touch of jealousy.

"Is *that* what you're thinking?" Colin wondered aloud. "Me? With Barbara Palmer?" It warmed his heart to find Amy so covetous of his person. He shuddered expressively, as though the mere thought of sharing his bed with such a creature were abhorrent.

Amy laughed. "How long have you known her?"

"We knew one another in exile, and she was all of fifteen when she took up with Lord Chesterfield. She went straight from him to Charles—with some overlap, I suspect, since her oldest daughter, although recognized by His Majesty, bears a striking resemblance to Chesterfield." Colin's voice took on a melodramatic tone. "So, you see, I never got my chance with her." He sighed theatrically.

"Oh, my," Amy said. "What scrumptious scandals are to be discovered by attending Court!"

"Enjoying yourself, my dear?"

The voice was resonant and impressive—'twas King Charles, talking to *her*. She turned and gazed up at him in disbelief. As tall as Colin, or perhaps an inch higher, he was even more extraordinary standing next to her than he had been upon his throne. She grinned and nodded, the only reply she was capable of at the moment.

"Amy is a bit overwhelmed, I'm afraid," Colin answered for her.

"I am *not*," she retorted, finding her voice again. "I am having a splendid time, Your Majesty."

Charles smiled down at her, his even white teeth flashing beneath his black mustache. "We're so pleased to have you here, Lady Greystone. A new face, and such a lovely one at that."

Amy colored, becomingly, she hoped. However, to her great consternation, she seemed to have lost her ready wit. "Thank you, Sire" was all she could manage.

"The next dance is a minuet. Might you know it?"

She remembered Robert scoffing at her dancing lessons. The elegant minuet was staid enough even for a pregnant cow. " 'Tis one of my favorites," she volunteered.

Colin discretely elbowed her in the ribs. Before coming to Court, he'd explained that ladies were supposed to ask the King to dance, not vice versa, and she had duly noted the information. But she'd not expected to make use of it. Was His Majesty hinting that he wished to dance the minuet with *her*? She looked up at Colin, and he nodded circumspectly.

"Would—would you care to dance the minuet with me, Sire?" she stammered out.

King Charles was a superb dancer. As he gazed into her eyes, Amy realized with a start that although his looks were far from the classic English standard, he was the most blatantly sexual man she had ever met. 'Twas no wonder he'd already sired eight acknowledged Royal bastards, plus, most assumed, an undetermined number of unacknowledged children as well.

Charles possessed many talents, not the least of which was an uncanny ability to put his companions at ease. By the time he returned Amy to Colin, she was laughing along with him as though they had been the best of friends for years.

"Tell me not that you've fallen in love with him, too?" Colin teased. He turned her so they were both facing Charles, wrapped his arms around her, and leaned her back against his tall body. "You'll not be the first, and you'll certainly not be the last," he warned with the easy grace of a man unconcerned with offending a fast friend, no matter his rank.

Bright color flooded Amy's cheeks, for he spoke a partial truth: She was halfway in love with King Charles already, and there was nothing for it. His charm was too powerful to resist, and the prospect of a friendship with the King of England, albeit platonic, was too delicious to pass up.

Charles laughed in response. "Worry not on that account, Greystone. Your prowess with a sword is legendary, and something tells me you would not wear a cuckold's horns gracefully."

Colin smiled wryly and dropped a kiss on the top of Amy's head. "Neither," he said pointedly, "would Lady Castlemaine."

Charles threw back his head, and a rumble of laughter poured forth. "You're quite right about that. And I've no wish to be skewered by either of you!" Though no one would dare challenge the King for any slight either real or imagined, they shared a laugh at the absurd scenario. Then the King sobered, took Colin by the arm, and pulled him aside. "Will you come into my laboratory with me? I've something important to show you."

"Of course. Amy?"

"I will be fine, Colin." In fact, the Duke of Buckingham was already making his way toward her. It seemed Barbara was right. The courtiers were dying for a diversion, and having danced with Charles, her popularity was a *fait accompli.*

Hands behind his back, the King paced determinedly through the Long Gallery, a dozen of his beloved spaniels yapping at his and Colin's heels. "I need to beg a favor from you, Colin."

"Anything, Charles. You need only to ask. What is it?"

His Majesty eyed the busy passage. "Wait 'til we're in the laboratory; 'tis the only chamber in all of Whitehall where I'm afforded privacy." Frowning, he paused on the threshold to the Royal Bedchamber. "Od's fish, how did they get here before me?"

With a sigh, he shouldered his way through the cluster of courtiers who gathered there day and night, competing shamelessly to do him the smallest personal favors.

"Would you like your slippers, Sire?"

"A warming brick for your bed?"

"A cup of chocolate?"

"No. No, thank you. No." He beckoned Colin after him, the spaniels darting in their wake. "Quick, into the laboratory before someone offers to hold my chamber pot for me."

Colin laughed as they shut the door behind them, the clamoring courtiers and barking dogs safely on the other side. "And why not? I hear tell the French Court obliges Louis so."

"Louis XIV I'm not," Charles said dryly. "I can wipe my own arse, thank you."

After the confusion of the public areas, the laboratory seemed eerily quiet. Colin's gaze swept over the profusion of paraphernalia. "Ford would have the time of his life in here," he said, making a mental note to secure him an invitation.

King Charles only nodded distractedly. The ill-synchronized chiming of his clock collection accentuated the expectant silence. Colin leaned back against a counter, almost knocking over a telescope in the process. As he whirled to right it, Charles drew a deep breath.

"I'm certain you've heard about our embarrassment at the hands of the Dutch."

"I've been out *in* the country, not out *of* the country," Colin replied in an attempt at wry humor. The King seemed so very serious.

Just two days earlier, the Dutch War had escalated, with disastrous results. Aided by a lack of defense money and interest from the English government, the Dutch had cruised right up the River Thames, burned three of the biggest vessels of the Royal Navy, and sailed back out to sea with the pride of the English fleet, the flagship the *Royal Charles*, towed behind them as a prize. It was, so far, the most humiliating moment of Charles's reign.

Yesterday, Charles and his brother James had been on the scene, supervising the sinking of ships in the Thames and its creeks to block a second attack. But 'twas too little, too late. Nobody commented upon Charles's hard work in defense of the Thames. To the contrary, the talk in London was about how he'd spent the night of the catastrophe dining with his son Monmouth, in the company of his mistress Castlemaine, where they all passed a merry evening hunting a moth around the chamber. He was suffering mightily for his exaggerated reputation of pursuing pleasure over responsibility. The Dutch War must come to a conclusion, and soon.

"The first step toward peace is to detach Louis from the Dutch," Charles explained, revealing his plan. "With the French as our ally, the Dutch will be forced to negotiate a treaty."

"Why should Louis want to side with us?" Colin asked. "Because he's your cousin?"

"One cannot rely on family relationships in foreign policy. At present, Louis covets their territory more than he desires our colonies." Charles picked at some lint on his velvet surcoat. "He has no real quarrel with England. Indeed, there has been only one actual battle between us, and Louis emerged such a clear victor that he must be inclined toward cooperation now."

Colin frowned, confused. "I've heard of no fighting with France," he ventured cautiously. He walked around the chamber, skimming one hand over microscopes, magnets, and air pumps.

" 'Twas a social battle," Charles conceded with a sigh. He started pacing. "Since the fire, I've grown weary of the complicated fripperies we adorn ourselves with here at Court. Plumes, periwigs, lace, ruffles, ribbons, chains . . .'tis all quite ridiculous, do you not agree?"

Colin could not have agreed more, as evidenced by his pared-down version of Court apparel. Still, as Charles himself had brought the dandified fashions from the Continent, a prudent man would not be too quick to assent. "One could look at it that way," he said guardedly.

"Last October, I designed for myself a more reserved costume. A long black coat, slashed here and there to show a white shirt, and a close-fitting waistcoat to match. Quite practical, I thought."

"And?" Colin failed to see what this had to do with the Dutch War, or a supposed French War, or any war at all.

"Well, Louis heard about it and promptly dressed all his footmen in my new uniform. I'm afraid the new style was blown out of existence by a gale of laughter," Charles lamented. He stopped pacing and turned to Colin. "A surprise attack, and a clean victory."

Colin had to choke back laughter. Louis XIV, the so-called "Sun King," had pulled off a practical joke of such unmitigated virtuosity, it turned Colin green with envy. What a coup!

"I suppose 'tis just as well," Charles said mournfully. "Even though the Court, naturally, followed my lead, I heard later that they all felt like damned penguins."

They both shared a laugh over that, which was a relief to Colin, who was about to explode anyway.

When the last chuckles had died away and the King's face had settled back into worried lines, Colin asked carefully, "And what is it that I can do for you?"

Charles took a step closer. "I need you to carry a letter to my mother in Paris. I cannot correspond with Louis directly; 'twould raise suspicion."

The last thing Colin wanted to do now was leave Amy, pregnant and vulnerable, to travel back to France, a place full of sad childhood memories. He hated France. And there was the debt—what would happen to the estate's productivity without him there to oversee it?

He took a slow, deep breath and looked up from the pendulum he was playing with. "Why me? Why not Buckingham, or Arlington or Lauderdale? Such missions are part of their position. I'm not involved in Royal intelligence."

"Exactly. If I sent any of them to the Continent, they'd be followed. 'Tis imperative these negotiations remain secret—if the Dutch suspect my designs, they will present counterarguments to Louis before he even considers my plan."

"But there must be someone else. Someone with a lower government appointment, whom no one would notice."

"Why so reluctant?" Charles flashed a teasing grin. "The Chases have never hesitated to do my bidding before." Serious now, he put a hand on Colin's arm. "I'm sorry, but I've considered this carefully, and you're the perfect candidate. No one will question your visit to my mother; you were always close to Henrietta Maria, almost like a foster son. And no one will question when she visits Louis, her favorite nephew, afterward."

The plan was flawless, except that Colin wanted no part of it. He swallowed hard and moved away, rearranging some bottles of chemicals. "This is a bad time to leave Amy." She'd seemed so melancholy of late, but she refused to talk about it.

"Ah, I see," Charles responded with the sort of genuine sympathy that was an integral part of his charm. "You needn't stay long; no one would expect it, with a child due soon. Just across the Channel, a short visit, and back. Three weeks—a month at the most."

Colin picked up a bottle of cloudy green fluid. A month. A month of the precious time he had left before he'd be forced to fail Amy . . . before everything would fall apart.

"Amy will be fine," Charles said. "I'll send her to Greystone with a Royal escort. I want you to leave tomorrow."

The bottle clinked to the counter as Colin's head shot up. "Tomorrow!"

"This is very important, Colin," Charles said gravely.

"What about Jason?" Colin asked wildly, casting about for any possible replacement.

"Jason would never holiday in France without taking the twins—everyone knows he takes them everywhere—trying to be the father they never had, I suppose. To leave them home would be out of character, and to bring them along, too visible."

"Ford, then."

"Ford was a child at the Restoration. My mother would not even recognize him after all these years."

"Do you not think people will find my leaving Amy at this time a mite suspicious?"

"No one who would be watching knows you well. You must admit: for a courtier, you keep a low profile. Your reluctance surely took me by surprise. Marital happiness is not assumed these days, I'm afraid."

Colin was silent. Defeated. His family had always been there when the Stuarts had needed them, and vice versa. When Colin had asked him, King Charles had granted Lord Hobbs's license without so much as a blink of his Royal eye.

But he was torn apart inside. He couldn't take Amy on a sea trip, seven months pregnant, and he couldn't leave her home . . . he just couldn't . . .

Charles put a hand on his shoulder and said quietly, "I'm asking you, Colin, as your monarch and *as your friend*, to do this thing for me."

He had no choice.

Chapter Twenty-seven

"My lady, do you not think you've seen enough?" Benchley looked down his beak nose at Amy standing at the edge of Greystone's quarry. She scanned once more over the site, smiling at the view of the quarrymen dotting the stepped-down ledges. The blows of their hammers rang through the air as they toiled in the hot sun. She watched a huge slab of dimension stone begin to crack away from the face, mentally adding its value to Greystone's ledgers.

" 'Tis doing well," she murmured, satisfied. Treading carefully on the uneven ground, she made her way down the rise and back to the two-seater caleche.

Benchley trailed behind. "In your condition, I cannot imagine why you insist on dragging yourself all over the estate. I'll take you home now."

"Nonsense—I'm pregnant, not ill. I've not yet inspected the sheep." She tried to hoist herself onto the seat, then convulsed in laughter, holding out a hand for his help. "God in heaven, I think my girth has doubled in the three weeks since Colin left for France. I've been wondering if he'll recognize me upon his return." At Benchley's wide-eyed look, she couldn't resist shocking him some more. "I've also been wondering how a babe this size can possibly fit out of me, but Lydia assures me it will work."

The tips of Benchley's ears turned red. He picked up the reins and clucked at the horse.

"I try not to think about it too much," Amy added brightly.

"Excellent plan," he choked out, staring straight ahead.

During the thirty-minute drive from the quarry perched on one side of Greystone to the grazing fields bordering the other end, Amy digested what she'd seen. Though but a small portion of Greystone's income, the tiny quarry it was named for was producing well. Sky-high stacks of newly cut wood from the estate's abundant forests waited to be sold. The crops were coming in nicely, though she was glad Colin would be home for the harvest—she'd not a clue what to do about that.

She'd brought the ledgers up to date, delighted to discover that Greystone had become self-supporting and then some. There looked to be a small profit due in the fall. She wondered why Colin had seemed so worried; did he not realize it?

She could hardly wait for him to come home so she could tell him. She missed him fiercely, his reassuring smile and the heavenly feel of his arms around her, especially when she lay alone at night in their big bed. She missed him more than she missed working with gold and diamonds. God in heaven, she loved him. When he came home, she'd tell him so—a million times. Maybe he would have missed her, too. Maybe he'd be truly happy then.

The caleche rolled to a halt. While Benchley went off to hail a shepherd, Amy lowered her ungainly body to the ground. The long summer grasses seemed to undulate on the rolling hills; their fresh scent tickled her nose. She perched carefully on the low fence and swung her legs over. 'Twas quiet out here, the silence broken only by the occasional bleats of the sheep. When a lamb came toddling up and butted his head against her skirts, she reached down to let him lick her hand.

"Lady Greystone?"

"Yes." She turned and smiled at the shepherd; no apple-cheeked nursery rhyme boy, but a grown man much taller than she. "I trust the sheep are doing well?"

"I . . ." Lifting one weathered hand, he removed his

cap and rubbed his bald head. "Know you anything of sheep, my lady?"

"No. No, I do not. But—"

"That youngster there has bluetongue." He kicked a pebble and pulled the cap back over his brow. "I'm sorry, my lady."

"Sorry?" She looked down at the fluffy animal nuzzling her hand. "Bluetongue?"

"An illness. Swelling of the nose and lips, bleeding in the mouth, and—"

Grimacing, Amy pulled her hand away. "Mucous," she finished for him, wiping her palm on her skirt.

"My lady!" Benchley rushed to unearth a handkerchief and thrust it into her hands.

The shepherd knelt to pry open the sheep's mouth. "See?"

"Bluetongue." Amy took a deep breath and wadded up the sticky handkerchief. "Or bluish-tongue, anyway. What does it mean?" She ran her fingers through the animal's thick wool. "Are they all ill? Surely we can still shear them come time?"

The man stood up slowly. "Those that still live." With a sad smile, he patted the lamb on the head. "More than half of the ill ones have died already, and more fall sick every day."

"What?" Amy's heart sank. The profit she'd calculated depended on projected income from the wool. She'd assumed the production would be consistent with last year's. "Can you not make them get better?"

"I know of no treatment." He shifted on his feet, took the cap off and replaced it again. "Lord Greystone, he keeps up with the newest ideas, but he hied himself off to London and has yet to return."

"Did . . . did he know of this?" Perhaps this was why Colin had seemed so melancholy.

"No. He left before it started. It spreads very quickly."

"Oh," Amy said blankly. "Th-thank you."

"My lady." The shepherd bowed and touched his cap.

She would never get used to that deference, she thought vaguely as she watched him walk away, the lamb following at his heels.

"God in heaven," she breathed, making her way back to the caleche. "Colin will really be unhappy now."

"Pardon, my lady?" Benchley raised a hand to help her up.

"Nothing, Benchley. Just talking to myself." Her stomach felt leaden at the thought of Colin's homecoming. Now instead of greeting him with good news, she'd be reporting a sure loss of income and the need to replace expensive livestock.

She couldn't stand it, she thought as she plopped onto the seat. She really couldn't stand it. After all the years he'd worked this land, now to be saddled with her and a baby on the way, plus unexpected monetary problems . . . well, 'twas just not fair. Colin deserved better than this. After all he'd done for her, was there nothing she could do for him?

She folded her hands over the mound of her stomach. Damned if there wasn't.

Colin looked again at the crumpled paper, then up at the street sign. Quai de la Tournelle. And there was the shop, Talbot Joaillerie. For people driven out of England, the Talbots had certainly managed to land in a luxurious location. A plaque with Louis XIV's warrant was prominently displayed in the window.

"This is it," he said, stuffing the paper back into his pocket. At the cabbie's blank look, he uttered a quick *"Merci"* and thrust a few coins into his hand.

He pushed on the door, but the shop was locked. Was it past six o'clock already? Colin absently patted his surcoat, looking for his pocket watch, then froze as he remembered.

The blasted highwaymen had taken it. What a trip—one disaster after another. He should never have come back to this place.

He plucked the sleeve of a passing pedestrian. *"Excusez-moi, monsieur. Avez-vous l'heure exacte?"*

The man walked past as though he'd not seen him. Damn Parisians literally wouldn't give you the time of day. Colin couldn't wait to get home. No matter if the crossing were as rough on the return as it had been on the way here—he could puke his guts out and be happy for it.

He pounded on the door. And pounded. And pounded. 'Twas five minutes before a petite, attractive middle-aged woman pressed her nose against the window. *"Il est six heures et quart, Monsieur,"* she scolded, pointing to the sign that listed their business hours.

"I need to talk with you," Colin called through the glass.

"By God, you're English!" she exclaimed, moving to unlock the door. She ushered him inside. "Come in, come in! I've nothing on display, but—"

" 'Tis you I wish to see, not jewelry, madame. You're Elizabeth Talbot, I presume?" She nodded her dark head, puzzled. "I'm Colin Chase—"

Understanding and delight lit her blue eyes. "Earl of Greystone and my Amy's husband," she finished for him. "I should have guessed. She described you in her letters as devastatingly handsome."

Colin felt his face heat under his tan. "Madame Talbot—"

"You must call me Aunt Elizabeth. Will you not come upstairs and have a cup of tea?" As she turned, a soft jasmine scent swirled into the air.

"Tea?"

"Oh, I know 'tis a frightfully expensive delicacy, but a stuffy marquise gifted me with a supply after we designed a diamond collar for his poodle. These French!" Listening to her giggle as she led the way upstairs, Colin felt a personal connection for the first time in weeks.

"I'm so glad you saw fit to visit me," she said after she'd hung a kettle of water over the fire. "You did not bring my Amy, did you?" She said it with mock disapproval, craning her neck as though he might have hidden Amy behind his back. "No, I can see you did not. I shall have to make do with you." She collected two porcelain cups, studying him with a sidelong glance as she set them on a tray. "My, but you're nice to look at. I think you'll do fine, after all."

Colin laughed, favoring her with one of his grins. He would swear she was flirting.

"Come into the sitting room, will you?" She handed him the tray, sailing past him with a swish of her skirts. "You're here on King's business, are you not?"

Trailing after her, he almost dropped the tray. "How . . ."

Her musical laugh filled the air. "You'd be surprised what I know of you, my boy." Her lips twitched in amusement as she took the tray from him and set it on a table, waving him into a chair. "How did it go?"

"Not well, at first," he said carefully. How much could she know? "On the ride from Calais, my stagecoach was beset by highwaymen."

Gracefully seating herself, she raised a brow at him. "Not an auspicious start."

"To say the least." He hitched himself forward. "As I was carrying little cash, the damned felons took my ring—the ring Amy made for me." He rubbed the spot where it used to be, more angry every time he thought about it. "I would have run them through with my sword, but there were three of them, bearing pistols, and one of me—"

"Amy would think you could handle them."

"She might at that." Her teasing expression coaxed a smile. "In any case, I know better, and none of the other victims seemed inclined to help."

There was an expectant silence. Elizabeth smoothed her skirts. "And Henrietta Maria? How did it go with her?"

Colin's jaw dropped open. "What has Amy written to you?"

"Not to worry." She waved a hand. "Only that you

were visiting the King's mother on King's business. No details." Elizabeth cocked her head. "Does she know any?" Colin nodded. "Then she knows how to keep her mouth shut. As for writing of you . . . you know how 'tis when you're young and in love, and you look for excuses to say—or write—your loved one's name."

"I cannot say that I do," he said wryly. "I surmise I was never young and in love at the same time." He rose, pacing to the fireplace. "In any case, the Dowager Queen did not see fit to be in residence. I cooled my heels for ten days, waiting for her return. After all that, I would not have been surprised had she refused to act on her son's letter, but fortunately, that was the one thing that went right." He toyed with a shepherdess figurine on the mantel, its frilly pink skirts reminding him of Henrietta Maria, who he trusted was on her way to Versailles to visit her nephew.

"And then?" Amy's aunt fixed him with a penetrating look. "Come on, boy, spit it out. I'm sure you'd not go out of your way to visit an old woman for the joy of it."

"Old woman, eh? Now you're fishing for return compliments." He laughed. "I can see right through you, Aunt Elizabeth."

"And I can see right through you. You're concerned about something, are you not?"

Uncomfortable under her knowing gaze, he walked to a window and swept aside the lace curtain. He stared down at the bustling Parisian street. "Madame—Aunt Elizabeth—I came to ask a favor."

"Anything, my boy."

"If you could see your way clear to accompany me to Greystone for a visit, I'd be more than grateful." His hand dropped, and the lace fell back to shroud the window. "As I'm sure you know, Amy is due to bear our first child soon, and your presence would make it much easier."

He turned toward her slowly, surprising himself with a sudden wish to confide in someone for the first time in his memory. But he could find not the words to begin.

Elizabeth stood up and came near. Her jasmine scent reminded him of someone . . . his mother? She smiled. "I suspect you may need something stronger than tea for this discussion. May I prevail on you to squire me out for supper? With William away in Antwerp, I find myself weary of dining alone." Her hand brushed his arm, and she raised a brow. "What say you to La Tour d'Argent?"

"*Restaurant* La Tour d'Argent? With no notice? I hear tell duels are fought to obtain a table there."

"Not to worry, my boy, you'll not have to fence for your supper." Elizabeth's eyes sparkled. "The owner's wife has been coveting a bracelet in my window . . . I'm sure we can strike a bargain."

"Anguille des bois, madame." The server set a pewter plate before Elizabeth with a flourish. "*Et pour vous,* Lord Greystone,"—Colin smiled at the hacked pronunciation of his name, but gave the man points for trying—*"Poule d'Afrique."*

The savory scent of the delicacy wafted to Colin's nose, but it failed to entice him. He sighed as the server walked away. "As I was saying, Amy is unhappy. She'll not speak of it, but she broke her vow to wed me, and—"

"Her vow?" A frown appeared between Elizabeth's blue eyes.

"She promised her father—your brother . . ." She nodded, indicating that she was not too fragile to discuss him. "She made him promises. To continue the traditions of Goldsmith & Sons. To save her inheritance for future generations. There's more, and to hear her tell of it, 'tis like promises signed in blood. She's miserable, and there's not a damned thing I can do about it."

"Nothing?" Her bejeweled fingers toyed with her pewter goblet. "Nothing at all?"

"Not without giving her up." His voice caught, and he looked down to his plate, slowly cutting a bite of his hen. "She cannot run a shop and live with me at

Greystone. And I cannot seem to make her happy there." The delicious entree could have been boiled wood chips for all it appealed to Colin. He chewed and swallowed, then brought his gaze to Elizabeth's. "I thought love would be enough, but it seems not to be. Not enough for her."

"Colin—"

" 'Tis my fault, not hers," he said through clenched teeth. A sip of his wine failed to compose him. "I manipulated her into this marriage—tricked her into saying yes because I couldn't stand to lose her." He took another gulp. " 'Twas a bad idea. A bad, bad idea. I knew all along that a nobleman has not the luxury of wedding for love, but I lost my mind over your niece. Now everything is a bloody mess."

Elizabeth took a dainty bite of her eel, waiting.

He looked out the window by their table. The Seine glowed orange in the sunset. The last rays glinted off the spire of Nôtre-Dame, making his eyes water. "There's more . . ."

"Yes?" Her voice came quiet.

"Did Amy mention I'd been betrothed to someone else?"

"You'd be surprised—" Elizabeth started.

"What you know of me," Colin finished dryly, looking back at her. "Well, I'd wager you know not that I owe the woman's father a fortune—even Amy knows not of that. Due at the end of the year."

Her delicate eyebrows rose. "And . . ."

"I cannot pay it." His hands fisted under the table. "Bloody hell, I cannot pay it. I'll be forced to use Amy's inheritance to avoid losing Greystone." His breath came hard and fast. "By God, she'll *really* hate me then."

"Will she?" Elizabeth murmured. He watched her graceful hands as she rearranged her cutlery. Jeweler's hands, like Amy's. "You're asking Amy to give up everything that made her what she is—that made her the woman you love. Would you give up everything for her?"

"Give up Greystone? If it were Greystone or Amy?" Had the pewter goblet been glass instead, 'twould have broken under his grip. He set it down, lest he spill on the snow-white cloth. "There are expectations in my world. For God's sake, the *King* granted me this property, this title . . . how can I fail him? What could I offer my children? I grew up without a home. I know what it feels like."

"From what I know of your story, you grew up without love as well . . . and which was the greater loss?"

Below the window, a boat drifted lazily by. Its passengers' lighthearted laughter swirled through the open shutters, melding with the conversational buzz that filled the elegant candlelit room.

Had he ever been so carefree?

If it were Greystone or Amy, which would he choose? His stomach clenched. Hell, it *was* Greystone or Amy. He had to choose.

"I will not take Amy's gold," he blurted, vaguely wondering if he looked more surprised than Elizabeth. He drew a deep breath. "If I do, I will lose her. Emotionally, even should she choose to stay. So I'll not take it. I just will not." With a motion that bespoke of finality, he speared a bite of chicken and forked it into his mouth. "There."

"Do you reckon it must come to that?" Elizabeth's words were quiet and thoughtful.

"Yes. I gave her my word. I cannot betray her." He shifted on his chair, returning her gaze. "Yes."

I think not, she mouthed, or maybe he just imagined it. But her features softened with a gentle smile, and she raised her goblet in a toast.

"Well, my boy, when do we leave for England?"

Colin poked his head out of the carriage, frowning at the unmistakable sounds of construction. His gaze followed the circular drive as he slowly stepped to the gravel. Atop the Great Hall, a new slate roof glistened in the sunshine.

He leaned against the carriage. Sweet Mary, if she'd spent his small savings on a new roof, thinking to surprise him . . . but no, it mattered not. Not now that he'd decided to forfeit Greystone, regardless.

His attention was diverted as Amy slammed out the front door and bounded toward him, as fast as her swollen girth would allow. "God in heaven, Colin, I'm so glad you're home!"

She threw herself at him, the mound of her stomach bouncing off his solid form. With a shaky laugh, he reached to set her aright, then crushed her against himself, burying his nose in her rose-scented hair. "By God, I missed you."

She pulled back, a radiant grin on her face, then lunged at him again, as though to convince herself he was really there.

He half-laughed, half-groaned, the gravel crunching under his feet as he shifted. "Wh-what the devil's going on here?" he finally stammered out, gesturing at the roof.

Her grin widened, then she froze when she looked past him. "Aunt Elizabeth?"

As her aunt stepped down from the coach, Colin ventured a small smile of his own. "It seems we both had surprises for each other, love."

"Oh, Colin! Aunt Elizabeth!" As she let out a cry of pleasure, enclosing her aunt in an enthusiastic embrace, Colin's smile turned genuine. She was such a joy . . . how could he ever have considered betraying her, even for a moment? Any sacrifice was worth it, so long as he retained her trust. And her love. Suddenly, the old fear started melting away. Here with Amy again, it seemed marrying for love was the best thing he could have done for himself and his children, no matter the consequences.

She tugged on his hand. "Wait 'til you see the inside! Did you notice the new windows as you drove up? The downstairs chambers are ready for furniture, and our suite upstairs is almost—" She stopped when he didn't budge.

He couldn't budge. He felt rooted to the ground. He didn't want to see all the improvements, his home restored like he'd dreamed, only to hand it over to Hobbs. The buzzard.

He backed up and sat on the carriage step. "Amy, love . . . just give me a minute to get used to this."

"There's more. I bought more sheep, and the thresher. And the mill is fixed." He squeezed his eyes shut. "Colin?" She jiggled his arm. "Colin, are you all right?" She gave a nervous giggle. "I'm the one who's supposed to feel faint these days."

"I'm fine," he whispered. "Did you spend it all?"

"Spend it all?" Her laugh rang through the courtyard. "Have you any idea what those diamonds are worth? Or how much gold a trunk will hold?"

His eyes flew open. "Diamonds? Gold?" Why did she always make him feel so dense?

Her laughter tapered off into the heavy summer air. "Did you think I would spend Greystone's accounts?" she asked slowly. "Without asking?"

"I . . ." He rose, but his knees felt weak. "Are you saying, then—"

"I want you to have it, Colin. I want you to be happy." Her hand moved to the bulge of their child. "The gold was meant as security for my son, was it not?" She gazed up at him, her amethyst eyes shining with tears. "What could be more secure than an earldom and acres of land? The fortune will be there, in the crops planted in the fertile soil, in the stone walls of the castle and the shingles on the Great Hall's roof. I should have realized it months ago." One tear escaped and traced a path down her cheek. "I'm sorry."

"You're sorry . . . ?" His hand came up to wipe away that one tear, warm against the pad of his fingertip. A peculiar grayness crept to fog his vision. He scooped her against him, holding her tight. Holding himself up.

She was the pregnant one—he'd be damned if he was going to faint.

Chapter Twenty-eight

His expression unreadable, Colin approached their bed the next morning and handed Amy a letter decorated with an all-too-familiar red seal. A pain clenched her middle as her eyes scanned down the page, past lines of neat, flourished script, the product of many years of tutoring, to the bottom, where 'twas signed, "Your very loving friend, Charles R."

"God in heaven," she groaned. The parchment rustled as she dropped it to the bed. "Not another summons, another favor."

Colin's laugh boomed through the chamber. "Read it, lazybones." He stalked to the window and pushed open the drapes. " 'Tis only a letter saying a treaty with the Dutch was signed three days ago at Breda, and thanking me for service performed on behalf of England."

She blinked against the sunshine flooding the chamber. "Thank God for small favors." When he came to kiss her on the forehead, she flashed him a mischievous smile. "I would have thrown you into the oubliette before I let you go this time. Six weeks you were gone . . . and we've not even made love yet." She laughed at the hungry gleam in his eyes. "I do not remember going to bed."

"You fell asleep in the middle of a sentence last night. Been lying awake missing me these weeks past?" He bent to kiss her again, and his teeth nibbled at her bottom lip, sending her pulse racing. A soft moan escaped her throat.

He smiled against her mouth. "I never got the chance to thank you for sharing your inheritance—"

"There's no need—"

"—and for saving Greystone."

"Saving Greystone?" She struggled to sit up. "Perhaps I made things a bit easier for you, but Greystone would have done well in the long run. 'Tis a fine estate."

"A fine estate, yes." He sat on the bed and took her hands. "But 'twould have been Lord Hobbs's fine estate."

"Lord Hobbs's?"

"I owe him money. From Priscilla's dowry, due at the close of the year. 'Twould have been Newgate Prison for me, or Greystone for him." He gave a rueful laugh. "Coward that I am, I'm afraid he would have ended up with Greystone."

"But there was always the gold—"

He quieted her with a kiss. "I promised you I'd never take it, love."

He'd been willing to give up everything for her. Tears flooded her eyes, and she blinked them back. "A Chase promise is not given lightly," she murmured, hearing Jason say so in her head. Back at Cainewood, almost a year ago. It seemed like a lifetime had passed.

"No, 'tis never given lightly," Colin agreed. "Most especially to those we love. Now, get some rest while I check on the estate."

One more kiss, his lips soft, lingering on hers. "Tonight," he promised in a tight voice as he backed through the door, eyeing her belly with undisguised apprehension.

Smiling, she caressed the swell of their child. "Tonight."

One hand on the doorjamb, he paused. "Are you happy?"

"Happy?" she asked in a daze. "I've never been happier in my life."

At that moment, 'twas true. The smile transformed

her face long after Colin's footsteps had faded down the corridor.

He loved her.

"You should be resting, child." Elizabeth came in and settled herself on the study couch. "Your time is near."

"I felt a sudden urge to straighten this desk." Amy sorted through the heap of yellowed receipts she'd found crammed in the bottom drawer, then held one up. "This is dated 1660, the year King Charles granted Greystone to Colin. My husband is a secret slob." She grinned. "Besides, I'm not made for resting; you know that."

"Your Uncle William says the same thing about me. The Goldsmith curse, he calls it."

The paper fluttered to the desk. "The Goldsmith curse," Amy repeated in a whisper, thinking not of the work ethic, but her cursed promise. The Goldsmith curse.

"What did you say, dear?"

"Nothing. 'Tis nothing."

The room fell quiet but for the rustle of paper. Amy felt Elizabeth's gaze following her as she moved back and forth, filing the receipts.

"What is wrong, child?" Elizabeth asked at last, her voice heavy with loving sympathy.

Amy's eyes filled with tears. Her emotions were so close to the surface these days; she was either violently happy or in the depths of despair; there seemed to be no middle ground.

"I know not, Auntie." She leaned both palms on the desk, staring down, studying the grain in the wood. "I was so happy this morning."

"This wouldn't have something to do with a 'vow' to your father, would it?"

Amy watched a tear splash onto the scarred surface of Colin's desk. "How did you know?"

"Colin." A long sigh escaped Elizabeth's lips. "You've not discussed this with him, have you?" Amy shook her head. "For God's sake, child, how can you let a promise to a dead man stand in the way of your happiness?"

"He told me I cannot have everything," Amy said in a tiny voice.

"Colin said that?" Elizabeth sounded incredulous.

"No, Papa said it."

"Oh, Lordamighty. My brother was a lot of things, but open minded wasn't one of them."

Amy flinched with a sudden cramp in her middle. "Yet 'tis true, is it not?" she said when the pain eased. "I'm with Colin now, and I have so much. I must learn to live with the fact that I cannot have everything."

"Poppycock. Hugh couldn't possibly have foreseen your future. He's dead, Amy. The shop is gone." Her voice softened. "You're a countess, child. Were your father here today, do you honestly think he would withhold his blessing?"

"I know not." Amy dropped into Colin's chair. "Goldsmith & Sons was everything to Papa."

Sighing, Elizabeth stood up. "You *can* have everything, if you'll but listen to your heart. You need only to talk to Colin—"

"About this? He's already told me—"

"He's not your father. Talk to him. You can live up to your vow—perhaps not literally, but the spirit, child. You can live up to the spirit of your vow, if you'll only approach your husband with open trust. He deserves that much, Amy."

She walked around the desk and leaned to kiss Amy on both cheeks. "Think about it. Now, I'm an old woman who has traveled many miles, and I think I need a nap."

Sniffling, Amy ventured a shaky smile. "God in heaven, Auntie. An old woman, indeed!"

Another cramp shot through Amy, but that meant not that the baby was coming. He couldn't be coming—Colin had left to spend the whole day inspecting the estate. Besides, she'd been having cramps—contractions, Aunt

Elizabeth called them—for almost eight weeks now, and they'd never meant anything before.

Greystone hummed with productivity. Colin rode toward the fields, certain the sheep and crops would prove as well maintained as the lumber operation and quarry already had. Amy was a hell of an estate manager. Almost as good as she'd been a jeweler.

A jeweler . . . He looked down to his hands on Ebony's reins, at the band of white skin that marked where his signet ring used to rest. After all these months, he felt almost naked without it, or as though part of his body had been amputated. And Amy . . . Amy could make him another.

He smiled to himself, remembering her pride in her craft, the glow in her eyes when she shared the treasures in her trunk. Her joy at discovering the identity of her wedding ring. Her fingers absently caressing the necklace she'd worn to Whitehall Palace. For certain, she'd enjoy making him another ring.

He reined in as the realization stole his breath away.

Bloody hell—what an idiot he'd been! She missed her craft—'twas in her blood, as much a part of her as her amethyst eyes and her quick smile. She'd make him another ring, and then . . . Holy Christ, he knew how to make her happy.

Colin wheeled Ebony toward the castle and dug in his heels. The rest of the estate could wait for an inspection. He couldn't wait to see Amy's face when he told her. The distracted, sad look would leave her eyes. She'd throw her arms around him, kissing him all over his face in that exuberant way of hers, and he would return every kiss, every caress.

Tonight be damned. He'd have her in his bed within the hour. Perhaps she was still there, resting. Waiting.

Damn, he hoped he could find a way around the mound of their child.

* * *

"My lady," Lydia called from the door. "Dinner is ready."

With a fierce effort, Amy opened her eyes and unclenched her fists.

"Milady?" Lydia's eyes widened until they were round blue circles. "Is it the baby?"

"No." Amy leaned against the desk. " 'Tis only another one of those little cramps I've been having."

"Are you quite certain?" Lydia pressed. "This looks—different."

"Yes, I'm quite certain," Amy snapped, her face impassive although her middle knotted in the most painful contraction yet. God in heaven, it felt like a steel band were squeezing the very life out of her. "I'm quite certain," she repeated through gritted teeth. "But I will take dinner in my bedchamber. I could use a nap." She turned to walk from the chamber.

"Milady," Lydia called, alarm in her voice. "You're *waddling*."

Amy whirled around. "I am *not* waddling. There is nothing wrong with my legs. Waddling is for pitiful pregnant ninnies who want to draw sympathetic attention to themselves."

She was glad no one was in the corridor to see her, because 'twas almost impossible to make it to the bedchamber without waddling. She fell onto the bed in an awkward fetal position, but before she could get comfortable, a pale straw-colored, sweetish fluid gushed out of her.

She knew what that meant. Lydia had related every detail of her previous five ladies' birth experiences with maximum drama, leaving Amy in a wild state of alarm. Then, last night, Aunt Elizabeth had explained everything in a very calm, clinical manner. Amy didn't quite know what to believe, but one thing was clear: When the bag of waters burst, the babe was coming. Period.

Hot tears squeezed from beneath her closed lids as she curled herself into a ball. The babe couldn't come now. Colin wouldn't be here for hours. And she'd not talked to him yet; Aunt Elizabeth was right—she had to talk to him. She had to trust him. She wasn't ready for this baby.

The fact that her son was ready, that Aunt Elizabeth had said he'd come this week or next, was beside the point entirely.

When another white-hot spasm clenched her insides, she moaned in pain and frustration. All at once, Lydia barged into the bedchamber, a dinner tray in her hands.

"I knew it!" she exclaimed, staring at the sopping mass of sheets. She dropped the tray forthwith, and Amy would have laughed had she been able.

But her womb tightened more. "He's not coming out now," she forced through clenched teeth. "I'll not let him. I'll keep my legs stuck together."

"But, my lady—"

Amy had never felt so out of control. "My body wouldn't betray me this way," she snapped, struggling halfway up as the pain subsided, determined to put an end to this madness. Then the truth dawned in a burst of anger and inevitability, and she fell back to the pillows.

"This child is coming whether I want him to or not," she wailed. "There is nothing I can do to stop him. Nothing." Lydia's face looked blurry through Amy's fresh onslaught of burning tears. "Send Benchley to find Colin," she said weakly, closing her eyes. "And wake up Aunt Elizabeth. Wake her *now*."

"I already did," Lydia said. When Amy forced her heavy eyelids open, Lydia amended with, "Wake your aunt, I mean." She bent down to gather everything back onto the tray.

Aunt Elizabeth arrived then, stepping over the broken crockery and taking charge.

"I'm hot and sweaty," Amy complained, and Aunt Elizabeth peeled back the covers.

"I'm chilled," she said, shivering, and Aunt Elizabeth piled them back on.

Amy felt nauseated, certain she was going to vomit, then she forgot her queasy stomach as waves of drowsiness overwhelmed her. She jerked awake when the next contraction seized her, and the cycle started again. Through it all, Aunt Elizabeth kept up a knowledgeable, reassuring patter.

"You're so nice and helpful, Mrs. Talbot," Lydia said frantically.

Amy opened her eyes long enough to glare at her.

"Oh, heavens," Lydia breathed, her eyes widening. "Milady, I can see it!" She moved closer and stared between Amy's thighs, but Amy cared not enough to be embarrassed. " 'Tis a shilling-size circle, covered with slimy black hair."

Amy grimaced, half in pain, half because she'd never heard anything sound quite so disgusting.

"Hush, Lydia!" Aunt Elizabeth admonished. She craned her neck to see Amy's face over the mound of her belly. " 'Tis your baby's head, Amy. He's ready to be born."

Aunt Elizabeth signaled Lydia closer and instructed her to hold Amy's hand.

"Push now, Amy," she encouraged. "Push as hard as you can."

Amy took her words to heart. She pushed with all the might she could muster, wanting nothing more than to get this horrible business over with.

"Ouch!" Lydia jerked back, but Amy tightened her grip. When the contraction ended and Lydia reclaimed and massaged her hand, Amy felt guilty. Then it started again, and Lydia leaned over her, sweeping the hair off her forehead and clucking reassuringly.

"Will you stop touching me," Amy spat. She seemed trapped on a seesaw of emotions, unable to control herself. As the pain peaked, she squeezed Lydia's hand again, and she couldn't care less if she were hurting her or not. A tiny part of her was shocked at her behavior, but not enough to change it.

She rested, panting, then pushed, then rested and pushed again. She pushed until she was certain her insides would spill out onto the sheets, but still her son remained stubbornly stuck in her womb. When the urge to push subsided, she closed her eyes, but the tears were leaking out all over again.

"Push, Amy, push," Elizabeth yelled.

Oh, no, 'twas coming again, so soon. Frustrated, Amy's tears flowed faster. This was so unfair! Her nails dug into the palm of her hand that wasn't clenching Lydia's.

"This is not the place for you," she heard Elizabeth say firmly. "Pour yourself a brandy and wait in the study."

'Twas more than confusing, but Amy's eyes were shut tight, and she was concentrating on the pushing and the pain.

"No," a deep, masculine voice countered. "I must talk to Amy."

Her eyes flew open. "Colin?" she moaned through the pain.

He hesitated, his breath coming heavy as though he'd been running. He glanced from Amy to Elizabeth and back again.

"I just want you to be happy, love." His fingers drummed against one thigh. He looked to where Lydia's gaze was rooted, and his eyes widened, then he tore away his gaze and focused on Amy's face. "I have something I need to ask you, tell you. This is important to me."

When the pain waned, Amy nodded. "Come here. Tell me."

"I miss my ring." He moved toward her, smiling, absently rubbing the spot where it used to be. "Do you suppose you could make me another one?"

"Colin, not now," Elizabeth growled.

Though the pain had ended for the moment, Amy was convinced her heart had stopped instead. "You . . . you want me to make you a ring?"

"We can build a workshop. I was thinking by the kitchen—"

"Oh, Colin!" Tears sprang to her eyes for the countless time that day. "How did you know? 'Tis just—" A pain ripped through her, and she grabbed his hand, shutting her eyes, pushing, pushing, pushing. Her son was coming; she could feel his head stretching the entrance to her body. 'Twas a miracle.

"Will you teach our children your craft?" Colin asked. "Your blood—your jeweler's blood—it runs in this child's veins as much as mine."

" 'Tis your blood will be running if you don't leave," Elizabeth warned.

"No, don't leave!" Amy panted, squeezing his hand.

"And if you don't mind living simply—"

"I don't! I've told you that," she wailed as the pain subsided.

"Then we'll save to replace your inheritance. And someday, a younger son who cannot inherit will open the finest shop in London. 'Twould be a much better life than soldiering or preaching."

"A younger son?" Lydia scoffed, mopping Amy's brow. "Cuds bobs, d'ye think she'll have another after going through this?"

"If you can all shut up for one minute," Elizabeth interjected, "this baby is about to arrive."

"Colin," Amy breathed. She had so much she wanted to say, but the urge to push distracted her.

"Amy, 'tis time," Elizabeth encouraged. "Push."

She pushed hard then, harder, harder still—and her babe slipped out into the world.

" 'Tis a miracle," she managed to choke out. "Everything." Then laughter bubbled up from her throat, even as tears flowed down her cheeks. And their babe's cries added the sweetest sound to the emotional confusion.

Colin moved toward the foot of the bed, his eyes registering sheer disbelief as the child of his loins was wiped off and wrapped in a blanket. Aunt Elizabeth set the wriggling bundle on Amy's abdomen and opened the blanket halfway. She used clean linen strips to tie the cord in two places, then Colin touched his child for the first time, holding it still while the pulsing lifeline was severed.

" 'Tis a miracle," Amy whispered to herself. Her precious son. Colin's wonderful compromise so Goldsmith & Sons would rise again. Her love for Colin and—the biggest miracle of all—his for her. All of it—a miracle.

Colin handed her the warm bundle. She held her babe snug to her chest, afraid to crush him, but afraid to let him go. Ever.

She gazed into Colin's eyes, fresh tears of joy flowing from her own. "Would you mind very much," she whispered tremulously, "if we called him Hugh, after my father?"

The warm sound of Colin's laughter brought a smile to her lips. "If it is very important to you, we will, love," he choked out, "but I'm afraid the other little girls might tease her."

"The other little girls?" She blinked, confused. "This child is a girl? *A girl?* Impossible." Tossing Colin a sidelong glance, she opened the blanket a bit. " 'Twould be just like you to play a practical joke like this."

But there she was, pink-toed and perfect. Amy tore off the blankets and cradled the sniffling child against her own skin, rocking her instinctively. "How could I ever have thought she was a boy?" she wondered of a sudden. "She was a girl all along. This infinitely precious girl is mine."

Her daughter quieted then, cuddled against Amy's familiar body, her ear on Amy's chest, listening to the heartbeat that had sustained her for nine long months.

Elizabeth beckoned to Lydia, and they slipped from the room.

"I can teach her to make jewelry?" Amy asked, staring up at Colin.

His eyes bore into hers, unblinking.

"Will it not look . . . unseemly?"

"Are you trying to talk me out of it?" He smiled, that old devilish smile that made her heart turn over.

"No." She took a deep breath. " 'Tis just . . . too good to be true, Colin. Papa said I couldn't have everything, but I do. I have everything."

"Well, I don't," he said flatly, trying and failing to hide the humor in his voice.

Amy worried not for a second. "You have me," she pointed out. "And our beautiful daughter. And Greystone—" She broke off as she saw his eyes turn that darkest green that melted her inside.

"Every day we were apart," he said in the heart-wrenching husky voice she'd waited six long weeks to hear, "I dreamt of making love to you. 'Twas the one thought that kept me going, minute after minute, hour after hour, day after day. And now—" He shrugged next to her, and that single expressive movement held all the pent-up frustration of a love that had gone unfulfilled.

No, he couldn't make love to her, Amy thought, not right now. But soon . . . soon. And, "You can kiss me," she invited, her lips already tingling at the proposition of that talented, well-remembered mouth on hers.

He did. Thoroughly.

When he pulled away, their daughter opened her eyes, to gaze unfocused at her parents for the very first time.

Her emerald eyes mirrored Colin's own. He stared at her, then reached out to touch one little hand, his heart in his eyes as her tiny fingers wrapped around his big one. "What a precious jewel," he murmured.

Amy met his gaze, her heart swelling in the shared moment. He was right. Of all the jewels she'd ever made, their daughter was the most precious.

"Jewel," they whispered together.

Epilogue

Six years later

The little girl climbed down the ladder and set it against the wall. Quietly, so her mother wouldn't hear. Then she squeezed through the door—carefully, carefully—since 'twas only open a tiny bit, just enough for a slip of a six-year-old pixie to fit through.

Jewel skipped through the kitchen, pausing to grab a warm tart from a fresh-baked pile, then across the Great Hall and down the corridor to the study. Hesitating, she wiped the crumbs from her rosebud mouth and swept the disheveled ebony hair back from her heart-shaped face. Then she placed a delicate hand on the latch and pushed, bursting into the chamber.

"Papa, come quick! Mama's burned herself!"

Colin jumped up from behind his desk. "*Holy Jesus*," he said under his breath. Jewel retraced her steps, this time at a run at her father's heels. She hurried to keep up.

"Lord, let it not be bad," Colin whispered. The blast furnace in the workshop could rise to such incredibly high temperatures. "Please let it not be bad."

The workshop door was slightly ajar. He pushed it open—*scrape, bang*—and a deluge of frigid water drenched his head.

Behind him, Jewel dissolved into hysterical giggles. His wife turned around from her workbench, the wax model she was working on still in her hands.

"She got you," Amy said. "Again." With one look at

Colin standing there, his hair plastered to his head and hanging to his shoulders in thick wet tendrils, she burst into laughter.

Colin reached back and pulled his still-giggling daughter into the room. With a violent shake of his head, he sprayed droplets of cold water onto her small head and shoulders. "Jewel Edith Chase," he said with mock severity, "this is getting way out of hand."

"I owed you. For the lemonade." Last week, Colin had promised Jewel a cool mug of lemonade after a vigorous fencing lesson, but the concoction he'd given her had been double-strength, no sugar. The pucker on her face had been priceless.

He chuckled now, savoring the memory. "*That* was for the hay," he protested. "How did you do that hay thing, anyway?"

"I'm not telling. We're even now."

"Like hell we are."

"Colin."

Amy's gentle attempts to limit his blasphemy in their children's presence were mostly for naught, and she knew it. Colin smiled to himself, then narrowed his eyes at Jewel. "Is it not past your bedtime, young lady?"

"Mama said I could cast my ring tonight."

Amy laughed. "Good try, Jewel, but you spent the evening balancing a bucket of water."

Colin knelt and hugged his daughter to his side. "You can cast your ring tomorrow."

"If I go to bed now, will you tell me a story?"

Colin groaned. "What is this, a negotiation?"

"What's a negotayshun?"

He ruffled her hair. "A negotiation is when—"

" 'Tis when you bat your pretty eyes at your father"—Amy's own eyes glittered with mischief—"and he gives you what you want."

'Twas Colin's turn to protest. "Amy!"

"Tell me a story, please," Jewel begged, her eyes sparkling with hope—those emerald eyes that were exactly like his. Amy was right; he could never deny his daughter when she gazed at him like that. "Tell me the one about when you were in France for the King, and your coach was stopped by hackneymen."

"Highwaymen."

"Whatever. Tell me, *please*."

Those eyes. "As you wish. Get ready for bed, and I'll come up in a while and tell you about it."

"Can Hugh hear it, too?"

Jewel's brother Hugh was a strapping boy of four who followed his father around like a shadow. The next Earl of Greystone. And then, of course, there was Aidan. Colin glanced at the sleeping child snuggled in the corner of the workshop. At six months, he still needed Amy near. And he would learn his trade here; his future was here.

"Papa . . ." His gaze moved from the cradle back to Jewel. "Please, Papa. Hugh loves your stories—you know he does."

"Very well, sweetheart." Emerald eyes sparkled again, and Colin's heart melted a bit more. Would he never get over the wonder of these precious beings entrusted to his care? "Now, go. I'll be along directly," he told her with a sigh.

She went, skipping out into the kitchen as if she'd not a care in the world. Which was true. And Colin hoped he could keep it that way for a long, long time.

He closed the door and turned to his wife. "Did you see how ingenious that was?" he asked, amazed at his daughter's creativity. "Look how she connected the bucket's handle to the door latch with a rope, so 'twould not hit me on the head when it fell off the top of the door. Perfect. Just perfect." He shook his head slowly in admiration. "Our daughter is so incredible."

Trust Colin to equate intelligence with a well-executed practical joke, Amy mused, rising from her workbench. She, too, was convinced their daughter was a genius, but her opinion stemmed from Jewel's reading ability and thirst for knowledge.

"I know what she did." Amy pushed the wet hair off

Colin's face, wrapped her arms around his waist. "I was here, working."

"And you let her do it, anyway."

"Of course—you deserved it after the lemonade. Besides, she thinks she went unnoticed. She was quiet as a mouse, and I kept my back to her the whole time."

"So you're an accessory to the crime," Colin accused, with that devastating smile that made Amy's heart turn over, even after all these years.

"I suppose one could conclude that."

"Which reminds me: How did she manage that hay trick? You must know."

Amy did know. Jewel and Benchley, whom she'd long ago charmed into acting as her willing accomplice, had placed a board against the open wardrobe and stuffed hay behind it, then closed the door most of the way, pulled the board and slammed the wardrobe shut. When Colin opened it to hang his shirt on a peg, he'd been turned into a human haystack. Watching from their bed, Amy had laughed herself sick. Jewel had run in, crowing with delight, prompting Colin to initiate a wrestling match that resulted in an explosion of sweet-smelling hay spread about the chamber. And after Jewel returned to bed, Colin had picked the strands of hay from Amy's hair, one by one, running them down over her body . . .

Amy shook her head to clear it. No, she hadn't the right to give away Jewel's secrets. "I have no idea," she said coyly. "Jewel doesn't confide in me." But Benchley does, she amended to herself. Benchley was forever boasting about Lady Jewel's accomplishments. To everyone but Jewel's father, that was. Benchley was loyal to a fault.

"Are you quite certain?" Colin asked, his lips against hers.

"Quite."

Colin's arms tightened around her; his lips pressed closer, warm and demanding. Her mouth opened beneath his, and his tongue plunged deep, exploring possessively. Amy's knees turned to pudding, and she felt the blood coursing through her veins, spreading the familiar tingling weakness to every part of her body, but most especially the part that was reserved for Colin.

His hand reached down to tug at her skirts, and then 'twas under them and his fingers were cupping her. She throbbed, unbearably so, and if Colin's arms weren't supporting her, she would surely have slipped to the floor. His kiss intensified, claiming her as his alone.

Amy's senses spun, and her heart pounded so loud she was certain Colin could hear it. She vaguely wondered how she could feel this way—her, a grown lady of twenty-nine, with three children. But inside, she felt no older than when Colin first kissed her, so many years ago. And his kisses still affected her the same way, only more so.

"Amy . . ." Colin murmured into her mouth.

"Hmmm?"

His hand stilled and he pulled his mouth from hers, but he pressed her even tighter to his hard body, his other hand in the small of her back. "How did Jewel do the hay trick?"

His lips brushed hers teasingly, his hand a warm promise under her skirts. And she almost told him . . .

"Lord Greystone?" A sharp knock came at the door.

Colin jumped away, groaning. "Yes?"

Lydia opened the door and stuck her head in just as Amy smoothed down her skirts, her cheeks flushed hot with arousal and embarrassment.

"Lady Jewel says you were supposed to tell her a story?"

"Oh . . . yes . . . I did promise her a story, didn't I?"

Lydia kept a straight face, but Amy hid a smile. She knew she and Colin shared an unconventional marriage. Colin laid down the law with each new servant: One did not just open a closed door when Lord and Lady Greystone were in residence. It mattered not whether 'twas the bedchamber or the buttery, one knocked first—or risked being sorry later.

Lydia turned, hurrying back to her charge. Colin

groaned again. Amy knew he would follow—he would never disappoint his precious Jewel. A Chase promise was not given lightly.

"This will be continued," Colin promised before going to his daughter. His deep, husky voice held a challenge, and she knew he was referring to the hay episode and what he undoubtedly considered an ingenious, delicious new method of inducing her to confess what she knew about it.

But, her body still tingling, she interpreted his words in an entirely different context. *This will be continued.* For a long, long, long time. Forever.

Author's Note

When I read a historical novel, I always find myself wondering what and who (besides obvious people like the King and Queen) might actually be real. In case any of my readers share this curiosity, I thought a bit of information might be welcome.

The King's mistress, Barbara Villiers Palmer, Countess of Castlemaine (and later, after this story takes place, the Duchess of Cleveland) was indeed real. As King Charles's mistress off and on for at least ten years, she bore him four sons—all of whom he created dukes—and a daughter. Charles granted lifetime annuities of £6000 a year for Barbara and £3000 for each of their sons. These were amazing sums at the time and more than he granted any other mistresses or children, yet he must have known Barbara had many other lovers—a vast string of them, including not only many English and French courtiers, but also actors, a playwright, a Groom of the Bedchamber to the King, and even a rope dancer!

I tried my best to recreate Barbara's vibrant personality from contemporary accounts of her life. I will never forget the first time I read one of her early biographies, as a college student in the library at UC Irvine. The book, almost 300 years old, was much too valuable and brittle for them to lend out, but—unbelievably!—they did let me touch and read it. I remember my hands shaking—I found it so incredible that someone's words had come down to me through all that time. Years have passed, and I now have several very old books in my own library, but I still touch them reverently—such is the power and endurance of the written word.

Barbara Palmer presented Charles with more children than any of his other mistresses, but many others shared his bed—he eventually acknowledged nine sons and five daughters, and it is assumed that he had more. Sadly, Queen Catharine never did present him with legitimate offspring, but at long last a descendent of his is poised to sit on the throne, since Princess Diana and her sons are descended from Charles II and Barbara, through their son Charles Fitzroy, Duke of Grafton, born in 1663.

As for Frances Stewart, the gorgeous but empty-headed courtier that Barbara and Colin were gossiping about, Charles did decide to forgive her for marrying the Duke of Richmond and eventually succeeded in wooing her as well. Unfortunately, shortly thereafter she fell ill of smallpox, and the resulting facial disfigurement seems to have cooled Charles's passions. But Charles was ever kindhearted, and she remained his friend. Before Frances succumbed to the dreaded disease, Charles's sister described her as "the prettiest girl in the world," and Charles immortalized that famous beauty when he had her pose as Britannia: Frances's face and torso still grace English coins.

Cainewood Castle is loosely modeled on Arundel Castle in West Sussex. It has been home to the Dukes of Norfolk and their family, the Fitzalan Howards, since 1243, save for a short period during the Civil War. Although the family still resides there, portions of their magnificent home are open to visitors and more than worth a detour to gape at.

Greystone was inspired by Amberley Castle, also in West Sussex. Charles II visited the castle in 1651 and 1685. The then tenant, Sir John Brisco, commemorated the second visit by commissioning a mural of Charles and Queen Catharine, which can still be seen in the Queen's Room, now a gourmet restaurant. The castle has passed through many hands and is now run as a country house hotel. The walls exude the spirit of dreams and legends, and a stay there is the stuff memories are made of, well worth the splurge.

For their London town house, the Chases have borrowed Lindsey House bordering Lincoln's Inn Fields. Attributed to the esteemed architect Inigo Jones, it is the only original house left in the square. The house takes its name from Robert, third Earl of Lindsey, who purchased the property in the 1660s from the family of Sir Theodore Mayerne, who had been doctor to James I and Charles I. There have been various distinguished occupants since, including James Whistler, who painted the famous portrait of his mother there.

If you enjoyed *Amethyst,* you won't want to miss the next marvelous romantic adventure from the talented Lauren Royal! In *Emerald,* Colin Chase's older brother Jason, the Marquess of Cainewood, takes center stage as his strong sense of responsibility leads him on a wild quest for justice—and into the arms of Caithren Leslie. Is she a notorious lady bounty hunter? Or a Scottish heiress whose striking beauty is matched only by her stubborn independence? Filled with laughter and danger, wit and passion, *Emerald* continues Lauren Royal's jewel trilogy, and demonstrates once again that she is one of the brightest new voices in historical romance today.

Turn the page for a special preview of *Emerald,* a Signet paperback coming in the fall of 2000.

Chichester, England
Thursday, August 1, 1667

"Jason, you cannot mean to kill him."

Jason Chase stopped short and wrenched his arm away from his brother Ford's grasp. He spun on his heel to face him. "By God, no." He shifted a glance over his shoulder toward the man in question. "But I'll know why he did this and bring him to justice if it's the last thing I do." Trembling with rage, his hand came up to worry his narrow black mustache. "I can still see sweet little Mary lying still as death, and her mother's torn clothes and bruised face as she chanted Geoffrey Gothard's name, over and over." His hand fisted and dropped to his side. "My villagers." He met Ford's gaze with his own. "My responsibility."

"You've plastered the kingdom with broadsides." Ford's blue eyes looked puzzled, as though he were unsure how to take this new side of his oldest sibling. "The reward will bring him in."

"I'm bloody well satisfied to bring him in myself."

Jason turned and continued down East Street to where Chichester's vaulted Market Cross sat in the center of the Roman-walled town. The most elaborate structure in all of England . . . but the beauty of its intricate tracery was at odds with the evil that lurked inside.

An evil that Jason intended to deal with.

Scattered businessmen, exchanging mail and news beneath the dome, paused to glance his way. The Gothard brothers were instantly recognizable from the descriptions Jason's villagers had given him: Geoffrey, tall and slim, with a stance that bordered on elegant; Walter, shorter and rawboned. His eyes on their hated faces, familiar from the broadsides he'd had printed, Jason strode up two steps through the open arches, his own brother following quickly behind. In their wake, people seemed to stream from all four corners of town, hurrying to catch the show.

Walter Gothard scurried back like a frightened rabbit. With a click of his spurred heels, Jason came to a halt and drew an uneven breath. He pinned Geoffrey Gothard with a savage gaze. "I'm taking you to the magistrate," he snapped out, surprising even himself at the commanding tone of his voice. For a fleeting moment Ford seemed dumbfounded, then he stepped away to allow Jason room, stretching out his arms to motion back the crowd.

Jason's hand went to the hilt of his sword. "Now, Gothard."

The other man's gaze held hard and unwavering. " 'My nearest and dearest enemy,' " he drawled in response. A line Jason recognized from Shakespeare. The man was not uneducated, then—indeed, his bearing was aristocratic, and his clothes, though rumpled from days of wear, were of good quality and cut.

Confusion churned with the anger in Jason's stomach. "What do you mean, your 'enemy'?"

Gothard looked Jason up and down, as though he knew him. "The Marquess of Cainewood, are you not?" The insolent words seemed to spew from the pale lips set into his squarish head.

"I am." Jason's words were clipped, through gritted teeth. A man of peace, he wanted nothing more than to go home to his calm routine, back to his estate, his life. But he could think only of little golden-haired Mary following him around the village, begging him for a sweetmeat, her blue eyes dancing with mischief and radiating trust.

Blue eyes that might never open again.

And there in dappled light stood the man who had battered her, shadowed by the pale limestone of the Gothic structure overhead. Right was on Jason's side . . . no matter that it was burning a hole in his gut.

"I've done naught to draw your ire—we've never met." Jason squinted at the man in the shadows. Gothard and his brother were pale, with the type of skin that burned and peeled with any exposure to the sun—and it looked as though they'd seen much exposure lately. Jason's jaw tensed. "Stand down, and consign yourself to my arrest."

Geoffrey Gothard's blue eyes narrowed. Jason blinked. He seemed to know those eyes. Maybe they *had* crossed paths.

The eyes went stony with resentment. "To the devil with you, Cainewood."

Jason squared his shoulders, reminding himself why he was here. For justice. Honor. The questions could wait—for now. He counted to ten, slowly, focusing on the fat needle of a spire that topped the old Norman cathedral across the green. As responsibility weighed heavily on his mind, his hand tightened on the hilt of his sword.

Father would have expected this of him. To defend what was his, stand up for what was right—no matter the personal cost.

Deliberately, he drew the rapier from its scabbard.

"Damn you to bloody hell." Gothard pulled his own sword with a quick *screak* that snapped the expectant silence. "We will settle this here and now."

Jason advanced a step closer, slowly circled the tip of his rapier, then sliced it hissingly through the air in a swift move that brought a collective gasp from the crowd. The blade's thin shadow flickered across the paving stones. His free hand trembled a little at his side.

With a roar, Gothard lunged, and the first flash of steel rang through the still summer air.

The vibrations shimmied up Jason's arm. Muscles tense,

he swung and thrust, and again steel clanged against steel. He twisted and parried, danced in to attack, then out of harm's way. His heart pounded; blood pumped furiously through his veins. Like most noblemen, he'd been taught well and spent countless hours in swordplay, but this was no game. And his opponent was trained as well.

Two blades clanked with deadly intent in the shadow of the Market Cross.

Adam Leslie dipped his quill in the inkwell and carefully added "My" in front of "Dear Sister," frowned, then squeezed in "est" in the middle. "My Dearest Sister." There now, surely Caithren wouldn't be miffed at his news after such an affectionate greeting.

Gazing up at the dark paneled walls of the Royal Arms, he flipped his straight, dark blond hair—so like his sister's—over his shoulder. That he'd not be home soon shouldn't come as a surprise to her—'twas not as though he'd spent more than a few weeks total at home these five years past. But 'twould not hurt to be loving when he imparted the news . . . he did love her. And he knew that she loved him as well, even if he was rarely home.

Och, Scotland was boring. He was happy to leave the running of the Leslie lands to Cait and their father. He chuckled to himself, imagining Da's latest ineffective efforts to marry her off.

"Are you not finished yet, Adam?"

He looked over and smiled at his friends, John and William, the Earl of Balmforth and Viscount Grinstead, respectively. Dandies, they were, dressed in brightly colored velvet and satin, decorated with jewels and looped ribbons. Though he kept himself decked out in similar style, he considered himself lucky they let him keep their company, untitled as he was—at least until his very-healthy father died sometime in the distant future. Da was naught but a minor baronet, so Adam wasn't entitled to call himself anything but Mister.

"Adam?"

"Almost done," he muttered, pushing back the voluminous lace at his cuffs and signing his name to the bottom of the letter. He set down the quill, sprinkled sand to blot the ink, then brushed it off, and precisely folded the parchment.

"An ale for my friend!" John called.

Adam nodded; this was thirsty work. Hell, any work was thirsty work. He preferred not to work at all.

He turned over the letter and scrawled *Miss Caithren Leslie, Leslie by Insch, Scotland* on the back. After dusting the address with sand as well, he rose and walked across the taproom to the innkeeper's desk, pinching the serving maid on the behind as she sauntered by with his tankard of ale. She giggled.

"Have ye any wax?" Adam dropped his letter on the scarred wooden counter and dug in his pouch for a few silver coins. "And you'll post this for me, aye?"

The ostler blinked his rheumy eyes. "Certainly, sir."

"Adam, come along!" William shouted. "We're fair dying of thirst."

Laughing, Adam pressed his signet ring into the warm wax, then went to sit with his companions. He lifted his ale and leaned across the table. Their three pewter mugs met with a resounding clank.

"To freedom!" William said, shaking off the foam that had sloshed onto his hand.

"To freedom!" Adam echoed. " 'Til Hogmanay!"

"You told her you'd be gone 'til the new year?" William asked, aghast.

"At the least." Adam swallowed a long gulp and swiped one hand across his mouth before the froth dripped onto his expensive satin surcoat. The taproom's door banged open. "We've the week's hunting in West Riding, then Lord Darnley's wedding in London come the end of the month. Wouldn't care to miss Guy Fawkes Day in the City. Then I might as well stay through the Christmas balls, ye think? No sense in going home, then leaving straightaway."

"No sense at all," John said slowly, staring toward the entrance. "Will you look at what just walked in? Think ye that might be the notorious Flora MacCallum?"

Their gazes swung to the tall woman and followed her progress as she sat herself at another table.

"Nary a chance." Adam's chair legs scraped on the wooden floor as he pushed back and raised his feet to the table, crossing his silk-clad ankles. He contemplated the contents of his tankard for a moment, then tossed back the rest of the ale and signaled the serving wench for another. "Flora MacCallum dresses like a man."

"She's carrying a knife," John argued in a loud whisper. "And she looks hard. Like the sort of woman who'd track outlaws with a price on their heads."

William let loose a loud guffaw. "You're in your cups, Balmforth. Flora MacCallum carries a sword and a pistol."

"Flora MacCallum would kick your sorry arses." Adam tugged on the lacy white cravat at his neck. "And mine, too, I expect."

They all burst out laughing, until another bang of the door caught their attention.

"Duel at the Market Cross!" came the scratchy voice of an old-timer.

And that ended the discussion of Flora MacCallum. One wouldn't want to miss a duel.

As they both fought for better footing, Jason hurried out of his midnight blue surcoat and tossed it to his brother, his gaze never leaving that of his foe. Geoffrey Gothard smirked as he lunged once again, barely giving Jason time to adjust. Gothard was fleet, but Jason was faster. They scrambled down the steps, and the crowd scurried back. Gothard was cornered, but Jason was incensed. He edged Gothard back beneath the dome, skirting the circular stone bench that sat in its center as they battled their way to the other side of the octagonal structure. Gothard took sudden advantage, and Jason found himself retreating as their blades tangled, slid and broke free with a metallic twang.

His arm ached to the very bone. Perspiration dripped slick from his forehead, stinging his eyes. But the other man's breath came ragged and labored.

All at once, a vicious swipe of Jason's sword sent Gothard's clanging to the stones, skittering down the two steps to the cobbled street, far from his reach.

Jason's teeth bit into his own lower lip. "I came not to kill today, Gothard, but merely to see justice done." He sucked in air, smelled the other man's desperation. "Yet I say to you now, surrender or die."

Sweat beading on his sunburned brow, Gothard stepped back until his calves hit the round stone bench. Frantically he scanned the mass of people still pouring from the surrounding establishments. Jason's gaze darted to follow Gothard's focus. Three more men stumbled out a taproom door and crossed the dusty street to the dome, the bright rainbow colors of their clothing marking them aristocrats.

Their leader pushed through the crowd, clearing a path for his two friends. "Come along, Balmforth," he yelled.

Gothard's eyes narrowed as he honed in on the voice. In a flash of movement, one of his arms snaked toward the man, the other down to the wide cuff of his boot, where the curved handle of a pistol peeked out.

Jason's jaw tensed; his knees locked. Time seemed to slow. His surroundings seemed impressed on his senses: the heated babble and musky scent of the excited onlookers, the cool dimness in the shaded dome, the bright green grass and streaky sunlight beyond. As Gothard rose from his crouch with the pistol glinting in one hand, Jason rushed headlong, his sword arm rigid. Simultaneously, Gothard jerked the newcomer in front of him as a screen.

Jason tried to check his momentum, but his blade forged ahead, piercing satin and flesh with an ease that came as a shock to a man unused to killing. A body was so much more giving than a shield, or even a tight-stuffed sack of hay. As long as he lived, Jason would never forget the astonished look in the man's hazel eyes.

The sword pulled free with a gruesome sucking sound that brought bile into Jason's throat. The man collapsed, his eyes going wide and dull as his bright blood spurted in a grotesque fountain that soaked Jason's shirt and choked his nostrils with a salty, metallic stench.

Stunned with horror, Jason watched the blood pump hard, then slow to a trickle—a spreading red puddle seeping into the cracks between the stones. The dead man's face drained of color, to match the pristine white lace at his throat. Geoffrey Gothard raised his arm, cocked his flintlock, and pulled the trigger.

The explosion rocked the Market Cross, momentarily startling everyone into silence. "I'll see you at the gates of hell," Gothard muttered into the void. He turned and pushed through the crowd, signaling his younger brother to follow.

Jason's vision tunneled, darkening to black as the onlookers' gasps and accusations became garbled in his head, then faded into an ominous quiet.

Ford Chase rushed forward when his brother, the thirty-two-year-old Marquess of Cainewood, clutched his chest and crumpled to the ground.

Pontefract, England
Friday, August 23, 1667

Her back to the other passengers straggling in and queuing to rent rooms, Caithren Leslie stared at the innkeeper in disbelief. "Are ye telling me there are no horses for hire in this village?"

He rubbed a hand over his bald head. "That is what I am telling you, madam."

Mrs. Dochart took Caithren by the arm. "Come along, lass. Mayhap the situation will change on the morrow." With her other hand she set down her valise and dug inside for coins. "We'll take a room upstairs, Mr. Brown."

Caithren shook off the woman's hand and leaned farther over the innkeeper's desk. "Are there no hackney cabs, either?"

"No hackney cabs."

"But Pontefract is a stage stop!"

"We've extra horses here for the public coach, naturally. But they're for the coach . . . not for hire."

Behind her, Caithren heard impatient feet shuffle on the gritty wood floor. "Hurry up, there," someone grumbled.

"Hold your tongue," Caithren shot over her shoulder. "I've spent eight days shut up in a hot coach"—with a crotchety, meddling old woman, she added silently—"just to get here and visit my brother at the Scarborough estate in West Riding."

Rubbing his thin, reddish nose, the innkeeper slanted her a dubious look. "The *Earl* of Scarborough's estate?"

"Aye, the same."

He shrugged. "You can walk. 'Tis nice enough weather."

Mrs. Dochart craned her thick neck to see out the inn's front window. "How far would it be?"

"Naught but a mile or so." The man opened a drawer and pulled out a thick, leather-bound registration book. "Out there, then head east. The road will take you straight past the Scarborough place. 'Twill be set back on the right side, perhaps a quarter mile from the road. A huge stone mansion—you cannot miss it." With a dismissive thump, he set the book on the desk and opened it to a page marked with a ribbon. "You may leave your satchel if you'd care to. Should Scarborough invite you to stay"—his tone betrayed what he thought were the chances of that happening: nil—"I reckon he'll send a footman calling for it." After pausing to give Caithren one more considered look, he waved her aside and the next person forward.

"Come along, lass. We'll be losing the light soon. We

should leave now." Mrs. Dochart set her own bag alongside Caithren's behind the desk. "Unless ye'd prefer to wait for the morn?" she added hopefully.

Caithren reached up a finger to twirl one of her braids. "Nay, I wish to go immediately." *Without* a chaperone. "But I'm . . . I mean to say . . . well, I expected we'd part company here. Not that I've not enjoyed yours," she rushed to add, waiting for a lightning bolt to strike with that lie. She couldna remember ever uttering a more blatant falsehood.

The old bawface looked dubious, but 'twas clear she'd no wish to tramp over the countryside. "Your cousin hired me to look after ye, lass, and—"

"Only so far as Pontefract. He was well aware I was getting off here, ye ken. My brother can see to my welfare from here on out. He'll hire a chaperone for the return trip."

Mrs. Dochart sniffed and patted her gray, coiffed head. "If ye're certain, then—"

"I'm certain." For want of another way to end their association, Caithren executed a little curtsy. " 'Tis pleased I am to have met ye, Mrs. Dochart, and I thank ye for keeping me company." That lie might have topped the first one—she wasna sure.

"Ye take care now, lass."

"I will, thank ye."

Feeling a great burden had been lifted from her shoulders, Caithren crossed the inn's taproom and headed out into the waning sunshine and down the road.

She'd not progressed ten feet when the woman's voice shrilled into the quiet street. "Ah, Caithren, lass!"

With a sigh, Caithren composed her face and turned back to the inn. "Aye, Mrs. Dochart?" The bawface stood framed in the doorway. A cracked wooden sign swung in the light wind, creaking over her head. "I told ye I shall be fine."

"But the ostler said east. 'Tis west ye're walkin'."

"Oh!" Her cheeks heated. "Right."

"Nay, left."

"Right. I mean to say, aye. Left, east." She hurried past, murmuring "Thank ye" over her shoulder. Though she'd have sworn she heard the woman muttering under her breath, she was soon relieved to be out of earshot.

The evening was warm, and the slight breeze felt wonderful after the stuffy, confining coach. 'Twas passably pretty country, the land green and flatter than at home. She much preferred the harsh contours of Scotland, but after all, she didna have to live here. She could enjoy the land for what beauty could be found.

Her heart sang to be free at last, on her way to meet Adam, perhaps rest a few days, depending on the returning public coach's schedule. In two weeks time she'd be back at Leslie, signed papers in hand, giving Cameron the tongue-lashing he deserved for saddling her with that irritating old woman.

Following what promised to be her first decent meal in weeks, tonight she'd luxuriate in a big tub of clean, steaming water. She couldna wait to wash off the dust of the road. And she couldna wait until tomorrow morn, when she'd be snug in a soft feather bed at Scarborough's, imagining the public coach rattling down the road toward London with that bawface tucked inside. The thought was so vivid and appealing, she almost missed the gravel drive that led to a yellowish stone manse in the distance.

The sun was setting, and she tucked her plaid tighter around her black bodice and skirt. When Adam saw her dressed in mourning, he'd understand right off how completely he'd neglected his family and home. 'Twould be a simple matter to convince him to sign the papers MacLeod had drawn up.

In the fading light she hurried along the path, marveling at the way 'twas so raked and pristine. Scarborough must employ an army of servants.

But they werena here now. The mansion was shut up tight as a jar of Aunt Moira's preserves.

The sun sank over the horizon as Caithren stared at the heavy, bolted oak door. She heard the call of a single hawk overhead, apparently the only living creature in the vicinity.

So much for her happy daydreams. Caithren stifled a sob. She would have to stay the night in Pontefract, steel herself to climb back on the coach in the morning, and then somehow survive the eight days 'twould take to reach London.

She counted on her fingers. She should arrive on the day of Lord Darnley's wedding, just in time to present herself as an uninvited guest. 'Twas the only place she was certain she'd be able to find Adam. Touching her amulet, she prayed there'd be no summer storm or something else to delay the coach, because God only kent where Adam would be headed the morning of September first.

Was that scuffling she heard on the roof? Probably some sort of wee animal. Or rats.

Caithren shuddered. "Set a stout heart to a steep hill-side," she said aloud, imagining her mother saying the words. She squared her shoulders and was turning back toward the road when there came the snort of a horse and an answering neigh.

Horses meant people. Her spirits lifted. Mayhap Adam and his friends were here after all, and they'd just been out hunting. Even were it strangers, mayhap they could spare her the long walk—

She heard a muted *thump* and the crunch of gravel, as someone apparently dropped from the roof of the building. Then another *thump.*

"Sealed up. Damn it to bloody hell." Coming from around the side of the manse, the man's voice was cultured. But he was cursing a string of oaths the likes of which she'd never heard. She scooted into the archway that housed the front door and pressed herself against the cold stone wall.

"Sealed up," he repeated. "Cannot even get inside and take a few trinkets to pay our way. Hellfire and damnation!"

"I'm glad 'tis sealed up." The second man's voice was

whiny, but none the more pleasant. "I don't fancy taking things, Geoffrey."

"Everything here is yours, Wat. Or should be. You crackbrain."

The man called Wat didna respond to the insult. "But Cainewood's horses? What about those?"

"These are rightly mine." The first man kicked at the ground, or at least Caithren thought he did. 'Twas difficult to tell from around the corner. "We had to take them. We were low on funds with no way to get here. Can you not get that through your thick skull? Did you want to walk here? Sleep in the open and beg for our supper?"

"We could have found work."

"Work? When hens make holy water. Should we stoop to chopping wood for a living? Baking bread? Shoeing horses?"

"Geoff—"

"Enough!"

Caithren heard the crunch of gravel beneath someone's shuffling feet. "So. Lucas is gone. What now, Geoffrey?"

"He'll be at the London town house, I reckon." Caithren heard the sound of pacing, then a prolonged silence, followed by a low whistle.

"What?" Wat sounded wary. "I do not like the look in your eyes."

"We will go to London." There was a significant pause. "And we will kill him."

He was planning to *kill* someone? A chill shot through Caithren, though the night was still warm.

Wat apparently felt the same way. "Kill him?" he squeaked.

"He's got it coming, and you're next in line. When you're the earl, we'll be sitting pretty." Wat had nothing to say to that. Or maybe he was shocked and speechless. "Besides, 'tis all his fault for kicking us out. His fault we're in this trouble. And his money we'll use to get out of it." There was more silence from Wat. "With

Cainewood's death on our hands, we've nothing to lose. Come along," Geoffrey growled.

Caithren's heart pounded as she listened to the noises of men mounting horses. 'Twas not long afore they rode around the corner of the manse at a slow walk, heading straight past the front door where Caithren hid. She scurried into a corner of the arched entry.

"I cannot do it." Even through Caithren's fear, Wat's whine was grating on her. 'Twas a wonder the one called Geoffrey didna put killing him next on his list of misdeeds.

Apparently Geoffrey chose not to listen, because he ignored the protest. "We've gold enough left to pay for one night at the inn. We'll let everyone see us."

"See us?"

"We'll leave for London come morning. People will remember us here, and if we ride like the dickens, no one will believe we could have gotten there in time. We'll not be suspected of murder."

"Geoffrey . . ." Wat's voice was so drawn out and plaintive, Caithren almost felt sorry for him. As they rode before her and then past, she risked inching forward to get a look at them.

Two men, both rumpled and sunburned. Brothers, if she didna miss her guess. They spoke like quality, and looked it, too—overly proud, even if their clothes could use a washing. But they were murdering scum. English scum. Cameron had been right about Englishmen.

Though the men's voices were fading as they moved down the drive, their words, however muffled, did nothing to calm Caithren's heart rate. "Now let us go find some women." The last of Geoffrey's words drifted back, faint but intelligible. "That new kitchen maid that was hired on before we left—she was a comely one, was she not? If she's not visiting her mama, she must be staying in Pontefract."

Women. The scum were in search of women. Caithren hugged the tops of her crossed arms in a futile attempt to stop herself from shaking.

England was as evil a place as she'd always heard. What was she doing here all alone? She should have let Mrs. Dochart accompany her to Scarborough's. Or Cameron—she should have let Cameron take the trip. In the name o' the wee man, this had certainly been an ill-conceived undertaking.

Though she couldna hear another word the men said, she was still shaking when they disappeared from view, still shaking when she started the long, lonely walk back in the dark. Still shaking after she'd reclaimed her satchel, paid for a room at the inn and extra for a bath, and trudged upstairs to wash off the dust of a week's travel.

She slipped into her plain room, shut the door, and leaned back against it, a palm pressed to her racing heart. She had to get herself in hand.

Nothing—leastwise a couple of scummy Englishmen—was going to stop her from finding her brother.